Also by Laurie Fox

Sexy Hieroglyphics:
3,335 Do-It-Yourself Haiku

My Sister from the Black Lagoon

A Novel of My Life

Laurie Fox

Simon & Schuster

SIMON & SCHUSTER
Rockefeller Center
1230 Avenue of the Americas
New York, NY 10020

Simon & Schuster and colophon are registered trademarks
of Simon & Schuster Inc.

Designed by Jeanette Olender
Manufactured in the United States of America

1   3   5   7   9   10   8   6   4   2

Library of Congress Cataloging-in-Publication Data
Fox, Laurie Anne.
My sister from the black lagoon:
a novel of my life / Laurie Fox.
p.   cm.
I. Title.
PS3556.0936M9   1998
813'.54—dc21   98-6466   CIP
ISBN 0-684-84745-0

Page 336 constitutes an extension of the copyright page.

Acknowledgments

My thank-yous are lush and go back many years, well before the formal beginnings of this novel.

First, a deep bow of gratitude to those earliest muses and generous supporters of my writing life, Donna Bulseco and Randall Babtkis, wonderful writers themselves, and to Charlotte Gusay, who has ardently championed so many writers and artists. To novelist Constance Warloe, early reader of the work, whose bright wisdom was of invaluable assistance. To my friend Frederick Johntz, whose short film *Toast*, which he adapted from a chapter in this book, was a gift to me as well as a revelation. To my three beloved, wise cheerleaders, whose weekly sustenance, lively readings of the work, and heaps of faith helped more than they can know—Tanya Freeman, Claire Farrington, and Sue Bender, my fairy godmother up in the North Berkeley hills.

To my dear colleagues and friends at the Linda Chester Literary Agency—Joanna Pulcini, whose ongoing enthusiasm for this work is a wonderful force to behold; Judith Ehrlich, whose sensitive reading of the material yielded such keen insights; and Gary Jaffe, whose daily esprit de corps is unmatched. And to Linda herself—incomparable friend and literary agent of one's dreams. Thank you for saving my life more times than I can count. Your passion is the greatest gift of all.

To my dynamic, radiant editor, Mary Ann Naples of Simon & Schuster—a huge dollop of thanks for your big vision and most sage guidance. And a bow to editorial assistant Carlene Bauer, who aided me in countless thoughtful ways. In turn, a deep curtsy to Carolyn Reidy, David Rosenthal, and Laurie Chittenden of Simon & Schuster for their spirited early support of this work. Also, a knowing wink to Gypsy da Silva, Carol Catt, and Leslie Jones for their behind-the-scenes magic.

Grateful acknowledgment to David Bianculli for the gift of his book *Dictionary of Teleliteracy*—it's a gold mine.

Last, a world of gratitude to my husband, D. Patrick Miller, for having the courage of *my* convictions; for taking such extraordinarily good care of me; for reading and listening to this book a hundred times over, and for supporting my hopes and dreams. I am certainly and profoundly blessed.

Author's Note

This novel is semi-autobiographical. Although the family at its center is drawn from real life, some of the other characters in the work are composites and others are inventions. Many lifelong friends do not appear herein. In turn, some of the events are imagined in order to explore certain themes. To maintain artistic freedom, it was necessary for me to write this story as a work of fiction; nevertheless, the emotional truth remains constant throughout.

To Mother, Daddy, and Leslie,
my family of origin

To Patrick and Chloé,
the family who found me
and took me home

Contents

Part Three

I am a human being: nothing

human can be alien to me.

—Terence

Let Me Entertain You

I was born into a mentally ill family. My sister was the officially crazy one, but really we were all nuts.

The first memory I have of things nutty—and I don't mean cute and screwball but, rather, things malevolent and indelible—is looking at a photograph of my sister, age three, sitting grimly on the toilet.

"This is the moment I realized that she wasn't like us," Mother said, pointing at Lonnie's vacant eyes in the photograph. It was 1956, I was an awkward four-year-old and completely mystified by this snapshot of my sister. "You can see she wasn't all there, wasn't with the family," Mother added softly to herself.

Here, in a photo that refused to lie, was a little girl sitting on the toilet, wearing a frown that could launch nuclear missiles— a look of possession and depth that was equal parts alien and recognizable. As if she were reconsidering being born. Surely Lonnie danced to the beat of a different drummer, only I had yet to hear the confounding music. Later, when I heard Stravinsky and, even more so, Karlheinz Stockhausen, I could glean the beat, I could even dance to it myself—something I did at age nineteen, when it was permissible to dance the dance of disso-

lution. Until then, I made an art out of normalcy: composure, logic, balance. I didn't fool anybody, because my chewed-up nails looked as grim as my sister's face.

No longer "with the family" myself, I grew my own sort of frown. It came on in my late teens and replaced the hideously normal smile I'd cultivated my whole life up to that point. I wonder now whether I can still change my face, whether I can grow another look that telegraphs what I know, not just what I have endured. A face isn't something you can train, but I want to grow old without wincing at the future or brooding about the past. My past shouldn't determine my future. I should have a choice about my face and my fate. I should be able to say that I was born into an unfunny family, and laugh. But seriously, folks, I was born serious. And even though I thought I was the star of my life when I was four, I soon learned that I was just another character in "The Lonnie Show." Lonnie was the sound and the action, the script and the special effects. There was no other theme or arc or subplot. Life with Lonnie was the only story. Until this story, which I hope to God is my own.

Part One

Toast

1958

ulia, my mother, looks like Rita Hayworth, but she is prettier and more real. She is loyal to me and my sister. This morning as I go off to school, she prays that I won't be lonely, won't be nervous, that I will be "okay," because there isn't room for another problem in this family.

At the breakfast table there's already a problem. My sister is refusing to eat toast. It hurts her in some way we will never know, but I believe her. Surely Coca-Cola hurts as it slides down the throat and mushrooms are extremely disagreeable, even monstrous, when you stare them in the face.

Lonnie's screaming bloody murder at the toast lying buttered and helpless on the Melmac plate. It offends her senses. Mother coaxes Lonnie, "Just try the toast." (She wants to say "the damn toast" but she's not going to blame the toast or fly off the handle; it's way too soon.) All this noise arouses my father, who enters the room with his big stomach, the little hair he has left flapping in the air. "What in Sam Hill is going on here?" he booms.

"Lonnie is frightened of toast this morning. She refuses to eat it," my mother explains.

"EAT THE TOAST," my father bellows.

"NOOO!" Lonnie howls. "NO. NO. NO. NO."

"What do you mean 'no'? What's toast going to do to you?" He shakes the slice like a rattlesnake.

"I've tried everything, Burton. Just let her be." Exasperated, Mother draws her long, freckled hands through her coppery, shoulder-length locks; she likes peace the way I like peace.

"*I'll* get her to eat the damn toast," my father insists, palm outstretched in Lonnie's direction.

"Get your hands off me or I'll strangle you and leave you for dead."

My sister is direct. She's taken to talking like a thug to get her way. Too many Cagney films, Daddy says. But I don't get it. Where does this toughness really come from? I don't have an ounce of tomboy in me, and Lon's filled to the brim. Dressed in bright plaid Bermuda shorts and a crisp cotton blouse, she almost passes for a girl. But that telescope slung over her shoulder and that Buck knife clasped to her belt make people uneasy. They make *me* uneasy.

"Please, Lon," I plead. "You'll like the toast with peanut butter on it."

"No! It's got sharp edges!"

"You want to see sharp edges?" my father threatens stupidly, the side of his hand cutting the air.

Lonnie runs from the table, shrieking and pushing a stuffed animal with three legs and two heads in his face. She has tailored this creature to fit her idea of the universe: the world has two kinds of creatures, freaks and normal people, normal people being the scarier and far more dangerous species. They kill the freaks and make them do irrational things. Like eat toast.

Lonnie and her two-headed friend scramble down the hall, my father close behind with his hairy arms extended. Lonnie makes it to her room and begins to circle frantically, an animal panicking in her cage. Huddled in the hallway, Mother and I listen to some tragedy take place. Everything is a blur when we peek into Lonnie's room.

"Stop, Burton," my mother implores. "Let her be."

"Daddy!" I scream. "Plee-ease. Lonnie doesn't *have* to eat toast. Not everybody likes it." I am not a little peacemaker. I can't even be heard above the din of arms and legs and howling mouths.

I have stopped breathing. Now Mother and Daddy are fighting each other, quarreling over what to do next about Lonnie and the toast. While they confer in the hallway, Lonnie springs onto her mattress, fists clenched.

"I'll kill ya, I'll kill ya, I'll drag you in the gutter. I swear I'll get you an' drain your blood on the pavement. I mean it. I'll get ya when you're sleeping." Then she laughs maniacally, not like a mentally ill person but like a cartoon villain. She drools and spits to scare us, and it works. We know she is the consummate actress and loves to play everything to the hilt. But we also know this blond little girl with a Buster Brown haircut and a murderer's imagination is to be taken seriously.

Later, when I come home from elementary school, I see that the cold, butter-stiff toast is still on the table. I lift it up to my lips. I'm hungry, but will eating toast change that? I decide at the last second that the toast is ruined.

Lonnie lumbers into the kitchen like George Raft. "Oo-zy! Ooze!"

Oozy is her special name for me. She calls me Oozy because, when we play cats, she makes a deep *ooze* sound through her nose instead of the traditional *purr*. Somehow she associates this sweet, contented sound with me, her baby sister. But I don't feel very sweet today, just beat.

"What?" I snap.

"Ya gotta spend time with your good-for-nuthin' sister."

To stave off my guilt, we drink chocolate milk from the carton and eat Cocoa Puffs from the box. To stave off my loneliness, we play with dolls and stuffed animals, and wrestle like all siblings do. Except that Lonnie crunches me with so much love I wonder if I'll live through the afternoon.

Leon the Leopard

1959

am riding in the backseat of our cream-colored Chevrolet, en route to my sister's dark-haired, dark-hearted therapist. We make the trip twice a week, but I am *not* good about going. Lonnie's even worse. She has put out a contract on Mrs. Mancini because this therapist—her fourth—doesn't put up with any nonsense. My mother and I put up with all manner of nonsense; we are afraid of being less than good, and frankly it's messing up our lives.

The Heinz-Heinz Clinic is far away from Burbank. Studio City must be in another country, and there is no freeway yet. We go the long way through the flatlands, past NBC and Warner Bros. studios. I am only seven years old, so the long way is hard on my sense of time and history. Surely I have other things to do at this age, but my vote doesn't count.

Today, as we approach the Cahuenga Pass, the last stretch of undeveloped land connecting Burbank to Studio City, the hillside is a blur. I see five separate moving clouds of dust; they portend some sort of magic. Within seconds, wild horses emerge from the dust clouds; they run riotously every which way. Mother says somebody must be filming a cowboy movie, and my eyes widen. I consider the movies a reason for living! Ever since I was five, I have inserted myself into every movie I've seen and gratefully, humbly found succor there. I've not been on this planet long, but the idea of "elsewhere" appears to be the definition of a happy life. I've learned that "here" is a major disaster, a massacre of possibilities.

The unruly horses are now streaming toward the highway like they might not stop in time. I imagine being trampled to death, metal and horsehair mingling. Lonnie's yelping "Ya-hoo, ride 'em cowboy!" like a wild thing herself. Animals seem to soothe her, the wilder the better. Just before we will be certainly mowed down, the horses change direction, and our Chevrolet crosses over the pass undeterred.

By the time we get to the clinic, the day has become a pressure cooker. Lonnie's upset over the idea that we won't buy her a monkey or a Tokay gecko. She tears off in the direction of the corner drugstore to drool over the latest monster magazines and ogle the Nestlé Crunch bars. Mother drags her back by the wrist, and for half a block Lonnie's screaming, "Meeshy, those horses are going to mash your face with their hooves! They're going to get you for giving birth to me, because I'm a stupid, stupid creature who has to attend this hell-house for maniacs instead of going to a *real* school—like Oozy."

"You're not stupid," I protest, both hands raised to the heavens like some actress wearing a toga in a biblical movie.

"Oh yeah? Then why am I the only schlemiel who's gotta get his brain scanned and body wrapped in bandages like the

Mummy? Why do I gotta go to the torture chamber to be probed by Dr. Mayhem?"

Lonnie's always trying to scare us big. I cover my ears and blink away tears; movies have not prepared me for her brand of savagery. Gazing up at my mother, hoping she'll play God here, I see a woman who, like me, can't quite believe her bad luck. She's stuttering, "I . . . I," and petting Lonnie's white-gold locks. Fear and kindness make her lips twitch. "Such a pretty girl," she says to my sister. My mother is a saint.

"Grrr!" Lonnie exposes her fangs to prove she's the picture of ugliness. "Don't call me a girl. Call me Mad Dog!" She flings Captain Eyeball, the stuffed animal she's been toting every-where for weeks, into Mother's eyes full throttle. Mother smiles a strange, close-lipped smile that's at odds with her sharp hand movements. Captain Eyeball is newly quaran-tined in her navy leather purse, while Lonnie brays like some animal I've never heard.

I   ▮   I

The Heinz-Heinz Clinic gives me the creeps. Sunlight floods the place, but its dark core manages to bleed through. In the waiting room I squirm on a pea-colored Naugahyde couch; my butt squeaks noticeably on the fabric. Those little flecks of dirt on the Naugahyde just might be boogers. Mother distract-edly rubs my hand while she tells Lonnie to settle down, settle down. Shyness tugs at me like a strong tide, threatening to pull me under. I need a disguise, because I want it made abun-dantly clear that I'm not one of *them*—one of the patients.

Lonnie has been a patient here for the last million years. She began her biweekly trips to the Heinz-Heinz—Bloody Ketchup Clinic in Lonnie's lingo—at the age of four. Although she's nine now, two years older than me, she's both my older *and* younger sister. Older in years and because she physically overpowers me—she can have me at the mercy of her gyrating fists in two seconds—and she's smarter too. Although she's been put in a class with mentally ill children her age, she can read and write at the twelfth-grade level. Her vocabulary is astonishing—words like "reticulated," "Australopithecus," and "inhumane" fall off her tongue. But she's my younger sister because she's worse than a baby when it comes to controlling her feelings. They spill out of her body and flood our house all day long. I mean, we're soaked. And younger because, as much as she hates to hear it, a babylike sweetness leaks through her tough-guy stance when she's not on guard. In public, I am sworn to protect my "little" sister; if anyone even looks at her funny, I will clobber them. Well, I'm a wimp so I do my clobbering in a silent, private way.

After five years of brain picking—both Lon's brain and my parents'—the Heinz-Heinz doctors can't decide what's wrong with Lonnie. The director says she's "schizophrenic," but Daddy says that's a bunch of baloney. "Lon does *not* straddle two worlds. She's definitely in one world, albeit her own irrational, insane little universe." The Freudians blame Lon's troubles on The Environment—"the home environment," they told Mother during last week's session, whispering so as not to offend. The non-Freudians believe my sister's problems are chemical, that her chemistry got gummed up inside Mother's womb and that she was autistic for the first three years—before she could express this unique chemistry. One lone doctor insists Lon is "borderline," which doesn't sound so bad to me. When he added, "With paranoid tendencies," he winked in a way that made me want to do some of that silent clobbering. But Lon likes the sound of "paranoid tendencies"; she calls it "piranha tentacles" and laughs a little too heartily to be convincing. All of these diagnoses enrage Daddy—he has little faith in "headshrinkers"—and they make Mother feel so guilty that she also regularly sees Mrs. Mancini at the Double H.

My own idea of what's ailing Lon doesn't count for much, but Mother says it's the most creative. Basically, I think Lon is onto something big. That she knows stuff we can't even imagine. Like what's out there beyond the Milky Way or what goes on where the deep blue sea turns black. Even what's behind our eyes when we shut them tight and see stars. But all of this magical, wise stuff that she picks up like a TV antenna gets mixed up with the drab, normal junk of life and creates static in her head. That's why she makes sense half of the time and the other half she's so bizarre that no one will give her the time of day. Poor Lon. She may be a genius like Albert Einstein and no one will ever know.

Lonnie is intently studying the person directly across from us, her eyes bugged out in obvious pleasure. Hand propped under her chin, she looks like a thoughtful scientist. Hiding unsuccessfully behind *The Saturday Evening Post,* the tall object of her scrutiny has her hair pulled back in a shaggy ponytail; her legs are clad in worn, soiled dungarees. Now the figure's staring back at Lon, equally amused. When the ponytailed lady abandons the magazine, Lonnie's confronted with a confounding beard.

"Are you a man or a woman?" Lonnie asks with utter sincerity, moving into range of the mystery figure.

Mother gasps and covers her mouth with both hands. "It's . . ." She can't spit it out. I do a double take. "It's Gary Cooper," she whispers to me, biting tangerine-shaded lips.

"Who?" I whisper back, trying to be polite.

"The actor, the actor," she sings softly.

Lonnie is now pulling on Gary Cooper's ponytail, examining him like he's an exciting new species. He appears to enjoy her sense of confusion. "I'm a movie actor who's getting ready to play a part," he graciously explains.

"But are you a man or a woman?" she insists.

"Well, I guess I'm a man." He chuckles. "I'm Gary Cooper."

"Oh," she responds neutrally, not offering any sign of recognition. "You sure look funny."

I am dying of embarrassment. What's a movie star doing in this place? Is he crazy too, or just waiting incognito for a loony friend or a wacko wife? I look away to give him all the privacy he needs, feeling badly that he's been found out. It's then my mother tenderly explains that *I* too will be seeing a therapist today, because . . . well . . . she can't explain.

I'm suddenly as small as a hand grenade and very, very furious. Mother gets her voice back. "Honey, the clinic feels it's in your best interests to be tested, in case you need some help coping with your sister. We want to provide that for you."

"Yeah, I'm so bad, Oozy, you might need shock treatments just to live with me. Or get your blood sucked out and replaced with acid." Lonnie pulls the worst possible face. All the light goes out of her milky skin, and she pretends she's a monster coming to eat me, or worse, to spend time with me.

I shoo her away in a wimpy fashion. But Lonnie is invincible; she doesn't stop for anyone. "Not now!" I explode.

Whimpering like a dog, Lon retreats to the toy chest in the corner of the waiting room and fishes out a yellow plastic gun. Hurt by things I can't express, I lick my lips too many times and scowl at the wallpaper's repeating patterns. Staring at paisley would make anyone bonkers. "Why do they need to test *me?*" I ask Mother, as if she's just slapped me hard. "Aren't I okay?"

"Yes, dear, you are just fine—perfect! But they're testing the whole family to make sure that living with"—she nods in the direction of Lonnie—"hasn't upset us too much. They tell me it will be fun—games, stories, dolls."

"Dolls?" I light up.

A pretty woman appears from nowhere and introduces herself. "Lorna, I'm Miss Deary." She extends a hand with pointed, red-lacquered nails—an actress' hand. I shake it gingerly, wondering why my hands already look older than hers.

"Honey, you are just going to have the greatest time! Let's go into the playroom and I'll show you all the wonderful things we have in there. Do you like Tiny Tears dolls?"

Maybe. I dunno. Are dolls that cry real tears supposed to cheer you up? Reluctantly, I follow Miss Deary into what I imagine will be a hall of fun-house mirrors that make you appear stretched out and stretched in, fat and screamy looking. In all the times I've been forced to accompany Mother and Lon, I've never passed through these doors, where all the crazies go. My stomach is in an uproar, but I do what the adults say.

Miss Deary has full, puckered lips like Ann Blyth, the mermaid in a movie I saw when I stayed up too late one night and Daddy forgot I was in the room. She's so gorgeous that I want to kiss her and take her home like Mr. Peabody, the fisherman in the movie, did. Sporting a cute pageboy swept back by a stretchy chartreuse headband, she escorts me into a small room with a grimy linoleum floor. On the floor is a rust-colored throw rug littered with junk: jacks and red rubber balls, a catcher's mitt, a dollhouse, a scratched-up race car, an icky, unfamiliar doll—probably an off-brand—and a mangled, pop-up storybook. Also three tissue boxes in case the "fun" gets out of hand. I sit down Indian-style and await instructions.

"Go on," Miss Deary waves her arms theatrically. "Play!"

Just like that? Wouldn't that be a little odd? I interlace my fingers and press my hands together until they ache, staring at the pearly-pink nail polish curling off my left thumb.

"Honey, feel free to play with anything you see. I'm going to visit another child for a second, but I will be right back." She winks a little too broadly.

I gaze up at Miss Deary's mermaid face and wonder how she can stand it, working with peculiar people, when she's so beautiful. It hurts me that she's already going away when we've just begun. Maybe I'm here to be ignored, just like at home. But I want to show her how darn flexible I can be, so I nod okay and pretend that the threadbare storybook is one of the ten wonders of the world.

"You're sure you're comfortable, honey?"

"Uh-huh," I peep and decide not to make my move until she's all the way down the hall. I notice that the weirdo doll actually has a very sweet face that's comforting. I take her up in my arms to check out her hair. It's thinning and stinky; the doll has been pawed to death by children with problems, which makes me kind of sick. But I can't abandon her; she needs me. So I raise her face up to meet mine and let our cheeks rub each other, like sisters do. I feel the warmth of the doll's soft plastic and press her more forcefully into my face. Then, feeling superselfconscious, I lay the wrecked doll in my lap. After a minute, I pick her up again and peek under her dress. The doll doesn't have any panties on, so I quickly pat down her frock to make it look fresh, even springy. To help her out in this place I decide to give her a name: Sarah? Becky Sue? Suzy Sadhead? On the rug, a tiny comb with missing teeth catches my eye, and I use it to comb out the newly dubbed Mindy's messy hair. When I've made her into someone respectable, I imagine her interacting with my other dolls. Without warning, Miss Deary breezes in with an enormous, severe smile.

"Hi, sweetheart! How are we doing?"

"Okay," I confess. I place the doll on the floor face down.

Miss Deary sits down next to me and smooths out the tight tweed skirt that demurely covers her mermaid "legs." "We're going to tell each other stories today. Do you like stories?" She doesn't wait for my answer but forges ahead with instructions. "I will begin a story and you will jump in and finish it—got the picture?" I nod my head.

"So Lorna-lee, here-we-goooo! A princess is very sad because she's never had a true friend. Her dog, Pesky, is her only pal. One day, while crying her eyes out, she comes upon a thick oak tree with a very old woman sitting at the bottom of it." Miss Deary leans into me and whispers, "Your turn, missy."

"Um," I say, "the princess asks the old lady for a lunch sack 'cause she's really really hungry. The old lady says no. No, no, no! The princess faints from hunger. But she's so light, she rises into the air and . . . um, flies above the head of the old woman. She buzzes around the old woman's head like a buzzard or a lovely bluebird or a bee with a mean old stinger or—"

"Yes?" Miss Deary encourages.

I realize that this is a setup. If I am too clever or violent or inventive, she will have my head on a platter. If my story is too plain, I won't have any fun at all. If my story is halfway neat and halfway normal, I will pass this test but have a dumb time doing it. This is the first time in my short life that I see how thin the line is, the one between the okay people and the not-okay ones.

"I don't feel too good," I tell Miss Deary.

"But your story was very powerful," she lets me know, running her ruby-red fingernails through her perfect pageboy fluff.

"It's a story about an angry girl, isn't it?" I chew on my hair while she reads the inscription on her pencil and appears to find it compelling.

"Oh, I don't know. Do *you* think so?" I don't answer, so she begins again. "The next story is about a little boy in a wheelchair. His mother loves him but she is very tired of pushing her boy around. She's just pooped! What happens next?"

"Uh . . . she decides to wrap red velvet ribbons around the wheelchair. She gives the ends of the ribbons to a flock of birds [uh-oh, I gulp, birds again!] who lift the chair off the ground, higher and higher into the sky. The boy floats above the clouds and makes friends with everybody else who's flying that day."

"And the mother?" Miss Deary interjects.

"The mother, who is very sweet and loving, gets a day off from pushing around her son. She goes dancing with the father of—"

"Of?" Miss Deary's eyes widen, like I'm onto something important.

". . . of her son's best friend. He makes dancing shoes for a living. The mother and the man slip on sequined dancing shoes and waltz around on the ground at a grand French park while their boys are floating above them in the sky, happy at last. The mother and the man kiss a whole lot and decide to start a school for handicapped children. But they don't have to work there. They don't have to do anything but dance."

"Really?" Miss Deary looks pleased at this one. She takes a long breath through her upturned nose. "Last story. A little girl hates her life on the farm. She decides to run away and become a . . ."

". . . a dashing skywriter, writing love poems in the sky with her handsome boyfriend pilot. They write in loop-de-loops and, before long, everyone sees their special message."

"Which is?"

"I dunno," I shrug.

"Oh, surely you can think of something?"

Eyes closed, I can see only a swarm of blinking blue and yellow dots; then the words form in my head. "Their message is: Leave us alone forever! We're happy and in love and will *never* come down!"

Miss Deary scribbles hastily on her notepad, a sign that something I said was peculiar. "You're quite the storyteller," she says in a bright, warm voice. "Now tell me about Lonnie. Is it hard for you to live with her?"

"Yeah," I reluctantly admit, "but she can't help it." I study the loops in the throw rug and imagine hiding within their deep shadows.

"Tell me what it's like to live with her."

"Oh, you know." I twist the Mindy doll's hair around my forefinger.

"No, honey, I really don't."

"Oh, she screams all the time because everything is wrong in her world. Certain colors and foods and noises make her nuts. She hates to hear babies cry. She hates *me* sometimes because she thinks I'm better off than her. But it's not true. I'm just luckier." I suck on my lower lip; my eyes begin to fill with water.

"Does she make you nervous?"

I shake my head vigorously up and down, tears jumping off my cheeks, as if I've just turned Lonnie in to the police.

"Would you mind drawing a picture of how Lonnie makes you feel?"

Miss Deary hands me a box of Crayolas and a clean sheet of manila paper, then runs out of the room without explanation. I take up the crayon labeled "Flesh" and draw a huge head surrounded by whacked-out, straw-colored hair. I fill in the head with a face that's both ghastly and pretty: one eye true blue, the other dipping down and purple; a mouth that's howling and laughing and hopeful, and a brain that's planning a major escape. Then I add a background of violet bows and bluebirds. When I finish, it's clear I've drawn something vaguely familiar: it's the Mindy doll imprisoned in this clinic.

Miss Deary rushes in and abruptly snaps up the portrait. "Thank you, Lorna. Well, time's up! Your mother is waiting for you." I know I look crushed, because she adds, "This picture is just wonderful—will you sign it for me?" I print

"Lorna Person" over the face I've drawn and imagine Miss Deary tossing it into the wastebasket as soon as I leave the room. Holding hands, we walk down the hall in silence; I can feel the weight of her sorrow. In the waiting room, she tells Mother that I am a good sport, that I'm a real artist and a gifted storyteller. Mother is pleased.

Miss Deary hugs me good-bye; her skin smells like stale flowers and baby powder. But I don't get to kiss her mermaid lips. "Oh goodness, wait a second!" she shakes a finger at my nose. Hobbled by her tight skirt, she scurries over to the receptionist, who hands her a crinkled brown shopping bag. Her arm disappears all the way into it, and I prepare myself for candy. Instead, out of the mysterious bag, Miss Deary produces some kind of stuffed tiger or lion or leopard. "The Heinz-Heinz Clinic would like you to accept this gift as thanks for spending time with us."

With us? She presents the animal like a peace offering. I decide that it's a leopard; it's got the kind of fur that, when new, is deeply thrilling. Plush with dark brown spots, he'll be something good to smush into my face on a bad night.

As she delivers the leopard into my tiny palms, Miss Deary commends me for my courage: "You are a brave little girl." But I catch her shaking her head as if she knows my future isn't going to be so sunny. How could she know this? Did something in my test tip her off?

I take the gift like I'm supposed to, but the animal makes me shy. I hadn't expected a souvenir, and I'm not that fond of stuffed animals. Couldn't she see I'm the doll type? Nonetheless, I've earned something big today. I grab the leopard, put it back in the sack, and hug the sack to my chest on the long drive home.

I   ∎   I

I make a life for the leopard at 114 Bethany Road. I name him Leon—Leon the Leopard—because it sounds noble. Leon sleeps near my face every night for months, a soft reminder of having my sanity questioned. Gratefully, he's a prince of a stuffed animal. For one thing, his loyalty is without peer. It doesn't matter if I cry too hard or pick my nose in front of him or plunge my lips far into his fur; he is steadfast. I'm sure he will keep my secrets until I can no longer remember what he might or might not know. Even if his fur becomes ragged and yellow, I will love him unconditionally. But frankly, I don't know how to create a personality for a jungle cat, not like the detailed lives I invent for my fashion-plate dolls.

Tonight, after a hundred nights of Leon sleeping on my pillow, I realize that the question he poses is growing old and irritating. Though he's a toy that exudes calm, he is also a nagging reminder of what I fear most: that I am deeply, truly crazy and have gotten away by the hairs of my chinny-chin-chin.

Afraid to answer Leon's question, I hide him away in a dusty shoe box. "Really, Lorna," I scold myself, "you're getting way too mature for stuffed animals!" I place the shoe box high up on a shelf in my closet, and climb into bed without my leopard for the first time in months.

But it's no use; I hear a rumbling in the shoe box where Leon fitfully sleeps. *Sorry,* I say to the ceiling. *Sorry,* I tell God. Confused, I step out of my covers and tiptoe over to the closet. I stretch my arms as far as they will go to reach Leon's box. Maybe I should allow Leon back on my pillow. Maybe I should be a better friend. The guilt is killing me, but the guilt is familiar. I leap back into bed and sit on my hands. Leon will be liberated only when it's safe—maybe when I'm ten years old—and then only for a few minutes at a time.

Miss Universe

1961

rs. Fisher must be fearless. She arrives at our house every Saturday night to bear witness to our lives. She acts regular in a house that looks and sounds and probably smells weird. A classic little old lady who could have been sent from Central Casting, she comes with the requisite blue-gray bun and wrinkles. She even twinkles! Though no cooking is required of her, she ties a gingham apron around her tiny waist the second she arrives. But no matter; she gives me faith in the idea of calm or perhaps has given me the very idea. Though spindly and slow, Mrs. Fisher's a good egg, and so soft to the fingers. Her cheeks crumble under my touch. When she gets steamed, she says "Oh fudge!" (it took me years to realize that "fudge" and "fuck" were interchangeable), and flaps her arms up and down in a regrettable way. I

feel ashamed and scared when this happens; she's so fragile she might topple over, and we don't need another catastrophe on our hands.

Already, Lonnie has exhausted a string of capable sitters, young women who couldn't bear the noise or the responsibility, and veterans whose spirits were crushed by too many evenings of insane-asylum antics, hellish screams, and absurd, bone-chilling death threats: "Lemme outta this godforsaken joint or I'll tie you up and leave you for the maggots!" "Lemme have another Hostess Twinkie or I'll make this your *last* supper!" Lonnie's accustomed to getting her way, and our sitters aren't willing to test this.

But Mrs. Fisher never lets on that this assignment at 114 Bethany Road has been the worst in her long, stellar career. She's been extraordinarily patient and kind with us, sloughing off insults and attacks like a priest (or someone deaf). She calls us "darling" or "dear," and Lonnie calls her "Fish Face" or "Fish Eyes." Out of respect (and for balance), I call her "Mrs. Fisher." I'm not sure how old people handle nicknames. If I was bolder, I'd call her "Grand Duchess"—something elevated. If I was really bold, I wouldn't stay in this family.

Every Saturday night my parents bail out of here in Daddy's black Ford Galaxie. They go to the latest movie and eat the latest kind of food at a neighborhood restaurant that's offering a two-for-one deal. I'm not jealous, though; I know they deserve a break from who we are together.

While Mother and Daddy are away, I try to use the time well. I ask Mrs. Fisher to show her commitment to me in a very personal way. "Can you cut out some clothes for my paper dolls?" I usually mumble, unsure of my demands. Mrs. Fisher never complains about these assignments; she seems almost grateful. Last week, she liberated Peggy Lee's entire wedding trousseau, cutting neatly around the flaps like she really cared.

Tonight, I've given Mrs. Fisher the daunting task of cutting out every outfit in my new Lennon Sisters paper doll book. Tomorrow morning, like magic, each sister—Diane, Kathy, Peggy, and Janet (my pet)—will have something divine to wear. On the coffee table, I've lined up each doll alongside her ensembles in hopes that Mrs. Fisher will apply herself, truly outdo herself, and provide four times the usual number of paper frocks, sequined gowns, picnic togs, modest bathing suits, and filmy boudoir attire. As Mrs. Fisher artfully attacks Janet's alpine outfit, I sit next to her on the couch for moral support, breathing in her Evening in Paris perfume. We're poised to watch the Miss Universe Pageant, and I can't allow anything to divert me from this goal. It's a two-hour special that should keep me hooked and calm.

This year I am pulling for Miss Argentina. Because she's a brunette, she's far more vulnerable than the blond contestants; her dark, velvety kindness leaks through the TV screen. During the swimsuit competition, she radiates compassion; in the talent competition, she offers a moving soliloquy as Anne Frank—although everyone must see she's a bit old for the part. But during the critical question-and-answer sequence, she positively soars.

The emcee has asked the five finalists the ultimate question: "If you are crowned Miss Universe, what will be the most important service you can offer the world?"

Miss Argentina licks her glossy lips, lowers her head like she's praying, then smiles defiantly at the judges. "I plan to use my title as a springboard for working with poor and disadvantaged children. I want to touch and change as many lives as I can."

I fiercely applaud Miss Argentina, while Mrs. Fisher snorts, "They all say the same thing! Can you believe this nonsense?" Mrs. Fisher is rooting for Miss Norway (a blonde!) and can't identify with the poor and disadvantaged—her family life on a farm in Iowa was the picture of normalcy. But I am stead-fast in my love for Miss Argentina; I want to touch lives too.

During a Breck shampoo commercial, I begin planning my own acceptance speech. I do this every year to see if I'm worthy. In my head I conjure up a vertiginous moment of applause, sweeping orchestral music, and a veil of real tears. My knees wobble as the emcee (James Darren? Tab Hunter?) announces my name, but I accept my tiara with a grace that has risen from unknown depths:

As the proud candidate hailing from the great state of California, and the even greater nation of America, I want to thank all the world's people for believing in me—*a big-nosed, flat-footed girl from Burbank, California. Believing in me enough to see past my oodles of flaws and stupid sensitivity. And for recognizing my potential for greatness. Yes, even at my tender age, I do a few things well: I doodle pictures of girls' faces. I can draw a variety of hairdos. I write stories about girls who fend for themselves, and I'm destined to become a fabulous actress, given half the chance. You people are amazing (and a little bit suspect) for seeing something growing inside of me. Thank you. You are too much. I hope I won't let you down. If I haven't already.*

My schmaltzy reverie is demolished by the presence of Lonnie; she's blocking the TV set, waving a headless Lennon Sister (please God, not Janet!) as the supreme taunt. She can't stand that Mrs. Fisher's attention has been redirected to me, a person who she believes has the world at her feet.

"Oozy, turn off that frilly girl show. You always get to do what you wanna do. You can go to a real school and you can drive and vote—"

"I'm only nine!" I insist.

"And you can go out on the town with your ugly, normal friends—"

"I don't *have* any friends!"

"That's because they're all afraid to come over here and meet *me*, the Creature from the Black Lagoon. Your friends are afraid they'll catch my disease."

"And what disease is that?" I ask sarcastically. "Scales, gills, and third eyes?"

"Heh-heh-heh," Lonnie laughs, always pleased when I support her ghoulish image of herself. "Yeah, scaly-itus! It's like scoliosis, but worse!"

Now I see that Lonnie hasn't really snipped off the head of my paper doll; she's just bent it down so that the doll appears headless. "Give me back my paper doll!"

Mrs. Fisher nods her head in approval; I think she's been cowering behind me the whole time. After a fidgety silence, she intervenes. "Lonnie. The doll is Lorna's. You know that, darling."

I make a face at the "darling." Lonnie's still a young girl like me, but with her wrinkled brow and precocious biceps, she appears to be carrying the weight of Khrushchev's Russia. She's sporting a freshly buzzed-off haircut that's absolutely freaky. Last week, in a secret act with Daddy's electric razor, she shaved her straight hairline into a widow's peak, hoping to join the club of vampires that live in her head. Her pretty white-blond hair is now sticking straight up like a Fuller Brush man's scrub brush. My sister, who only a month ago could pass for Hayley Mills in *The Parent Trap*, is now so distorted that I have to look away: I have seen this hair before in a documentary on concentration camps that aired on *The 20th Century*. I couldn't look at those women either.

"Lonnie dear, please give Lorna her doll and I'll give you some buttermilk and a Fig Newton in the kitchen."

Lonnie scowls at me like a Dead End Kid, then flings my once-fresh paper doll on the rug as if it's smelly garbage. To scare us out of our skins this evening, she's adorned herself with a shark's tooth necklace, a ghastly shrunken head on a cord that she bought at Pacific Ocean Park, a cheap plastic skeleton ring, and her ubiquitous flesh-colored earplugs. Noises, especially the giggles and girl talk of the Miss Universe Pageant, annoy her no end. Unfair, because the crude sounds of wrestling and boxing matches are like music to her ears. At the cries of babies, she cringes, but during baseball games she revels at the outcries of opinionated old men. I am onto her and she knows it. Still, I protect Lon from the "bad" sounds as much as I can—otherwise, she'll make bad sounds of her own.

"Oozy can't have all the fun, Mrs. Fisher. Ya gotta save some leftovers for me!"

"In due time, in due time . . ." Our baby-sitter pats her tightly wound bun and takes a shaky, shallow breath.

"Listen up, Fish Face! I wanna watch *Thriller*, not this girly crap with voodoo dolls walking all over the stage showing their tushes!" Lonnie lunges at Mrs. Fisher as if she's going to bite off her powdered nose.

Mrs. Fisher flutters her eyelashes and makes little wiggly smiles. "I promised Lorna she could watch her show. It's only on once a year and *Killer* comes on every week. Let's give Lorna a chance, dear."

"Okay, I'll give Lorna the chance of a lifetime: I'll give her her *last* chance to live by letting me see my show. Or else something really terrible will happen to her when she's sleeping."

Standing within an inch of Mrs. Fisher's dainty waist, Lonnie flexes her cute, bunched-up muscles. In a surprise attack, she bolts onto our plastic-encased davenport and makes a show of bouncing on its tired cushions. Taller than Mrs. Fisher now, Lonnie appears to take up more room in our house than I thought possible. Fists protecting her face, she tightens her body into a defensive position and holds it so long that she begins to quiver.

Still, I'm numb to her threats tonight: Miss Argentina just got crowned third runner-up, and I'm clapping like I'm right there in Miami Beach, out of my head with excitement. "Yay! Yay! Yay!"

Lonnie and Mrs. Fisher have taken their standoff into the front hall, which has been freshly painted by Daddy in some newfangled process called Zolotoning. Mrs. Fisher's voice is unusually loud, and I can't hear who the first runner-up is. "Shut up, Lonnie!" I snarl. (I could never ask Mrs. Fisher to pipe down.)

"Oh yeah? You prissy pink princess!" Lonnie shakes her fist at me like a mobster. "I'll clam up for good and then you won't have *me* to ruin your evening ever again, 'cuz I'll be dead and six feet under!"

Lonnie pantomimes her tragic death, stake-through-the-heart style, and I begin to fill with regret, already picturing myself weeping at her grave. Before I can tell her that I love her and that she shouldn't even *think* of dying, Lonnie has bounded out the front door, into the thrill of the Burbank night. I hear screams up the street and wonder if that's my big sister or if the whole world is having a problem tonight.

Mrs. Fisher grabs her purse and my left arm, and we fly out the front door, racing up the hill and past the cozy-looking tract houses. I wish I had a disguise for these occasions, a way to be related to my sister that didn't show. I feel Mrs. Fisher's hand trembling in mine and realize that she doesn't have a clue as to where Lonnie has gone. I am frantic, studying the driveways of all the neighbors, who, I suspect, can't stand us— because we're Jewish or because we have a crazy person in our family, or maybe both. The shadows aren't friendly; I hear stupid little dogs whining and the brassy sounds of TV sets. Oh fudge, I've just missed the announcement of the new Miss Universe.

I see the flickering image of Ginny Merkle, a girl in my class who has always seemed standoffish, as if I emit some kind of rotten fumes. She's moving back and forth in front of her kitchen window, laughing and drinking soda with another girl. Their giggles pierce me; I'm convinced they're laughing at me, scampering up the street with an old lady in tow.

Mrs. Fisher wraps her yellow cardigan around her thin, white frame and warbles into the hot summer wind. "Lonnie, Lonnie, dear! Sweetheart, come back! You can watch your little show. Honey, please come back!"

My own squeaky voice has got fear written all over it. "Lon? Lonnie? Lon-neeee! Please come home . . ." I can't see anything in front of me except hulking cars and the swaying skeletons of trees. I turn around to make sure that Mrs. Fisher is keeping pace with me and discover she's a half step behind. We look into each other's eyes and see the same thing: cloudy irises and tears.

"I'm terrified," she confides. "Whatever am I going to tell your mother? That I lost her daughter? Good God! Sweet Jesus!"

I have never heard Mrs. Fisher swear and wonder if I am going to lose *her* to the night too. Then it will all be up to me, sweet Jesus, Moses, or whoever. I must find some courage, I must find my sister. "Let's go up higher," I tell her. "Lonnie's gone into the hills."

"How do you know?" Mrs. Fisher tugs at my arm. "It's so dark, she can't see her own feet."

A shiver passes up my thighs, even though it's too hot for goose bumps. And then I detect something a few yards in front of me that's shaped like a human being: it's a father coming home late to his happy family, kissing his wife hello on the doorstep, and expecting something tasty for dinner. Mrs. Fisher and I walk and then run as quickly as we can up another whole block. The incline is getting steeper, and we are huffing and puffing like two old ladies.

Straight ahead, an animal sound startles us. "Listen to that," I instruct Mrs. Fisher, who looks as worried as a guy strapped in an electric chair.

"It's a coyote," she whispers.

"No," I shake my head. "It's her!"

I get a sense of what's going on now. Lonnie thinks like an animal. Like a frightened wolf or fox or bobcat, she plans to scramble into the Burbank foothills as far as she can go. She's always got to make a whopping big point: *I am not human, guys, remember?*

"Look," I point dead ahead. My eyes follow a tall moving shadow as it washes over a backyard retaining wall and merges with the shiny rocks behind it. Mrs. Fisher cautions me not to trespass. This is not a tract house like the ones on our block; this house belongs to somebody with money, and maybe they will come out and shoot us to protect their fancy trappings. Now the shadow is climbing the rugged face of the hill.

"Oozy's gonna get bitten, Oozy's gonna get bit."

Thank God, it's Lonnie. "Lo-onn!" I yell. "Get down here! Now!"

"No!" she bellows. "You wanted me dead and now I'm going away for good."

"Please?" I beg.

"Forget it, murderer. Oozy is a killer, Oozy is a killer," she chants.

Mrs. Fisher is beside herself and can't speak; she's looking at the ground like this is not happening. Unexpectedly, I fill with a strange kind of love: maybe Lonnie *should* live in the hills. She's suited for them. The salamanders and snakes and insects respect her. Maybe we've been trying to cage a wild thing for too many years.

The shadow climbs higher, until I can see nothing but bare rock and the occasional weed. Then, small stones rain down on us, and I hear the screech of a baboon. Mrs. Fisher is biting her lower lip so hard, I think I see blood. She motions stiffly. "C'mon, let's call the police."

"No," I caution, oddly in control. "They can't do anything, they'd only make it worse. Lonnie's not afraid of cops, and she'd happily go out with a big bang."

"What do you mean, 'Go out'? 'Big bang'?" she repeats, hands on her chest, trying to still her heart.

"You know—make a scene, do something dramatic." I tend to forget that not every family knows drama like our lucky clan.

"Dramatic?" Mrs. Fisher's voice cracks. "More than *this*?"

"Yeah, a big Academy Award type of scene. She might act like a rabid dog or a berserk wolfman. The police could shoot her if she does her wolfman act."

"W-wolf?" Mrs. Fisher stutters.

Now I've succeeded in frightening both of us. Meanwhile, Lonnie has stopped pitching rocks. I can't see a trace of my sister; the silence almost hurts. "Lonnie?" I query, "I'm gonna count to ten and then call the police. I swear it."

More silence. Then the truth. "Lonnie, this is really upsetting me."

"Good!" she blurts out from some unknown place at least fifteen feet away.

It's then I decide I can't take any more of this. I am a wreck. I am a nervous wreck, just like my parents, and there's little hope of changing this. I will live my life as a wreck and forever be searching the hills for my sister in the middle of the night. I will always bite my nails and feel ashamed of my hands. I will always eat my dinner too quickly and hardly taste it. Till the end of my days I will hide in my room and wonder if I'm really okay or just faking it.

In the midst of my terror, Mrs. Fisher kisses my ear. She shouts in the direction of a large bush halfway up the hillside that's bobbing suspiciously, "Well, good-bye dear, we really are too tired to stay out all night." We make sounds as if we're leaving.

"Yellow-bellied cowards!" Lonnie roars.

So she wants to be saved after all. I smile and try the only approach that's left: shtick. "Lonnie, get your big *tookis* down here, you *meshuganah* Creature from the Black Lagoon."

"Heh-heh." Her classic cartoon laugh.

"I'll let you watch your schlemiel monster show and let you eat as many chocolate-covered matzoh balls as you want. Your wormy little sister will crawl under a rock while you have a monster bash and barbecue my paper dolls on the hibachi."

Mrs. Fisher wrinkles her nose like I'm speaking Spanish. She doesn't realize how much I've flattered Lonnie by entering her world. She doesn't know Lon's got a yen for Yiddish.

As my sister makes her way down the hill, she shakes her head of wigged-out hair and makes fake mountain lion sounds. I answer with a poorer version of growls and roars. By the time I spot Lonnie's wild-eyed face in the moonlight, both of us are howling at the moon in unison. I give her a bear hug, but she shakes me off violently. Without warning, the back-porch lights of the fancy house flick on, and we are forced to hush up. Like common criminals, we hustle out of the backyard and silently make our way down Bethany Road. Holding hands, Mrs. Fisher and I practically weep with relief, while Lonnie grins like the Cheshire Cat. Her cheeks are smudged with dirt like an orphan in the movies, and she's got twigs and leaves in her hair and on her Peter Pan collar.

As we approach the driveway to our house, Mrs. Fisher mumbles a brief, unrecognizable prayer. I am praying too— that no one has seen or heard us. Lonnie jabs me in the ribs, cracking herself up with the stalest jokes: "Home sour home, Oozy. You know that home is where the fart is." We've left the front door wide open, and the screen door's flapping back and forth in the eerie Santa Ana wind.

Lonnie saunters in like she owns the place and turns on the television. She tunes in *Thriller* and plops down on the couch, a little too close to my Lennon Sisters. In minutes, she's hissing at the set, foamy drool spilling out both sides of her mouth. Disgusted, she turns off the TV and stalks into the kitchen. Mrs. Fisher and I run after her like prison guards.

"What's happening now?" I shout in Lonnie's ear. Nothing more can happen. I won't allow it.

"I've seen that episode," Lon whines. "It's slow and silly and cheap, cheap, cheap! It doesn't feature the type of sophisticated monster I like." Lonnie throws open the refrigerator door and snatches a carton of buttermilk from the shelf. She takes a swig of milk and wipes her chin. "Gotta go drinkin'," she announces, and plods down the hall to her room, gripping the milk carton like a beer can.

With Lonnie our captive, Mrs. Fisher locks every door and window she can think of, then sits down on the sofa to catch her breath. She nervously flips through an old *Saturday Evening Post*, sucking a lemon drop she's removed from her purse. I sidle up to her on the sofa, my butt sticking to the plastic casing we keep on the cushions for protection. Is it too much to ask of her now, to cut out clothes for my Lennon Sisters? Before I speak up, she sighs, "Oh, Lordy."

I decide to leave her alone and retire to my room. Good night, Grand Duchess, I want to say. " 'Night, Mrs. Fisher." I kiss her on the cheek and get a noseful of Evening in Paris.

" 'Night, Lorna," she answers melodically. For a fleeting moment, we stare into each other's eyes and she winks; it's as if we've been through a war together.

In my peppermint pink room, I tear off my clothes and throw on baby-doll pajamas decorated with pictures of petite hamburgers and hot dogs. I turn down my covers and turn off the light. Norwood, my best and only friend, my extra-fuzzy gray kitty, has been waiting for me—an especially happy lump on the bed. We snuggle in the dark; he's purring, I'm just trying to calm down. But some kind of lunatic laughter interrupts us. Through the common bedroom wall, I can hear Lonnie cackling.

I shudder in the dark on this hot, windy night. Then my thoughts turn to myself, to my odd, unlucky life. Could a person be disqualified from the Miss Universe Pageant for harboring a crazy sister? No, I reassure myself, realizing that, for me, the pageant's many years away. Even though I'm snug under a single cotton sheet, more doubts bubble up: Will I be prettier when the time comes? Will I be more deserving?

I pull my stiff floral bedspread over my head and decide to work on my acceptance speech. To beef it up where I can, here and now.

Normal

1962

addy is Zolotoning the living room ceiling in an inspired rage. He's pretending he's a mad artist, the van Gogh of housepainters, with a little Daffy Duck thrown in to make me squeal. "Daddy, please stop it!" He loves to make me die of embarrassment. The more I ask him to stop, the more he prances girlishly with his paint gun, abruptly turning into a trigger-happy cowboy. Lustrous flecks of gold flick onto our ceiling from the gun's nozzle. Noxious fumes fill the air.

"This ceiling's not big enough for the both of us!" Daddy boasts with an exaggerated John Wayne accent. He's decked out in an old bowling shirt with "Burt" embroidered above the single pocket, and stained, baggy swim trunks that have dropped well below his stomach.

Daddy's clearly in top form, toting his bulky gear around

like a big shot. This weekend he's already sprayed our bathroom a pukey peach color and the kitchen walls a moody vegetable green. Mother says Zolotoning gives him something to do that's completely different from his job as an accountant at CBS—something blissfully separate from us, the family. But that's okay with me; separate is good, and the Zolotone gives our home texture. The paint doesn't cover our walls with just one color, it endows them with a wide range of possibilities. Gray, red, and green mingle to make our bathroom the idea of peach. I'm convinced that Zolotone warms the surface of our house; it covers up the bad spots. It's the newest thing in paint, and we have it before anybody else. I can't help feeling a little special, a little superior. All this space-age business is thrilling.

Last month, Daddy was equally inspired. He completed a breathtaking mural of the ruins of Pompeii on the far living room wall. Tracing a wall-sized image with a stencil kit and then coloring in the shapes by number in the most sensitive way, he created a scene of unparalleled beauty and high drama. But I'm not sure this scene belongs in a living room. I mean, doesn't it depict the aftermath of the world's worst volcanic eruption and the loss of thousands of lives? It seems strange to me that what's considered beautiful is often brutal.

At least Daddy didn't stencil in all the dead bodies that must have been pinned under the glamorous ruins. I know how much he hopes to bring a slice of paradise into our lives. That is why I will remember to ooh and aah over his mural until he feels his work has been fully appreciated.

I'm an artist too. My young fingers itch with talent! When Daddy gets testy and shoots off his mouth ("Everyone clear the joint, I'm taking over the dining room!"), I hole up in my room to fill my drawing pad with picture after picture. I begin by drawing the same five circles I've made since I was four. The game is called Making a New Family. I like the surprise of making families; you fill in the circles with face parts, mixing and matching features until the children have a combination of their parents' good looks. See, I'm giving the father a big nose but thin lips, straight brown hair, and squinty eyes, and the mother full lips, big eyes, curly blond hair, and a pug nose. The little girl gets the straight brown hair and large nose of her father, and the big saucer eyes of her mother. The little boy gets the full, girlish lips and wavy blond hair of the mother, and the bulbous nose of the father. I take a pause, then fill in the baby's features: pug nose, full lips, two hairs. Voilà, and on to the next family!

"Ooze, come out of there and play with me or I'll twist your neck off!" It's Lonnie, the scourge of the hallway.

"I'm busy, Lon. Give me a few minutes alone."

"You're so busy you'll work yourself to death!" she complains. "Let me in. It stinks out here!" Lonnie pummels the door with her fists, and since it really does stink, I have no choice but to let her in. She pushes her way into my bedroom and wrests the drawing pad from me. "What are these clown faces, Oozy? They're ghastly, heh-heh!"

"I'm making new families," I reluctantly confide. I explain my technique of drawing circles with colored pencils, and filling them with endless combinations of facial features.

"Very clever, Ooze. You're a mad scientist, creating new life from dead faces! Doctor Oozy Frankenstein!" Lonnie doubles over with laughter.

"Hey, what's so funny? My families aren't monsters. They're my beautiful creations."

"And you're *my* creation, Oozy. I made you in the laboratory, which is why you're so twisted!" She points at me knowingly, as if she has privileged information.

"Cut it out, Lon." I yank the drawing pad out of her hands and hide it in the closet. "Beat it!"

Lonnie cuddles up to me, the fawning, purring cat-sibling.

"Sorry, Ooze, didn't mean to make you jump out of your skin and leave it in a pile on the floor. Can ya play with me now? I'm a lonely, desperate creature." She purrs against my cheek for emphasis and holds my wrists a little too tight.

"Okay," I sigh. I cannot deny her. "Let's play school."

"Yay! I'll get the mob." Lonnie races out to round up her motley crew: goofy, threadbare stuffed animals; Ken dolls whose heads have been removed and replaced with much larger heads with burned-off hair, their bodies painted silver. Even jars of floating yellow goop!

I venture into the depths of my closet and remove my badly scuffed, black patent-leather doll case. I open the lid. Okay, I haven't taken very good care of my own dolls. There are too many disembodied legs here to make me feel like a good mother. The tiny clothes are a shambles. An air of decaying rubber and musty cotton rises from the doll case and makes me gag. "Sorry," I say out loud to no one.

I pluck Tressica from the heap of splayed bodies. She's the leader, the one with all the power. Then I remove Becky, the classy Madame Alexander doll with the radiant white complexion, carrottop locks, and spray of freckles. Too bad she's nearly bald; silken clumps of hair have dropped off her head as if she's been exposed to an atom bomb (or Lonnie). Then there's Joanne, sleek and aristocratic, with the hardest of boobs—a cheap knockoff of Barbie. And finally, my sweetie-pie Midge doll—a nicer, flatter, and more wholesome doll than Barbie could ever be. I've never owned a Barbie and don't care to. She's too sharp featured and unfeeling. I can't help but think that Barbie wouldn't like me much either. She'd consider me a wimp, a doll owner who feels too much, who'd surely force her to do the same. Could Barbie feel sorrow? Could Barbie understand what it's like to be plump, lonely, Jewish?

I line up my dolls against the closet, primping their dresses and tamping down their stray hairs. Lonnie rushes in with her gaggle of beasts. The monkey gang is out in full force today: there's Captain Eyeball, the monkey astronaut, who wears a spacesuit; he's a reasonable creature, and often, when things get out of hand, I can appeal to Lonnie through the Captain. Then there's Jocko, the big cheese, the gang leader who bosses my dolls around as if they were slaves. Come to think of it, Jocko acts suspiciously like Daddy when Daddy throws his weight around. But Jocko talks more like Jimmy Cagney and Daddy acts more like Jackie Gleason.

Over the last four years we've noticed that Lonnie has developed a thing for thugs. A big thing. I don't understand why a soft-cheeked, angel-faced girl would pretend she was the toughest thing around, but this is her strategy. "Lorna excels at sweet and Lonnie excels at tough," Mother says. Lon and I bicker about this all the time; she calls me a "pushover," and I call her a "pushy pig." She's determined to win an award for being the opposite of everything that little girls are supposed to be.

In addition to the monkey gang, Lon contributes a few more students: Pyrozykees, a doll of unknown origin with a giant alien head or swelled brain. Frankly, I don't know *what* sits atop its shoulders, but I have gotten used to it. Pyrozykees is one of my best students, a brain in every sense of the word. Then there's Bad Dog Benjy, a fiercely comic hound; Harry the Horsehead, a hand puppet of rare depth; and Junky Jerry, a clown whom Lonnie has outfitted with extra arms and legs. As I prepare to lead the class, using Tressica the doll as my official stand-in, Lonnie's creatures tear the place apart, arguing amongst themselves and tossing each other around mercilessly.

"School is in session," Miss Tressica Scott announces wearily. "And I forgot my shotgun," she adds tartly. She already knows she doesn't have the inner resources to handle this crowd. "Welcome back after Easter vacation. Did everyone have a good time?"

"Yeah, man!" Lonnie's brood raves in unison. "We had a blast!"

"Good, good," Tressica tells the class. "So I'm sure you're ready to work hard now and focus on your studies."

"Study *this!*" Jocko bellows and slams Bad Dog Benjy hard against the ceiling. All the animals guffaw and encourage more of this play.

"No roughhousing in my classroom!" Tressica insists. "Or you're out of here!"

"Yes, Miss Scott," the animals sing. "We'll be so good that you won't recognize us," adds Pyrozykees.

"Fine," Tressica continues. "Now, I'd like all of us to draw a picture of what we did over the Easter break, then dress up our pictures with interesting titles. Okay?"

Lonnie forces all her beasts to nod, and I make my dolls agree like ladies: "Yes, Miss Scott, we'd *love* to."

A furry brown hand waves frantically in front of Tressica's face. "Yes? What is it now, Jocko?" she says crossly.

"Can I draw a pitcher of my gang terrorizing the neighborhood? The slugfest that went down last Tuesday? Or how 'bout a pitcher of me robbing Becky of her last cent? Heh-heh."

Tressica draws in a long breath and struggles with her answer. "Sure, Jocko, you may draw anything your heart desires."

"My heart desires *you*, doll!" Again, the stuffed animals roar and begin to punch each other in the face. I stick my tongue out at Lonnie and set Tressica down so I can distribute manila paper and crayons to the class, just like a real teacher. Then, as Miss Scott instructed, I draw a picture from the point of view of each doll—a pleasant portrait of everyone's vacation experience. Becky surely went on a picnic to

Griffith Park with her best friend. Joanne most certainly went shopping and ate finger sandwiches in the tea room of May Company. Midge was magnificent as Lady Macbeth in some Shakespeare play. At the bottom of these drawings I add captions: "A Day in the Park Proves Perfect"; "Ladies at Lunch"; "Acting Means Everything to Me."

Holding Tressica again, I peer over Lonnie's shoulder at the drawings she is quietly creating for her brood: "Jocko Goes to Jail"; "Captain Eyeball Leaves the Earth in Search of a Better Planet"; "Junky Jerry Kills the Ringmaster at Barnum & Bailey's Circus." The last image is particularly unnerving: a blur of elephants and tigers, and a slain man wearing a top hat, a deep red stain nipping at his shoes.

"Now it's time to share our work," Tressica announces brightly. "It looks like you have created some very special drawings. Midge, would you like to go first?"

"Yes, Miss Scott. This is a picture of me as the famous Lady Macbeth. Um, could you guys quiet down a little?"

Midge is distracted, as are all the dolls, by an annoying buzz spreading through the classroom. Lonnie's animals are whispering and smirking and pointing in the direction of the teacher. When the disturbance is too great to continue, I pick up Tressica and scream, "Pipe down! I can't hear what Midge is saying!"

"Midge doesn't have room in that little head to say much!" Bad Dog Benjy blurts out.

"Out of the room—now!" wails Tressica. The animals continue to spread some dark secret amongst themselves, and I begin to feel hot and humiliated. "I said, out of the room, Bad Dog. You're expelled!"

"Don't let her speak to you like that, Bad Dog, not when she's a you-know-what," Jocko instructs. From the animals, giggles and snorts all around; my dolls sit stone-cold silent.

"Excuse me, Jocko Monkeybrains. I don't believe I know

what you're getting at." I stare at Jocko with renewed hurt, waving Tressica in the air like a baseball bat.

"Uh, Miss Scott, you know what everybody says about you . . . that you're not exactly *human*, ha ha!" Again, the animals bust their guts with laughter.

"And why is that, pray tell?" Lonnie really has me going.

"You know why." Jocko looks me in the eye. "Tressica isn't a real doll, she's a—"

"What? Spit it out!"

Jocko swaggers up to my face and, dangling in midair via Lonnie's machinations, spits at me. "P-tooey! C'mon, get real. Everybody knows that Miss Tressica Scott is an *android!*" The entire classroom is delirious with this accusation, animals sniggering, dolls outraged.

"That is most unkind," I counter as Miss Scott. "That's completely untrue."

"Then why does she have a string on her back that controls her hair?" Bad Dog sneers at me.

"Show us her string, show us her string!" the animals chant. Before I can stop him, Jocko has swiped Tressica and pulled her dress up over her head to reveal the doll's awful secret. Okay, she *does* have a string that sticks out of her back, a special rigging that helps me change her hairdo from long and flamboyant to short and pert. I have always maneuvered this string in private and never knew it was the subject of such derision. I am as shocked as Tressica; to be found out is a terrible thing.

The sound of overexcited stuffed animals and highly offended dolls pierces the air. The classroom din is off the charts, even more headache producing than usual.

"Well, I've never been so insulted!" cries Tressica.

Joanne seconds this with a response that is deeply personal: "All of us have our beauty secrets—a string, a special makeup to cover our pimples, high heels to make us look taller. You have no right!"

Becky begins to cry, and Midge, the picture of kindness, strides right up to Jocko and scans him from head to paw. "You should be ashamed of yourself, you big galoot!" She makes a move to kick him in the knees but decides against it at the last second. Midge turns her back on the monkey and sashays back to her safe circle of dolls.

Jocko, newly incensed, trails after her and drags her by her soft-plastic head over to the corner where all the animals have now assembled. "Oh yeah? If I'm such a galoot, then let me prove to ya how gentle I can be."

"You? Gen-tle?" Midge stutters. All the dolls laugh shrilly.

"Ya mock me, eh?" Jocko challenges. "Well, get a load of this," he pokes Midge in the chest, "I can be your sweet-loving man if ya just give me the chance."

The overweight simian glances at his gang for approval, and they chime in on cue: "Yeah, Jocko's a sugarpuss when he wants ta be!" "Jocko's got so much sugar and spice in him, he's practically a cupcake!" "Jocko's so gentle, he's a girlie-girl."

At that, Jocko turns on his cronies and hurls Bad Dog Benjy at the ceiling with born-again spunk. Bad Dog giggles spasmodically in a rich blend of fury and delight. Then Jocko grabs Junky Jerry by a leg and whips him through the air three times. This only seems to fuel Jerry's lust for blood. "Cowabunga!" he cheers. A familiar dark cloud passes over my classroom.

"Lon, quit it!" I break character. "I've had it with disruptions. I want a civilized school!"

Lonnie hisses at me and continues to play recklessly with her brood. In her own voice, she taunts me: "Oozy's got a big tush! Oozy has a *tookis* where her heart should be." She picks up Becky's drawing of Griffith Park and rips it into three parts. Ritualistically, she stuffs each part in her mouth and, like a savage, chews it. Saliva runs down the corners of her mouth; she lets the slime drip onto my floor in some sort of dare.

In their corner, the dolls huddle noiselessly, expecting an explosion that will soon alter their destiny. Experience tells them this classroom is not a stable environment. But instead of making sparks, Jocko's gang unexpectedly makes for the door.

Left alone with their collective fear, the dolls return to their dormant state; they lie supine on my rug as if electrocuted. After a few anxious minutes, I get off the floor and put away the crayons and extra sheets of manila paper. I tidy up the room and even muster enough detachment to design a new hairdo for the badly maligned Tressica. While my attention's focused on creating a mile-high do for her (to manage this, I've had to draw out the full mass of hair that issues from the now famous hole in Tressica's head, which conversely pulls in her string all the way), I'm hardly conscious of the low rumble outside my door. But there it is: a threatening hum, the scuffle of stuffed animals.

Lonnie thunders into my room, transporting Jocko, Jerry, and Benjy by their necks. "Lock up your daughters!" the beasts threaten in unison. "It's time to rape and plunder Dolltown!"

In a biblical movielike frenzy, the gang of three rampages through my room, overturning the doll case, stomping thoughtlessly on doll clothes and doll shoes, maliciously shredding the student drawings, and physically overpowering my dolls. I scream—as myself, as Tressica, as each one of my dolls. The shrieks only seem to egg Lonnie on; her animals tirelessly maul my dolls, pulling on their hair, peeling off their clothes.

With a power-drunk battle cry of "Away with the android!" Lonnie's gang whisks Tressica out of the room, the doll's shapely legs pointing toward heaven, her elaborate coif bobbing toward hell. I follow them out of my room, but I'm too late: Lonnie has locked her bedroom door. I can only stand in the hallway, feeling helpless against the unimaginable crimes she's committing in the privacy of her blue room. I picture my Tressica with her hair chopped off, her limbs unhooked. Or worse, with some alien head on top of her curvaceous body.

I pound on Lonnie's door. "Lon, lemme in! Give me back my Tressy!"

"Forget it, this one's all ours. She's the grand prize!" The commotion beyond Lon's door gives me the chills.

"I said, you better give her back or I'll . . ." My threat trails off into nothing. I cannot come up with anything forceful to say. I sit down Indian-style in front of Lonnie's door, hoping to regather my strength. I will calm down by *pretending* I am calm. I learned how to do this last week by observing an actress on *The Mike Douglas Show.*

I tap gently on Lonnie's door. "Lon, it's Oozy. Please treat my doll well, okay?" So much for calm; I am next to tears.

The commotion stops. Then, an entreaty: "Ooze, ya better treat *me* right or I will *kill Tressica!* Ya better show some RE-SPECT!"

I nod in response and then remember she can't see me. I twist my hair around my fingers, wishing yards of it would issue out from a hole just like Tressica's. But it's been fashioned into a short, Hayley Mills pixie, which is totally wrong for my long face.

"Oozy, didja hear what I said? Respect is the name of the game."

"Uh-huh," I answer. "I will treat you with more respect. Whatever that means."

"That means that I get to make my animals as wild as possible," she lectures. "Ya get it? And you get to make your dolls as civilized and sissy as ya want 'em to be."

"Okay," I consent. "I will allow your animals to be their stupid selves as long as they don't hurt my dolls."

"Hurt! My guys here were *loving* your dolls. That's affection in my book. Jocko's gang sees how bee-u-tiful the girls are and just flips. Except for that android. Everyone can tell the Tressica broad is a total fraud. Hey, I'm a poet and don't I know it!"

I sniffle in the sunless hallway, freshly damaged by this new charge against Tressica. "My Tressica is no fraud. She's just learned to adapt, that's all. She had an operation to help her make it in this world."

"Aw, she's a freak and a half!" Lonnie howls.

"So, don't freaks deserve respect?" I ask pointedly. No sound from the blue room. "Huh, Lon? Don't freaks deserve respect?"

After a few more beats, I hear her pacing back and forth. "Yeah, yeah, we freaks deserve *everything* we can get."

The door cracks open two inches and a naked doll with absurd, out-of-proportion tresses is tossed into the hallway. I pick up Tressica and cradle her in my arms; she must be awfully cold. I am especially careful to hide her string so no further insults will be hurled at her by passersby. I sniff at her body. The rough touch of the gangster monkeys has surely tainted her; she even smells gamy.

We hurry back to my pink room and crawl under the bedcovers together. She sleeps while I sulk. Ever the loyalist, Norwood the kitty bounds onto the bed to join us, rubbing against Tressica's mane and inspecting it like I did.

Through the thin padding of my comforter, I hear Daddy bellowing like a fat opera singer: "O-solo-mio! O-Zolo-tone-o!" He's still speckling the ceiling, and the Zolotone stink is wafting under my door. Now I'm afraid that Daddy will make our house a little *too* special.

I curl deeper under the covers and conjure my own sort of living room: crisp white walls hung with the seductive pictures of everyday life that my dolls just drew. I know what beauty is; I am surrounded by it.

Certifiable

1964

onnie has just punched her hand through the glass shower door. She's staring at the unsubtle trails of blood snaking down her arm, admiring them with awe and respect. She loves bloody things, and now she is one of them. Mother's screaming in Daddy's ear, "Burton, do something!" Daddy's growling, "Stand still, stupid, so I can bandage your arm!" And I'm making hysterical little-girl noises. Lonnie's the only one who is perfectly quiet.

The shower door has cracked into a million veiny pieces, just like a windshield after an accident. "Safety glass," Mother points out.

"Why is Lonnie bleeding if the glass is so safe?" I ask, adding to the confusion. Daddy shoves me out of the way so he can inspect the damage.

"Because your sister is an idiot!" he answers, his voice taking up all the space in the tiny bathroom.

"Aw, *you're* the idiots for giving birth to a defective creature like me!" Lonnie seethes, attacking my parents and herself in one fell swoop.

I run out of the war zone with its glass-littered floor and take refuge in my closet. Squeezing my frame into a tight ball, I attempt to launch myself into fantasy. But my trusty imagination fails me. I can imagine nothing in this cramped, cobwebby space. Desperate to replace the garish bathroom images in my head, I work even harder to re-create my favorite bedtime reverie: I'm Wendy from *Peter Pan*, taking expert care of Peter and the Lost Boys. I love being the center of attention—all these cute orphan boys need me! First I do the nurturing and then I let Peter return the favor. Our romance blossoms in record time; within minutes, I'm not only Queen of the Lost Boys but Queen of Peter's Heart.

After sustained glances during which we drink in each other's essences like foamy milkshakes, Peter says, "Wendy, you are the most wonderful person in my life, but I can never go back to London with you. My place is here with the Boys."

I give him a bittersweet peck on the cheek and seductively pull down the hood of my velvet cape. "Peter, my life is here with you and yet my life is in London too. I will have to straddle both worlds, split myself in two. I'm sorry that I can't stay with you and the Boys indefinitely. It's just . . . Never-Never Land is so stifling! There's no theater here, no movies."

"We could start a little playhouse, you and me," Peter suggests, a lightbulb going off above his head.

"Of course we could." I pat his shoulder, swathed in soft green felt. "But I'm not a country girl, I could never survive without a decent department store. Yet I do love you so!" I kiss him delicately on the nose, and before he can decide to leave Never-Never Land with me once and for all, I hear

Daddy and Mother quarreling in the hallway, right outside my door. My fantasy crumbles like the shower door, into a zillion jagged pieces.

"Julia, we both decided that if there was one more incident like this, Lonnie would end up in Camarillo. We promised ourselves we'd hang tough, that we wouldn't let her sway us from this decision." I notice that Daddy is speaking extra loud to make sure Lonnie picks up every word.

"Burton, we can't give our own daughter away! We promised ourselves, remember? That we'd do everything we could—everything—before Lon would have to, you know, go away. We'd try a different clinic, a new special school." Mother's voice quivers with fear; thrashing sounds from Lonnie's bedroom underscore the quivering.

"Yeah, yeah, how about a new can of paint? We've *done* everything. *You* can't take it, *I* can't take it. Lorna can't even stay in the same room with Lonnie when she loses it. It's over. *Do you hear me, Lonnie? It's over!* If you can't wear a dress and act normal, we can't allow you to live with us."

I double over in the closet with the stomachache of the century. I want to vomit but nothing comes out. As much as Lonnie is impossible—and everyone agrees that she is—she's still my dear, sweet, lumbering big sister, and you can't give away a sister!

"Do you hear me, Lonnie?" Daddy taunts. "You're going off to Camarillo State Hospital in two days. Better start packing!"

"Oh my God, no!" Mother gulps. "Please, Burton! Don't scare her. Please don't scare her."

I hear Mother knocking on Lonnie's door, "Sweetheart, don't worry. He doesn't mean it."

"The hell I don't!" Daddy growls.

Through my closet door, I hear more thrashing from the direction of Lonnie's room, as if there was anything left to thrash. By now, all of her furniture must be pulverized. I crawl out of the closet like a toddler and cross over to my bedroom door. It's like I'm riding a conveyor belt, being drawn against my will to some unspeakable tragedy. I crack open my door and peek into the hallway. Daddy has vanished and Mother's now inside Lonnie's room. I crawl down the hall and peek into my sister's bedroom. Mother is sitting on Lonnie's bed, cradling her with those familiar freckled arms, vigorously rocking her back and forth. "Lon, this is very, very temporary. As soon as you can calm down enough for Daddy, you'll be back with us. I swear it."

"Yeah, Daddy's the villain, isn't he? *He's* the one with the problems."

Mother smiles with tight, closed lips. "Yes, he has some problems. We all do."

"I'm gonna go away so Daddy can work on his satanic anger. Only when his tongue's tied in a knot will it be safe to come home. Am I right?" Lonnie looks up at Mother with blue saucer eyes.

"Right," Mother chuckles warmly, "it's a deal." She hugs Lonnie so firmly that my sister practically disappears inside the hug. I can't remember a hug like that but I'm not sure I want one.

I   I   I

Lonnie has thirty-four paper crocodiles that she's drawn by hand, colored in, and cut out. Each one has a name: Scalawag, Sr.; Scalawag, Jr.; Bitsy Scalawag; Itsy Scalawag, and so on. The smallest is barely a half-inch long and the largest is over three feet long. I like to play with the crocs because they are sweeter than the monkey gang and are generally in a good mood. Johnny the Crocodile is not the largest croc, but he's the leader of the pack and the most humane.

Sometimes the paper crocs ride around in our shoes when

we play Hollywood Freeway in the hall. Or we line them up by size, from largest croc to infinitesimal, and make them slither into the living room. When the crocs venture into the plastic wading pool with us, Lon and I confer their identities onto rubber thongs (we put their paper versions away to keep them from turning into soggy clods). This transference is not easy to explain to our parents, but Lon and I get it and that's what counts. Only the most popular crocodiles get swimming privileges, because we only have eight thongs. Newly evolved into thong-crocodiles, they bob in the water, their true home.

Lon and I excel in the water too. I may be getting a little old for splashing around in wading pools, but Daddy has erected the latest spiffy model, and Lon appreciates the company. Our favorite game is called Don't Go in Too Deep. I play Carille, a pretty ingenue crocodile who repeatedly ends up in the "deep end" and must be saved by the heroic Johnny (played by Lonnie with a throaty, manly voice).

Here's the drill: Carille swims around innocently but aimlessly until she no longer recognizes her surroundings. Realizing that she has strayed too far from home, she finds herself in a lagoon that's uncommonly deep and sinister. Unnerved, she screams, *"Help, help, help!"* She panics until Johnny appears. Three seconds before she would drown—signaling 1-2-3 with her claws poking through the water—Johnny scoops her up in his muscular arms and carries her back to her home lagoon. Deposited at last in a safe place, Carille flushes with warm feelings for the handsome boy croc. Like an older brother, he affectionately pinches Carille on the arm and ends the game by wagging a claw in her face. "Now don't go in too deep!" he warns. Then the noble crocodile swims off into the sunset. Of course, Carille is motivated to disobey him and repeat history all over again. Lon and I have a tradition of playing this game until we're exhausted. Sometimes Johnny saves Carille twenty times in one afternoon before we call it quits.

Today, Johnny is late and Carille is about to buy the farm, to visit Davy Jones' Locker. Gulping "salt water" and trying desperately to stay afloat, I can't believe that Johnny is nowhere on the horizon. "Help, Johnny! Help!" I cry. But Johnny refuses to come to my rescue. With her wide, husky back to me, Lonnie's pounding the water with angry fists, trying to empty our wading pool. "Lon! What are you doing?" I holler. No answer. Bewildered, I abandon my role as Carille and paddle over to the other side of the pool. "Lon, look at me." I place my dripping hands under her chin and lift her face to meet mine. "Hey, it's me. *Oozy.*"

"Yeah, it's Oozy, my pudgy little sister."

"What's cooking, Lon?"

"You're lucky to be a Homo sapiens, Ooze. Me, I'm a Homo *mutation!* Well, guess what? Somebody's gonna pay! Somebody's gonna die!"

When she says this stuff, I usually think "Yeah, sure," but this time I believe her. This time she's being shipped off to Camarillo.

"I know, Lon. It's awful, just awful. I'm gonna miss my big sister." I give her hulking body a wet hug.

"Ooze, I'm not a *sister*, remember?" She buries her head in her chest and stoops over like a caveman.

Since last Chanukah, when she asked for and received a boy's dress shirt that buttoned on the left and a pair of denim dungarees with those silver buttons that travel all the way "down there," Lon's no longer content with just speaking like a boy—she's dressing and pitching her voice low like one too. But I think she acts more like a puffed-up superhero, with a little Charles Atlas thrown into the mix, than a sporty young man. Yesterday, Mother tried to explain this recent change:

"Lon believes that guys have it made, that they have all the power. She's probably mimicking her father, the most powerful force in her world." I still don't get it; I think boys have a terrible life, catching balls and climbing trees, and stuffing their tears when they really want to wail. But I comply with Lon's request, "Yeah, okay, you're not my sister."

"That's right," she responds, "so I can't go to that planet where all the mutations are sent—I'll never come back!"

"Oh, honey," I say just like a mother, "you're scared." I try to pat her on the neck but my hand gets caught on her shark's tooth necklace. Seeing that she's shivering, I wrap my arms around her broad, athletic back.

"Your big, bad brother is scared out of his wits," Lon confesses. "I'm a spineless, gutless creature. After I'm eviscerated at Camarillo, you won't be able to find my guts."

No, I scream inside my head. But I squeeze her hand and whisper, "Oh you'll come back. I promise you will." Then I splash water in her face and shout "Prom-isse!" This is an old ritual of ours, but she doesn't smile or splash back.

"Hey, Lon, how about changing our game today for the first time in a century?" She looks interested. "This time Carille will save Johnny the Crocodile. Not because he's weak but because he accidentally swims to an island where only girl crocodiles live, where they put boy crocs in jail. Carille happens to be swimming by when she discovers that Johnny's been locked up. She tells the Queen Crocodile that Johnny is her best friend in the world and that he's saved her life at least a million times—which is the truth, you know. The queen gives Johnny a medal for bravery, and then Carille carries him back to his lagoon."

"Aw, Ooze, I don't need nobody to carry me!"

"Okay, okay. Carille doesn't carry Johnny—she's his special guide, that's all."

"Well, all right. As long as Johnny's not a wimp!" She holds her chest and arms defensively like a linebacker.

"Yeah, yeah, no wimps."

"Okay, Ooze, but only once. You can rescue Johnny only once." We shake hands on this and then paddle to opposite sides of the pool to get into character.

I ■ I

Lonnie's whole world has been packed in the trunk of our Ford: jelly jars of dead and dying bees, her circus of stuffed animals and deformed dolls, a really neat topographical map of the world, a worn baseball glove and ball, a box of her way-out drawings and stories, her Beany and Cecil hand puppets with the intentionally ruined voice boxes, and, oddly enough, a half-finished oil painting of Mother's. I'm a bit jealous because I've always loved this portrait of a stylish woman wearing a wide-brimmed, hot pink hat, and can't imagine what Lonnie sees in it. Secretly, the thing has always upset me; it bothers me that Mother never found the time or focus to finish it.

I decide to register a complaint about this spectacular injustice, blowing through the kitchen like a pint-sized hurricane. "Muth-er, you never even offered the picture of the lady to *me*, and I love ladies!" I place my hands on my hips and chew on the insides of my cheeks.

Mother appears genuinely remorseful and bends down to face me. "Lorna, I, uh, didn't know you cared about this painting, and I'm a little stretched here." She wipes her hands on her cotton apron, over and over as if to dry them, and removes a tissue from a pocket to dab her nose. "Besides, Lonnie needs the painting more than you right now. She wants to alter the face a little. You know, have some fun with it."

"Fun?" I object. "Lon's not talking about painting in a goofy mustache or Alfred E. Neuman ears, Mother. She's got her heart set on giving the lady two more eyes, some gross fangs, and a dozen horns. Maybe even Martian antennae!" I walk off in a huff to take refuge in Norwood's fur, knowing I don't even want the stupid painting; I just want Mother to finish the thing.

Mother runs after me; she's the only person in the world who responds like a person ought to. "Really, Lorna!" she scolds through my bedroom door. "I'm surprised. It's just a picture. I'll paint you another."

"Well, I'm surprised too!" I shout back, packing my Mexican straw purse for the imminent trip. "I'm *surprised* that Lonnie screwed up so bad she has to leave. Surprised at you guys for giving up on her. And then there's me. How could I even *think* about having a better life? We're all ugly traitors!" I want to slam the door but it's already closed.

I I I

We are taking the drive I never thought we had the courage to take. En route to Camarillo State Hospital in our once-stylish Ford, my family appears frozen and dumbstruck. There's a chill despite the eighty-degree valley temperature. I stare out the right window, avoiding eye contact with anyone in our car. Daddy's got the radio on loud enough to block out our thoughts. But they manage to leak through, the anxious thoughts of a family that's losing a member to an unknown planet.

I'm more than a little worried. Lon, who normally would be bouncing off the walls like Speedy Gonzales, is sitting peacefully next to me, hands in her lap, light giggles and half melodies issuing from her mouth.

"What's going on?" I whisper in Mother's right ear, accidentally tapping her gold hoop earring.

"What do you mean?" she says at full volume.

I cock my head in Lon's direction and raise my eyebrows.

"Oh," Mother whispers back. "Lonnie's been sedated. So she can more easily make the transition."

This is the first time I've heard of Lonnie taking drugs. "I wonder what it's like to be calm?" I ask forthrightly, but nobody answers. I know the Heinz-Heinz Clinic gives Mother and Daddy pills to help them cope. I'm the only one who goes through life without any extra help.

After driving past endless residential tracts that have gobbled up the landscape, we finally reach the country—soft, rolling hills blanketed with wheat-colored grass. Daddy says we are out of what's called the "megalopolis," but no one breathes a sigh of relief. Lonnie's listening to the music inside her head and Mother's chewing gum and nodding as if engaged in conversation—except that no one's talking to her. We begin climbing steadily, leaving the known world behind. When our Ford reaches the crest of the tallest hill in the Valley, I hold in my breath like I'm riding an elevator. The sun strikes my window, almost blinding me, and holds my face in its gaze. Craning my neck out of the car, I can't believe what I see down below: a miniature valley—like the molded terrain of a train set—with a storybook farm and farmhouse nestled in its belly. A place a person could live. "Daddy, slow down!" I urge. "Look at that farm. Wow, it's so neat!"

"Do ya see any animals, Oozy?" Lon asks dreamily.

"Nope. We're too far away to really see anything. All I can see is . . . perfection!" I settle back in my seat and close my eyes: I'm a milkmaid napping in the soft meadow grass.

I must be smiling, because Lon says, "Hey Meeshy, Oozy's got a stupid grin on her face. Watch out!"

I swat her with my *Betty and Veronica* comic book, and Lon swats me back with her *Famous Monsters of Filmland* magazine. She seems to be coming back to life. Then I remember the poem I had endeavored to show Mother this morning when she was packing Lon's things. She'd promised to take a couple minutes off to read it. But the moment she did, Lon began to protest and Mother said, "You'll have to save the poem for later."

"Mother, um, can you read my poem now?" I ask in a voice barely above sea level.

"Yes, I'd love to!" She takes the wrinkled page from my hands and makes a big deal out of spreading it on her lap—as if it was a treasure map or an expensive napkin. "So what do we have here?"

I crumple up in the backseat, not sure whether I like her making a fuss. Mother announces the title of my poem, " 'The Destiny of Tina.' Ooh, sounds good!" she cries a little too energetically.

"Muth-er. Please read it to yourself," I instruct.

"Hey, girls! I can't hear a damn thing." Daddy cranks up the radio and begins crooning "Moon River" along with Andy Williams. Lon looks tired, almost ghostlike; she is fidgeting with something I can't see. Then smoke fills our nostrils. Lonnie has lit a whole book of matches and is waving it behind Daddy's thinning hair.

"What the hell?" Daddy pulls our Ford into the emergency lane and slams on the brakes.

"I'm not going to that godforsaken place!" Lonnie drawls, her medication making it impossible for her to sound too threatening.

Mother has already grabbed the matchbook and dipped the whole thing in her coffee mug on the rubber floor mat. One by one, the doors of the car fly open, and everybody steps out so the smoke can leave the premises. Daddy doesn't waste a second. He stalks over to Lonnie, hoping to scare her with his big stomach and equally imposing swagger. When she tries to mimic him, she's too out of it to do any harm. Daddy shoves both of her shoulders to remind her who's in charge. Mother cries, "Burton, no!" During this standoff, I crawl into the front seat of the car and retrieve my poem. It's hopeless: Mother will never be able to finish reading my poems and stories. Mechanically, I dunk the poem in her coffee mug and watch the ink wash out and the paper turn brown. Mother is going to feel really bad about this, and for good reason. Maybe someday when I'm grown up, I will give her a second chance. I have a copy of "The Destiny of Tina" back at the house that will never be destroyed. If I can watch my temper.

■   ■   ■

For two months, I've had Mother and Daddy all to myself. But I was totally wrong about how it was going to be. My crystal ball predicted nothing like this bland, desertlike existence.

I had imagined an almost pastoral life in the middle of suburbia—more rose bushes and fuchsias, more friends, perhaps a new kitten. Life without Lonnie was supposed to be a life of peace and quiet. Of multiple trips to department stores; of new madras shifts and T-strap shoes; of long, unbroken conversations with Mother, and nights without screams echoing down the hall from Lon's insane asylum. I hadn't anticipated the meteor-sized hole left by the absence of her screams, the sadness of Lon's perpetually closed door. During this time, I continued to bite my nails at the same speed and still went to bed with all the covers pulled over my head. I continued to eat too fast at dinnertime and worry my way through sixth grade. I still didn't know if I was or could be normal, and I didn't become super outgoing or popular either.

Much to my surprise, Mother and Daddy's "conversations" about what to do with Lonnie continued as if she were still around. One morning, while Mother was still in her bathrobe, they took their debate outside. Daddy was pulling away in the Ford, late for his job at CBS, when Mother ran out in the driveway and insisted that Lon come home. "Burton, it's time and you know it!" Mother pounded on the hood, which I took as a good sign.

Reluctantly, Daddy rolled down the window, shaking his head to underscore how wrong Mother was. "Julia, you just don't get it. Lon will remain at Camarillo long enough to put the fear of God in her, and that's that. Case closed."

Eavesdropping from our kitchen door, I didn't understand Daddy's criteria; Lon's fears were already at an all-time high. So I ran out in my bathrobe too, my bunny slippers looking silly in the sunlight. "Daddy," I croaked. "Um, I agree with Mother. The doctor said Lonnie's wearing dresses at least five days a week now—so she looks like a girl just the way you want her to. The doctor said her 'boy phase' is almost over. Isn't that good news?"

Daddy scratched his long sideburns, a rather hip hairstyle that was tolerated in the TV business. Then he rubbed his bald spot and stretched back in his black upholstered seat. After a pause that was so pregnant it must have had twins, he spoke very slowly to us, as if we were foreigners. "Good news? Hell, I'd like to think so. But I'll bet all the money in Vegas that your sister is making these changes just to impress me. So you see . . . I'm not so sure they'll . . . stick." Then he rolled up his window and backed out of the driveway without saying good-bye. Mother and I retreated into the house and got dressed. I remember that we both skipped breakfast that day, leaving even our orange juice untouched. The subject of Camarillo and food do not mix.

As a newly conceived family of three, we've tried our best to approximate what peace and quiet looks like. These last two months, Daddy has listened to his Esquivel records and bowled with his buddies more often; Mother has had more time to spend with her best friend, Thelma, and with Thelma's prolific problems.

While my parents have been preoccupied, I've spent long hours at my sketch pad, drawing an entire ballet corps and manufacturing tempestuous relations between the dancers. I can't say I've been happier, but life has been a tad more pleasant, if uncomfortably so. I've had to feed my sister's menagerie—goldfish and geckos, pythons and boa constrictors—all manner of disgusting food. Lon's ghost still demands a lot of attention.

I   I   I

Today's the big day. Lon's doctors have declared that she's a model patient: subdued, compliant. Drugged. And she's been wearing dresses full time. When Daddy saw this with his own eyes, he agreed she could come home from Camarillo—sort of on a test drive. The joke of the morning is, now that Lon's returning, things can get back to normal. Daddy said this at least five times to crack me up. I'm surprised he's in such good spirits, but Lon did promise she'd put on girl clothes at least six days a week.

Of course, I couldn't go with Daddy and Mother to pick up Lon—way too disturbing, just the idea of that place. Over the last two months, I've created a huge gulf between Camarillo and me so I won't catch what Mother calls a "mental cold." A part of me still believes that mental institutions are crawling with highly contagious germs.

Yesterday, I got my hair cut in a bowl shape to resemble the Beatles. I think Lonnie will approve. I'm wearing daisy-patterned pedal pushers and a lemon-yellow crop top with two rows of ruffles that brush my belly button. Kind of unfair, since Lon will be forced to wear dresses.

Already weighted down by a waffle breakfast, I approach the fridge and pull out last night's lime Jell-O mold; I have my eye on those floating, festive cherries and pineapple chunks. With a tablespoon, I carve away at the Jell-O to unearth the pretty fruit. In no time, I can see the bottom of the mold. I stop before the whole thing's gone and return it to the fridge. Then I approach our ceramic cookie jar on the kitchen counter; it's shaped like Shirley Temple's head, so I pretend I'm carrying a baby into our living room. I count the number of Fig Newtons inside the jar—eleven—and decide to eat four of them. When I have finished the fourth, I decide to eat one more and then return the cookie jar to its hallowed spot on the counter. Despite being stuffed to the gills, I flit around the kitchen. Is Lon going to be quiet enough, changed enough?

I put on my favorite record in the whole world—Hayley Mills' "Let's Get Together"—and try to dance myself into a cheerful mood. I have finally mastered the twist, the fading dance sensation, which I learned by aping dancers on *The Lloyd Thaxton Show*. I swivel and bend and watch my ruffles bounce up and down in rhythm with my tiny breasts. In what my ears confirm is a flawless English accent, I sing along with Hayley: "Let's get together / Yeah yeah yeah / Two is twice as nice as one," twisting my torso lower and lower, screwing myself into the carpet.

But I lose my balance and topple over. Then I laugh at myself in a good way. For once, I have done something utterly normal, a dance that millions of young people do.

Without warning, the front door flies open and the three Persons tramp in. Already they're engaged in an argument:

"You will too wash your toes while you live here. I can't stand seeing the disgusting dirt wedged between them!"

"Yeah, man, I'm disgusting. Daddy's right, I'm a no-good dirty rat!"

"Stop it, you two. Just stop it right now! No more talk about toes. Let's choose a more pleasant subject."

"Yeah, Meeshy's right. How 'bout talking about heads. Heads without bodies!"

"Now Lon, you know I didn't mean that."

"Oy vey!" I say to myself. "Here we go again." I run into the entrance hall and greet Lon with a major squeeze. "Welcome back, you big lug!"

Lonnie's sporting a humiliating new attire—a white dotted-swiss dress with a navy-blue sailor collar and tie. "Hey Oozy, it's me, the Black Plague!" She laughs so hard she bends over like a gorilla.

"You silly thing," I tease her and check her out. She's not exactly the same sister who went away two months ago. I see she's picked up a couple of new facial twitches—rapid eye-blinks and anxious lip-puckering, probably lifted from fellow inmates—and she seems more amped up than usual. Her arms are covered with a scabby blemish I've never seen before, and her face looks heavier, as if she's been eating a lot of starchy food.

"Hey you, it's your favorite holiday," I say with false optimism.

"Hollow-weenie!" she sings and lands a sisterly punch to the stomach.

"Mother bought some really choice candy to hand out," I add.

"Yeah, man, poison! And I'm going as the Hunchback of Notre Dame."

"The hell you are," Daddy jumps in.

"The hell I *am!*" Lon counters, then uncharacteristically backs off. "Aw, I'm getting too old for that kid stuff." She turns her back on us and marches off to her bedroom, as if to demonstrate she's no longer a wildebeest.

Daddy's not convinced. "Two weeks," he says to Mother. "I give her two weeks."

Mother looks crushed. "Burton, she'll never get better as long as you think badly of her."

"It doesn't matter *what* I think. Her situation is congenital.

It's fixed." He plunks his ample rump on the sofa and immediately gets lost in the *Herald Examiner*, his face, shoulders, and belly hidden under a paper tent.

I stare a hole in Mother's head, imploring her to say something, do something to show Daddy he's wrong. But she's too tired, anyone can see that. Mother exits to the kitchen and unwraps some bloody ground beef. "Daddy?" I take two steps in the direction of the sofa.

"What now?" he groans without putting down the sports section.

"Lon has just proven that she has the ability to change. That's more than most adults can do, you know."

"Implying what?" he challenges, throwing the paper down on his lap.

I gulp back tears. "Um, implying that we now know what she's capable of—that she could someday calm down. Mother thinks so too."

"Uh-huh, and if we pray hard enough, pigs will fly and horses will dance on the heads of pins."

"Isn't that angels?" I peep. But I better not question his mangled proverbs.

"Lorna, I've had enough for today. Leave it alone. Soon rug rats will be ringing the goddamned doorbell."

Then I remember that Daddy hates Halloween with a passion—all the trivial interruptions that prevent us from eating our meal, the idea of grabby children at the door. I chew my left thumbnail and decide to hole up in my room until dinner.

"Hi, you fuzzy-buzzy thing," I greet my faithful cat, Norwood. He's sleeping on my bed without the faintest notion that Lon has returned. I pet his plush, gray coat and let him know that the Earth is back on its axis, that we have to suffer a house full of crazies again. But instead of going bananas, he purrs loud enough to shake the rafters. We curl up against each other like two lovers in the movies.

█ ▐ █

Dinner is on the table—fragrant hamburgers, iceberg lettuce salad with giant sliced tomatoes and Girard's Italian dressing, tall glasses of Lipton iced tea. It's Lonnie's first night back, but in spite of her legendary hunger, she hasn't emerged from her room. We're holding our breaths because we don't want a situation on our hands. Finally, after we've all taken huge bites out of our burgers, Lonnie blesses us with her presence.

"Welcome," Mother says genially.

"Oh no you don't," Daddy shakes his head.

Lonnie's still imprisoned in her white sailor dress, but around her neck she's slung Hades the python, the pet she's most fond of. She's also flaunting a fake, rubber ax planted expertly on her back, and her face is completely hidden by a hideous Phantom of the Opera mask. "Hey there, hi there, ho there," she greets us. "The kids at the door will love it when I give 'em their candy. Hades will scare the wits out of 'em, and the parents will die of fright, heh-heh!"

Daddy rises menacingly from his chair, about to rip the snake off her neck. But his scowl curls into a smile, and he shrugs. "Go get 'em."

Relieved, Mother says, "Lonnie, you're up at bat. Our official candy giver-outer."

"Yeah, I'm gonna rot the teeth of every tiny tot in Burbank!"

"Lon," I beseech her, "please don't scare anybody too bad with that snake."

"Aw, Oozy, you're such a pansy."

She's right. For all my preposterous fantasies, I'm always embarrassed when it comes to Lon's inventiveness. And she's in top form tonight, at the height of her powers. The hamburger goes down my throat in untasted, unchewed clumps; my big cuddly sister is back.

Nutcracker

'm straightening my left wing for the fifth time. My pink tulle tutu needs to be fluffed at the butt; it's lost its oomph over the last year. My right wing droops and threatens to detach. Mother doesn't think it'll make it through another round of "Dance of the Sugar Plum Fairy."

I'm a failed fairy. My Halloween costume, which hung in the closet this year while Lonnie flaunted her Lon Chaney mask, has served me well up to now. Every Saturday when Mother's down the street visiting her blond-bombshell friend, Thelma Wasserman, and Daddy and Lonnie have sworn to visit every tropical fish store in the Valley, I've put on wings. Although I've wriggled into my costume like it's an embarrassment, I've also felt its potential. Some costumes give you hope.

With respect and a bit of bumbling, I shake *The Nutcracker*

Suite LP free of its sleeve. I click on the power to our state-of-the-art stereo and place the shiny black disk on the turntable as if it were a sacred gold coin. Daddy has taught me to worship the stereo almost as religiously as the TV; I turn up the volume as loud as I can stand it, just the way he does.

The needle hits the disk and, gingerly, I travel with it. In mere seconds my clumsy torso becomes talented. The Lorna I know and loathe leaves the premises, and her gifted stunt double takes over. This costume confers upon me vast balletic powers, the chance to live in a different story. I'm a girl who moves like silk, who has grace and courage and strength and purpose.

The Nutcracker is an old story. I don't understand all the goings on in it. I don't even know who all the characters are or if they are happy. But the music tells me what to do and how to act, and when I follow it precisely, I arrive somewhere new. I have a huge need to express myself with arms and legs, the ones I keep folded away.

I know I look stupid. I have no formal training. I am not ballerina-skinny or even close to being a lovely, swoony, swan-necked creature. I have sensationally flat feet. Daddy says I can't make it down the hall without bumping into the walls. He's too polite to say how pathetic that is. Maybe he's not polite; maybe he's just too busy telling Mother and Lon how wrong they are instead of telling me. I *am* wrong for this part. But my net-and-wire wings allow me to forget that. So when "Sugar Plum Fairy" begins, soft and expectant, when it beckons and swells, I wade out into the cool stream of sounds. I glide. I flutter. Even feign *en pointe*. I perform fake pirouettes and fake pliés, and once in a great while I attempt a real leap: I burst through the living room walls and become an honest-to-God ballerina!

The air on my wings feels good. Nobody can doubt my physical strength and Giselle-like beauty. My command of my body slays the critics. I am an international star at the dawn of her career. My body is happiness; my life a warm, embracing sun.

All dolled-up—I'm wearing Mother's blue eye shadow and coral lipstick, and my own translucent wings—I spin past the scenery, orbit past the curtains on stage right, and twirl right into Peter Illich Tchaikovsky, the famous *Nutcracker* composer. I buss him on the cheek. He is stunned but says, "To think I am complete at last! I have found my true Juliet, the lead dancer for my next ballet!"

I decline the role, explaining with a flurry of hand gestures that I must finish my studies at Ralph Waldo Emerson Elementary School, that I am a serious student. Peter swears something in Russian as I toss back my hair to show off its strawberry-blond highlights (my tight ballerina bun has unraveled from all that spinning). But he is in the worst tizzy and pleads with me, "Lorna, you must come back and dance your heart out for me! I need you more than you can know!"

I run off without looking back, hoping I haven't damaged him too badly. He's really sensitive—the way I like men—but I have to return to America. Peter doesn't realize I have a different calling: I am going to be an actress, not a dancer. In movies, I will express my sorrows with words and be even *more* specific. Hollywood wants me and that is that. Hollywood and my mother.

"Lorna!"

I run into the kitchen with the finale from *The Nutcracker* taking up all the room in my head. My scratchy skirt gets caught on the telephone stool; I've torn a little hole in it.

"What, Mother, what?" I hadn't heard her come in and feel totally exposed. Mother is crying but pretending she's not. I hate that; I'm not good at not noticing.

She clears her throat and straightens her poufy bubble

hairdo. "I can't take the sound. Please turn it down so I can *think*."

I dash into the living room and turn down the volume on the stereo to a hush, then rush back into the kitchen to make things better in there. "I was dancing to 'The Nutcruncher'— that's what Lonnie calls it." She doesn't smile. "Are you all right?" I ask.

Mother shakes her head up and down, but I notice beads of sweat on her upper arms, as if she's been running. I sit down and join her at our gray, fake-marbled kitchen table, propping my hands under my chin to better focus on her woes and her magnificent, coppery hair.

Mother's aquamarine mascara is all matted up in her eyelashes, and her button nose is swollen on top. I think of how large my own nose is and ponder the unfairness of this all over again.

"I was talking to Thelma about how unhappy she is. That's all. You know she has her hands full with the two sets of twins. And her husband's so passive, he doesn't help her with anything! Her unhappiness just makes me cry sometimes." In a grown-up sleight of hand, Mother pulls a fresh tissue from her rolled-up blouse cuff and dabs at her cute nose. It's undeniably small. "I can't really help Thelma. She should get professional help."

"A maid?" I say to make her laugh.

"No, honey. A therapist like Lonnie has. Thelma needs to talk to someone other than me. I'm exhausted by her problems!" Mother finally recovers enough to notice me through her runny eye-makeup. After taking inventory of me from head to toe, she releases a high, edgy giggle.

"What?" I blurt defensively. "Is something wrong with me?" I jump up from the gray vinyl chair and play nervously with the tendrils of my dance-dampened hair.

"Honey, you are *so* sensitive. I was just noticing your get-up. Woo-woo! We have a regular ballerina in this house!"

I sink back into the chair and stick to its surface; the humiliation of being caught in the act of pretending, at my age, is "what's wrong." My flouncy fairy skirt is forced up to my neck, and I imagine taking a scissors to it.

"Are you exhausted by *my* problems?" I ask, looking directly into the centers of her reddened eyes.

"No, Lorna, I *love* your problems. I mean, I love to help you. I am just not a bottomless helper." Her voice is quavering, about to break up.

"Why don't I take off this ridiculous outfit and make you a grilled cheese sandwich?" I say like an adult. Remembering that the tiara that completes this fairy look still rests on my head, I yank it out of my hair and hurl it to the floor.

Mother looks up from the gray swirls on the Formica tabletop and bends over to retrieve the sequined crown. "So pretty," she sighs, then begins to stroke my hair with a firm touch from my forehead to my loosened bun. I realize that I am cringing under her fingers and don't understand why. When I move out of her reach, her hand falls off my head.

Some muscle in her face collapses. "Honey, I can make us both grilled cheese, and then we can go shopping for a real leotard and toe shoes."

"Are you kidding?" I screech. "I can't *really* dance. I'm a spaz."

Mother looks crestfallen. "That's just not true. Maybe you're a little wobbly on those feet you inherited from me, but you have a special grace all your own."

This parent type of lie makes me boil. "You just don't get it! I am a complete dork in the moving department. I can hardly walk, so don't say I can move like a dancer, because I can't. I have defective parts! Anyone who has eyes can see!"

I run out of the kitchen with tears of my own and hide behind the walls of my bedroom—which I notice are sickeningly pink like my costume, like the little girl I once was. I crush my pillow and squeeze the life out of it. Norwood, who had been dozing serenely on the bed, eyes me mournfully and, loyal to the end, nuzzles my arm. I shrug him off like a mosquito.

"I give up, I give up!" I hear Mother chanting in the hall as she makes her way into the master bedroom.

There, I've done it: I *have* exhausted her with my problems. I'm so confused that I'm furious with her and sorry for her at the same time. Teeth clenched, I unhook my wings, then shed my pretend-silk costume with the irritating tutu. I rip off my panties and training bra, and wrap myself in my terry-cloth bathrobe. I slip my unstable feet into fluffy, fake-fur slippers. Jeez, they're pink too! I'm pink, my mother's nose is pink. I am surrounded by this color and forced to surrender. In one jerky, unballerinalike movement, I lurch off my bed and tumble onto my daisy-shaped rug, grateful that it's a tolerable shade of blue.

I'm sitting smack in the center of my tiny, nothing world, next to naked in the middle of the afternoon. And then I notice: there's almost a peacefulness inside these pink walls. So I pray to them. I tell them how sorry I am and how grateful. Eyes lowered and palms touching, I pray for confidence and for talent and a modicum of fame. Oh, is this awkward! I'm not a person who knows *how* to pray. I can't press my hands together in some cornball religious gesture. A gesture has to be original and true! So I wrap my hands around my waist— like a lover—and squeeze the air out. I squeeze and ask for something or somebody to take away Mother's problems. Or at least to give her a vacation from them. Straining for an answer, I realize I can't hear anything while I'm breathing. So I stop.

Daddy and Lonnie pull into the driveway in our Ford Galaxie. I hear the engine stutter and the two of them arguing about who's more powerful, who's stronger and more indomitable. This is not the answer I was hoping for. My pink walls come tumbling down.

Conflict, My Love

1966

ot everything in my life was difficult, mind you. I'm just hard put to remember the other things, those times of high spirits and rollicking fun. My heart became heavy and my eyes moist at an age when most children discover the joys of family life. I would gratefully list these joys for you now if only I had a handle on them. Instead, I can provide a litany of sorrows: watching the neighbor children frivolously stone my sister; watching my sister make a monster of herself by brutally chopping off her hair and wearing shrunken-head necklaces in place of ivory cameos and silver hearts; watching myself become a shy, tortured girl who wouldn't cross the street if anyone within blocks was looking; watching TV as if my life depended on it; and finally, watching my parents do nothing about any of this.

I began, then, to live a life of the mind. I devoted thousands of hours to this pursuit, crafting a parallel existence more glamorous than my own, like most young girls, but with a twist: I devised a fantasy life of incomparable complexity. That's right, I invented even *more* problems! My fantasy life turned to romance but offered story lines of bottomless tension, layers of conflict that Shakespeare would have been proud of. If I dreamed up a boyfriend, I made him someone who had loved and lost me, lost himself in the process, but was crazy-in-love enough to cross heaven and hell to win me back. By the end of childhood, I had multiple dream-boyfriends who had suffered with me across several continents. It was closeness and distance that intrigued me. And nothing simple, God forbid, was real. The more complex the relationship, the more fulfilling and authentic. I mean, if a boy just fell in love with you without any complications, your plot would come to an abrupt halt. What would two happy people have to talk about anyway?

I distrusted ease with all my heart. Simple people bored me. And healthy simple people were like creatures from Mars. Problems gave you depth, I reasoned (and I was twenty thousand leagues under the sea). All through grade school my favorite fantasy had been one worthy of a child born in the shadow of the A-bomb. The United States would be in the first phase of World War Three, all my classmates forced to live underground in gorgeous, mere inches-away proximity. Of course, I chose an A-list of characters to populate my tribe, special girls and boys whom I longed to include in my new, improved nuclear family. Within this group, I would pair off with the smartest, deepest, wittiest boy, eventually pressing my body against his (in the dark of my bedroom, my pillow substituting for his warm, caretaking body). This daydream was presexual, of course, an attempt at building another family—one less crazy and more predictable.

Suffice to say, I never really wanted our country to go to war, but if war was conflict, if conflict was complex, and complexity was reality, you could say that all I knew about family life was war. By the age of thirteen I was a veteran of a million soul deaths—deaths pantomimed, threatened, and always cleverly invisible. My father, that brigadier of bombast, spent joyless weekends marching around our circular floor plan to Sousa's greatest hits. He barked desperate, empty orders, while my mother, the shell-shocked soldier, silently prepared our meals, occasionally retreating to her bedroom. For the pièce de résistance, Lonnie, a kamikaze in the truest sense of the word, dive-bombed her way into our living room at least once a week, showing off her penchant for death like an expensive new suit. She's the only one who could ever out-suffer me, and believe me, I'm good.

It's extraordinary that in this atmosphere of verbal attacks, sirenlike screams, and suicide raids, I never put on armor. I just lay on my bed and took it. When I could manage, I'd retreat into fantasy, but mostly I just took it. Until I went off like another kind of bomb. The bomb of dismemberment, of no memory of wholeness. The kind of explosion where you lose your mind and cannot feel your body.

I ▪ I

Summer is upon us. This means I will have to plan my days with the technical precision of a war room commander, securing enough dates with girlfriends to give off the aura of an active life. But I have too few friends to pencil in over the twelve weeks, something Mother is sure to pick up on. She so much wants a bustling social life for her introverted daughter. Alas, her daughter can't convince those junior high girls who pal around with her in school to view her as take-to-the-movies-and-go-shopping material.

It's not that I'm disliked. Everybody at school seems to

more than tolerate me. Because I am amiable at first glance and smart at second, I have wildly popular acquaintances as well as colleagues who are ordained pariahs—and a few others like me who fall untidily between the poles of shiny prom queen and cootie-ridden weirdo.

But you can guess whom I find the most stimulating company. Whom I wouldn't mind being stranded with on a desert island. You might say I'm into conversational geniuses, those girls who can discuss the literary merits of the Oz books and put forth strong opinions about the guests on *The Mike Douglas Show*. Girls with whom I'm not afraid to confess my crush on William F. Buckley, Jr. (yes, his blazing intellect blinds me to his looks). But there aren't enough of these girls with which to fill the gaps of summer, and Mother is surely going to worry herself sick about me. I am already worried sick myself.

Two weeks into the ninety-five-degree heat of the San Fernando Valley and I have only one date with a friend pinned down: on Tuesday, Beth Feirbaum and I are scheduled to see *A Man for All Seasons* at the Cornell Theatre. We plan to discuss the film to death over a fabulous meal at Bob's Big Boy. The discussion promises to be very filling; we can't go wrong with fried food. Beth likes onion rings dipped in Thousand Island dressing while I prefer the traditional french-fries-and-ketchup combo.

I admire Beth a lot. She's on the plump side, cerebral, and, like all truly interesting people, socially questionable. Miles deep into Dickens, she hasn't a clue that she's been labeled a "bow-wow" by the girls at John Muir Junior High. As such, she is more content than me, a person who still cares about the evil social realm. You see, it's Saturday—three days from Tuesday—and my schedule is looking frightfully nude. Horrified, I have fabricated a few errands to dress it up, and if it wasn't for those choice shows on TV, my nights would look equally grim.

This summer, *Peyton Place* comes on three times a week, which is a lifesaver—more than I care to let on. The show's all about Feelings, my favorite subject. And I get to hear, and then try out, the quiet, faintly British accent of Mia Farrow. Before Mia, I'd never realized that softness could have an appealing, even manipulative quality. That softness produces results! All these years I thought my own softness only translated into spinelessness; that, in terms of character, I resembled a flimsy leaf. Convinced my breathy voice exposed a shameful lack of nerve rather than a slow-burning sensuality, I assumed I was invisible to boys. So what a gift it was to discover that boys find flimsy leaves desirable! For a girl in search of a way to be in this world, Mia Farrow has become a powerful teacher. She's living proof that the meek will inherit the earth—*and* carry top-rated television shows.

After the date with Beth on Tuesday, my schedule shows nothing. Zilch, nada. I can't force these girls to call me. I can't force myself to call them. Embarrassed by this fact, I crumple my schedule into a ball and bitterly throw it at my bedroom ceiling. But it pops back in my face, taunting me further. It's 7:30 P.M. and not only do I have nowhere to go and no one to be with, the boob tube is a major let-down. *Peyton Place* is being preempted all week by baseball games, and as for tonight's programming, there's nothing on the horizon except reruns of *Candid Camera* and World War Two documentaries. God, I am tired of creating activity out of thin air. The truth is, I am not an active teen and need to face it. Need *Mother* to face it. I prefer my own company to almost anybody's anyway.

Sliding open my closet door, I scan the contents for some object that could fill my night with fun or, at the very least, fill twenty minutes of the Void. Someone like Mickey Dolenz to share a laugh and a Coke with, or a time tunnel for escaping my present condition. Mickey could accompany me into the time tunnel, and we'd leap out into an eighteenth-century English landscape—a place and time where John Muir Junior High doesn't exist.

When it comes to fun, my closet fails me. Old clothes just remind me of old, bad times. Shoes long out of fashion make me wince. Then I spot two tiny feet sticking out of my scuffed patent-leather doll case and wonder who's aching to get out. It's Becky, the formerly redheaded, freckle-faced Madame Alexander doll—my favorite doll of all time—who is now screamingly bald. I give her an automatic kiss, but when she doesn't reciprocate, I throw her down hard and bury her under a mass of tiny doll clothes. She's no help.

I spot other body parts peeking out from the case—random heads and legs and arms—and wonder why I have been neglectful, so inexplicably cruel to these childhood friends. Running out of my room in a panic, I tear down the hallway and into the living room. The bodies of Mother and Daddy and Lonnie are draped over our two sofas like the lazy, melting watches in that outrageous painting at the Los Angeles County Museum of Art. I recall that Lonnie, the family visionary, really understood this painting. "That's reality, man!" she had blurted out like that beatnik on *Dobie Gillis*.

I'm in an advanced state of torment as I make my living room entrance, but no one looks up to greet me. The family is in a rare mute mood, engrossed in a scratchy sci-fi movie without any discernible stars. Usually this is forgivable: science fiction serves as an opiate for us Persons, helps keep us sedated.

Daddy is greedily plunging his hand into a Tupperware bowl of bridge mix, a seductive assortment of malted milk balls and green mint disks. Lonnie's on the floor inhaling a mountain of vanilla ice cream the height of Mount Everest, while Mother daintily picks at grapes, too high-strung, really, to ingest a mountain of anything.

"Sit down, Lorna!" Daddy commands. "You're forcing us to watch *you* instead of the movie!"

"Yeah, Ooze, your butt's the size of the Titanic. Sink it!"

"But I'm not even in front of the set!" I defend myself, arms flailing in the fuzzy, blue TV light. And then, turning up the volume on my hostility, I stick my butt directly in front of the screen to illustrate the difference. "*Now* I'm in your way. *See?*"

"Uh, Julia," Daddy waves his hand as if someone died and made him king, "will you ask Gidget to sit down or leave the room?"

"Honey, why don't you join us?" Mother asks sweetly. "The monster looks like spaghetti and meatballs. I don't think you'll find him too scary." Mother pats the space next to her on the smaller sofa, suggesting that I land my tush precisely on this spot.

"Yeah," Lonnie weighs in, "this is some cheesy space opera! *Monster*-ella!" Everyone chuckles but me. Can't they see I'm in the middle of an important fit?

Aggressively showing off the wiggle I lifted from our sexpot neighbor, Miss Mayo, I cross over to the large divan and plop down next to Daddy. That's where the good food is. He hardly stirs, which confirms I'm invisible. My family could care less that I'm here or that I have no one to play with.

My fingers burrow deep into Daddy's bowl of bridge mix and scoop up at least a hundred pieces. Okay, I am as greedy as my father. Rolling around a malted milk ball in my mouth, I get a faint pleasure from reaching its airy, honeycombed core. I collapse it on my tongue in slow motion. I follow the first piece with nineteen others and become lost in the rhythm of dissolving the balls, one by one, until I forget how wrapped up I've been in my own misery and am ready to feel something else.

"Lorna," Mother interrupts my consumption at the commercial break, "what's on tap for tomorrow, sweetheart?" She's trying to sound upbeat but I know she's scared to ask this potentially explosive question.

"Um, nothing's for sure. I guess I'm gonna make some calls and see who's available. You know that Judy is on vacation in Tahoe, right? And that I'm seeing Beth on Tuesday?"

"Mmm . . ."

"Well, I guess I'd like to go to The Broadway and Bullock's to check out their sandals, if you don't have to do anything with—" I nod in Lonnie's direction, crushing a sticky malted milk ball in my palm. "I mean, could you take me to North Hollywood in the afternoon, and leave me off to wander around the shopping center?" I'm thinking it would look a little weird to be seen with my mother on a beautiful summer day, when I should be moving about in a cloud of gabby girlfriends.

"Well, Lorna, I promised to take Lonnie to the Griffith Park zoo to visit the monkeys."

"And marsupials!" Lon chimes in.

"And I thought—I hoped—you would want to come with us." Mother fidgets with a grape, accidentally squirting juice in her eyes.

"Well, you're wrong! Everyone's wrong!" I fold my arms to demonstrate my absolute sense of rightness.

Mother rises from the couch and sits down next to me, patting me on the back as if I'm choking. "Honey, Lonnie's been waiting to go to the zoo for weeks, and I thought you would find something there of interest."

"Like a heat stroke?" There, I did it. The girl who's known to one and all as a Goody Two-shoes is an undeniable brute with her mother. "Mother, I couldn't possibly find anything interesting in you guys' company. Isn't that a contradiction in terms?"

At this, Daddy wakes up from his sci-fi reverie, bringing his hefty presence to bear on me. "You want attention, Lorna? Here's attention!" He digs his fingers, which smell pleasantly of chocolate, deep into the flesh of my upper arm and looks me hard in the eye. "You, Miss Person, will go to the zoo with your mother and sister—"

"I'm not a sister, remember? I'm not a girl!" Lonnie corrects Daddy.

"Shut up!" Daddy barks. "Lorna will accompany her mother and sister to the zoo, and she will figure out how to have a good time there, using that fertile imagination she is so famous for. And right now, she will apologize to her mother for mouthing off. Then she will leave the living room so we can watch our movie without a teenage girl ruining it for us." The fingers let go of my arm but leave vibrant red marks in their place. A part of me hopes these marks will be permanent.

I sneak a glance at Mother, who looks hurt and dazed. "Sorry, Mother," I mumble. "I didn't mean to say those things. It's just that it's all so predictable." I shrug and hang my head low.

She looks up, stung by my words but still interested in my opinion. "What's so predictable?"

"You know. I can never ask you to do anything with-out . . . you know." More sheepish shrugging.

"What? What? I don't know."

She really hasn't a clue? This time my shoulders point in Lonnie's direction. *"You know.* There's always something that comes before me, something that puts *my* things on hold."

"Oh," she says softly. "Sorry. Sorry, dear."

I leap up from the sofa, "I *know* you're sorry!" Then, to pro-tect her from my thoughts, I scramble out of the living room, stomp down the hallway, slam my bedroom door, and fling my stomach full of candy onto the bed. My young breasts receive the full brunt of the fall. "Ow! Jeez!" I hiss. Norwood, who had been snoozing blissfully on the pillow, bounces in the air. After landing, he tries rubbing his cheek against my hand, but I shove him off the bed. "Beat it!"

Finally alone, I say at full volume what needs to be said. "Sorry is the most used word in this family. You're the sorriest person on the planet, Mother. You really can't help it. Sorry is what we are. You're sorry, I'm sorry, we're *all* sorry. But we gotta do something to change this! *Sorry isn't enough!* Sorry doesn't make things right. I'm sick of being sorry, aren't you? Aren't you?" After this private soliloquy, I break down and dampen the pillowcase with my stupid, sorry tears.

In the brief pause between my third and fourth round of sobs, I hear a low chanting: "Oh God, oh God." It's Mother's voice from the hallway. The voice sounds genuinely disturbed, like it really heard me. I listen to Mother clearing her throat; she's trying to assemble some words.

"Lorna. I know your sister demands most of my time. Well, all of my time. I know that's hard on you. You really deserve more, no question you deserve more. I tell you I'm sorry because I don't have the words to tell you how unfair all of this is—for you, for me, for your father, and most of all, for Lonnie."

"So Lonnie comes first again—in the unfairness department!"

"No, that's *not* what I meant. You're trying to trip me up instead of listen to me! I meant that Lonnie can't change her condition like we can."

"Okay, so let's change it," I demand through the door, my mouth practically swallowing the doorknob. "Let's change our condition."

"O-kay," Mother agrees, heaving a huge sigh.

"Why don't you change your plans tomorrow and take me to The Broadway? That would be a change."

"Lorna, you know I can't do that. I promised your sister."

"But you don't understand!" I wail.

"What? What don't you think your mother doesn't understand?"

"I don't have anything to do!" I cry. "Do you get it? I don't have anybody who wants to do anything *with* me."

"You have Beth," Mother counters, always trying to be helpful.

"Yeah, once a month Beth wants to see me for a couple of hours, but I don't have a real friend who wants to spend a whole day with me. Can you imagine that? Can you imagine how that feels? I'm like a leper! I guess I'm just so special and so smart and so interesting that everybody is too jealous of me. Did you know that I hate myself, Mother? I hate myself more than everybody else who hates me!" I begin to slam my pillow—which usually substitutes for a loving boy or a smitten movie star—on my head, then against the wall, then on my head again. The noise alarms both of us.

"Lorna? Don't hurt yourself!"

"I must have something so wrong with me, something so heinous and putrid that I have missed it entirely. And here you and I thought I was special—ha! And did I mention how *ugly* I am?" My speech breaks down into pathetic staccato hiccups.

Mother timidly opens the door as if a mad, snapping tortoise lived inside my room. Consumed by my anger, I still feel badly for her: a mother with *two* daughters who are out of control.

"Lorna," she whispers, extending one arm to her crumpled heap of a daughter who's been dazed by too many blows to the head. She lifts my arm over her shoulder and positions me to sit up beside her on my wreck of a bed. I look up at

Mother's face, her cheeks streaked with aquamarine mascara and lips smeared with Revlon Goldbrick lipstick. I realize we both look terrible. She strokes my hair affectionately, gently fussing with my rubber band, which is hanging by one strand, my ponytail destroyed.

"You are not ugly to me, do you hear me?" She holds my chin up to her face to make sure I've heard this. I nod to make her feel better, still privately believing that I have a weird, not-of-this-time-period look. "You are a beautiful young woman who is coming into her own. I promise you: You will not go unnoticed in this life."

"What about in this *house?*"

"You do *not* go unnoticed in this house. There's just not enough of me or Daddy to take care of you girls sometimes. Not enough time for Daddy and me to take care of ourselves." I can tell she is talking to herself now, but that's okay, we all do. "I love you so much, Lorna, but Lonnie seems to be taking more of everyone's time than we ever expected. We are seriously considering placing her in a home this time . . . a home with others like her." She bows her head; I know shame when I see it.

"No!" I protest, horrified. I can't bear to think about what this means: that we have failed, that my selfish demands will deposit Lonnie in a home that's one step from hell. "No!" I squeal once more, this time with arms held up to the sky like Medea, or maybe like a bad actress.

"We haven't actually made up our minds. But we're close. We're getting close to a time when we've got to save ourselves. Can you imagine a time when I could spend the whole day with you, shopping and eating out and helping you with your homework?"

I don't answer. I remember the last time we tried sending Lonnie away and how nothing really changed. Mother looks into my eyes for something I can't give her.

"Can you imagine this house without the rages, the fights?"

"No," I answer truthfully. "I can imagine a lot of things, but that's beyond my imagining. I mean, life without Lonnie— isn't that illegal?" Mother shakes her head no. "Then it's very, very sad, that's what it is."

▌ ▌ ▌

They're gone, all gone. Here's my chance to commandeer the living room and then refuse to give it up. Mother and Lon have trundled off to the zoo, where it's always too hot, too crowded, and unpleasantly littered with the turds of un- known species. Lon will spend at least an hour in the Snake Hut, lost in serpentine reveries, and another hour watching the chimps cavort like a gang of Jerry Lewises from *The Nutty Professor.* During the day, Mother will field at least a dozen questions about why Lon can't drag another python home and why we can't be a board-and-care home for rhesus mon- keys. Daddy is off to May Company to pick up more Frank Sinatra LPs and a couple Rosemary Clooneys (a stereo enthu- siast, he's likely to bring home ten records in one blow), fol- lowed by a trip to White Front, the humongous discount house full of unappealing, cheap stuff. He intends to buy a slew of backyard plants and a bag of barbecue coals the size of the Hindenburg.

When I'm certain the coast is clear, I race like a ferret from my bedroom to the record cabinet in the dining room, then carefully fling every Broadway musical we have in our arse- nal onto the carpet. I don't know why I run, maybe it's a teenage thing. Or maybe I'm scared that I will run out of time to be alone. I do sense that my time alone is nil, that every second counts. But I'm not any more relaxed when my family leaves the premises; they always leave behind some kind of life-inhibiting humidity that no one can see. I think it's called tension.

For today's performance, I'm dressed in a pink denim wrap-around skirt and hot-pink madras blouse; my Sugar Plum Fairy wings have been permanently retired. With religious reverence, I lightly finger the first stereo record we ever bought: *My Fair Lady,* the original Broadway cast album with Julie Andrews and Rex Harrison. After years of practice and devoted study, I'm a pro at playing feisty Eliza Doolittle. I can lip-synch her part more expressively than any other, mimic her Cockney accent to a T. I'm an expert at capturing her inner nobility, her bruised pride.

I clean the record with a tiny sponge and a drizzle of clear fluid, the way Daddy has successfully programmed me, then place the disk on the spinning turntable, awkwardly skipping the needle to "Show Me," the song where Eliza oozes venom at Freddy Eynsford-Hill. Because I have a lot of venom myself, this song serves me well. "Words! words! words! / I'm so sick of words! / I get words all day through, / First from him, now from you! / Is that all you blighters can do?" This is the anthem I fiercely subscribe to.

But today I'm uncomfortable with the spiteful tenor of this song, so I advance the needle to the finale, "I've Grown Accustomed to Her Face." This is Professor Higgins' swan song, the curtain-closer in which he confesses and curses his addiction to Eliza. He's a sad, egomaniacal fellow. Still, as much as I want to despise this character, I am in awe of Rex Harrison's acting chops. Rex can't sing to save his life, which gives me tons of hope for my own career in the theater.

Ever since I opened my mouth to sing in kindergarten, it's been a crushing blow to discover that I have no vibrato—really no singing voice at all. How could this happen to a person who has whole medleys in her head? Musicals are my life! Someone upstairs has made a whopping, career-killing error and I have never gotten over it.

While my Broadway show albums spin circles on the

turntable, I lip-synch all the parts—not just the female ones. I take on the men's roles, sing both halves of duets, embody whole choruses. And I provide inventive (though sloppy) choreography. My audience gets their money's worth. I flail, kneel, plead, reel. All this emoting tips me off, reminds me that I've some pretty powerful latent talent. Because I feel my characters from the inside. Because I am onto their truth. For longer than I can remember, I've been convinced that actors—good actors—are special conduits of feeling; their ability to express themselves can radically change the world, just like politicians and scientists do. I realize this sounds a little inflated, but Broadway is a place that can withstand inflation.

At the close of "I've Grown Accustomed to Her Face," the doorbell rings. Instinctively, I crouch low to the carpet and creep stealthily down the hall to go cower in my room. After what feels like ten minutes, I hear the beat of retreating footsteps. I sneak a peek through my lacy eyelet curtains and spot a man and a boy, both dressed in dark, stiff suits and ties, making their way down our driveway. They look suspiciously happy and both carry Bibles in the crooks of their arms.

I return to my post in the living room, worried that I have lost precious time and will be forced to cut the afternoon's complement of songs. The next musical on tap is *South Pacific*, starring Mary Martin and Ezio Pinza. In the theater of my mind, I'm the spitting image of Miss Martin as I perform a rousing "I'm Gonna Wash That Man Right Outa My Hair." I shampoo my hair in a crowd-pleasing pantomime and affect a look that says I've sworn off guys. Then I skip the needle to the poignantly hesitant—or is it hesitantly poignant?—"Dites-Moi." But I don't really hit my stride until I belt out "I'm in Love With a Wonderful Guy." Here I am able to reach untapped levels of ecstasy. Arms stretched toward the sky, I radiate as if there actually *was* a wonderful guy in my life, filling the combination living room / dining room of our mod-

est tract home with such overheated bliss that the walls expand to contain it, and then barely do. Strangely enough, I
have convinced my body—hormonally, psychologically, theatrically—that love is taking over my protons and neutrons
and electrons, so it must be halfway true.

"Hello," I say softly when the song stops. "Hello, love!"

I float with this feeling for a minute, beaming at everyone
and at no one, before I waltz over to the stereo and replace
South Pacific with *Man of La Mancha*. Despite my chaste status, I always get mileage out of playing Aldonza, the fiery
prostitute with the banshee voice. The ghosts in my living
room applaud this choice. At 114 Bethany Road, my acting
range is boundless. But portraying a lady of the evening is a
serious undertaking. I really don't know her sexed-up world
of one-night stands with travelers. I can't know her anger at
being sliced open and ravaged, as if she were a doll with no
feelings. It's entirely unfair of me to guess, and then fake, her
level of humiliation.

So why do I enjoy playing a character who walks around in
a sweaty, stinking world of men and drink and dung? I suppose it's her passion and instinct for revenge I relate to. Plus,
trying on a personality so opposite to my own is very liberat-
ing. Aldonza is outwardly bad, while I am *inwardly* bad. She
is sexual, while I am innocent. She gets to spit and I get to
chew gum. I'm sure that Mrs. Mancini, Lonnie's psychologist,
would only see therapy here. But I want my performance to
transcend therapy!

And then I remember that this character, who demands respect despite her ignoble origins, gets to storm the stage and
have her big star-making moment, the kind of moment that
steals everybody's heart. And it occurs to me again that I am
greedy, just like Daddy, not just for food but for attention. I
could eat the whole bowl of candy *and* grab the spotlight on

the stage of my family's life—and would *that* be enough? I guess Little Miss Generosity is a selfish bitch.

The feeling of being found out is so startling that when "To Dream the Impossible Dream" balloons to its goose-bump-inducing finish, I can hardly chime in. I feel too soiled by my greediness and need to be special. All my life I have been a prostitute seeking attention, the right *kind* of attention.

Stricken with guilt but still mindful of my performance responsibilities, I position myself shakily in the center of our living room and bend down on wobbly knees. If I have to fight my way to center stage for a crumb of attention, I'm sure I'll be forgiven. *We theater people are damaged,* I will tell my biographer. *We have holes in our hearts plugged with applause and tossed bouquets. Our fans expect us to be broken, to give more than we get. In the theater, emotional baggage is compulsory. Compulsory.*

I take a humble bow in the direction of our backyard, nodding to Norwood, the one creature who has faithfully attended all of my performances. To honor his vigilance at the screen door, I blow a feeble kiss his way. Then, with the clock ticking and the orchestra swelling to crazy, unheard-of extremes, I manage to squeak out the last word of the finale— "dream." I hold this note, breathing into the word, as if I had a voice that mattered.

I sustain this note until the cows come home.

Hollywood Babylon

ith all the stock I place in the imagination, a person might think that *I* think artifice is everything. But that's really not true. I know that fantasy can never substitute for a superior reality. It's just that there's a dearth of superior realities to go around. Seriously, I'm waiting. I've yet to meet a reality that could match the fantasies served up by the stage or silver screen, or summoned up by the desperate mind. I swear, the day that reality lives up to my expectations, I will throw in the fantasy towel. I will try harder to interact with real people and real objects and real environs. Until then, my feeling is, you've got to believe in the power of stories—stories breathed into songs, movies, poems, novels—to keep you ambulatory and away from razor blades and Valium and bridges. Until a more compassionate reality interrupts your nothing world and your fantasy life feels embarrassingly thin. Only then will you be brave enough, protected enough, to surrender your stories and step into the world without the velvet cloak of the imagination. The cloak you conjured up to keep you warm, luxuriant, and falsely lovely.

■ ■ ■

Daddy is trying his best to bond with me. I'm trying my best not to resist him. I suppose this could be a red-letter day, a day when my most extreme fantasies meet the reality that is Hollywood and become enmeshed, become one. Daddy and I are en route to the Hollywood Palace, that show-bizzy temple to the stars, to witness a secret taping of the Dave Clark Five. Lonnie could care less about coming, which suits me just fine. I am too nervous about making contact with five of the world's grooviest guys—musicians only a guitar lick less famous than the Beatles. So nervous, in fact, I can hardly listen to Daddy's rant about his new job at ABC. He is so worked up about this job, he barely notices the light turning green.

"Lorna, I'm at ABC eight weeks and already I'm sick of working for these horse-headed, acne-faced punks whose music would wake the dead. These English bands are arrogant, talentless nobodies in my book!"

After toiling for such dignified fare as *Rawhide* and *Gunsmoke*, Daddy's been assigned the plum task of head accountant for *Shindig!* the world's first prime-time rock and roll TV series. Besides being a feather in my personal cap, the perks of his assignment—complimentary singles ranging from recordings of complete unknowns to the number-one groups of our time—have formed a bridge between us. It's not that Daddy and I use his new position to discuss the fine points of rock and roll, but rather that, finally, Daddy has something to offer me. It doesn't even matter that most of the singles he showers me with are from mystery groups who will never amount to anything; I am pleased he has something for me that's tangible. Something I can honestly thank him for.

"Now Lorna, you gotta remember this taping has not been announced to the press. You didn't tell any of your girlfriends, right?"

"No," I reply studiously, wondering when I can let this cat out of the bag. What good is meeting famous people if you can't live to tell your story?

"You see, the producers want to make sure the Dave Clark Five can fly into town without anyone noticing, tape the damn show, and make it back to the airport by five o'clock. Screaming girls will just slow down the process. So instead of taping at ABC, we rented the Hollywood Palace. Later, this footage will be seamlessly edited into the show and it will appear that Dave and his dirty rat pack are playing in front of the *Shindig!* audience. Good editing can make you believe anything."

"Daaa-dy," I object on cue, "they're *not* dirty! You're thinking of the Animals or the Stones—the Dave Clark Five are super clean-cut. You'll see."

"Uh-huh, and your mother and I are from Liverpool." He clicks the radio on, as if we're not deep in discussion, and dials in the kind of wallpaper music that parents are nuts about.

"Daddy?" I clear my throat. I am determined to discover one thing that makes him happy. I haven't a clue, but he always lights up when he's approached as an expert.

Daddy glances sharply at me, then glowers at a driver who is dangerously close to our bumper. "What a schlemiel! This cockamamie Cadillac wants to kill me!"

"Daddy, I want to ask you something."

"Yeah, yeah. Ask, ask!" he shakes his chin up and down, always short with me, as if the meter's running.

"Well," I bow my head like a dope, "do you still have a

dream to create your own TV show?" He studies the horizon instead of looking at me. "You always had a way of telling a story. You always could see the whole thing in your head."

Without a word, his right hand reaches across my lap and I flinch, as if we are about to crash or he is about to smack me. I don't know why I do this since he's not in the habit of hitting me. I guess I'm mimicking Mother; she always pulls back when Daddy manufactures a little affection to make her forget all the yelling.

With his left hand on the steering wheel, Daddy wrestles with papers in our glove compartment with his right. He pulls out a ragged business card bearing the handwritten address of the Hollywood Palace. At the red light, he looks over at me and grins; at last he looks genuinely interested.

"Well, Lorna," Daddy cocks his head like a guy who stocks hundred-dollar bills in his wallet, "I just happen to be working on something at this very moment. Something top secret." He raises an eyebrow for comic effect. "I haven't been able to discuss it because I need government approval before I can proceed."

"I won't tell a soul!" I promise.

"Well . . . I guess I can confide in you, since you haven't told a soul about today's shoot." He winks at me like James Bond signaling a lady spy.

I fidget in my bucket seat, the teenage stool pigeon. I did casually mention to Beth that I was going to see a world-famous rock group this weekend. But I didn't say who. I just had to tell somebody, so I chose the most intellectual girl I know. Anyway, to my glamorous news she responded, "What's the Hollywood Palace?"

"Tell me! Tell me!" I squeal in Daddy's right ear. "I have a real sharp sense about what makes a strong story."

"You do, do you?" But his attention is drawn to a noise on the left. "What in Sam Hill?" Daddy presses a button that lowers his window, allowing the air-conditioned air to spill out like liquid gold. "Hey you, *schmegegge!*" he verbally assaults a driver who's nearly scraped the side of our new Thunderbird. "Drive much?" he asks, his voice leaking sarcasm and superiority. With a theatrical flourish, Daddy presses the button that raises his window. Then, in an attempt to show his daughter that he's still up for a good time, he punches a set of buttons that electronically shift his seat up and down and sideways. I watch as his head grazes the roof; then his whole body dips down until he's as short as Billie Barty. Next, his body lurches all the way left, then all the way right, practically into my lap, while the steering wheel remains oddly in place. I always reward his silly behavior with giggles, but this little stunt makes him look positively Martian. When the light turns green, he maneuvers his seat back to center and proceeds along an unfamiliar street.

"Okay, it's time to spill my secret," he stage-whispers with uncharacteristic relish. "You see, for a long time I've wanted to create a pilot for a series that's about an elite international peacekeeping organization—"

"Like the Peace Corps?"

"Exactly, except I had my idea *before* Kennedy, thank you very much. Now it looks like *my* idea was stolen from him, but that's not the case. Anyway, *my* Peace Corps–type hero would be assigned to various countries, presumedly to teach medicine or agriculture, but in fact, he would be an operative."

"Like James Bond?"

"No, he's American, remember? A wholesome, Midwestern, married guy."

"Clean-cut?" I rib him.

"Of course, clean-cut, not like those mangy rock groups. But here's another twist: he was orphaned as a baby and brought up by a Louisiana gambler, a con man. So not only does he have CIA training, he's been trained in the con arts too!"

"Like James Garner in *Maverick?*"

Daddy makes a sour face. "Okay, Miss Know-It-All, *you* try to invent something absolutely new. Everyone knows there's only a handful of stories to be told." He scowls at me, then brightens, "A handful of stories in bottomless variations! Anyway, my operative is black—so there! Did you guess *that*, smarty pants?"

I shake my head no and try to look supportive; I dare not mention the fact that Bill Cosby in *I Spy* is a black operative. "Wow, the Peace Corps plus spies plus a black leading man! Sounds really strong, Daddy."

"Yeah," he sighs dreamily, eyes closed for a second to savor his scenario, "it's going to be an important show. It will deal with social issues, political issues, but be fun, fast paced, suspenseful. I want a Steve McQueen–type to head the cast. A black Steve McQueen."

I close my eyes too, forcing myself to see what he sees. "But Daddy, why do you need the con man angle? Isn't it enough that the guy poses as a Peace Corps volunteer? Does he have to be practically a criminal too?"

Daddy swings our Thunderbird into a gravelly parking lot that must serve the Hollywood Palace; for a few seconds the crunch of gravel consumes our thoughts. Then abruptly, he flips off the radio and presses a strategic button that dips his bucket seat back severely. He's in his trademark thinking position. To fill time, I fish out my vinyl Barbie autograph book from my pink patent-leather purse and consider the impressive names I will fill it with today. With my hairbrush, I tease the crown of my head and perfect my flip, which is threatening to go limp from the strong Santa Anas. All the while,

Daddy stares out the driver's window, head turned away from me in obvious disgust. Or maybe he's considering my suggestion.

Finally, without turning around to face me, Daddy speaks in a low, passionate voice. "It's this simple, Lorna. You *need* a complicated hero. You *want* a guy who's been bad and turned good. It gives him a dark side, the potential to turn bad at any moment. This creates your suspense. If your guy is one hundred percent good, then you always know how the show will turn out. Your guy has to be tempted, to be somewhat seduced by the bad guys. And"—Daddy waves a forefinger in the air above his head—"if he's been a con man, he *knows* what makes bad guys tick! This gives him insight, gives him an edge. Edge is everything . . . everything."

Daddy gives me the cue to exit the car, and I hop out, my heart beating like a poodle's. The Dave Clark Five must be rehearsing mere yards away, and I forgot to practice my introductions on the way here. Only hours earlier, in the privacy of my room, I had tried out a couple of greetings, just in case the opportunity presented itself:

Modest: "Hi, I'm a true fan. Would you mind signing my autograph book? I would be deeply touched for the rest of my life."

Respectful: "You know, I would love to have the courage to actually talk to you, but seeing that you are in a rush, I ask only for an autograph and then I will disappear into the afternoon, never to be seen again."

Bold: "You are geniuses! You must tell me how you create your music. I'll get you all some beer and we can have an intimate conversation."

The truth is, in this heightened social situation, I will be reduced to abject voicelessness. If I can find a voice at all, my greeting will be sadly realistic: "Hi [painful smile], thanks for, well, you know [giggle, cough, fade into the furniture]."

My feet crunch the gravel while I listen halfheartedly to Daddy's instructions: "Do not speak to anyone as you enter the building. Do not confirm that the Dave Clark Five are inside. Do not acknowledge that anything important is going on in there. Do not act excited. Look straight ahead as we enter. And don't dawdle."

"C'mon, Daddy, I'm not a child. What if someone asks me if I have permission to be here?"

"Tell 'em you are Burton Person's daughter—that no one will get paid this month if you're given a hard time."

I nod and try to appear like I'm a Hollywood Palace regular. But my stomach's in an uproar. I tighten my grip on my chain purse strap, hands trembling as if I'm about to take a math test. And though I have created an abundance of rich scenarios for meeting the Dave Clark Five, I cannot remember a single one. Perhaps it's best to be invisible—the thing I hate most—in order to survive my first brush with fame.

I lag a few feet behind Daddy, wiggly smiles breaking out on my face like new blemishes. When I really should be rehearsing my greetings, all I can think about are my patent-leather T-strap shoes—insufferably stiff, they're pinching my toes as I waddle down Vine Street (and here I hoped to look hip, smart, and *très chic*).

At the entrance to the Hollywood Palace, a once-glorious playhouse now draped in nostalgia and faded red curtains, I am overwhelmed by the buzz of activity. Apparently somebody, many bodies have found out about the shoot. A gaggle of girls my age scream in that over-the-top fashion Daddy predicted; the girls seem to bounce off the walls, jumping up and down without the benefit of pogo sticks. As Daddy and I navigate the teeming mass of teens, I bow my head as low as it will go. I would never want to be suspected of having special privileges.

Before I can make it to the heavily guarded doors, I freeze

in midair the way the Road Runner does when he races off the side of a cliff, then slams on his "brakes" before plummeting tragically to the ground. I really don't belong at a secret taping, not as much as these die-hard girls do. I could never scream in the presence of *rock* musicians. Maybe I'd raise my voice for Julie Andrews, Mary Martin, theater people.

"How'd *you* get in?" "Hey! Who are *you?*" "Can you get me in to see Dave?" "You've *gotta* help me!" Absurdly, the girls surround me, as if I had influence in this world. I shrug my way through the crowd, mumbling the words "my father" in a feeble effort to explain. By now, Daddy is in the lobby, hoping to hunt down his wayward daughter; he shakes his head in disappointment when he spots me. When I reach the towering glass doors, a hand reaches out and presses into the flesh of my upper arm, dragging me into a handsome lobby with gold fleur-de-lis patterns on the crimson carpet and wallpaper.

I throw off Daddy's claw and primly pat down my wide-wale corduroy jumper. "Give me a break, Daddy! Those girls were actually jealous of me! It wasn't easy to ignore them, you know."

"You didn't follow instructions. I could get in trouble if you told one friend about this shoot." He mops his forehead with a handkerchief like an overworked comic, then uses this same swatch of linen to polish his Pat Boone-ish white bucks. Just when I think I'll have to confess, the lobby lights begin blinking. "Show time!" Daddy says with renewed vigor.

I smile to make him feel like a big shot. Daddy hustles me into the darkened hull of the theater and instructs me to sit in row 7 so I won't be too obvious. He excuses himself to talk to a colleague in row 1, but not before bragging, "You ain't seen nothing yet!"

I curl up into what looks like a red velvet love seat. The whole theater, which is quite modest—nothing like the vast sea of seats on *The Hollywood Palace* TV show—contains only fifteen rows, really series of love seats. When the lights brighten, I discover that these love seats are connected like one long couch and merely separated by armrests. How strange.

On stage, a mysterious team of longhaired, string-bean guys stealthily fool with the equipment. Roadies, I note with excitement. I watch these lithe figures with a mixture of awe and perhaps a nascent shred of lust. Their bodies sport tight, worn Levi's and T-shirts that are three sizes too small. Yummy. On all sides of me I pick up the sound of English accents and imagine I smell English Leather cologne wafting through the air. Finally, the *Shindig!* director hollers, "Right-o, let's go!" and the roadies leave the stage. For a second, the silhouettes of a drum set and giant amps hold our attention. I'm so jazzed, I'm going to explode.

Without warning, two men rush the stage and position themselves behind bulky, insectlike cameras; another man frantically repositions a spotlight, then runs off to points unknown, cussing all the way. I rearrange myself on the love seat to make sure I won't miss a single note. Without fanfare or introductions of any kind, five Beatle-coiffed guys storm the stage. Actually, they saunter on as though this were a Sunday picnic and take their places at discreet, masking-tape X's on the stage. It's then I realize that while everybody knows Dave, recognizes Dave, the other four band members are nondescript. Such is fame, I note philosophically. How weird to be collectively famous and yet not known yourself. I decide that when the concert's over, I will give the other four guys equal attention—maybe even more.

The Dave Clark Five run through their sparky, Beatle-ized repertoire of hits; "Glad All Over" and "Bits and Pieces" make me especially giddy. I clap animatedly at the end of each song, but the sound I make is hollow; the whole place is empty save for a few men in suits (the brass), me, Daddy, and maybe a few other daughters I can't see. When the director calls "Break!" I shift my weight around in the plush velvet seat and try to appear casual. I dive into my purse to find something to keep me occupied.

Oh God. Out the corner of one eye, I spy one of Dave's Five within talking range; he seats himself only one love seat down the row from me. My heart thumps audibly like a sound effect on *Dark Shadows*. The guy smirks like he knows he's hot. He drags diamond-ringed fingers through his damp, mahogany hair, then shakes his mop-top like a wet dog. Is this some sort of cue? Maybe I should acknowledge the guy's musical talent. But I can't remember which instrument he played. What do I have to say to a famous English person anyway?

The fellow stares me down, an amused but jaded expression taking possession of his lips. My eyes dart away to regard the inner mysteries of my purse—where's my Bonni Bell frosted-pink lipstick, my cola-flavored lipgloss? Still he presses on. I bet he's checking out my skirt length (is it short enough?) and my overall shape (I hope to God I have one). With a rush of heat to my head, I lift my chin and smile back wanly, wondering if I'm the "bird" for him.

"Gotta fag, luv?" His accent lilts just like Ringo's as he pats his pockets, a casually desperate man. I shake my head no, and my flip bounces convincingly.

Within seconds, all five of the Five have seated themselves in my row, lighting up "fags" and sharing in-jokes. I crumple into a socially retarded ball and twist my body in the opposite direction. I don't want these rockers to think I'm *that* interested. Despite my attempt at nonchalance, my ears pick up all kinds of hip music lingo and a generous usage of the F-word. Maybe I should just ask the guys if they'd like some Cokes; their throats must be awfully dry. When I next sneak a peek, I see two heavily made-up women—Jean Shrimpton and Marianne Faithfull look-alikes—collapse their sleek, miniskirted frames into the laps of two of the musicians. In the half-lit auditorium, I detect some heavy petting going on and hear the sound of juicy kisses, the kind where tongues dart in and out like Siamese fighting fish. In response to this showy display, I place my hands neatly in my lap, the chaste little princess in a den of iniquity.

When I can no longer keep my attention drilled on the limp velvet drapes to my left, I look up to find the mop-top who first addressed me suggestively straddling the armrest between us. His cowboy boots practically touch my lips. I watch the denim patch at his crotch pull away from the pant seam. He sees that I see, and smirks wide enough to show off his bad dental work.

"I suppose you want an autograph?" He yawns.

"Well," I answer, astonished to discover that I have a voice, "no, not really. I'm not that kind of girl," I chuckle.

"You don't say?" he cocks his head, the ends of his mouth turned down like a snooty butler's. "But I'm such a gear, far-out bloke, am I not?" he sneers, making fun of English slang.

"Oh, I don't doubt that for a second. It's just that, well, the experience of hearing you is enough of a gift [yay, my morning rehearsal paid off!]. I guess it just seems silly—to steal a piece of you. It's kind of like an invasion, an American invasion."

"Listen, luv, you don't have to be so polite. Everybody wants one." He bends over within kissing range, allowing me to check out the thick bed of chest hairs peeking out from under his T-shirt.

"Oh, I really mean it! I totally had wanted an autograph, but now that seems pretty lame. An autograph's not the same as knowing you, of course. All of a sudden, it doesn't hold any fascination, any . . . cachet. I don't mean to offend you, but you guys seem so much like real people. I thought you would be different, like a different race or something."

"Eh, what's ketch-up . . . cashew . . . whatever?" The sex-bomb musician looks nerdy as he struggles to get an intellectual hold on things.

"Cachet? Oh, it means essence, perfume, charisma."

"Oh yeah, that. Yeah, I see now." Undeterred, he swings his cowboy boots over the armrest and lands firmly in my love seat, an obvious ploy to intimidate me. "You're a strange bird, you know?"

I look up at him, squinty-eyed; he must be over six feet tall. The musky scent of his sweat clouds my mind. "Strange?" I question. "Thank you. I guess that's *my* essence."

To that, he screws up his face as if *I'm* the weirdo and hastily scoots down the aisle to his more comfortable world of blokes and fashion models. Despite my outward show of casualness, my heart is pumping overtime and my armpits are soaked. I run to the ladies' room to pee and check out my sweat and my flip, which by now I'm sure is a flop.

On my way back to the auditorium, Daddy appears as a vision in the empty lobby. But it's really him; he just seems out of synch with the whole rock scene. "Well, teenaged daughter," he announces formally, pulling on his sports coat lapels for emphasis, "pretty impressive, no?"

"Daddy," I say softly so that only he can hear, "the music was great. But these guys, they're just guys. I thought they'd be special."

"You mean like gods?"

"Yeah. I guess I place too much importance on intelligence. I bet Dave Clark, the leader, is smart. John Lennon and Paul McCartney are total geniuses, you know. Guess I'm kinda shocked that fame doesn't make you necessarily smarter. Maybe I'm barking up the wrong tree."

Daddy almost hugs me; I can tell he feels something stirring inside. "Lorna, Lorna. The tree is fine. There's nothing wrong with the tree. It's good to have goals. Bark away. Write your poetry and act in your little plays. Just be willing to give it up when you're older."

"Why? Why should I give up my dreams?" I say louder than I intended to.

Daddy recoils; his eyes make a jerky, 360-degree sweep of the lobby. "Because sooner or later all of your energy will be channeled into making a living, taking care of a family. Trust me, there will be no energy left for creative pursuits. Look at me."

"But Daddy, you're planning a huge TV pilot on the Peace Corps—with spies!"

"Right. And you're Doris Day."

I throw a bitter look his way; a fire begins to take up residence in my head. "What? You don't plan to do your pilot?"

For untold seconds, Daddy refuses to look at me; he's lost in a bad, dark place. Finally he whispers, "Let's get out of this cockamamie theater. C'mon." He tugs roughly on my jumper.

As our four feet crunch the gravel on the way back to the car, Daddy's a total deaf-mute. Deaf to my questions, my protestations. The moment we settle into the Thunderbird, he floors the accelerator and abandons the lot like a bat out of hell. Gratefully, we're stopped in our tracks by a red light at Hollywood and Vine, that mystical intersection crossed by all movie stars as they make their rounds about town. While he guns the engine in neutral, Daddy rests his arm along the top of my seat like a real father. "Hey you, don't listen to what I just said. Okay?"

My flip jiggles up and down in accord, and we sit there for another eternity. Then Daddy bolts upright in his bucket seat. "What the hell? The stoplight's out for chrissake!" Daddy clicks on the radio to fill the dead space. His favorite Muzak station is playing a numbingly bad version of "Love Me Do," and Daddy hums along cheerfully, as if he liked rock and roll and lanky British musicians. The light eventually blinks green, and again we blast our way through town.

Over the Cahuenga Pass, Daddy hums whatever melody comes on the radio, but I don't make a peep. I spend the time reviewing the faces of the Dave Clark Five. I have to admit, I can hardly recall their features. I can hardly remember my conversation with Mister Cowboy Boots or which songs were sung. But I do remember that my rehearsed scenarios failed me. Like I said, I've never met a reality that surpassed the fantasies conjured up by the yearning, churning heart.

The long drive home is uncommonly fleet. As we fly through the flatlands of Burbank, I'm silent and engaged in a kind of prayer. Hands clenched together, eyes closed, pink purse snug in my lap, I make a promise that I know I will keep forever: *I vow to the gods of celebrity and the gods of anonymity that I will not give up my dream of becoming an actress or a writer. Right now, I can't guess which way the fates will point me. But I know one thing for certain: no matter how great an artist I become, I'll never be an asshole. I will stay true to my bright, dorky self. This I promise.*

Glinda: The Early Years

y the time I was fifteen, I had been cast as Glinda the Good Witch three times. Everyone said I was a natural, that I must have a Ph.D. in Goodness. Drama teachers said I had the part locked. But this sure thing, my ability to be instantly viewed as a dead ringer for the Good Witch of the South, was a double-edged sword. While I could taste this goodness myself—compassion seemingly oozed from my pores—I also watched in horror as I began, on a daily basis, to terrorize my mother and give my father the cold shoulder. I saw myself recoiling in public at Lonnie's behavior and strange looks. I began to feel my shame come up in ugly little burps.

So while others saw me as Lorna the Good, I was not clear on the concept of my goodness, for it seemed to be both true and false. In fact, I seemed to have untold compassion for everyone *but* my family, and I included myself in this equation.

I ▮ I

At some time in her young life, every girl falls hard for *The Wizard of Oz*. A handful of girls relate best to the character of Glinda, the witch of kindness and gentility, or, in the rarest of cases, to the bullying, monstrous witch. But most of us feel like Dorothy on the inside: homeless, clueless, lost—yet open to possibility! I am merely normal in this way, having always maintained belief in magnificent opportunities, especially ones that spirit you away from your family of origin. By my mid-teens, then, I found the idea of a stunning atmospheric change—like the tornado Dorothy Gale survived—nearly irresistible.

With my dreams pinned on becoming an actress, my thoughts naturally turned to *playing* Dorothy rather than *being* her. Appearance being destiny, though, I had to admit that my face just didn't read "perky." Nor did I appear to be one hundred percent American, with my aquiline nose and closely set eyes. Though my big bowl eyes telegraphed "innocent thing," I could never beat out the girls who were deemed Obviously Pretty—the ones too pretty to ignore when it came to casting the Dorothy Gales, the Sleeping Beauties and Pollyannas.

Never cast as an ingenue, I began to cultivate a vast repertoire of character roles: tiny tots (*You're a Good Man, Charlie Brown*), queens (*Cinderella*), and mothers (*The Skin of Our Teeth*). It didn't take me long to see that ingenues and princesses were dullards, that such roles were as deep as the paper they were written on. Still, with those coveted parts came costumes to die for, comely wigs, and alluring makeup, while the mothers I played were usually plain (or worse) and the queens haughty, old, or silly. With some discipline, though, I consoled myself that character roles were meaty, sweaty showcases for my superior acting chops. Let the princesses be swooned over; they don't pick up the choice awards when the curtain comes down.

Despite these rationalizations, by the ninth grade I had exhausted the gamut of mother, queen, and tot roles. I longed for a serious departure from these Goody Two-shoes parts. Learning that Mrs. Doggsley, our veteran drama teacher, planned to mount yet another production of *The Wizard of Oz*, it took me two weeks to screw up the courage to try out for the part of the Wicked Witch. Certainly, after two and a half years of worshiping Doggsley, of donating every pound of raw talent—and there were a lot of pounds then—to her Broadway-caliber musicals, she would see fit to award me a role wherein I could chew up the scenery. Whole tables and chairs! Munchkins! Pretty girls!

"Lorna, please take the stage and read for the Wicked Witch. Sam will read the part of the Monkey King." Mrs. Doggsley nods at Sam and me like we're The Chosen People.

I scramble onstage, trying to muster every evil feeling I've ever had, seen, or heard about. I think of Hitler, Mussolini, and the mean girl up the street who never looks me in the face. I think about how furious I am when Lonnie destroys my stuff, about how unfair my life has been to this point. Unfortunately, this last line of thinking makes me sad, not angry. I doubt audiences will accept a sad Wicked Witch.

Mrs. Doggsley asks Sam and me to read the scene where the Wicked Witch summons the Winged Monkeys to her castle. With broad strokes, I mime taking the Golden Cap from the cupboard and placing it on my head. Then I lift my right foot in the air and say, "Ep-pe, pep-pe, kak-ke!" Standing on my right foot, I chant, "Hil-lo, hol-lo, hel-lo!" and then, with both feet on the ground, I cry, "Ziz-zy, zuz-zy, zik!" A crowd of menacing monkeys (seventh grade drama students) closes in on us, enveloping us in a blur of flapping wings.

The Monkey King looks me in the eye and says, "You have called us for the third and last time. What do you command?"

I suck in enough air to get through my lines. Imagining witchy poison coursing through my bloodstream, I demand, "Go to the strangers who are within my land and destroy them all except the Lion. Bring that beast to me, for I have a mind to harness him like a horse and make him work till he drops dead!" Then I let go with an awful shriek, on loan from Margaret Hamilton, who played the Wicked Witch in the film version.

Everyone in the auditorium laughs, including my beloved mentor, Mrs. Doggsley. The monkeys giggle and smirk.

"What is it?" I break character and search the audience for an answer.

Finally, Mrs. Doggsley speaks up, a faceless voice echoing through the proscenium arch: "Honey, you're the sweetest Wicked Witch ever to set foot on my stage. No one will believe you have an ounce of evil in your body. I'm really sorry. But please try out for Glinda."

I roll up the script in my hands; I can play Glinda in my sleep. Mrs. Doggsley asks me to read the scene where Glinda grants Dorothy's last wish. She asks Melissa Swenson, the blondest girl in the ninth grade, to read the part of Dorothy. Melissa, it turns out, is an experienced actress; she's been acting since the age of five and already has developed more confidence and bigger breasts than anyone in the drama department. I would have chosen her for Dorothy myself if she wasn't such a heartless creature.

Both of us approach the apron of the stage and clear our throats in unison. Melissa looks me levelly in the eye; I gaze timidly at the ground. "Good luck, Lorna," she whispers.

I look up, surprised and sincerely appreciative. "Thanks," I say, "you too."

"Aw, I don't need luck. I need to get out of this shitty school."

"Places," Doggsley calls. Gripping our scripts like lifelines, we begin. Melissa manages to project a virginal quality (how *does* she do it?); I feign a wand in my hand, the picture of grace.

"What can I do for you, my child?" I inquire as Glinda, voice drenched with honey.

Melissa, who is rumored to take pills and has a boyfriend in high school who drives a Porsche, gushes, "My greatest wish now is to get back to Kansas, for Aunt Em will surely think something dreadful has happened to me, and—"

"Stop!" Doggsley hollers. "Girls, can you get closer to each other, relate to each other more intimately?"

"Something dreadful *has* happened to me," Melissa confides under her breath. "I'm going to be cast in this crappy play." She inches closer, waits a beat and, as Dorothy, repeats loudly: "For Aunt Em will surely think something dreadful has happened to me and will put on her mourning clothes. And unless the crops are better this year I am sure Uncle Henry won't be able to afford the farm." On cue, Melissa makes plaintive, gurgling sounds that are truly obnoxious, a parody of real pain.

Per the script, I lean forward to "kiss the sweet, upturned face of the loving little girl." "Bless your dear heart," I say.

Melissa takes two steps backward and wipes off my kiss with her palm. "Your lips are wet!" she hisses.

"Stop!" Doggsley again. "Girls, girls, the chemistry is off! Please concentrate. Let's move to the lines about the ruby-red slippers." She lets go with a smoker's cough. "Places!"

I close my eyes to concentrate on the essence of Glinda, but Melissa taps me lightly on the shoulder as if to signal an apology.

"Yes?" I say.

"Are you Jewish?" she inquires without a trace of emotion.

"What?" I gasp.

"I said, are you Jewish?"

Too shocked to respond, I unroll my script to have something to look at. But the pages are shaking. "Um, yes," I finally say. "Are you?"

But Melissa's safely back in character, a perky, hateful thing: "You are certainly as good as you are beautiful! But you have not yet told me how to get back to Kansas." She bats her eyelashes, and the boys who played the monkeys swoon in the front seats.

I take a deep breath, bite my cheeks, and let the script fall to the floor. Addressing Melissa's forehead, I proclaim: "Your ruby slippers will carry you over the desert. If you had known their power, you could have gone back to your Aunt Em the very first day you came to this country. The slippers can carry you to any place in the world in three steps, and each step will be made in the wink of an eye. All you have to do is knock the heels together three times and command the shoes to carry you wherever you wish to go."

"Stop!" yelps Doggsley. "Lorna, I must see you immediately."

I shade my eyes to locate her in the darkened auditorium, but my sight is hindered by an unwelcome wave of tears. From out of nowhere, Doggsley gallops onstage and motions me to step behind the curtains. I follow, dumbstruck.

"Lorna, I have never been moved before by Glinda. Dorothy, yes. The Scarecrow, yes. But Glinda, never. Look!" She points her wizened index finger at my waterlogged eyes. "Even *you* are moved by your performance! I shouldn't tell you this until tomorrow," she intimates a little too loudly, "but you definitely have the part. Now go sit in the audience and be absolutely mum." Doggsley slaps me on the behind and jogs to center stage. "Okay, next Wicked Witch, please step up to the plate!"

Part Two

You Move Me

1968

or years our family's been itching to move away from Burbank, depressing little smog town that it is, home to the oppressors. For the last three years we've devoted Sunday afternoons to checking out every tract-house development that's sprouted in the San Fernando Valley basin. As I've collected the various brochures of the model homes we've toured, I have poured myself into each new world and modeled myself a brand-new life. For each home and its attendant city, I have given myself a new identity, a personality that should prove more successful than the present one.

I've decided that if we move to Encino, I will put more wiggle in my walk, more inflection in my speech, more oomph into my exclamations. If we move to Woodland Hills, I will lose twenty pounds, try harder to tan, and grow my hair to new lengths. If we move to Northridge, I will suppress my smarts (if I can) and relate to boys like the other girls do (flirt). The idea of starting all over again—developing a personality that works—is awfully seductive.

But when Daddy announces to the family that we are really—no lie—moving to Tarzana, I am crushed. Though Burbank has always treated us Persons badly, I can't help thinking that Daddy is destroying my theatrical career in a terminal way. I've just begun Eisenhower High, and though I find its ruling class of jocks and cheerleaders nauseating, Mrs. Doggsley, my beloved drama teacher from junior high, has been drafted as head of the drama department. She's promised—well, alluded to—a long string of juicy roles for me. In other words, I can't leave at the very moment my life is scheduled to begin! I still don't have a boyfriend or any dyed-in-the-wool girlfriends, and I'm still a bona fide misfit, but I believe that life onstage can compensate for that. It had better.

I ▪ I

Mrs. Doggsley has just announced to our Theater I class that she will be mounting a revival of *The Fantasticks,* the longest-running play in the history of the American theater. I slump in my seat and mutter "Oh great," while the rest of the class claps approvingly. Of course, I love musicals, but she's forgotten that I can't sing. What am I supposed to do—take a sabbatical until heavy dramas are back in fashion? Just as I'm leaving the auditorium, trying to look cheerfully courageous, Doggsley flags me down and pulls me backstage, her old ploy.

"Lorna, look me in the eye." I raise my chin and see an Amazon woman of sixty who still wears her gray hair long and loose, and pines for her golden days as a Ziegfeld Follies showgirl. She looks more formidable than ever, with her over-the-summer weight gain. "I couldn't help but notice how down in the mouth you are," Doggsley says huskily.

"Oh, Mrs. Doggsley, I think the choice of *The Fantasticks* is . . . um . . . fantastic! I don't really know the play, but I'm sure it's—"

"Shush." She cups my mouth with her perfumed palm. "In fact, I don't expect you to say a thing in this play."

"Wh-what?" I stutter.

"I want you to try out for the part of the Mute, that whimsical creature who uses pantomime to paint a whole world of feeling. It takes a special sensitivity to play the Mute, and I couldn't think of a more perfect actress."

"Oh, Mrs. Doggsley!" I blush. "Thank you! Thank you!"

"Stop genuflecting and get ahold of the script. I don't have time for grateful girls." With that, she swoops into her tiny backstage office and summons the young man who's been waiting anxiously for a conference with the Supreme Being.

"Mister Dickens," Doggsley's voice booms through the door, *"entrez!"* I watch as lanky Roy Dickens with his cool sweep of surfer bangs cowers before Doggsley. "First of all, Dickens, you have no reason to be acting. Please reconsider this. Second of all, you have every reason to build the set for our musical. Seriously consider *that*."

Through the window in her office door, I see the young man's mouth drop open and the textbooks he's been cradling drop to the floor. As he stoops over to retrieve his belongings, only his butt appears in the window. Before I can blink, Doggsley has playfully slapped his behind. While Roy regains his balance, Doggsley toys with her pearl drop earrings and pats stray hairs back in place.

"Gee, Mrs. Doggsley, I really think I could nail the part of El Gallo. Lemme show you something." He fumbles with the buttons of his shirt, but Doggsley turns her back on him. Before Roy can reveal why his shirt is coming off, Doggsley has whirled around to place an outsized hammer in his hands.

"Dickens, this should occupy those hands for a long, long while. Get my drift?"

"But Mrs. Doggsley, just take one look at my chest. Honest to God, it's El Gallo's chest." He opens his neon-orange surfer shirt with yellow piping to expose a well-defined upper torso that is growing an abundant crop of thick, dark hair.

"Impressive, Dickens. No doubt you're a man's man. I just think your real talent lies in building things that have character, rather than playing characters who . . . Damn it, I can't complete this analogy! Just take my word for it, all right? The theater needs Roy Dickens, but offstage. *Offstage.*"

I hear Roy Dickens chuckle along with Doggsley as she escorts him by the elbow out the door. "Bravo, Dickens. Now take care of those hands, they're extraordinarily gifted."

I imagine Doggsley showing Roy how to place his gifted hands around her waist. I imagine her offering instructions on how to nibble her ear and kiss the lined, tender skin of her neck. My fantasy upsets me until I realize that I want Doggsley to be loved the way I want my mother to be loved. Or could it be that I want Roy Dickens to squeeze me tight too? He's such an oaf, how could that be? I try to shake off the ticklish, squiggly feeling that travels up the inside of my thighs, that same constricted sensation I feel between my legs when I kiss my pillow. But Roy Dickens? No. I can't believe that I wouldn't have control over this feeling, that I can't *choose* who makes me feel sexy.

I ▮ I

The Mute is a pivotal character but hardly a stretch for me. I am wearing a black Danskin leotard that betrays a little too much stomach, holding a stick that represents a wall between two lovers, and trying my best to stay in character while my mind wanders. I'm thinking about our move to Tarzana—it's for certain now, and no amount of protest will reverse Daddy's decision. I want to take this stick and bop the heads of the two lovers—shoot, all my talent has been channeled into playing a wall! But before I can mull over my reasons for wanting to remain in Burbank, I am feeding the heroine lines; she's as blank as a newborn baby. Because the Mute is not a speaking role, it takes all my concentration to not crack up. It also takes a lot of nerve to whisper the lines so that only the heroine can hear them. When the hero's eyes are about to pop from the strain of waiting for the heroine to speak, I curl into a ball at their feet and, like a bad ventriloquist, project the last line of the scene all the way to the last row. The lights blink out, and we scramble offstage, sweat flopping off our foreheads.

Later, during the finale, when the cast sings "Try to Remember" in an all-out assault on the heartstrings, Mrs. Doggsley makes her backstage rounds, urging the crew to chime in. "I want a lush, full sound!" Doggsley commands, waving her hands in the air like propellers. Then she grabs me forcefully by the shoulders and confronts me with her famous deadpan. "You too, Person."

I confront her with my famous worried look. "But Mrs. Doggsley," I whine, "I'm the Mute, remember? It's out of character for me to sing. I'd be breaking a cardinal rule of the theater."

"Sing!" She turns on her heel and makes a beeline for the sound crew, who, to my ears, are singing too enthusiastically. But instead of singing my brains out, I use the time to review my life here in Burbank, allowing myself to mourn every acquaintance I've made during the last four months in the drama department; every part I would have played if only I'd gotten the chance; my deep and abiding respect for Doggsley—dare I call it love? Tonight, the wise guys of the crew seem more dear to me than usual; the very steps to the stage appear to have more bounce; the hull of the theater glows from within. Do I have a gift for sentimentality!

Okay, I'll chime in. For Doggsley and for the sacred rite of passage from Burbank to Tarzana, I will open my mouth and force out the last words to this bittersweet song: "Try to remember the kind of September / and follow / follow, follow, follow, follow, follow."

The principal cast members trot offstage, breathless, and then I join them onstage to take our bows. Tonight the applause sounds tinny, faraway. In my head, I am already packing my clothes and shoes, my sketch pad and poetry notebook. I am out the door, so to speak, and on to something new that has no sound yet, no picture. I stare at my round dancer's calves as if they'll offer up clues to my future.

Ollie Jonson, who plays one of the two fathers in *The Fantasticks* and who has played the Wizard of Oz as many times as I've played Glinda, approaches me with open arms. "I'm sorry that you're leaving us, Lorna," he says bashfully, then crushes me with a powerful, damp hug. "You were always my favorite actress. My favorite person, actually."

"Really?" I light up.

"Yep. You have something that sets you apart. I think it's called depth. It's like you really know how to feel stuff! Maybe I'm wrong, but—" He shrugs when words fail him.

"Gosh, thanks," I shrug back.

"I have depth too," he winks, then pats his ample stomach.

"Ollie," I say hesitantly, "you're also one of my favorites. May both of us lose our depth someday, if you catch my meaning." I point melodramatically to my thighs. "But seriously, folks, I always thought you were one of the Special People. One of the rare good eggs. I know we'll get our just deserts, our big revenge. Someday our creativity will wake people up."

"Yeah, like really loud alarm clocks!"

"Maybe . . ." My voice breaks and I cover my face with my fleshy hands.

"Lorna, what is it?" He puts a sweaty arm around me, but I wriggle free.

"Oh, Ollie, I'm completely lost tonight!" I raise the back of my hand to my forehead like a comical diva to obscure the fact that I really mean it. "Do you think, like, maybe you could help me get through this?" I smile and wince simultaneously.

"Heck, Lorna, *I* don't even know how to get through things." Ollie scratches his ruddy cheeks. "But, um, maybe I could give you something like the Wizard gave the Cowardly Lion?"

"Wow, I could really use some courage."

My dear friend Ollie, short and already balding; Ollie with the divorced parents, the plague of pimples, and the imagination of twenty students, dips into his pockets and pulls out a small, see-through marble.

"It's a clearie!" I gasp, clapping my hands. Reverently, I take the glass ball proffered by Ollie and roll it between my palms.

He regards my simple happiness. "Hey, Lorna, I won't tell you to chant 'There's no place like Burbank,' because I get the feeling that you don't consider this place your home. But the clearie will allow you to see clearly, right? So when you're confused, just peer into it, and uh, maybe think of me." He winks again.

I bend over to give Ollie a peck on the cheek and he reddens. "Thanks, Ollie, this is the best! Believe me, I will cherish this thing." Before I tuck it under the tight sleeve of my leotard, I peer into the marble one more time and see the blinding stage lights reflected in its whorled glass. And then I make out a face that looks a little less ugly than usual. It's *my* face. It looks scared and a tad garish with stage makeup, but it's halfway decent. Passable. I will take this face to Tarzana and maybe not create an entirely new personality. A few crumbs of the old one may come in handy.

■　■　■

Daddy is carefully unpacking his *Gunsmoke* shot glasses, his *Combat* wine goblets, and a campy *Shindig!* serving platter— all souvenirs from shows he's crunched numbers for. He places them on a display shelf in our new den for all the world to see. I hate glasses with guns on them, but I am proud of Daddy's work in television. Despite his domestic temper, I know his work away from home is marked by a cool intelligence.

Almost tenderly, Daddy lifts his bowling trophies out of a carton marked "Burton's Personal Things" and seems to ponder each one for its golden memories. More evidence of his life away from us. I feel sad watching him inspect each trophy for scratches; the perfect world he deserves has gotten away from him. In the kitchen, Mother's making her special tuna salad with hard-boiled eggs and celery, and Lonnie's downstairs in her "groovy new pad" with the cottage-cheese ceiling, helping her snakes adjust to their alien environs. All morning long her TV's been blasting away at full volume as she loyally watches one cartoon show after another. I hear her mattress squeak, followed by squeals of her own. As I knock on her door, she yells, "The bastards!"

"Are you okay?" I ask.

"Yeah, Oozy, get your *tookis* in here, the Dodgers are winning!"

"No more cartoons?" I tease, lifting an ironic eyebrow.

"Cartoons are for kids!" Lonnie enlightens me and leaps off the bed, holding her body low to the ground like an Australopithecus, her current obsession. We just moved in the day before and already she's Scotch-taped her "Time-Life Evolutionary Time Line" to the wall.

"I don't understand," I goad her. "If cartoons are for babies, then why do you watch them?"

"Shut your pie-hole, Oozy, and say hello to my boa." She

gently transfers the boa constrictor, which had been hanging like a heavy necklace around her shoulders, to my shoulders.

"Hi, Lugosi," I say with great effort, and then begin to sniffle.

"What's a matter, Ooze? Snake got your tongue?"

"I hate this place!" I confide sotto voce, and pet the snake as if it were a cat. "This is the end of me for sure."

"But it's a wild place, Ooze. Just look out the window."

It's true. Tarzana is on the cusp of civilization; only months earlier our lot had been a sheep meadow crawling with taran-tulas. I gaze out Lon's window to take in the unfamiliar back-yard; the steep, terraced hill is blanketed with pink-blooming succulents and buzzing with insects. It *is* a wild place. In the front yard is a kidney-shaped swimming pool, the thing I blackmailed Daddy to get. If we were forced to move, I needed something very powerful to lure me here. So I got a pool in the middle of nowhere. Big deal, I tell myself, and pet the snake harder.

"Oozy, be careful! Lugosi's just a tiny creature."

"Tiny?" I scoff. "He's a giant!"

Lonnie removes the boa from my body; it was halfway un-der my sweater and I hardly knew it. And then my resentment pours out, the dark stuff I thought I had securely stowed away. I now know that I must punish Mother and Daddy for taking me away from Eisenhower High School, a place that had offered few pleasures save for the drama department, a place where I was sinking socially. But here I am in the new place, already feeling like nothing, and someone must pay. If I can cry longer than I have ever cried, I may be able to hurt my parents so badly that . . . I don't even know what I want. I just want to hurt someone.

Like a zombie from one of Lon's horror films, I stagger to my new bedroom; it also boasts a cottage-cheese ceiling, but the window looks out on my hard-won pool, a real in-the-ground one, not one of those inflatable jobs we grew up with. I roll onto my bed and begin what will become a six-hour crying jag, the longest on record anywhere. I don't even know where I got such deep resources, but I push out as many tears and as much noise as I can.

Midstream, Daddy pays me a visit to see what all the ruckus is about; over the long afternoon, Mother pays me three. But neither of them is as wounded as I had hoped: the more I howl, the more staunch they appear, standing firmly behind their decision to give us Persons a better life. They promise that, in time, I will understand. Mother says that we all needed to get away from the sorrows of Burbank, but she still looks sorrowful, so I'm not convinced. Although I want to make her pay for this move, a small part of me believes she is right. Burbank is the town that couldn't tolerate our "difference," that threw stones at my sister's body and words at her face, that made me the shyest thing around. Tarzana has no history of hurting us. Not yet.

Completely exhausted by my attempt to punish my parents, I hide under my Flying Nun sheets and invite Norwood into the cave I've molded. He enters obediently, turning his motor on so loud that the newness of Tarzana is drowned out. I'm comforted by his familiar vibrating fur. Here we are, I tell him, two displaced creatures who have only each other as touchstones. In no time, I slink into a creamy sleep and dream of walking hand in hand with a boy who's alternately lanky and brawny. He looks a little like Luke Halpin from *Flipper* and a little like Paul Petersen from *The Donna Reed Show*. We never hug or kiss, just stroll idly in a golden meadow. Then we walk peacefully in circles around the bases at Dodger Stadium. When I wake up, the feeling of holding the dream-boy's hand remains palpable. My hands tingle with warmth and belonging. I can't explain it, but the feeling that I am accepted is the most thrilling sensation. I didn't have to speak well or be smart or pretty to be accepted. I just was. My hands hug my waist to keep this feeling alive, moving awkwardly to my breasts to test the feeling there.

I step out of my sheets and prop open the door to my bedroom. The house actually smells good. Upstairs, my family is having dinner without me. Three different drinks are set up in front of Lonnie: a tall glass of buttermilk, a mug of regular milk, and a plastic cup of orange juice. In front of my plate a tall glass is waiting for me; it's filled with skim milk. Daddy's drinking Verner's ginger ale, and Mother is having skim milk like me. On Lonnie's plate is a mountain of mashed potatoes, a snowcap of melted butter drizzling down its crown. It's her main course. Daddy and Mother silently tear at their barbecued steaks, as if picking at scabs. Nobody looks hungry.

"Hi," I offer. "Sorry I'm late."

Mother automatically springs up from the table and fills my plate with everything she's cooked. Daddy says, "Welcome to the horrible world of Tarzana."

"Yeah, Oozy, it's hideous here—you'll love it!" Lonnie shovels a spoonful of mashed potatoes into the exaggerated hole of her mouth. With her heavy-duty intake of butter and ice cream and buttermilk, Lonnie's once-slim frame has filled out and she's verging on becoming voluptuously stocky—what we Jews call "zoftig." Now eighteen and a formidable presence, she refuses to get within one inch of a dress. She wears the same thing all the time: Lee hip-hugger blue jeans that she can hardly zip herself into and one of Daddy's extra-large bowling shirts, which nicely camouflages her girth. Glued to her feet are blue rubber thongs; mysterious bones hang from a rope around her neck.

I sit down at my place, prepared to eat too much. "Sorry," I say softly to everyone.

"What? We didn't hear you." Daddy makes a big deal of this, his nervous right leg pumping up and down so violently the kitchen table vibrates.

"I said, I'm sorry I made a fuss."

"Ya see, I'm not the only monster around here," Lonnie adds pointedly.

"You're no monster," I object on cue.

"Yes I am! What else do ya call someone who can't go to high school?"

"How 'bout *Lorna?*" I throw my spoon down and watch it bounce off the table. "I can't go to school tomorrow, Mother. I'm terrified." With my fork, I shove a still-bloody piece of steak in my mouth. It's unchewable.

"You'll be just fine," Mother consoles, pushing her plate away from her. I can see she is worn out around the edges of her kindness.

"No I won't." I shake my head. The whole table falls silent again. "But it's not your fault, Mother. I just *think* it is sometimes." I look up at her heart-shaped face. Her eyes are so thick with tears I can hardly tell they're green. So this is the revenge I had hoped to exact. Not very satisfying, really quite awful.

"Great mashed potatoes," I say respectfully. "Yummy steak. Boss peas." When Mother's dessert arrives—a pineapple upside-down cake—I make a big fuss over how good that is too.

We Have Arrived

1969

y friends are waiting in the driveway, honking more times than necessary to make their point. Actually, Doon's Volvo is doing the honking, but I don't mind sounding a little surreal, a little vague. For I have never before been able to say with any certainty that I *have* friends and that they are waiting for me to do something. I have never had the pleasure of falling into the outstretched arms of a group of people who took me on face value. Being swooped up by a carload of teenagers has always been a distant fantasy, not the destiny of an oddball girl.

I I I

In my first week at El Corazon High School, when I'd expected to be fully ignored rather than decorated with medals,

I fell in with the most tolerant group of weirdos and normals. An institution only three months old, El Corazon was in its earliest stages of social development—there hadn't even been time for a popular group or football team to form. In fact, there seemed to be no caste system of any kind, and this breathtaking lack of hierarchy had created the most unusual cliques. The drama department was in its infancy too, and the same day I landed here, I was voted president of the Thespian Club. At first, I'd thought the joke was on me, that I was being served up on a very absurd platter so that others could snicker behind my back. But all the snickering was done in front of me, and the Thespians kindly let me snicker with them!

In a nutshell, no one wanted to be president, but everyone wanted some sort of drama club so they could ditch classes for rehearsals and costume fittings and set building. So when the drama teacher, Mr. Krassner, introduced me to the class and recited my hefty theatrical résumé (the Glinda gigs were a big hit with this group), a darkly dashing student approached and asked if I'd carry the Thespian torch. After coming to my senses (he looked like a combination of doctors Kildare *and* Casey), I accepted the assignment. The students even gave me an aluminum foil crown and scepter so I could rule my roost with a camp nobility. During my induction ceremony later that afternoon, where I was required to sit on an improvised throne and smile benignly, a strangely tall Asian girl with Medusa curls and piercing cat eyes loped around me three times, sprinkling red glitter and winking, as if to suggest that I was in good, though silly hands. As she extended her hand to me, its spidery fingers adorned with a silver Celtic ring and a gigantic amethyst one, she bent down on one knee and bowed her head. Her unruly raven tresses brushed my knees. I took her hand and, in my role as newly ordained Thespian queen, kissed both her rings. What possessed me to do this, I don't know; the students in Burbank would never have condoned such intimacy. The exotic young woman looked up, her smile sly and sage. "I'm Doon," she said in a thick New York accent. "Welcome to the New World."

Over the first two weeks at El Corazon, Doon introduced me to her eclectic circle of friends: actors, painters, hippies, Mormons, atheists, potheads, nice girls, bad boys. The amazing way everybody tolerated everybody else was the beginning of a new zeitgeist, a mind-set that stretched the concept of cool pretty far. But the real test for me was bringing my new friends home to meet Lonnie, something that had often before proved fatal.

Most of them passed the test with flying colors, trying their best to accept Lon but never remaining in her room too long. But when Doon first swept into Lon's rather shocking emporium of caged reptiles, caught insects, and movie monster pinups, she hardly blinked. "Hey!" she called to Lon, who was curled up in her twin bed with a scholarly book on werewolves.

"Hey-hey!" Lon echoed, lifting her nose from her book to meet Doon's out-of-this-world presence. Doon's frizzy hair—it turned out she was half Filipina and half black—stuck straight out as if she had been plugged into an electrical socket, a look that received Lon's instant stamp of approval.

"Hey-hey-hey," Doon upped the ante, seeing how far this game might go.

"Knock-knock," Lon sang, changing the rules abruptly.

"Who's there?" Doon asked.

"Knock-knock," Lon repeated.

"Who's there?" Doon asked again, feigning exhaustion.

"No one. Your insane mind is playing tricks on you!" Lon exploded with laughter as if some internal engine had blown a gasket.

Doon quickly wedged her fashion-model frame next to Lon

on the bed. She propped Lon's pillow behind her own head, stretched her long, hairy legs across the polyester bedspread, then pulled a Player's cigarette from a Victorian cigarette case taken from the pocket of her velvet pants. I ran to the window and shoved it open.

"Meeshy's gonna get you for this," Lon warned her visitor.

Doon lit up suavely and blew smoke in Lon's eyes, practically challenging her to a duel. "Listen, Miss King of the Underworld, no one—and I mean *no one*—is crazier than me. You got it?" Doon's full lips fashioned an elegant smoke ring; it captivated Lon and danced atop the white-blond hairs of her arm.

"Yeah, man," Lon conceded. "You win. I'm too tired to fight ya today. Ya got me when I'm down. But, hey, do ya wanna see my python and boa?"

Doon shook her fright wig up and down, and stubbed out her cigarette in a ceramic lunar landscape that Lon had crafted in therapy. "Sock it to me," she said.

Curiously, my female friends showed more interest in Lon's snakes than any of the guys; the males tended to offer colorful excuses for making quick exits from our house. When I shared this finding with Doon one day, she tore off the John Lennon glasses that perched on her tiny nose. "That's so fucking Freudian. Males are scared shitless of snakes because snakes symbolize the male member." When I'd scrunched my nose in bewilderment, she scolded, "The penis, Lorna, for Christ's sake!"

I still didn't understand. "Why would guys be frightened of something they already own? It's women who should be scared of snakes."

At this, Doon had flicked her wrist dismissively and told me to read Sigmund, because "she really didn't want to get into it."

I I I

The honking from Doon's Volvo hasn't let up. "Ooze, that pack of wolves is here to chew on your carcass."

"Thanks, Lon." In the entranceway to our Tarzana home, I squeeze Lon's baby-soft cheeks and tug at her necklace ringed with glass eyes. "Ee-yew, that thing's ghastly!"

"I've got my eye on you, heh-heh. But please don't go, Oozy!" she beseeches, hanging on to the waistband of my tight brown cords. "The night is young and so is your flesh."

"Sweetie, they're *waiting*. Can't dawdle." I pinch her muscular forearm to show her I'm not such a bad guy.

"I'm waiting too . . . for your stinky corpse to return! Then I'll show you a good time."

I shake my head, exhausted by this kind of talk.

"I guess your friends don't mind hanging out with a big-nosed mynah bird!" she adds as a postscript.

"At least I *have* friends!" I sneer.

"Yeah, you're all grown-up now, Ooze. Too adult to play baby games. Gotta go out and play astrophysicist and heart surgeon. Well, I'd like to perform surgery on *you*—you traitor!" She skulks off to her room and slams the door.

I throw my key chain at the space where Lon just stood. More honking. Laden with the usual sister-guilt, I gallop out the front door and nestle into the backseat of the Volvo between voluptuous, earth mother Claire and a bunch of Doon's art paraphernalia. Doon is at the wheel, and, beside her, Perry is quietly knitting something; it looks like a psychedelic muffler.

"Sorry I'm late," I wince. No one says a word. Doon cranks up the radio—it's "Knock on Wood"—and she begins banging on the roof of the car, pounding a little too militantly on the steering wheel and door. No one makes a sound, but I detect the gentle inhalation of smoke from a joint I can't see. The car smells musty; Gauloises cigarettes and grass have mingled to create an earthy fragrance—or is it Doon's homemade musk oil? The Volvo takes off into the night, destination unknown.

I unwrap a piece of Juicy Fruit gum and crack it tirelessly in my mouth. My friends, usually so affectionate and vocal, appear to be in a stupor. Their look of alienation suggests more than the habitual marijuana haze. I gaze out the back window as the Volvo negotiates one hairpin turn after another; we're adrift in half-rural Topanga Canyon. For once, the screamy radio takes the place of all conversation.

As the Volvo snakes through the sinister depths of the canyon, I take inventory of my new life in Tarzana, one with batteries and friends included. I marvel at the very idea of having pals. Tonight, we are a motley crew with one collective foot planted firmly in the counterculture and the other in nice homes with good stereo systems. Of the four of us, Doon has taken the most chances, or maybe she's taken the most emotional abuse and her personality reflects this. Tonight she's wearing those chartreuse peace-sign pants she sewed for Memorial Day; they're really loud and purposefully offensive to war veterans and most parents. Around her neck is a Celtic pendant that signifies something powerful about women. On her feet are those legendary shit-kicking boots that zip up the sides.

Perry, a heavily freckled, ponytailed young man, is our resident clown. He's so sweet-tempered that sometimes I wonder what's upstairs. I am not accustomed to fey, good-natured males. Just when I think Perry is a totally benign being, he articulates a complex thought and I am compelled to change my opinion. Claire Weinstein was the second friend I made when I arrived in Tarzana; her four-feet-eleven stature, beach blond, waist-length hair, and Indian bedspread skirt belie the fact that she's headed straight for Harvard Medical School. Although I try to encourage her artistic side (she sculpts, paints, writes vivacious short stories), her parents want her to save lives in peril rather than write about them. But Claire is the most "like me" person I've ever encountered; together we flirt with breaking all sorts of mores, mindful of how easily we still pass as perfect citizens of the republic. While I appreciate Claire's secret need for a respectable life—a real job and a couple of babies—somehow I feel a little more radical than she is. I think my parents removed the safety net at birth. Given my untrustworthy nerves, I'm not so sure that a secure job and a mess of children will make me more stable.

"Doon's in a snit," Claire announces, breaking our silence. "She's cruising for a bruising," she teases, patting Doon's shoulder. Doon extends a sleek arm to address the denizens of the backseat, and curtly flips us off. Nobody says a word for another five minutes. When I can't stand it any longer, I begin to pet Doon's ebony curls and purr into her right ear—the same way Norwood soothes me. Claire and Perry join in, purring ardently until the whole car is vibrating with sympathy.

With a dramatic swerve, Doon exits Topanga Canyon Road and navigates the car along a bumpy dirt road to nowhere. Moonlight reveals that we're on a narrow path leading to an old wooden shack. Within ten yards of the building, Doon stops abruptly and cuts the lights. "*Nous sommes arrivés. We have arrived,*" she announces. She pops her door open and struts out, parading her cool attitude, encouraging us to do the same. Of all my friends, Doon is the most mysterious, and for this I am grateful. She's tough as nails but elegant—basically the hippiest chick this side of the Rockies. Rail-thin, with nut-brown skin, she's the first person I've known intimately to allow her hair to do what it wants—and what it wants to do is stick out its multiple black tongues and tell the public to fuck off. She's never without her European pack on her back—what she calls a "rucksack"—and a carton of clove cigarettes and a carton of Player's. But for all her posturing and Eve Arden crustiness, Doon happens to like me. Her crusade to fly in the face of our culture's norms gives me permission to doff my mask of normality. Well, maybe pry it off a few inches at a time.

I sneak up behind Doon and, ever the sidekick, embrace her buoyantly from behind. "Whoa, Nellie," I say. "Just where are we headed?"

Doon whirls around to face me. She draws both hands like claws through her kinky curls and says, "God, Lorna! You ask too many questions." I must look crestfallen, because she adds, "Look, baby, I feel whipped tonight. My father is an asshole, my baby brother is fucked up, my stepmother is a cunt, and I am plainly fucked."

I nod as if I understand. "It's the American way," I say to make her smile.

She shakes her head no, and with a jerk, topples over in my direction. Claire and Perry rush over and prop Doon up against the Volvo. Claire's a "good girl" like me, but she doesn't share my respect for the absurd. "Let's get Doon back before this turns into a bad scene," she says.

"It's already a bad scene," chuckles Perry, who doesn't seem to comprehend the gravity of the evening. He ejects a Gauloise from a pack tucked in his shirt pocket and lights up, carelessly flinging his match into the heavily wooded area. Sitting down on a tree stump beside Doon, who has now draped herself seductively on the ground, Perry continues to secrete rude, hiccuplike laughs.

Claire, who has been coolly silent while Doon lies in the dirt, finally claps her hands like a scoutmaster. "Okay, gang. Time's up. Shall we make like a tree and leaf?"

Doon nods dreamily but refuses to move. With a twig, she draws a scary face with fangs in the soil. Under the face, she prints the words GET MY ACID, and I shudder. This evening has all the makings of a horror movie.

The three of us escort Doon to the cabin, Doon kicking her legs out in front of her to protest our manhandling. As we approach the front door, a flock of moths swirls insanely in the cloudy light of a lantern. The three of us knock on the door in unison, Doon swinging on my arm for balance. A thick, furry arm pulls back a lace curtain on the diamond-shaped window in the door, and a gruff, bearded face peers out at us. The face belongs to a weatherbeaten young man who has lived more dangerously than I can imagine. He opens the door—he's wild-eyed and shirtless—then moves past us into the yard as if he doesn't see us. After a round of spasmodic, chest-ripping coughs, he spits up on the dirt. When he returns to our group, his wits appear to return too. "Hey, Doon! How's it hanging?" He slaps her on the back like a football player.

"It's hung," Doon replies mournfully. The bearded hermit grins to reveal a broken set of teeth, then grabs Doon by the lapels of her jacket and kisses her sloppily on the mouth. She wipes off his spittle, then queenlike, commands him to take her inside to sit by the fire. As I enter the shack, a tingle of fear runs up my neck. The cabin reeks of old leaves and dust, sweat and kerosene. A sick feeling roils in my stomach. This is an evil place, it tells me. The five of us sit down on orange crates that encircle the fireplace, and Perry passes around an unusually chubby joint. Claire and I refuse it; Doon and the grizzly guy accept. After an uncomfortable silence, the young hermit points to his chest and says, "Mick, I'm Mick." He hands me a bottle of vodka to guzzle the old-fashioned way.

I sniff at the bottle's lip, then hand it back to him. "No thank you," I say bashfully. "I'm not a drinker."

He looks dumbfounded and shrugs. "Your loss." Then he drinks what I assume is way too much of the stuff. Too nervous to move, I manufacture a smile and survey the cabin. It's surprisingly quaint and romantic; the night and general bad mood have probably given the place an evil cast. That's when I catch Mick slipping a handful of pills into what's left of the vodka. Doon chugs it without noticing and uses her elbow to wipe a drizzle of alcohol from her chin. I find myself gawking at the two of them, knowing that, as hard as I try, I will never fit into situations that require a certain amount of sophistication or disregard for the body.

Doon eyes Mick suspiciously, and he kisses her recklessly again. Her dull cheeks flush with fire, and instead of drinking in his lust, she shoves him away. "Get off, motherfucker." Mick responds by tugging at her drawstring pants; as she struggles against him, he manages to jam a hairy paw down the front of them. God, I hope she's wearing panties today. I look helplessly at Claire; my eyes say "Do something," but she shakes her head. She believes Doon can hold her own.

Despite Doon's lack of focus, she pulls hard on Mick's greasy ponytail. He screams, "Bitch!" but he almost sounds gleeful. He withdraws his hand from her pants and holds it up in the lantern light as if it was a trophy. Then he makes a big deal of inserting three fingers deep into his mouth and drawing them out in slow motion. "Mmm, that's good pussy." Mick grins an awful lopsided grin and sidles up to Doon, who has retreated to the tattered sofa at the far end of the cabin. She looks lost in another world. Noting how out of it she is, Mick spreads her legs wide and nestles his head into her crotch area. "Sweet thang," he sings and begins tapping her vagina through the cloth of her pants.

My eyes grow huge at the repulsive sight of Mick invading Doon, and yet something unwanted stirs in my own body. I can't speak and I can't act. I have no experience with this kind of monster. Claire tugs at the back of Mick's sweat-drenched denim shirt, screaming, "Get off, asshole!" She climbs onto his back and is still clinging on when he rises.

"All right, back down, honey. I was only claiming what's mine." He shrugs her off.

"You think you *own* Doon?" Claire challenges, pretty manicured hands on her hips. She's much braver than me by leaps and bounds.

"I can give her what she needs. That's more than you schoolgirls do for her. Aw, what the fuck," he says. He prances over and grabs Claire's ample breasts, cupping one in each hand. "Let's get mellow."

A heavy clay ashtray, like something sculpted in elementary school, crashes into Mick's head, spilling ashes on his already dingy hair. The ashtray breaks into chunks and puffs of dust. Still akimbo on the sofa and only semiconscious, Doon has protected Claire's honor by lobbing the misshapen object at her questionable friend. But instead of turning up the volume on Mick's wrath, the attack seems to quiet him—or maybe the mixture of drugs and alcohol in his blood has altered his mood. Mick mutters, "Sorry, babe" in Doon's direction and pretends as if he's never seen Claire. "Want some fruit?" he asks us.

"Yeah," I answer. "Fruit is good."

This whole time, Perry has been no good at all. Wasted, gone, he stares glassy-eyed at the fire with no trace of recognition. I cover his shoulders with a Pendleton blanket from the bedroom. Having fully recovered from Mick's advances, Claire is now piddling around in the kitchen, making us a round of coffee. Though I have also wrapped myself in a blanket, I am shivering, Miss Utterly Uncool. As much as I have an affinity for the hippie life, I don't have a taste for its dark side. Why would I want to lose my mind in the woods? I put up with too much imbalance as it is with Lonnie.

Mick stumbles over to a vintage turntable, blows on the dust gathered on its plastic cover, and puts on a record that's lying next to it. Music's the perfect antidote to evil, I think. Puncturing the dreadful silence, young Stevie Winwood croons "Can't Find My Way Home," and the five of us find something in common. We sing along with Winwood, each praying in our own way to see the morning. I hug myself to keep warm, and hold Claire's hand as the fire goes out and the fear rises. Both of us sip our coffees, taking care to watch over our hip friends like the unhip angels we are. When Doon and Perry pass out on the sofa around 4 A.M., a sobering Mick helps us pack our friends neatly into the Volvo. Claire does the honor of driving us back to Tarzana. Under the promising dome of dawn light, I believe that I will see my home again.

In the front seat, Perry seems to be doing fine; wrapped in his half-finished muffler, he looks like a modern-day Mayakovsky. When he's not too fucked up, he's the sweetest fellow, really a dear. But Doon, well, I'm not sure if she'll ever tunnel out from her dark worldview, her poisonous anger.

Light-headed without alcohol or grass, I sprawl in the backseat, cradling my favorite lost soul; I hold Doon's frizzy, warm head in my lap and tenderly massage her scalp. It's incredibly late, but my parents are too preoccupied to worry. They're so grateful that I have friends, a place to go. Of course, they don't know I'm hanging out in Topanga Canyon with "drug fiends," but I didn't expect this either. I think they think I'm staying over at Claire's house; I wasn't altogether clear about my agenda and now can't remember *what* I told them. But really, they needn't worry. I never let myself go with hard drugs or alcohol, because inside my head, it's already more chaotic than I care to let on.

In an effort to shake off our intense experience, Claire and I sing a medley of ballads—"Clouds," "Suzanne," even "The

Cat Came Back"—until we realize that most of the lyrics are colossally depressing. When we arrive at Doon's ranch-style house, circa 5:30 A.M., I escort my charge to her room. As I deposit Doon's dazed body under a lacy coverlet in her incongruous little-girl bed, I whisper "I love you" in her ear. Although I have not had the good fortune of saying this to a boy, I relish the chance to say these words now.

Doon gazes up at me with sleepy cinnamon-colored eyes, eyes that, moments earlier, had been vacant and psychotic. She smiles benevolently like a good witch. "I love you too, kiddo."

I sit down on the edge of the bed and let out an exaggerated sigh. "You probably think I'm a lightweight. Not in your league."

"No, I think . . ." She pauses and I almost lose her to sleep. "I think I am very fortunate to have such a nice person in my rotten life."

"But I have nothing for you, nothing you haven't seen or heard before. Where you possess scads of interesting stories and expressions, and teach me about art and music and fabrics and tarot." I take inventory of Doon's bedroom walls; every inch is covered with sumi brush paintings, exotic weavings of beads and driftwood, handmade Victorian valentines. Everything but the bed seems laden with mystical meaning. "Doon," I wave my hands at her walls, "you give me culture. You *are* culture!"

"Oh pish, tosh," she slurs her words. "You're a heavy poet and a pretty mean little actress. You're only a lightweight on the outside. On the inside you're something else altogether."

"Yeah? What's that?" I fish.

"Sweetheart, I'm too tired to come up with something smashing right now. You gotta give me the luxury of sleep. Meanwhile, keep the baby, faith." She winks at me and disappears under her crisp white sheet.

I steal out of Doon's house, careful not to wake the family that she hates with a passion. As mad as she is at the universe, the fact is, she desires my company. A tall, worldly, profane person needs me to remind her that she is good.

When I finally crawl under my own covers, even in my state of exhaustion I am greedy for company. I want to go to bed untroubled and unfettered, alongside a body who cares for me. But it ain't gonna happen.

I think back on the events of the marathon evening. How I detest my goody-goody nature, the way I use it as a protective coating. I have tried to pretend that watching my friends pass out means nothing—that they are entitled to hurt themselves without worrying about my feelings. But I really do care; I just don't acknowledge evil when I'm face to face with it. All the bad things this world serves up slide right off my innocent skin. I can move among thieves and drug addicts and murderers with a smile on my lips and the knowledge that it's all a mistake. This is because I know that, deep down, no one meant anyone any harm. Like me, they only wanted love because only love is real. Well, let's not forget poetry and music and cats—cats are real. And the hurricane force of one's family.

But all my goodness doesn't protect me from being lonely. I must have no inner resources! To lull myself to sleep, I invent a fantasy not unlike the fantasies of previous nights: I am the star of my own TV show, *The Lives and Loves of Lana Pleshette*. In this morning's scenario, I have to deal with the pressures of stardom but also the problems of dating two of the show's male actors. Although they are Sears-catalogue handsome and extremely smitten with me, I am far more attracted to a shy, soulful cameraman who yearns to take photographs like Cartier-Bresson. I work hard to make all three men happy and secure in their talents, but my relating abilities are being stretched thin. After a terrible fire on the set that puts both actors in the hospital, I am free to express my love for the cameraman. We move to Paris, where he can work on his art photography and I can bask in the dusky light of anonymity. Of course, the moment we are the slightest bit happy, I am forced to conjure up a problem that has some meat on its bones. But before I can come up with something titillating, I nod off into a world that asks nothing of me.

I I I

Clad in my aging Glinda costume, I lie on my blue daisy rug, trying to calm my upset stomach. I've turned on the TV to help me cope. On *The Today Show*, Frank McGee chats with Barbara Walters about the upcoming moon shot. I notice how confident he is, how confident she is. Words just ripple out of their mouths. I tear at the hem of my billowing skirt and watch the tulle shred to pieces. Stock footage of Apollo 11 fills the screen. Only a knock on my bedroom door interrupts the ritual ripping of my skirt.

"Lorna? May I come in?" It's Mother, an expression of alarm pasted on her face. I don't have the strength to answer. She enters anyway. "Lorna, do you know it's 8:45? School has already started." I still don't have the strength to answer. "Honey, are you okay? Are you . . . in a play today?"

I robotically shake my head no and watch Frank and Barbara share a laugh. It occurs to me I've forgotten how to do that. Mother kneels down beside me and places her Jergens-scented hand on my forehead. "You feel cool. I thought you might have a fever or something." Again I shake my head. "Then what is it, honey? Do you need a day off from school?" She looks away so as not to embarrass her costumed daughter. "A mental health day?" She makes it sound cheery, like a holiday.

After a pause during which I bury my head in the folds of my massive skirt, I answer, "Yeah. Can't go on the field trip. Gotta stay home."

"Okay, Lorna. You know I always respect that. I won't force you to go to school. But what's this field trip all about? I don't recall signing anything."

"Camarillo," I squeak through the layers of tulle. "Camarillo State Hospital. My psychology class thinks it's real important to see how the other half lives. Like I need to go to Camarillo and learn something. Well, I won't go!"

Mother pats me on the back, but all I feel is the electric current of anxiety sparked by the word "Camarillo." Now I wish I hadn't said it. "Of course you don't have to go," she assures me.

"But it will look weird if I don't." I emerge from the yards of tulle and taffeta. "I mean, a lot of parents refused to let their kids go, out of fear and hatred of crazy people. I don't want people to think that we're stupid or that we hate the mentally ill."

"Then go." Mother stands and wrings her hands. "Go, go, go!"

"But I swore I'd never go back to that place. I *swore.*"

"Then don't go! But leave me out of it. *I'm* not one of those stupid parents." She exits with the kind of flourish I thought only I had perfected. Although I'm hurt by her abrupt departure, I'm impressed that she made a little scene.

The moment Mother closes my door, I unzip my bodice and step out of my Glinda getup. With some effort, I slip my growing thighs into hip-hugger jeans and throw on a clingy tube top that accentuates my full bust. I lace up my moccasins and adorn my pierced ears with gold, crescent moon earrings, the only hippie accessories I've chosen for today. I am going to Camarillo with the rest of them. Because it's important not to flinch. I must show the others that the mentally ill deserve our respect and that we must not look away.

■ ■ ■

Our school bus pulls up to the rolling green lawn that envelops the state hospital grounds. It's been five years since I've sucked in my gut to survive this place. Of course, I'm shaking; I knew I would. But that's the past. I have a brand-new chance to act like a grown-up.

As my classmates file off the bus, I hear the usual sick jokes about Camarillo. I even catch myself smiling at a real stinker. Just when I think I'm going to faint from the psychic fumes the hospital gives off, Doon and Claire catch up with me and each friend takes one of my hands. God, they must know what I'm going through; they must really get it.

"My family's thinking of vacationing here this summer," Doon says slyly.

"Oh yeah? *Our* family's got reservations for the penthouse," Claire adds.

"My, my," I chime in, "the Persons must be lagging behind. Actually, we've invited most of the inmates to spend Chanukah with us. I *know* we can make them feel at home."

We give each other corny high fives. Then Doon raises two palms in the air and shouts, "Gimme ten!" I oblige by slapping her palms. She slaps me back with one hand and replies, "Here's change." Although it's the oldest joke in our book, the exchange relaxes me enough to let out the old air in my chest and take in some new.

Like a group of dumb tourists, my classmates line up to enter one of the tamer residence halls. The students seem unusually anxious. Out of nowhere, an inpatient approaches—a young man who appears to be our age—and initiates a conversation with the female student in front of me. He's got a traveling eye and a blister on his lip. "You're pretty," he says. She backs away as if he has cooties. "Can I touch your beads?" he asks. She shakes her head no, gripping protectively at her peace-sign medallion. Then he approaches me, moving within inches of my nose. "Hi," he says sweetly.

"Hi," I reply. "Guess we're causing a lot of commotion today."

"Yeah, I was minding my own beeswax, and before I know it, all you guys are here, minding *our* beeswax!" He thinks this is funny and giggles louder than is socially acceptable. But I don't see the humor in being treated like a zoo animal.

"Um," I speak up, "we're here because we're studying psychology—the way the mind works, you know."

"Yeah, yeah, I know. I went to college. I studied anthropology and stuff. When I went to college my mind worked better." He knocks on his head like it's a door.

"Oh, I'm certain it'll work well again," I assure him.

"Naw, it won't. You're wrong." He giggles again, then picks at his cheek. "A fly touched me. Ick, it tickles."

I nod and take a few steps forward as our line inches its way toward his residence hall.

"Wait! I gotta tell you something." The young man kneels on the grass at my moccasined feet and extends his hands upward in a classic pleading gesture. Several of my classmates gather round to watch this piece of theater. "Excuse me, miss, but will you marry me? Would you mind? Please and thank you."

This just about breaks my heart. Before I can consider every nuance of the question, an excitable supervisor materializes and puts her hand on his shoulder. "Damon, leave the young lady alone. C'mon, son." She points him in the direction of his room.

"Damon is a demon!" he shouts at her. "Damon is a demon!"

The students try their best to stifle laughs but they fail miserably. I cover my face with my hands. Laughter was to be expected. When we finally enter the building and the line breaks up, I panic until I locate Doon and Claire in the lobby. They seem to be priding themselves on how well they fit into a loony bin. Claire's bragging, "I deserve to be here more than you. *You're* hopeless, while I can be rehabilitated."

"God, the truth hurts!" Doon clutches her chest as if pierced by an arrow. "In point of fact, I was assigned to the psychiatric floor at Mt. Sinai Hospital when I was thirteen." She tugs on her hair so it'll stand up and look even more freaky.

"My God!" Claire exclaims, hands slapping both cheeks. "Why were you put in the psycho ward?"

"Because someone tried to rape me, stupid! That's what they do when that happens."

Is this revelation true or just Doon's theatrics? The thought that it might really have happened stuns us and yet makes perfect sense. Doon's sarcasm, her outrageous hair and clothes have expertly protected her from further insult—and from the rabid libido of boys.

"I'm burned out," I announce to my friends. "Can we just sit outside and leave the rest of our class to embarrass themselves?"

My two favorite chums—a mythological siren who could drown men by looking at them, and a bohemian Gidget who is insightful and artistic and will probably discover the cure for cancer—accompany me into the fresh air. We sit under a majestic oak tree and share the contents of Doon's rucksack: one Kit Kat bar and one apple.

Eating too fast, I choke on a tough piece of apple skin. "There's no way a person can come here—to a place where everyone's sanity is questioned—and not feel borderline themselves. No way!" I blurt out. "It's like the flu. You come into contact with people who are ill and you feel what they feel. You begin to doubt yourself. You begin to feel more like *them* than the people you left behind. It could happen to any of us, you know. Craziness is just around the corner. I know, I've been to that corner."

"This place gives me the creeps," Claire moans. "They make it pretty on the outside so we can't guess it's ugly on the inside."

"All of us are ugly on the inside," Doon says wryly.

"Not me," Claire smiles, revealing a mouthful of apple.

I fold my body and become smaller, holding my knees to my chin. "All the kids were complaining about the smell of that ward, and I tried to pretend it didn't get to me. Like I was better than everyone else. The truth is, the place scared me too. Made me sick to my stomach. I'm no better than those idiots who were pretending to throw up. As much as I stick up for the mentally ill, I don't want to be associated with anything they touch or do. I like my illusion that I'm not one of them. I mean, how am I supposed to get to sleep at night?" I throw myself on the lawn and cover my face with my hair—in case I start to cry. My friends already think I'm a crybaby. In seconds I am crushed by the weight of one and then two women—we would never be caught calling each other "girls." My friends are bearing down on me in a gesture of silliness, in what I want to believe is an act of love.

"This is how you'll get to sleep: we'll squash you. Mashed Lorna. Like, totally," Claire ribs me. Then begins a round of tickling followed by an intentionally sappy group hug. Although it's obvious that Doon and Claire are teasing me out of my black mood, they don't know how good it feels to be crushed with the weight of another person. Presence means everything to me. The opposite of absence is very powerful.

Confessional

1969

addy's pacing back and forth, a steak knife in his hand. He's supposed to be tending the hibachi in our sliver of a backyard, adjusting the thick blobs of meat until he deems them minor masterpieces. But he's too distracted by his bad news: he's been "let off" from the network because three of the shows he works on have been canceled.

"I'm getting too old for this," he grumbles, his shoes wearing down the carpeted path between the living room and den. "Four times in six years. Four times in six years, Julia. This business is heartless, heartless! No place for an old man!"

"Burton, you're only forty-nine, for heaven's sakes." Mother runs in from the kitchen, wiping her hands on an apron that is longer than her trendy short skirt. She still has two pink sponge curlers attached to the crown of her head. "You'll make a comeback, just like before. It's not like the television industry is drying up."

"Well, it is for anyone who has an ounce of experience. All the young Turks are taking over. They're putting us old Turks out to sea." He waves the knife in the air menacingly.

"Burton! Watch the knife, please." He follows her into the kitchen. With her own knife, she slices a head of lettuce on the cutting board with uncommon aggression. "Um, maybe you should get out of the house a little more often? I can't take all the pacing, Burt. You're like a bomb about to go off." She looks up at Daddy with a sympathy that's been badly eroded. "I-I'm too nervous to eat tonight!"

Daddy rushes over to the kitchen counter and takes Mother into his strong, hairy arms. They sway in place. "Hey there, you with the stars in your eyes," he sings sweetly, rocking her like a baby to calm her nerves. They begin to box-step stiffly around the kitchen; their grip on their respective knives slackens, and Mother's gold thong sandals glisten in the late afternoon light. Then Daddy whispers silly stuff in Mother's ear and delicately removes the sponge rollers from her hair. She laughs silently, pulling away from him at the same time. I can't help but notice that she's cringing.

When their slow dance reaches the den, they both stop in their tracks. Not because I'm watching my favorite afternoon TV show and they respect this, but because Mother's face has fallen.

"Burton, let me go!"

"What the hell? I can't seem to do anything right, Jules. Tell me what to do and I'll do it!"

Mother's jaw opens but no words come out.

"Tell me, goddammit!" He throws her out of his arms.

"Burt, I-I just can't take care of Lonnie and . . . now, you too. It's too much!" She covers her eyes with one hand, the vegetable knife almost jabbing her cheek. "If I'm a failure at being a wife and mother, so be it!"

I notice she didn't bring up taking care of me. But that could be a good thing. My body's taking up the entire couch, decked out in size 33 Levi's and a form-fitting, scoop-neck tee. Daddy looks over at me with a harshness that scares me. I know he's ticked off by my bralessness. He hustles away to the living room and fiddles with the knobs to the stereo. Then he glides back into the den, swiveling his hips comically like Ricky Ricardo. Our house fills with the incongruous gay sounds of an old cha-cha record. It's Pérez Prado, one of Daddy's pet albums from the fifties. Without asking, he sweeps Mother up again in a dance of his own making. "Ugh!" Daddy shouts to Prado's syncopated beat, snapping his fingers in the air. Though Mother's gold lamé sandals follow his oxford shoes, I see she has gone off to another world.

Mother stops dancing and freezes in front of the TV screen. Maggie Evans, the pretty, beleaguered heroine of *Dark Shadows*, is completely obscured.

"Burton," Mother pleads. "Burton!" She puts her hands on his shoulders and shakes him like a woman at the end of her tether.

Daddy looks helpless. After giving Mother one of his signature hangdog looks, his face darkens and his mouth takes in short, scary breaths. When he finally speaks, his voice drowns out Maggie Evans and Barnabas Collins' love scene. "Whatsa matter *now*, Julia? I thought you *liked* dancing and *ro*-mance!"

I flee downstairs to my room, but can still hear them going at it. My ears won't protect me, they never have.

"I don't know if we should stay together anymore, Burt. I just don't know."

"Jules, we've been over this. You *know* you can't afford to take care of Lonnie on your own. You could hardly hold down a job with nerves like yours."

"Oh, that's really fair. Well, maybe you're right, but I could try. I could try!"

"Honey, you need me. Remember? You need me! And, I, uh, promise things will get better. Change is in the air. You'll see. I've got a pilot I've been working on that's going to knock the network's socks off! It's about a blue-collar bigot, his submissive wife, his foolish son, and his peacenik daughter-in-law—"

"But your bosses don't see you as a writer. They see you as a numbers guy. I don't know, Burton."

"It's going to be great, Jules. A Nielsen-ratings smash!"

"No. I mean I just don't know if . . . if I love you anymore. I don't feel much of anything. Just burned to a crisp. I don't know if I love *anything*."

Before Mother's words can threaten me with meaning, I decide to go to sleep. Sure it's almost dinnertime, but sleeping might be more important than eating right now. I tuck my head under the covers and watch the swirling colored dots that form when I shut my eyes tight.

"Hey guys, red alert!" Forget it, it's sister interruptus. Lonnie's running around outside, squawking about something burning. "Meeshy! Daddy! The whole joint's going up in flames. Better get your carcasses out here!"

I run upstairs. Through the sliding glass doors of the living room, I see Daddy fanning smoke with a rolled-up *Hollywood Reporter*, and I wonder if our back hill has caught on fire. And then I see him remove four black, shriveled fragments from the hibachi with his tongs. It's our dinner.

With the crisis of the day snuffed out, Daddy asks Lonnie to go for a ride in the Valley. "C'mon Lon, let's go get some steaks at Sizzler."

"Can I get a chocolate fudge sundae and a piece of chocolate cake?"

"Yeah, yeah. Anything your heart desires," Daddy says wearily, showing us all that he's a nice guy.

"Then beam me up!" She smiles radiantly.

"Okay, but you'll have to remove those skeleton rings and bones if you're gonna step one foot inside Sizzler."

"No way! They're a permanent part of me. It would be like removing my brain."

"Your brain's already removed," Daddy says hostilely.

"Hey, you think I'm going to ride around with a bastard like you?" She springs into a generic martial arts pose.

Daddy lifts his hand like he's going to do something awful with it. Then the arm returns to his side as if he's turned into a pussycat. Opening the front door, he hollers in a voice loud enough for our neighbors to hear, "Let's get outta here, Lon, and give your mother a chance to think about the rest of her life. Time to decide if she can cut it in the real world."

Daddy slams the door and lumbers outside to warm up the car. Lon apes his movements and slams our door a second time. She stalks down the front steps, skeleton-ringed hands hidden deep in her pockets, and takes Mother's seat in the car. The two baddest guys I know drive away, leaving Mother and me in peace.

I I I

It's a brand-new, ninety-degree day. But heat is a good thing: it tranquilizes us Persons, reminds us not to try so hard at life.

Daddy's cooling himself off at a bowling alley in Encino. Mother's inside our air-conditioned house, reading *Ladies' Home Journal* and whispering on the phone to the friends she left behind in Burbank. Lon and I have claimed our poolside turf, waiting for the "pool monster"—that horrid vacuum gizmo that maniacally loops its way through the water—to shut down and get out of the way.

Wearing a fairly modest bikini, a red bandanna print with

white piping, I'm baking on the steamy patio that rings our pool, working on a tan. True, I don't have enough melanin for the real thing, but Bain de Soleil has a tanning cream that has promised to help me; my palms are already orange from applying the stuff. On a beach towel with THAT GIRL printed in giant letters, I turn onto each side for ten minutes, like one of Daddy's flank steaks. I've got my transistor radio on full blast and am belting out "Suite: Judy Blue Eyes," eyes closed to the world. Next to my towel is a can of Tab and twenty-five carrot sticks. Today's game plan is to get by on five hundred calories, to shave off one more gelatinous pound of flesh. This is the fifth day of my radical diet, and though my willpower is strong, I am spacing out royally. Each time I lift my head to see what Lonnie's up to, I black out. When I got up to pee after the first round of tanning, I stumbled like a drunk on my way to the bathroom. Now, when I need a little more sustenance, the long trek to the fridge makes me queasy.

Resting my sun-dazed forehead against the cold refrigerator door, I steel myself. I'm not ready to encounter a Sara Lee pound cake or a bucket of gravy from Kentucky Fried Chicken. With haste, I grab a Big Stick Popsicle from the freezer and run out of the house like a thief. The fifty calories buried inside the ice and synthetic flavors are necessary ones, I tell myself. And anyway, I can swim these calories off. Twenty laps should do it.

Back on the towel, posed like a starlet on the beach at Cannes and hidden behind glamour-girl sunglasses, I see that a human shape has invaded the pool. So Lonnie has decided to join the pool monster. (Why wait to swim when you can have maniacal company?) I watch her husky body wade through the water like a rhino, watch her enormous D-cup breasts weighing her down, suppressing her natural athleticism. The pool monster moves perilously close to these breasts; it's petulant and impulsive. Afraid Lon might get strangled in its hose, I jump up to save her, but my vision conks out. Red dots blinking in a sea of black are all I see. Still, in my role as the sister-with-her-head-screwed-on-right, I'm able to holler, "Lon! Get outta there!"

"No way, José!" she hollers back. "I belong here."

When my eyesight returns, I chant, "Danger, danger, Will Robinson," hoping the kitschy sentiment will change her mind.

But she ignores the warning. "Come on in, Oozy, the water's fine!" Instead of splashing me coyly, she creates a minor tidal wave that nips at my towel and ankles.

"No," I say sharply. "You know the new rule."

"Yeah, Oozy only swims alone. Oozy has to have the pool all to herself 'cause she's a vicious shark. Mean and vengeful. Well, come on in and I'll make sure you're the *last* one who ever swims in this pool, ha!"

I shrink with humiliation and stuff another carrot stick in my mouth to shut me up. It's true; ever since we moved to Tarzana, I've had a very strong urge to swim by myself. I can't share the pool with anyone—I know because I've tried. It's not a law-of-physics thing; I can still float and do the back-stroke and the sidestroke alongside Lon and Mother and Daddy. But my daydreams won't stay afloat. Any fantasy worth its salt sinks the moment another human being shares the water with me. My TV-star scenarios evaporate. My romantic reveries shrivel up and die.

Lonnie emerges from the surreal blue-green water and shakes her torso like a cocker spaniel. I'm forever amazed. My formerly slim-hipped, lithe sister is now endowed with the stocky build of a sumo wrestler, and those pendulous breasts must really get her down. How can she pass as a male when they are so obvious, so glaringly female? In addition to showing off her de rigueur rubber flippers and diver's knife, she's flaunting a torn piece of yellow cloth tied around one of her biceps.

"*Qu'est-ce que c'est?*" I point to the arm.

"What? Oozy wants some Fresca?"

"No, *qu'est-ce que c'est.* That's French for 'What the hell is on your arm?'"

She laughs and parades up and down the deck like Blackbeard stuffed into a one-piece swimsuit. Now I recognize the yellow cloth. Lon has appropriated my Vietnam protest armband, a souvenir from my first student march on a chemical factory.

"Real cool," I say, too detached to get angry.

"Ya mean ya don't care that I *stole* something from ya?" she taunts me. "Guess the sun has blinded you and burned a hole in your brain."

"Yeah, sure," I answer lazily.

"Hey! The pool monster's stopped. I'm gonna ask you one more time, Ooze, to get in the pool with me."

"Naw, you go on," I wave at her.

"Is it because I'm too weird for ya?"

"No, *I'm* the weird one. I don't want to think or do anything. Just wanna stay inside my head."

Lon rests her burly body next to mine on the towel. Her wide shoulders block out the letters and, in my mind's eye, THAT GIRL now reads THRILL.

"So Oozy, do you think *my* head is different than yours?"

I am knocked out by this question. "Gosh, I don't know. What do you think?"

"I think the science inside my brain is all scrambled. The chemicals in there went haywire a long time ago. Ya know, in Meeshy's womb."

I gulp audibly and stutter like Don Knotts. "I-I just don't know, Lon." My own head has been beaten by the sun for two hours, and now this. I readjust my sunglasses and stretch out on my half of the beach towel, too nervous to make a peep. Lon rests her new Marine-style buzz-cut locks on my lap, and we begin to breathe in synch, the sun blocking out all rational thought. The long version of "Light My Fire" comes on the radio and carries me away with it.

"Oozy?" Lon interrupts my reverie.

"What now?" I sigh, studying the clouds.

"I know that I'm a mental case. I know I'm mentally ill, you know."

"Uh-huh," I reply. It kills me that she knows this and yet has never been able to get out from under this fact.

"I'm a mutation of science. Something went terribly, terribly wrong."

"Oh, honey." I pet her head. "Not that wrong."

"You don't even know," she says. "You people will never know."

I try to say something inspiring, but I know she's right. I have nothing new to say. Fortunately, "A Hard Day's Night"—already a golden oldie—follows "Light My Fire."

Lonnie squeals, "The Beatles! Yay! Better not exterminate them, Oozy."

"Wouldn't dream of it," I say, and then, in the privacy of my head, begin my weekly inventory of body parts—all the parts of me that work. Two eyes, two arms, two legs, two ears, two feet, one nose (but what a nose), one mouth, one stomach, two thighs. Oh, let's not even *go* there.

Ever since I was six and halfway aware that something about Lon didn't work right, I've been vigilant about this practice, counting the things I am grateful for. Or *could* be grateful for, if I were a good person. Just knowing I possess the requisite body parts, despite the fact that a few are deeply flawed, can bring me peace, remind me that I am conspicuously rich in ways that handicapped people are not. Of course, what always trips me up is whether or not to count my mind. This is a tough call to make and one I will leave to professionals. "At least you've got your health," Mother likes to remind me when I'm certain that Lon has destroyed my life. "Yep," I respectfully reply, thinking, *I've fooled everybody in the world. The only difference between Lonnie and me is that I'm a better actress.*

"It makes me feel all right!" the Beatles sing jubilantly, their song concluding with a clangy guitar lick. Lon leaps up from my lap and announces she's going to make some toast—at least four slices—and smother them in peanut butter and thick slabs of butter, her favorite lunch.

"Uh, please don't talk about food today. I'm trying to ignore the whole idea."

"Okay, Ooze. You got it! I won't suck any more of your blood. Too much carnage." She swaggers away in her one-piece swimsuit.

As I watch her enter the house through our downstairs bathroom, I remove my sunglasses and pull my stringy hair into a ponytail. Dispensing with the usual beach-babe wiggle, I throw myself into the deep end and carelessly displace the water. I spin in circles like a dervish, orbiting further away from the world I know.

When I'm winded, I pause to choreograph a new synchronized swimming routine. I point my toes out of the water, rotate my ankles, and make little circles with my feet. Then I dive to the bottom of the pool and touch it; although I don't care for these depths, I know that touching down means something in our culture, a mark of achievement. But all I achieve is a feeling of discomfort. Bursting up through the water like a rocket, I raise my arms above my head—I'm faking exuberance, trying to act like someone who actually loves her life.

When I catch my breath, I paddle over to the pool return.

Discreetly, I allow the intense current that gushes out of its hole to fill my bikini top and puff it out to the max. Then, making absolutely sure that no one is watching, I grab the silver pool bars and pull myself up higher, until my vagina is flush with the opening. The pulsating stream of water that jolts my vagina over and over again excites me in a way I haven't shared with anyone. It does more than tickle me—it seems to change my mood, no matter how dark. I feel so good, I can't tug myself away from this stream. So I close my eyes, but instead of seeing dots, I see flames.

Finally, when the feeling is too dangerous, I tear myself away from the opening and, with a butterfly stroke, swim to the shallow end. When I reach the steps, I extend my legs and arms as far as they will go in each direction—south, north, east, west—and swell with a curious happiness that has no name. With my arms and legs akimbo, my mind floats off. In seconds, I metamorphose into the classic Disney mermaid, the kind with the insanely long hair that, instead of getting tangled by seaweed, ripples like silk as she purls gracefully through the seawater. I am grace incarnate and have a date with a merman who loves me! Alas, he doesn't have a face. Not that he's a blank; I simply can't imagine *how* he looks. Handsome? I hate handsome. Rugged? I hate rugged. I decide that he refuses to reveal his face to me because it has been hideously deformed. This small fact doesn't deter me; it only makes me love him more! Of course, if I can love the merman hard enough and long enough, his face will heal. I have been taught to believe that this is true. Which is why I'm lolling in a pool instead of participating in real life. In real life, there's no guarantee about love transforming faces or hearts or even minds. Lonnie and I may be stuck with our imperfections for the rest of time. Unsettled by this idea, I swim three laps in my mermaid guise. Maybe my thinking is off. I haven't had a crumb of protein in five days.

I   I   I

I am writhing on the cool porcelain tiles of our marine-themed bathroom, using a sea-green rug for a pillow until its color makes me puke. I'm writhing at the bottom of a lake with seaweed coiled around my waist. Do forgive the mixed metaphor; my stomach hurts that bad.

I have eaten too much. This afternoon was like every afternoon: I came home from school and, without thinking, flung my books on the coffee table with the *Better Homes and Gardens* and *Variety* and *Life*. I did not pass Go or my mother or anybody. Without thinking, I found a huge tub of Lucerne cottage cheese that had my name on it. I smiled, recalling how much I liked the texture of cottage cheese, especially the creamy silk top that slides down your throat in a superior way. I recalled, too, just how much cottage cheese I eat every day, and how it does something good for me, like a friend who's consistent, dependable, generous, and kind. Then I recalled that what goes best with cottage cheese is a whole box of Triscuits or a whole box of Wheat Thins. The provocative salty sweetness mixed with the crackers is a very special experience.

So I threw open the cupboard that's highest and most painful to reach—in case someone in our family thought food was *pleasurable*—and reached for the Triscuits with a trembling hand. I managed to pry the box loose from a shelf packed with other boxes of completely unappealing food and, with the cottage cheese tucked under my armpit and a teaspoon sticking out of my mouth, retired to my bedroom to eat peacefully but greedily.

You take a heaping spoonful of cottage cheese on the tongue and, before it can possibly find your throat, stick in a Triscuit for some fun. The whole business is like building. Mortar and brick, brick and mortar. The texture is to die for. The texture makes you die later. But while you are building a monument of cheese and cracker, you get a tremendous boost from the maniacal activity, the unstoppable nature of your building. A brick of cracker is barely in your mouth before you add the cheesy mortar and get crammed with a weight that's so real, it's a downright presence! Something big is inside you, filling up the part that's not real, that's murky and full of vapors. What a comfort it is to cram a presence down you! Of course, it's a bit violent. It's forced, and force is violent. Oh, but I haven't even talked about the dark part yet.

At the same time that you're doing this architectural eating, you realize in a flash that it's wrong. Because you've read enough articles to know this is "crazy" behavior. You tell the devil in the cartoon balloon above your head to go away because you deserve this food, you deserve to have as much pleasure as possible. Sure, you were bad to eat half a box of Triscuits, but your life's so defective you *deserve* to eat the rest of the box, because you don't do other bad stuff like smoke or drink, do drugs or run away from home. You are so good; in fact, you're pathetically good. You *deserve* to ruin yourself. Besides, the pain in your stomach will soon match the pain in your head. It will make the invisible visible. You will finally have some proof.

The devil says, "Go ahead and self-destruct, I don't care. I'm not a fucking baby-sitter. You will become so distorted that no one will recognize you. Not even me."

Blinking away the devil like that cocky television genie, something more powerful gets ahold of me. A faint but urgent voice says: *Lorna, stop. I want you to put down the spoon.*

But I need the texture, I say. Get out of here!

No I won't. I like you, Lorna. I won't go until you stop. You can *stop, you know. You can fill yourself with drawings and poems, your fantastically Lorna-esque work.*

I smile at this. But my mouth wants more inside it. Poems and drawings don't have any calories, I tell the goody-goody voice of reason. I can't *chew* them. Can't wrap them around my body. Can't get *warmth* from them.

You can use them to remind yourself that you are already full.

Yeah, yeah. (I must have read this before in *Seventeen*.) Supposedly, I was born full; I am eternally full but have fooled myself into thinking the ache is real.

My stomach is beginning to react to the mess inside. I burp, and it tastes horrible, like death. Desperate to rid myself of a voice that would have me give up food, I cram another cottage cheese–laden brick in my mouth and, like the forty before it, hardly taste it. Ah, but the salt, the sweet wheat, and the milky bulk! This is good, this *works*. Then another, and another. Each time, I smooth out the remaining cottage cheese in the tub and make it look brand-new. I want a smooth appearance to my crazy behavior.

But the cheese exerts a magnetic pull not unlike the South Pole; no matter where I hide my hands, they are inexplicably drawn to the tub's dark center. (Has food never been tested for its magnetic properties?)

Disgusted, I decide to lock the whole business behind closed doors. In a trance, I return the cottage cheese tub to the top shelf of the refrigerator and the Triscuits box to the depths of the cupboard. I imagine a skull-and-crossbones decal pasted on each door: STAY OUT LORNA: THIS MEANS YOU! Before I can catch myself, the message quickly mutates into DIE, MONSTER, DIE.

But no matter how tightly I have sealed the waxy wrapper inside the cracker box and secured the lid on the tub, they appear to violently undo themselves, bounding out of their respective hiding places and leaping back into my hands—the hands of a killer.

So I complete the picture. I get rid of the evidence and begin—one more time with drumroll—to mash the cheese-laden crackers into the recess of my mouth, shoveling food until there's nothing left but the shell of the tub and the hollow cardboard box and the shiny teaspoon (which reflects the mad face of the killer). I lick up the remaining curds still clinging to the lid and avoid looking at the cracker crumbs now wasting away in the empty wrapper.

At last I am complete; my stomach is full and inflexible. For a perfect moment there's a stillness that's not filled with hatred—a feeling of solidity, of mass. I exist! And then the gas begins its silent campaign.

Shaken and ashamed, I crawl into the downstairs bathroom and cradle myself on the cool, tiled floor. There's a bomb growing inside me like an alien baby. I sneak a look at the full-length mirror and see a ghost. Then I curl into a ball like a pill bug. The cramps are mean, the body unforgiving. So this is the way the killing begins. I mean, I think I'm really going to die this time. If not from the food I've just forced on myself, then from my best of intentions.

You see, I had intended on eating everything in the world as a radical method of self-change. Because the other methods have failed me. I had *intended* on eating away at the membrane that separates me from the happy world—a way of punching through to the other side. The food was *supposed* to push me through to that serene place where I would become essence. Where I would evaporate into a see-through, floating, meaningful thing. So the disappointment is huge when all I get from food is bigger. And flatulent. And cruel. I can't tell you how sorry I am when this happens. All I wanted was to taste something better than the stuff around here. I'm not going to apologize for being hungry. I'm starving and I need some company.

Here Comes the Sun

1969

hen there was the boy. The force you've been waiting for your whole life to blow through the door, the magic you welcome and fear and cannot do without.

He was not so much a boy as a young man with stubbornly boyish features: high-top sneakers, button-fly Levi's, and an unsinkable, upbeat spirit. The hair was the longest my high school would tolerate, the body lithe and quick, the whole being deliciously angular. But it was the nose that ultimately sold me, that signaled true greatness—a narrow, witty beak of a protuberance, not unlike my own. A kind nose, a wise and biblical nose, a nose that would consider me in its gaze and let me stay awhile.

At first, Nathaniel was only a fuzzy notion, a boy on the periphery. A comrade of Claire's, he sat next to her in Govern-

ment and presumedly was a bad influence. Eternally combat-
ive and questioning, while sporting a permanent grin, he
daily assaulted the teacher with a more feeling logic, a more
humane way of considering things. Claire reported that
Nathaniel was "more different" than anyone she'd ever met:
"The guy's obsessed with finding the truth. Like it's something
you can chase after and wrestle to the ground." While this
made Nate companionable in her eyes, he simply pushed too
many of her buttons to be considered "romantic material."
Claire preferred to think of herself as "open" and "progres-
sive" but never "outrageous" or "radical," her candid assess-
ment of Nate.

Upon hearing this, I was wowed. "Outrageous and radical
sound pretty spectacular to me, Claire. I have little use for
conventional boys, and they have no use for me!" I made my
proclamation as we strolled arm in arm on the great lawn before third period.

"You just don't get it," she chided. "What disturbs me about
Nate is how wild he is. This morning he asked me if I was secretly unhappy—can you believe that? I mean, where does he
get off?"

"That's not wild," I defended this totally unknown entity.
"That's brave. You just feel a little threatened, but who
wouldn't? It sounds like his question hit a nerve," I teased
her, tapping a large vein on the side of her neck.

"No!" Claire wailed. "See, I love that he's weird, right?
Though I know other students who are more freaky-weird,
and some guys are more flamboyant or narcissistic. But Nate
is alone in his weirdness. When I insisted that I wasn't 'secretly unhappy,' he snorted like he didn't believe me."

"How awful," I said, becoming secretly very happy.

"He just cocked his head like some Lucky Charms leprechaun and said, 'Claire, I admit that I provoke people, but I
do it by loving them in my imagination, by embracing their

worst traits. Of course, this pisses everyone off.' Can you believe he said that? Well, it sure pissed me off!"

I took Claire's hand and escorted my petite friend to Social
Studies. Eager to meet the new "weirdo," I forgot to stuff my
face at lunch.

■ ■ ■

That afternoon, I was introduced to Nathaniel on the middle
lawn of El Corazon High School. He was shouldering an
enormous cardboard sign in the shape of a human hand. It
modestly instructed:

> **hand me the vote.**
> **nathaniel berman, your better**
> **boys' league president.**

The sign commanded the attention of all who saw it. Nate
was a candidate in some race that never had crossed my mind.
Formal school politics seemed square in these experimental
times; the so-called counterculture surely ran counter to Boys'
League president and the like. Of course, like everybody else, I
smiled at the sign. No doubt a goofy smile, because the sign itself was so goofy. But I flushed with admiration too; there was
something genius and brave about concocting a cartoonish
campaign. Didn't this guy hear the world laughing behind his
back?

Claire had warned me that Nathaniel *expected* everyone to
feel superior to a guy toting a giant hand. So when I saw the
hand with my own eyes, I understood Nate's political strategy; the boys might very well elect a president who posed no
threat to their hipness. He was too outré to be cool. For all his
creativity, Nathaniel was a safe, benign choice.

"Nate, this is Lorna." Claire made the briefest of introductions. "She's the most real person—besides *you*, of course.

You just *have* to know her." Claire smiled smugly at her cu-
pidic skills and hummed a suspect little tune.

I stared openly at The Nose. But Nathaniel looked me right
in the eye, without a trace of fear. His equilibrium at such an
historical moment was daunting.

"I admire your handiwork," I practically whispered into my
purple turtleneck sweater, grinding the rubber heels of my
Mary Janes into the grass.

"Yeah?" Nathaniel grinned at my pun. "Would you like to
touch it?" he asked, as if offering me the chance to hold his
frog or rock or some part of his body.

I reached out to grab the sign's long stick and lifted it high
over my head. "This feels nice," I blandly reported and
pumped the sign up and down like a giddy cheerleader. "Rah
rah, everybody wins." Then I set the whole business down on
the grass. With a happy adrenaline surge, I knelt over the
cardboard hand and pretended to read its palm. "Ah," I prog-
nosticated, "this hand will have a long life and much good
fortune. This is a hand with a future!"

Nathaniel bent down and peered into the palm as if he saw
what I saw. "By George, you're right! This is a winning hand!"
We giggled together and noticed that Claire, our official escort, had conveniently escaped our circle and was now a few
yards away, brushing sensuously against the chest of her new
boyfriend, Petey, a total airhead in my book. Nathaniel then
asked me the first of what would prove to be a thousand life-
threatening questions: "You seem sort of sad. Would you like
to walk home with me after school today? I'm pretty comfortable with sadness."

The sheer boldness of his statement floored me. *How dare
you*, I wanted to scream, but answered instead, "Yes, that
would be good. That would be possible." I swung my arms
nonchalantly, the corners of my mouth turned up to suggest I
possessed a terrific sense of humor.

"Good. Possible," he repeated my words.

Shit, Claire was right. He *was* completely invasive. *Sad*, ha! The word rattled in my brain. I had always hoped to project an ethereal, otherworldly grace. But a *positive* grace, not a morbid one. Morbidity I hid from the world. "This alleged sadness of mine—are you so sure about it?" I challenged Nathaniel.

"Oh, yes!" he avowed. "But I'm sure it's justified. I'm sure that it's necessary."

He watched me as if he already cared. Could that even be possible? If he hadn't looked so genuinely caring, I might have slapped him for being presumptuous. Is it kind to expose others? I wanted to ask him. Is it kind to say out loud what a person really is? I decided, on the spot, to suspend judgment until I knew exactly what he meant. Such a noble nose couldn't betray me. At least not yet. It was too early.

I ∎ I

Our walks home from school were doozies—frank, screwball, emotionally adventurous. Not long after our first tentative conversations, Nathaniel and I launched into juicy philosophical inquiries; we held spirited debates on all manner of lofty topics that other kids our age would have found tedious.

"Do you ever feel so totally alone that you realize it's your lifestyle?" I asked Nate one afternoon, two weeks after we had met. I spun a couple of circles in the hot, still air.

"Loneliness is an illusion," Nate answered with conviction, as if his opinion was an age-old maxim. We stopped to rest in the shade of a great oak tree, Nate insisting I alight on a special mound of earth he had cleared for me.

After a full minute of silence, I asked, "Do you ever wish you could fire your parents?"

"Nope, I wish I could free them." With that, he opened a brown paper sack, withdrew a single oatmeal cookie, and split it down the middle. He handed me the larger piece.

"What if I could read your mind?" I smiled, coyly twisting a lock of hair around my forefinger.

"You'd find out how happy I am to listen to your questions." Nate returned my smile. He seemed to be chewing his cookie with unnatural ardor.

"I see that your cookie's made you a happy guy."

"Yep. But not half as much as sitting next to you."

I blushed, shuffling my moccasins in the dirt. I bit into my cookie with teeth that were shaking. "Um, Nathaniel, do you think a person could know someone so well that he or she never had to speak to that person again?"

"Yeah, I believe that."

"No more talking? What kind of a relationship is that?" I said huffily.

"I thought you *liked* the idea of knowing someone that well?"

"Well, I changed my mind. Talking's very important."

"Naw. Not that important," Nate said with complete confidence.

"Ha! What's more important than expression?"

"There's just more than one kind of expression, Lorna."

"For instance?" I bent my head to one side like a puppy, pleased to hear my name spoken in Nate's soft voice.

Nathaniel took my left hand, which was still holding the cookie, and brought it up to his lips. First he bit off a tiny piece of cookie, then brushed his lips across the top of my fingers. The little breeze this caused surprised me.

"What if a person was, like, a whole world?" I whispered, averting my eyes to the meadow grass surrounding us. "Would there be enough time to explore him—or her?"

Nathaniel gently returned my hand to my lap, and from the pocket of his vintage vest, produced a magnificent timepiece. He flipped the watch open to reveal its elegant face. "Good news," he beamed. "The answer is yes. There's more than enough time." Then he kissed me on the cheek to further assure me.

We sat quietly under the great oak for another half hour, ignoring the Valley's smoggy horizon. Expressing ourselves only with lips and hands, we moved in the variety of ways young people figure out for themselves. My heart must have given me away, though, it was so loud with possibility.

This may sound grandiose, but my daily walks with Nate provided my first glimpses of reality. The walks made my bedtime fantasies appear weak and silly, and any exchange with my parents or Lonnie an out-and-out bore. Conveniently, Nathaniel and I lived within three blocks of one another. It turned out that we shared the feeling of being misfits, too, although Nathaniel was gloriously content with his condition and I was still undecided. It also turned out that he was the first perfect human being I had ever met.

Our walks were characterized by an improvisational friskiness that pleased me no end. It was clear, despite my appalling shyness, that I got by on my wits, my ability to make frantic but exalted connections between ideas, words, and images ("Tonight, the sunset's so Seurat." "So right?" "Yes, Seurat with me!"). And Nathaniel was my match in every way. He held forth for long minutes and windy paragraphs on all sorts of extreme ideas, yet was able to respond with immediacy and support to any number of my oddball notions.

But our frisky nature didn't end with intellectual parries. Nathaniel enjoyed physical comedy as much as I did; we were shameless about using our elbows, feet, and legs to make a point, shameless in our mugging to drive home some personal truth. For me, all this physicality was inspiring; I had always felt completely ill at ease and fraudulent in my attempts to act composed. God knows, in high school circa 1969, it was the fashion to be cool, which meant that emotion and expression of any kind was absolute proof of one's *un-coolness*. But all this hanging back, keeping one's arms and legs in tow, was a prison for me.

By 1969, Feelings had become my raison d'être. As much as my own emotions tortured me, I felt compelled to express every one that pricked the surface of my heart. I suspected there was something to be gained by being honest. (And what would Art and Literature be without feelings? Dead in the water, that's what!) I imagined that, someday, my poems would lovingly expose the fact that everybody wrestled with the same gremlins. Ever so gently, I'd encourage my readers to treasure their sorrows as much as their cars and record collections. Somehow, despite my own experience that strong feelings were poisonous (if not lethal), I trusted they had some usefulness, at least in art if not in life. Hence, on good days, I gave my sad feelings all the respect I could muster. On bad days, I still wanted to feel nothing—what I thought most people were wildly successful at.

Nathaniel was the first person I'd ever met who enjoyed *all* his feelings. He appeared to rejoice in them; there wasn't a single emotion that didn't amuse or intrigue him. Even despair and grief brought a faint smile to his lips. He felt affectionate about feelings because he didn't fear their power. He said feelings were part of the human condition and therefore as much a part of our bodies as feet and hands. So, within minutes of meeting me and discovering I had nothing but dark, bloodstained feelings to unload, instead of running the hell away (which would have been understandable though unforgivable), he approached even closer. Over our first weeks together, spent talking and kissing and walking, Nathaniel probed me for every sadness, like a brilliant surgeon whose fingers have remarkable intuitive powers. And I gave myself over to his science, crying all the way.

Secretly relieved that "Lorna finally has a boyfriend," my

parents soon came to believe that I had left one living hell, the family, for another, the beau. All they could see of My New Romance were the black mascara treadmarks down my cheeks, my pink-rimmed eyes and attendant bags—the puffy face of their daughter who had a genius for tears.

"What is this guy *doing* to you?" Daddy complained after I'd dragged in late one Saturday night. "Taking you out to funerals instead of the movies?"

"Yeah, Oozy," Lonnie chimed in. "Do ya go on grave-robbing binges together?"

"Oh no, Daddy." I flushed like a standard-issue teen in love. "It's incredibly wonderful with Nathaniel! We just talk. He helps me express all this stuff I could never say—about me, about you and Mother, and uh, Lonnie." I looked up apologetically.

"Oh no you don't, Ooze. You're gonna tell people I'm a combination of Charles Manson and Jack the Ripper. You'll ruin me!"

"No I won't, you've got to trust me. You see, no one's ever been this interested in me. Nobody's ever found me, us, *interesting!* You see, Daddy," I gushed, "I'm deliriously happy!" Then I let loose with a fresh supply of tears. I was like a fountain, Nathaniel liked to say—Renaissance-pretty and ceaseless.

Nathaniel bequeathed the greatest gift I have ever received: the time and the space to reveal myself—all the good, the bad, and the ugly, with an emphasis on the latter—without fear of being turned away or tarred and feathered. After our first month together, I developed a theory that maintained, if a person was seen and accepted for who she really was, she could die with a peaceful heart. Because Nathaniel was my first love and my first lover, I wanted all of time to stop right here. But I wasn't ready to die.

▌   ▌   ▌

"Lorna-loo, read that new poem again, the one about me!"

I am scratching Nathaniel's back with what little nails I have while he blissfully strums his guitar. We are both scrunched into the ridiculous space of his twin bed, happy as clams.

I clear my throat with a classic "a-hem" and pick up the ratty sheet of yellow paper at the foot of the bed. "Here goes something!" I announce with bravado and then read my rawest work to date in a barely audible voice:

Affinity
The woman would like to give
away the stones
that keep her mean the man
would like to keep
all the weight but not the taste
of his old sorrow
why
I could begin to tell you tales of how
they love how hard
they memorize the world's
sweet song
how hard they try to hear it

"That is so beautiful," he praises. "*You* are so beautiful. I am so beautiful!" Blushing like the proverbial rose, I clobber him with the poem. "You really think I have something here? Do you think this is almost a poem?"

"Jesus, Lorna! It *is* a poem, you are a poem."

"I know. *You* are a poem too! So beautiful, so fragrant, so thorny."

"You mean horny!"

I clobber him again with the newest object of his affection. We double over and begin to smooch extravagantly. I inhale Nate's Right Guard deodorant; the lime scent casts a spell on me, and I am grateful to be here, in a small, close-shuttered room in Tarzana with my new boyfriend, the hero. Just the notion that he waits for me to come out of my house each day makes me out-of-my-mind grateful. Daddy calls Nathaniel the "latest religion" but I don't think that's fair. Or true. He *is* godlike because he cares for me but—really—I don't have sexual feelings for God! I don't know if I have *any* feelings for God. He hasn't kept me going like poetry has. For a year now, it's been my belief that only poems are worth living for. I would have done myself in a long time ago if it weren't for these silly scraps of paper.

"A dollar for your thoughts?" Nathaniel nibbles on my earlobe while I stare into the out-of-control flame of the candle on his nightstand.

"Dollar? You *know* you don't have that kind of money," I admonish him.

"I mean, where did you *go*, Lorna?"

I love to hear my name spoken, but something is pulling on my mind, dragging me under. "Go? I dunno. Just wondering if I have the courage to say what I need to, if I have the skill to say what I want to, if I have anything to say, if poetry can be a whole life, if I can support myself by writing, if I'll ever win an Oscar, if you are going to leave me. You know, the usual stuff."

We laugh together at this, which conveniently conceals the fact that none of my concerns are funny. I play with the buttons on Nathaniel's white oxford-cloth shirt, unbuttoning and buttoning each one in succession. When I arrive at the button closest to his navel, I kiss the bare skin there and suck. This creates raucous raspberry sounds. Nathaniel raises his eyebrows like Groucho, then reaches over for the glass of water at his bedside; after one ambitious swallow, he produces a vulgar burp. All this business doesn't mask our nervousness.

With a look of inspiration, Nate bends over to retrieve his guitar from the floor and begins fooling around with it, trying out the chord changes to "Suzanne": "Lorna takes you down / To the river with her worries / You can hear her thoughts go by / You can spend all her money . . ."

"Very funny," I snort. "Very fucking funny. I happen to be thinking about things that really matter. My future, for one."

"What about thinking 'bout things that really matter in the present?" Nate croons with Dylanesque intonation, strumming the same three chords. "I matter, you matter, what's the matter, bay-bay?"

"Nathaniel!" I whine. "Things won't always be this good. You know that!"

He sets down the bulky instrument and crawls over his lumpy mattress to cuddle with me in the corner. "Why not? Why do things have to get worse? Who says *that's* the law?"

Nate wraps his arms securely round my waist, and my tension about the future eases. I sense we're more together than apart, chest pressed to chest, heads pressed together for warmth and proof. I am forced to close my eyes; the feeling's so good, it's painful.

■　■　■

I wake up to discover that I'm still in Nate's arms. It's clear he hasn't been sleeping; he's been watching me, readying himself for something we can only speak about euphemistically.

"It's time," Nate announces, gazing at me with the eyes and the face that I can't get enough of.

"Time for what?" I raise my eyebrows, knowing the answer.

"Lorna, I can't wait any longer. I'm dying out here! I feel like

I'm standing outside your door in the rain. It's time to let me in. I'm getting soaked. Please," he whispers in my ear, pulling on the lobe gently with his teeth.

I grin at his mop of sandy hair; I need to be inside him too: flesh hair eyes scent. My hunger embarrasses me.

"I-I don't have any stuff with me," I stutter, raising my head to meet his soft, expectant eyes. Lying alongside me with his shirt off, Nate looks brand-new, dewy. I swear I've never seen him before in my life. I feel shy, I feel wise, I'm a hundred years old, I'm three years old.

"Stuff? I'll stuff ya, baby," Nate says in a really bad Humphrey Bogart imitation.

This time I forget to smile. "I really want to, um, be with you, Nathaniel. I knew tonight was The Night, with your parents out of town and everything. I'm not afraid of making love." There, I've said it, unable to call "it" fucking or balling— I'm the good girl to the last drop. Nate parts my hair so he can look into my 'fraidy-cat eyes, my tight little window to the soul. "I'm, uh, just afraid of the pain. For women, there's pain, you know. But I want to, I want to."

He kisses the nose I thought no one could love and quietly, tenderly, slips off my thirteen-button wool navy pants—"thirteen chances to say no," he always teases when I wear these pants to school. My deep V-neck tee peels off automatically; I don't remember how it ended up near my toes in a heap. My fraying rayon panties follow the tee, and my ponytail comes undone as if a force of nature has blown through the room. Nate slips out of his jeans and Fruit of the Loom briefs, and before I can admire his luscious form, it is rocking me, its skin sticking freshly to mine, like Peter Pan's shadow. In seconds the nakedness feels right, feels safe; I don't understand what's so dangerous. I smile winsomely, letting Nate know that I am beginning to find comfort in being closer-than-close. But he sits up abruptly and I fall off his body. "What?" I gasp. Maybe he thinks I'm a mistake.

Nate bends his thin, Gandhi-like frame over the turntable next to the bed. He puts the needle on the disk—Led Zeppelin—and takes another gulp of water. I wait, unable to make an independent move. Then Nate burrows his legs under the sheet again, a shiver making its way up his shoulders. Looking at me in earnest, he draws his hands through my tangled plaits of hair, then grabs me urgently, as if we're late for something. *I'm not crazy about the music,* I think, *but if it helps you* . . . We slink under the top sheet and enter a humid, underwater cave. "I promise I will go easy. I promise," he repeats, but I have already wrapped my bright white legs around his waist and am squeezing hard, climbing him until I find a fit that is perfect, a place to call home. But I'm foiled again. Without warning, Nate scoots me up toward the pillow so my head has a soft place to rest. So I can breathe. With tiny pecks, he kisses my toes, arches, calves, knees. Just when I recognize the pattern he's making, he leaps to the dark-gold center between my legs, and I pull back, frightened yet ravenous. I must be chewing my swollen lips.

"Lorna, Lorna." My name again, proof that I exist. Nate stretches his slim, hairless torso over me, echoing my shape; I'm his shadow again. I buckle under his weight and, at the same time, love the sense of being crushed. My breasts especially love the pressure—the whole idea of Nate bearing down on me. I emit a squeal, and the sound surprises both of us. Wonder, lust, and joy mingle. But my center continues to pull away, afraid of being pierced.

"Lorna, I have something to say," Nate breathes into my mouth. I bite off his mouth, at least I think I do. But when I open my eyes, there's that mouth again!

"Lorna?" he questions me.

"Yes. That's the answer . . . isn't it?"

"Lorna?" He's fiddling with his penis in the vicinity of my vagina—oh God, where *is* that infamous hole? He's trying all sorts of maneuvers, as if I'm not cooperating. I'm trying, though. Trying to accept that I must go through with this because I adore him. Because it's the way of the world.

Rubbing his lovely warm dick on my stomach, he lunges for my lips, sucking them so hard I begin to drip down below, opening up without thinking. For once I am not thinking!

"Lorna," he begins again, "I will pull out so don't worry. *Please don't worry.*" He wipes some moisture off my forehead, the gesture a mother makes with her baby. I *am* a baby, completely artless and without guilt. But then something pushes into me, fills me with new mass, new meaning, and I expand with it and become some sort of blooming woman, not quite full-blown, but a thing evolving in slow motion, like a rose filmed in time-lapse photography.

"You smell so good," Nate lets me know.

"Mmm," I reply. "You're the good one." The rose is blushing with color and I don't want to think about the end of the rose, its petals falling listlessly to the ground, the stem growing brown and stunted and dry. No, the picture of love should be an endless film loop of the rose becoming itself, not leaving itself.

"I absolutely love you," Nate tells me, so happy inside the blooming rose-woman.

"I absolutely love that about you. I absolutely love that you love me," I say.

He looks once more into my smitten eyes and sees the telltale uncertainty at the edges. Undeterred, he presses his hips into my ample flesh, driving deeper, trying to make it through to the other side. Then he stops in midair and cups my wayward breasts, protecting them from the big bad world. "I can wait," he assures me.

I squeeze him from inside, letting him know that I'm ready. For one flawless moment I have banished the uncertainty. Now I'm ready to show him everything.

▌ ▌ ▌

Unbelievable. I've just had sex for the first time and I am walking through the front door of my house, not sneaking in through some basement window. It's still early, only 10 P.M., and my panties are so wet and sticky that I'm sure the whole world can see that I'm streaming with fluid. Blood, semen, a thick woman-juice that doesn't even have a name. Strange, no dogs pick up my scent, no parents rush in to accost me. I'm no longer a virgin, and does it matter? My hair must be misted with sex, my fingers coated with sex, legs lathered with it. But this house does not seem to care.

This house is full of men playing poker. So Daddy's invited his old Burbank buddies over to play cards. There is such a racket and so much food and drink sprinkled around the dining room that a once-virginal woman can pass through unde-tected, as if she's still chaste. I spot Lonnie crouched in the den behind the wall that divides this room from the dining room; she's listening intently to the blow-by-blow of the game. A nut for the off-color banter that enlivens card games, she loves to tape the men's extravagant curses on her mini tape recorder.

"Hey, Ooze, get your fat head over here!" Lon whispers hoarsely, flagging me down as I try to steal down the stairs to my bedroom. "Get a load of this," she boasts and replays a lively series of "damns," "hells," and a couple of "shits" that she recorded earlier in the evening. "I got some great stuff tonight, Oozy. Why don't ya stay here and spy with me?"

But I'm on cloud nine, coasting with the delirious beauty of my secret. I don't feel like hiding behind a wall to eavesdrop on a bunch of smoking, drinking men who say "damn it to hell." I'm fairly anxious about checking out the state of my panties, about showering and scouring my body to a new level of clean, about getting ready for the tidal wave of guilt to rush in. I mean, Ann Landers has warned me.

"No, Lon. Not tonight. I'm kinda tired."

"That's a stinky excuse. You stink!" she says and pretend-spits at the carpet.

I wonder if, under the circumstances, I really *do* stink. "Hey, Lonnie, it's no excuse," I protest. "I'm cooked. Dead tired." But my visible glow must be making me a liar.

Lonnie leans over her spy machine and speaks into its microphone with conviction: "Lorna is dead, Lorna is dead, Lorna is dead." Then she rewinds the tape and plays back her stupid mantra at full volume: "LORNA IS DEAD, LORNA IS DEAD, LORNA IS DEAD."

As I step away from her covert operation, Lon tugs on my right calf and pins it down. "You're going nowhere, Ooze. This is where it's at!" She twists my leg with an improvised martial arts move.

"Let me go," I command. "You're hurting me!"

"Guess I don't know my own strength, Miss Social Butterfly. Well, you're no butterfly to me—you're a killer bee, stinging me over and over again with neglect. Do ya hear? I'm gonna turn you in to the authorities for ignoring me. They'll lock you behind bars, and your vampire boyfriend will never get to ya!"

In her maniacal glee, Lon's not fully aware that she's pressing me into the carpet. The skin under my wool pants burns. But I'm too tired to object; my body's gone through enough for one night. Leg still twisted back, I process a stream of moving pictures. Abstract images of flesh careening in the dark replace the pain in my knee. I can smell him again; all I have to do is think his name and he's back.

"Ooze, are you listening? I wanna make a point here." Lon-

nie sticks her round, plump face in my angular one. For
weeks she's been tugging on her nostrils, hoping to widen her
nose to resemble a black person's, and I see that it's working—the nose *has* broadened. I'd tried giving myself dimples
lately, poking my cheeks with a soft lead pencil, but had not
met with success like this.

"Yeah, I'm listening. Give me back my leg and we can talk."

Lonnie releases the leg, but instead of freeing me, pins me
down with her considerable girth. She's wearing camouflage
pants, a khaki vest, and a utility belt, compliments of the local
army-navy surplus store. The Vietnam-soldier look has invaded our house. Her clothes jingle as she moves over my
body, tickling and taunting me. As she sits up on my stomach,
foreign coins, screws, and empty cartridge cases tumble out
of her open vest pocket.

"It's raining money, Lon," I point out, trying to cheer her
up.

"Yeah, but it will be a rainy day in hell before I get off of
you, heh-heh!"

"Muth-er!" I yell, but no one can hear me; a heated exchange in the dining room overpowers our own.

"Damn it to hell, Al!"

"Jesus! Put your cards away. It's quitting time, Sid."

"No shit. Stop now, Sid, or I'll call your wife."

"Marg has no say in this. Give me more cards."

"Christ, Joe, give him the cards."

"Hell no."

"Hey, is there any more Pabst?"

"Yeah, Pabst is on tapst!"

"Play ball!"

"Fuck you!"

"Hey, not in this house, Marv. There's kids here."

"Sorry, Burt. I thought we were alone."

"Boy, wouldn't that be nice?"

I recognize Daddy's voice, Daddy's opinion. *Yeah,* I want to answer, *that would be nice.*

Lonnie has also heard Daddy's comment. I watch her flex her muscles, ready to strike. Crackling with electricity, she leaps off my stomach and runs into the dining room, screaming like an assassin, "Yiiiiiiii-yiiii!" I follow her in and meet the dark-circled, bugged-out eyes of five men with stubbly beards; the whole lot of them look sloshed. Lon runs circles around our company, challenging each of Daddy's friends to wrestle with her. "C'mon, any takers? Are ya all sissies? I can take ya with my eyes closed, with my hands tied behind my back. C'mon, you yellow-bellied cowards. Let's fight to the finish!"

Instead of becoming enraged, Daddy's friends shake their heads approvingly and grin at Lon, admiring her style.

"I've got to hand it to you, Burt," Marv speaks up. "You got one hell of a floor show here."

"I'll drink to that, Marv. Lonnie's a regular ball-buster," adds Sid.

"Yeah, man," Lon agrees, not really understanding but liking the sound of it.

Marv lifts his beer glass and proposes a toast, "To Lonnie!"

The four guests follow suit, "To Lonnie!" But Daddy's drink remains on the table; he raises his eyebrows at Lon, signaling her to leave the room.

"Put it here, Lurn, er, Lon," Sid slurs his words as he rises on unstable feet to shake Lon's hand. She loves the recognition and extends her hand to each of the men, making sure they feel the undeniable power, the manliness of her handshake. When she arrives at Daddy's place at the table, she extends her hand with less assurance, fearing he will take this hand and lead it to her room. But Daddy's in a rare mellow mood, as schnockered as his pals, and doesn't want to rock the boat. He shakes Lon's hand lightly and lets it go so he won't be tempted to hurt her. Unfortunately, Lon's feeling her oats and forces her hand back into Daddy's. She begins to arm wrestle with him against his will. After the initial embarrassment of having his daughter force his hand down—twice—on the table, Daddy concentrates harder and slams Lon's hand down so hard the pistachio nuts and crinkly potato chips and chocolate mints fly out of their bowls. The poker chips bounce off the table.

"Asshole!" Lon screams and bolts out of the room.

Daddy's friends stare at him and at the mess on the table—like it's his fault. When they spot me just inside the doorway, I fake a warm smile. I know how much Daddy needs to show me off, his poster child for normalcy. But how can I be normal? I have just made love, got laid for the first time, and the thrill has to be overshadowed by the shame and absurdity of Lon and Daddy's antics. *You are assholes,* I want to tell the men, but I don't. Got to keep that normal thing going. "Good night," I wave to the guys, walking backwards out of the room. I can't kiss Daddy on the cheek because he may pick up the musky scent that betrays my new status.

" 'Night," echoes the room. But instead of going to bed, I mount the stairs to check on Mother. She always cloisters herself during poker games, tries to steal a few hours of quiet time. Still, it's odd that she didn't make an appearance when Lonnie screamed. She's usually the first one at the crime scene.

A hazy light peeks out from under the master bedroom door; I knock timidly. "Mother?"

Without permission I crack open the door, worried that I'll find an empty room with the second-story window open. Maybe on the very night I've gotten more out of life than ever before, she's had enough. But she's in her bed, reading light on, a *Ladies' Home Journal* covering her face. A tall drink and some white pills sit on her night table. I walk over to the drink and smell it—it's just Pepsi—and sniff at the pills. Bayer.

"Mother?" I remove the magazine, which had intentionally masked her expression. It's pained. She opens her watery, sea-green eyes, and I kneel beside her. "It's only me, Lorna."

"Hi," she says feebly. She's pallid; even her freckles look faded. "How are you?" she asks in a faint, cloudy voice.

This moves me beyond words: she always wants to know how I am, no matter how awful she is. "I'm great," I answer, and for once I mean it. "I think I'm going to be great."

"Good," she purrs and, noticing the magazine at her side, repositions it over her eyes. Her rust-colored hair, which is sticking out in stiff bunches on the pillow, has begun to thin. The beginnings of age, I think. Have we done this to her? What haven't we done?

"Mother, Lonnie had a big night tonight," I tell her, deliberately censoring my own news. "She went in to meet Daddy's friends but she got too excited. She arm wrestled Daddy and got hurt."

"I'm sorry to hear that. Really. But I can't do any more tonight." She curls over on her side and pretends I'm not here. This is not the mother I know.

"Mother!" I chasten her. "Lonnie may need you. She's freaking out because she thinks you're going to send her away."

"Too bad," she murmurs and slides under her satin bedspread.

Something big must have already happened today, something that did this to Mother. Or maybe just the usual stuff. I lift the *Ladies' Home Journal* that covers her face, bend down and kiss her cheek, then return the magazine to its place. I don't care if I smell of sex; Mother needs a kiss, and I have one left in me.

Creature Feature

1970

lone on a Saturday night, I decide to hold a mini film festival. In a rare turn of events, Mother, Daddy, and Lonnie have gone out for steak and lobster, followed by a movie at the Cinema Two. Because I refuse to see the latest Sam Peckinpah bloodfest, I get the pleasure of my own high-strung company.

I make more popcorn than necessary, as if I'm expecting someone fun or hungry, and throw on my vintage black sheath dress with the ripped-out zipper, pour myself into black Danskin tights, and slip into cotton Mary Janes from China. I look like a hippie version of a vampire, a ghoul who could benefit from a bra and a leg shave.

Nathaniel couldn't make it; his parents were holding a summit meeting to discuss their pending divorce. He regretted that his attendance was compulsory, but promised this was the last of such meetings. Doon said she couldn't come; her head was full of "thunder and lightning." Besides, she was on a diet. I took this to mean she was depressed. Claire had fled town with her parents to avoid being wooed by Petey, and Petey, who lived right around the block, was in a "righteous funk."

This left me. Earlier this evening, I had surveyed the *TV Guide* and settled on something romantic to watch, something unabashedly girlish and too corny for most of my hip and canny friends. The old chestnut *Funny Face* would suit my purpose to a T. *Funny Face* with Audrey Hepburn (gamine *sans pareille!*) and Fred Astaire (much too old for her, but dancer *sans pareil*) was the story of a plain Jane bookseller (Audrey) who is plucked from a Greenwich Village bookshop by a world-class fashion photographer (Fred) to become the next darling of the fashion magazines and Paris runways (and why not?). Admittedly not the kind of art film that is popular with my friends. Light, flimsy, apolitical. This was not going to be a four-star Fellini evening. I was about to go slumming with Hollywood fare.

I had decided to allow myself the luxury of a Hollywood musical as a supreme act of kindness. A guiltless evening of glitz and gowns, I told myself, might provide a tiny respite from an anxious life. And besides, I had always identified with Ms. Hepburn; there was a skinny waif lurking inside my thick skull and hefty thighs. For sure, Audrey was the epitome of European culture; judging from the majority of her film roles, one could assume that she viewed the world as a bright and gentle place where good fortune was just around the corner. Perhaps this was the result of being treated, for beginners, like a princess. I truly believed that if I had been treated similarly, I might have responded with matching charm, precision, and grace. If we were all treated more like royalty, we would all develop more endearing, even cine-matic, personalities. This was a theory I swore by, even as it began to dawn on me that movie stars had their own prob-lems with self-esteem and, all too often these days, tried to kill themselves.

In the bathroom, I roll a purplish shade of lipstick—Mad Mauve—over my lips and smack them on a tissue. With a plush fake-mink brush, I apply more rose blush than two cheeks can bear. I coat my eyelashes with a Maybelline mas-cara that promises to make them luxuriant and yards long. If the overall effect is a little tarty, I don't care; I'm sick of look-ing natural. Just when I'm about to administer a second coat of Great Lash, the clock in the den strikes six: my movie is about to commence.

I gallop into the den, not an easy feat in a sheath, and de-liver my tush onto our cushy couch. Norwood, my true-blue buddy, leaps onto my lap and settles in for the duration. It's tough bending over in this dress, but I manage to fish the re-mote control from the crack between the cushions, and press the magic number that should deliver me to Audrey and Fred . . .

A Crest commercial monopolizes the screen. My brand, the only toothpaste I've ever used and I've never had a cavity. I take a shallow breath and feel my waist strain the seams of my dress. I'm gaining weight just sitting here. Come on, Au-drey, let's go! The bright screen turns greenish gray and scratchy; I must have the wrong channel. Before I can verify this, the words *The Creature Walks Among Us* scroll down the screen in rhythm with mock-eerie, asymphonic music. The music tips me off that something out-of-this-world is about to happen. The Creature? Now I remember. He's one of Lonnie's fave-raves, the "Gill Man," that lonely hearts club member from the Black Lagoon. I dash to Daddy's bookshelf and speed-read the spines of his books on television and the cinema. There it is: *Milton Mertz' Encyclopedia of Film.* I rummage through the book alphabetically until my eyes target a whole slew of Creature titles. Voilà:

> *The Creature Walks Among Us* (1956). Director: John Sherwood. Story and Screenplay: Arthur Ross. Third in a series of "Creature" movies, beginning with *Creature from the Black Lagoon.* Just when the Creature is relaxing in his new home in the Everglades, he is confronted by a team of "enlightened" doctors who decide he'd be more content if he were able to walk among men. In the name of medical progress, the doctors brutally slice, stitch, and burn the Gill Man. Their goal: to help him adapt to everyday life among humans. Here, the pathos of the beleaguered Creature reaches new heights.

Is this my sister's story, or what? I slap the encyclopedia shut. It's the arrogance of our culture, our science, that's being put on trial in this movie. I had better wake up. I dash back to the den, remembering what Blanche Dubois said: There are no accidents. Actually, it was Tennessee Williams; I must give writers their due.

The Creature Walks Among Us turns out to be a classic persecution story, and I am fixated beyond belief. I am remarkably astute at screening out the hokey acting, only allowing ideas into my consciousness that make biographical sense: the unforgivable human crimes against the Creature, the unconscionable destruction of nature by the scientists, our race's inexplicable fear of anything primal or intuitive. Chills make their way up my legs, and the hairs on my nape prickle. I have never connected with my sister's plight in such a visceral way! Certainly this is impossible when she is near me. I could never allow myself to feel so wrecked around her; I would go limp with empathy and stabbing pains before I could let her know that her life feels unbearable to me. (And it's not *my* life to live.) But this low-budget allegory is holding me hostage, prodding me to confess that what happened to my sister in the womb—way before any of us could reach her—is the worst mistake I have ever borne witness to. No one is accountable yet everyone compounds the mistake. Just by staring at her strangeness they cast her back into hell. And the ones who secretly wish to burn and scrape her, and the ones who have ignored her gashes and fed her pills, they are as shameless as these scientists who say they are helping the Creature find its way among men. Shameless and accountable. And I suppose I walk among them too.

Just when I'm sure I am devouring this movie wholesale, a strange thing happens. My epiphany relaxes into sleep. At least I don't remember anything between feeling wholly riveted and wholly conked out. A cereal commercial blares at me as my head snaps awake. Something made of oats. I hate oats. Norwood is nowhere to be seen, but my black dress is blanketed with his gray fur. Before I'm conscious that the movie is over, I watch more credits streaming down the screen and hear the same distorted soundtrack. I seem to have lost a whole hour like a drunk who has blacked out. My hair is a mass of knots, and I've grown sleepies in the corners of my eyes. I stumble into the kitchen and drink a full glass of orange juice. My dark lipstick makes a sensual imprint on the glass, which reminds me that I am dressed for an Audrey Hepburn flick when I should be wearing fins.

I wiggle back to the couch in my tight cocktail dress, feeling a little queasy. I see the popcorn in the bowl hasn't been touched. Impossible! And then I notice I have struck gold with a double feature: the title *Creature from the Black Lagoon* fills the screen. So this is the original, this is what spawned a whole race of copycat films with copycat monsters.

The voice-over is especially moving: ". . . in the warm, murky depths of the sea, the miracle of life begins . . . in infinite variety, living things appear and change and reach the land . . ." I witness a different gaggle of scientists, including a very smart and beautiful lady scientist, discover a fossilized hand with webbed claws in the soil deposits near the Amazon. Then we privileged few see an oversized webbed claw emerge from the black water, reaching out for mere seconds before it recedes into its murky-depths home. Is it amphibian, Homo sapiens, the much sought-after missing link? My heart knocks about in my chest—well, it would if I were a child. I have to concede, tonight I watch with a heart that's a little jaded and too monster savvy. This film is brain-drainingly slow. I see the silliness of it all and yet the mythic parts still attract me, threaten to pull me along in their undertow . . .

The smart and good scientists feel they may have stumbled upon a significant aberration, a glorious mutation in nature. I hate when Lonnie calls herself a mutation; my interest is renewed.

"The Black Lagoon. Another world!" exclaims the handsome scientist who will no doubt live to see the end of the film. "Be careful. We don't know what's down there."

It is quickly revealed that the Black Lagoon has a deadly mystique; it is a place full of killers, of things that kill. We are told the legend of the man-fish, reminded that "the water has its secrets." And, over the course of an hour and a half, I see what Lonnie must have seen all along: that the monster just wanted to be left alone with its scaly, green self. It was happy in its singularity. This was no miserable wretch who needed company! But because the Creature was exotic and powerful and, worst of all, deep; because it erupted from our unconscious desires, from our connection with all-powerful nature, it deserved to be shot and set on fire. And studied to the max.

I gnaw on my thumbnail. In monster flicks the study of an alien species always involves a large measure of disrespect. I mean, these scientists are talking dissection, vivisection, and strategic bombing by the air force! But taking something apart to glean its power doesn't make sense, and Lonnie knew that. She always knew her well-meaning therapists were afraid of her power, of her relationship with nature. She caught on that their study of her was not meant to flatter her, nor was it an attempt to become more like her. She sensed she was the thing they most wanted to *avoid* becoming.

I pull at my draggy tights and rearrange myself on the couch. I have to admit there have been times I would have liked to shoot Lonnie myself and throw her back into the ancestral waters. Surely it's Lon who's always forced me to think such thoughts. It's sad, but after eighteen years I no longer think of her as innocent. She's not just a freewheeling girl swimming around in our deluxe pool; she's made herself into a much more threatening thing that dominates the landscape. The landscape of my life! Throwing her back into the water wouldn't be such a tragedy. Would it?

The Creature, shot by the selfish, mercenary scientist against the wishes of the well-intentioned ones, now sinks to the depths from whence it came. So the only good Creature is a dead Creature. I feel a draft from an open window. The unbearable weirdness of all creatures bears down on me. Can I be wiping tears from my sophisticated, Maybelline eyes?

I decide to make an appointment to do something with Lonnie. First thing in the morning, I'll take her out to a pet store or an ice cream parlor. I can go out in the world with the thing I might have become if a couple of my chromosomes had crumbled.

As end-of-the-film credits roll for the second time tonight and the warped music swells, I realize how lonely I am. I call Nathaniel, hoping I haven't interrupted his family powwow.

Thankfully, he answers on the first ring. "How's tricks?" he says.

"Okay," I lie. "I'm hungry and I know it's late but—"

"A fish dinner at Trident's?"

"No fish," I insist. "Mexican, Italian, Thai. But no fish."

"I love that about you," he coos absurdly. "You always know what you *don't* want."

"I want you." I burst into tears.

"Shit! You must be famished. I'm on my way."

I hang up the phone and run to my bedroom. I strip to my underclothes and slip on a yellow fifties frock with an eyelet lace bodice, a gathered waist, and full skirt. An Audrey Hepburn sort of dress. I look like spring.

A Whole Lotta Love

n the first day I met Nate, I had the unfortunate ability to picture the very last day: the complicated good-byes, the meaningful shrugs, the cold space left after love has left the premises. I guess it was my way of getting prepared, maybe years in advance. No one wants to be caught with her pants down, her heart seized up. Upon meeting Nathaniel Berman, then, and sensing we had an amazing future together, I also saw clearly a day when he would recede from the foreground of my life, becoming smaller and smaller until he was an unremarkable speck on the horizon. I did not accept the sheer unfairness of this, but I knew our parting was inevitable. For nothing good and happy had ever stuck around for the whole show. And as much as I believed in kismet, I also believed in its opposite: the inalienable fact of abandonment.

So for each day with Nate that looked something like the previous one in quantity and quality of kisses and deep conversation, I thanked my lucky stars. After five months of such gifts, Nathaniel did not appear as though he was going anywhere. Indeed, we seemed to be going to a place together, and although I could not bring myself to call him my boyfriend ("special friend" was our enlightened term), I began to imagine us bound by a special mission—one that had the staying power to last a lifetime. Silly me, was I about to believe in something bigger than abandonment?

▮ ▮ ▮

Nathaniel and I are munching tortilla chips at Casa de Brian, our favorite Valley haunt. As always, we share a few giggles about eccentric Brian Thornycroft and his hybrid of an eatery. Originally hailing from Manchester, England, Brian had always dreamed of putting his stamp on Mexican cuisine, adding mushy canned peas to his tostadas and pastry crust to his flan. Surprisingly, his hybrid took off in a big way, and nobody even noticed the canned beets that began to make their way into his culinary vocabulary.

As for me, Mexican food was a total lark. Because Mother's attempts to integrate it into our diet had failed (Daddy couldn't stomach it), I had had to wait eighteen years to get hooked on such fare. These new cravings resulted in weekly trips to "Brian's House" for me and Nate, and in regular crying jags for me. For it only took me about five minutes from the time we sat down in an old wooden booth to offer up my latest problem to Nate as an appetizer.

"Lonnie insists that I've forsaken her, that I won't stoop to playing games with her because I'm too grown-up now. She says I'm leaving her behind in the dust. That you have replaced her." I toy nervously with the tortilla chips in the red plastic bowl set before me and pull out a fine, crusty specimen.

"No, *you* have replaced her." Nathaniel utters this as a statement, not a question. He is always so damn prescient.

"Yes . . . you're right, you're *both* right. I finally have a life, and it's so obvious now. Lon sees that I'm moving away from her even though I live in the same house. It's like I've got a new address or something." I scoop up a little hot sauce in the unusually beautiful chip and unconsciously force the whole thing in my mouth.

Nate grins in the midst of my agitation, as if agitation was cute. I look away, up at the flaking ceiling and down at the chip-littered carpet, trying to stuff my unsociable feelings. In the uneasy silence, Nate plays with a pile of chips on his napkin, eventually building something that resembles an airplane. To get my full attention, he flies the contraption into my ear.

"You *do* have a new address," he speaks up. "It's called Lorna and it's a place where you can begin to devote some energy to yourself. You've got to tell Lonnie that if you practice happiness, you'll actually have more happiness and energy left for her. But if you comply with her every demand to play with her, talk to her, surround yourself with her disturbing stories and paintings, eventually there'll be nothing left—for her or for you. Tell her you have only so much gasoline in your tank and that when it runs out, it runs out for everybody who's riding in your car." Nate maneuvers his tortilla-chip plane in the airspace above our heads, waving it to drive his point home.

"But you don't understand. While I'm with my friends or by myself, if I even *think* about how lonely Lonnie is, I just pass out. This is a thought I can't even touch. It's too dangerous. And the truth is, I *do* want to get away from her. As far as I can. The whole idea of her just makes me sick—as much as I love her." The waiter, who has been hovering nearby, takes three steps back, as if I'm contagious.

"It's the guilt that makes you sick," Nate states with appalling clarity.

"Oh, yeah," I agree, fixated on a chip I've just lost in the hot sauce. "I can't bear to imagine that I'm as wicked and uncaring as most people are. I've always considered myself the embodiment of compassion, but obviously, I reserve that special stuff for my friends. Let's face it, I'm a phony. A truly compassionate person would be consistent, would *be* there for her sister." I break down, sobbing into the plate of cheese enchiladas that have just been delivered under my nose. At this, Nate registers no surprise; my tears have been putting out fires in spicy enchiladas for months.

"Just maybe you know more than Lonnie. Just maybe you know that you've got to save yourself *first*—that in your case, it's not selfishness, but lifesaving we're talking about!" Nate cradles his airplane-chip in his palm and feeds me its left wing. I open my mouth grudgingly; it seems like the time to eat has passed.

"You mean that in order to help myself, I have to hurt my sister? Or should I trust that somehow she understands and knows that my actions aren't meant to hurt her?"

Nate's head bobs energetically to signal yes.

"But what if Lonnie's like a dog and only understands that I'm leaving the house and has no idea if I'm ever coming back? What if she only knows how to be abandoned? What if—"

"Excuse me, excuse me!" Nate holds up his hand like a crossing guard. "Just *who* are we talking about here?"

"What?" I push away the platter of soggy cheese enchiladas, which have barely touched my lips, and raise my eyes to meet his. I bet they're as fiery as the hot sauce. "What do

you mean, 'Who are we talking about?' Obviously, we are dis-
cussing the fact that my sister does not possess a deep understanding of why I'm no longer available to her. All she knows
is that I'm here or I'm not. The way a house pet reasons." I
throw my fork on the floor for emphasis.

"Methinks we are in the presence of a major projection."
Nathaniel picks up his drink, an oversized glass of Pepsi, and
toasts me with an arrogant smile on his serpentine lips.

"Projection?" Heat rises off my neck, and I can't blame the
dinner. "I know you're an armchair psychologist and your
dad's the real thing, but please be careful when it comes to di-
agnosing me—you could be dead wrong!" I leave my chair so
quickly that it rocks in place as I run raggedly into the room
marked SEÑORAS and slam the door.

When I return to my seat, Nathaniel is downcast, head
propped on both fists. He won't look at me.

"Listen," I tell him, "this whole discussion has gotten a little
too close for comfort. I'm just a little tired of you being right.
Don't *you* get tired of being right?" He says nothing. "I mean,
I'm tired. Are you tired? I'm tired. I think that you are *probably* right, but I want to develop my own theories, my own insights, my own right ways!"

Seemingly self-absorbed, Nate draws on his straw until it
makes sucking sounds; there is no more Pepsi. I begin to
panic. I hate his lack of response; I am sure that it will kill me.
I will die in my favorite restaurant, head bobbing in hot
sauce.

Hysterical on the inside but bitterly quiet on the surface, I
glance down at my oval plate until I begin to make out some
kind of pattern. Someone has written in the red-brown enchi-
lada sauce, has created a finger painting of uncommon
beauty. It says: U R THE 1 4 ME. "ME" has been underlined
with a green chili.

This time the tears roll down my cheeks until I see nothing.

But I can feel Nate's hands wrapped around my waist, rocking me. He escorts me to his parents' Saab and rushes me home to his bed. Closing the shutters, he lights a thick white candle that releases a cocoanutty scent, and clicks on the stereo. As always, his first choice of music is Led Zeppelin's "Whole Lotta Love," which I consider puerile. Nevertheless it builds a powerful mood. I unbutton Nate's blue jeans, savoring the metal buttons that lead down to his crotch. I hate the word "crotch" but in this charged atmosphere, the thought of it makes me genuinely excited! I unbutton his oxford-cloth shirt, then pull his white T-shirt over his head, pausing to inhale the lime scent that lines it. I admire for what seems like minutes the curly hairs that travel from Nate's belly button down to the space between his legs. It thrills me, this difference. I will never tire of it.

I will never understand men. I believe that women are far more attractive in practically every way. Yet the mystery of maleness remains potent. I can observe it for days and still learn nothing. Men can be kind, men can be brutal, men can be impossible. Men can hurt you, then not hurt you. Men can help you, men can crush you. Men can make things better, men can make things worse. Men are full of it, men are empty, men can kiss you into oblivion, they can give you a world and a context and a space for fitting in. But men are not paintings or plays or poetry. They will leave you *even* when you're looking.

When I have finished pulling off Nathaniel's crew socks, he begins fiddling with my own, but I am not in the mood to be methodically undressed. I hastily throw off my own layers of clothing so I can press my nakedness against his before another refrain of "Whole Lotta Love" goes by. I am an urgent woman, and he accepts this: one more medal he has earned. I need to feel his heart beating and his penis swelling, to breathe in his hair and sweat. Lovemaking is interesting but nothing compared to being embraced. He squeezes me tighter than I can imagine, and when it's not possible to be any closer, he draws me in—within inches of his life, it seems. I begin to swell up too, with the deep heat of generosity that is love, that is kindness—what other people call sex. The big, heady God feeling where your vision blurs and you lose all your weight.

I begin to see that there may be a way to live in synch with Nate. Over time, the subversive inner voice that says "You are not Nate" may go away. But try as I might, he eludes me. His body feels like mine, but his mind—that damn barrier between us—acts like an impermeable force field! I brush my hand through the sandy curls on his forehead, hoping to poke through the force field and soothe the part that gets in the way of our togetherness. He looks sad. Why does he have to be something *different* from me?

I think of my own sadness at the restaurant—another barrier to being here now. Just seconds ago, we were not two minds; we were an embrace, and it was impossible to have separate ideas. But then I did and then he did. I hate that part, the release from being one and the same. I don't want to go back to my crummy world, the one without his body. He seems to sense this and presses me tighter; we flip over and face the wall, which is masked by a huge poster of Bob Dylan's rainbow-colored locks.

With one arm, I fumble under the bed for my book bag, and retrieve my plastic plunger, which has been prefilled with contraceptive foam. Plunger in hand, I make a seamless move for the bathroom, but Nate intercepts me and pulls me back into bed. "Forget it," he says sweetly.

"But—"

"Later," he instructs, taking the plunger from my fist and stashing it in a drawer on the nightstand.

I nod, believing he would never harm me in that way, the

way of all men. For I have been lucky in sex—at sex?—free of the guilt that plagued Mother's generation, and giddy with the knowledge that my "first time" was steeped in the tradition of true love. Still, the threat of getting pregnant looms like a poisonous gas cloud; the sensation of risk has been embedded in women's genes for generations, and I don't have the power to undo it. Besides, Nate isn't godlike enough to stop the flow of sperm. No man is.

Nate's gentle lips find mine—always a small miracle—and gently absorb my worries. I kiss him everywhere I can find a fresh inch of flesh and then return to his mouth for more suckling and smacking and nibbling and lip brushing. We are happy in our happiness. Nate is holding both of my breasts now, refusing to let them go in the most heroic way. Maybe he wants to come with me, to this place where we don't have to divide into two.

"Nathaniel," I whisper in his moist ear, swabbing it lightly with my tongue.

"What?" he breathes hotly in my eyes.

"I want to know if you feel exactly the way I do." I scoot up against the headboard and tuck a pillow beneath my head. I know that talking throws a huge wrench into sex, but I have to know the answer.

Nate offers me a stinging look and props his feet on the headboard. "Do I feel exactly like you? I suppose I do. I don't know. No, I guess I don't."

My heart sinks. "You . . . don't?"

"No. Because I was happy kissing you and experiencing you, but you want something else now. Something better." He rolls over to sit next to me.

"What could be better than that?" I ask earnestly.

"Apparently you think there's something that can surpass what we have."

"I'm just thinking about what happens when the kissing stops."

"We come up for air."

"No," I tug at his arm. "I mean, why can't we be just as close when the kissing stops? Why does there have to be a lessening of intensity? Why do we have to return to ourselves?"

Nathaniel pulls a hurt face. "Don't you take me with you when you go home?" He pinches my ass.

"Yeah, I always pack you in my bags."

"So do I. See, you don't have to worry—my luggage is hardy. You're in my special compartment. You'll never get lost."

"Thank you," I manage to squeak out before—surprise— one long tear rolls down my nose and drops into his mouth.

"You'll never get lost . . ." Nathaniel repeats, patting me on the back like an infant.

I try to imagine that he's telling the truth, that there's nowhere else to go but his arms. But in my doomed vision of the future, I can see the last day we are together, his arms nowhere near me, folded neatly against his chest. He looks like a man with a mission, a very separate mission.

The End of Nate

1971

he end of Nate was not the beginning of me. Unlike a protagonist in a feminist fairy tale, I did not flower when he disappeared from view. But I do not think my eyes were closed when it happened, nor my heart. It just happened. And despite all the warning bells that sounded as I studied the Great Books and Art Movies of the day, I did not feel properly forewarned. I neither acted composed nor reacted bitterly when facing the largest-scale disaster in my abbreviated romantic history. I did not keep my chin up or play the good sport. Instead, I whispered like an invalid whenever I was forced to speak, and lumbered along the streets like Frankenstein's monster. Worse, all the time that I *thought* I was facing the truth—staring it smack-dab in the swollen eye—I was protecting Nate's good name. I believed in him that much.

In retrospect, Nathaniel was like an evangelist who not only saves your soul but marries you too, only to run off with another woman or a lot of loot or with the Lord Almighty himself. In my case, Nate ran off with God because both of them left me high and dry; my belief in belief systems crashed. I had trouble believing in the present let alone a future where Nate and I didn't share top billing.

I never could see any evil in Nate's actions, though. In my mind, he remained a mensch through and through. But if he was a mensch and didn't want me anymore, that only made me less of a mensch! At some point in our history that had gone badly undetected, I had become undeserving of his goodness. I no longer rated. To be accurate, when Nate pulled away from me, he drained me of all that specialness he had so lovingly anointed me with. I had to work hard to replace all the good stuff he'd extracted and be careful not to replace it with bile.

∎ ∎ ∎

Wearing headphones protects you from the radioactive fallout of family life but does a piss-poor job of screening out the miseries of your love life. On the contrary, while you *think* you are cloaking yourself in songs that keep you warm and safe and distracted, you are actually homing in on every syllable from every song that has everything to do with your sorrow. You become a beacon for sadness, a magnet for woe. And do you stop? No. You continue to flog yourself with the Songs That Matter.

I am singing my brains out to Laura Nyro, echoing her whispers, screaming her screams: "I belong to the man / Don't belong without him / When I sleep without him / Loneliness."

Deep into her moody music, I am unconscious of all the racket I'm making. Simply, I am alone with Laura, experiencing her experience. Ever since we moved to the West Valley, away from the conservative turf of Burbank, the small-mindedness that threatened to turn me into an invisible girl, I have taken over the living room / dining room of our trilevel home. We really can't afford to furnish this vast space, and that has been to my advantage. The near-empty room has proved perfect for rehearsing my drama-class scenes and Isadora Duncan moves. Best of all, I don't have to pretend that I have privacy—I really do! With a formal dining room table taking up only a few yards at the southern end of the room, I can fill the northern end with my impassioned oration or gyrating torso.

But my most important hours here are spent bonding with our Magnavox stereo. Connected by headphones to the console, I can isolate myself from the family, can forget who and where I am. The curly black cord permits me to rise from my supine position on our olive shag carpet and, eyes closed, seriously lose myself while strutting my stuff.

My stuff these days is somber. Ever since Nathaniel went off to college (he graduated from high school a half year earlier than me), I've had a tough time getting off the carpet. Since the day he packed his bags for Berkeley—I believe his major is World Consciousness—I have seen him only twice. Regrettably, both occasions were rocky and fraught with my noisy, repulsive emoting. Try as I might, I failed to check my feelings at the door. To be fair, the first time I visited Nate in his dorm room, he was considerate and affectionate, if a bit mechanical. I could see that the geographical distance between us had made him too open to experiences that no longer involved me. I wish I could say this was unforgivable, but separation is the oldest story. It's as if I was from the Old World and he was a New World guy.

When I first entered his room, I could smell the difference. The Indian curtains and bedspread didn't have my scent on them. Everything was screamingly new or part of his room-mate's trappings. When I could muster the courage, I asked Nate why he had chosen a school so far away from his best friend—me. I didn't have the courage to ask if this choice was a deliberate ploy to disengage from who we were together. At the time, I still believed that everything Nate did made sense and was superior to any other way, especially my own. Privately, I held out for Nate to remember who I was over the long term; to accept that my influence extended well beyond our youth and comfortably into middle age. I was so sure that we would take this journey together. Though the flood of fears about him leaving me had risen menacingly to the banks, I still believed in the efficacy of dams. But the dam didn't hold. My essence ended up all over the place and, truth be told, there was major water damage.

I I I

Unlike Laura Nyro's songs, which are licenses to rant and rave, Joni Mitchell's music is a salve; her songs are woolen shawls in which I wrap myself like a widow. Her lyrics, in-candescent and sea-bottom deep, guide me like electric eels through my first dark nights of the soul. I have waited all my life to know an adult-strength emotion, and now that I have arrived, there is no turning back.

I am shivering in the middle of June, out of my mind with feelings that have no images to go with them. Parts of my body must be caving in, but I see nothing amiss, only sense the insidious slippage. I press the full length of my body into the carpet, listening to melodies that simultaneously pierce and feed the heart. The love stories Joni paints are all too common, about men and women who've been conspicuously unsuccessful at love. I nod along with her, letting her know that I finally understand this, but only as a terrible fact of life.

I really don't have a clue to why men and women fail. Don't they love being in love? Don't they enjoy leaning on each other in a world that promises only drift and upheaval? In spite of all the inconstancy around me, I know that loyalty is my strong suit, that I am capable of loyalty in the extreme. Sure, grown-ups believe that a woman my age is not capable of mature love. I'm aware of this. But I know they're dead wrong. Because my love for Nate is eternal, historical, unextinguishable! As mentally shaky as I have been lately, my feelings for Nate are steadfast, on terra firma.

But it's over. For some impenetrable reason, he no longer needs to live on a diet of my love. He's able to go on without me, to function on the empty calories of disconnection. This summer, he's come back to Tarzana without—can I say this out loud?—calling me, seeing me, touching my face. The idea of this makes me sick. I am choking on this idea. I can hardly make it. I pass out from sadness. The sheer weight of my sadness reduces me to something flat and useless. A crushed can of Tab. I refuse to try anymore. I must be very, very ugly and really, really gross. Oh yes, and just not smart enough, delightful enough, special enough. Oh, but Nate must have the finest reasons! He always has the best reasons, the most thought-out rationale for every action. There must be an answer to why he would slay his best friend in the world with total silence. I hate this about him. His completeness. How dare he be complete without me! Why can't he reveal his grand plan for living without me? Surely I deserve to know. Oh, but his reasons must be very right-on. So brilliant that I may kill myself. Do you get this, Nate? That you have done something so irresponsible I may never get over it? I may never recover from your excellent reasons for forsaking me.

Tears sprinkle down my cheeks; I'm still the poignant fountain Nate once admired. Now I know what it means to be at a complete loss. I have lost something that's irreplaceable. Rummaging around in my unconscious, I pick up the melody of Joni's lament. I think she's trying to deliver a personal message: "I can't go back there anymore / You know my keys won't fit the door / You know my thoughts don't fit the man / They never can, they never can."

I have a bomb in my chest that threatens to explode. It is ticking away the minutes; I'm a major cliché. Finally I can join the legions of women before me who fell apart and were never put back together again. All the Humpty-Dumpty women who cracked up, were disembodied by love. Angry, am I angry? Curiously, no. I'd have to find something to be angry *at*. But Nathaniel has left me no clues. It's the unknown that does you in, robs you of your sanity. I could deal with the known: Nate's need for solitude, Nate's need for a brief vacation from us. I would not deal with these things well, but over time, they would become the thing I'd tell myself.

I have nothing to tell myself now. I cannot imagine why my dearest friend of all time and space would not have the courage to approach me. Am I not reasonable? Am I not the celebrated empath of the San Fernando Valley? Known for her rare ability to talk things through?

The vertigo of not knowing has become the cornerstone of my new personality. I pound my head with my fists, hoping to drive out the earthquakes that slip and slide within. It's as if a novel kind of gravity has taken possession of the earth, one that pulls my head down to the ground and holds it hostage. I am caught in a force field of grief and cannot imagine a time of levity, of release. Without knowing how, I pray on the carpet. I don't need words and don't have any. I am so sunken that my weight, the full mass of my sorrow, becomes a prayer. I rip off my headphones and rip their cord from the stereo set. I wish I had the nerve to wrap this cord around my neck and once and for all end this suffering. But as much as I yearn to be a disembodied spirit, I remain three dimensional. I am cursed with dimensionality.

A bloody, severed hand is flung in my face. A dumb rubber hand. "Lonnie!" I screech. "That's gross."

"I've gotta *hand* it to ya, Ooze. Thought you'd appreciate my latest acquisition."

"Can't you see I'm too upset to notice?"

"Yeah, Meeshy and Daddy said you were down in the dumpster. I thought my hand would cheer you up. Ya know, put a smile on that miserable poker face of yours."

"Well, it won't. I refuse to smile. No one can make me." I hide my face in the tendrils of the shag carpet.

"Lemme give you a back rub. It'll change your tune." Lonnie stoops over my crippled body and animates the rubber hand, making it crawl up my spine like a crab.

I shake off the stupid toy and shield my face with my arm. "Go away. Find someone else to bug."

"Hey, that's not fair, Ooze. Ya know there ain't anybody else."

"What about Bernard? I thought you were best buddies."

"Yeah, well his parents removed him from our school for maniacs—they think he's all better now."

"Oh," I whimper, "do *you* think he's better?"

"Yep, he's better than me."

"Now, that's *not* what I meant!" I twist around to face her.

"I dunno, Ooze. I mean, I'm not gonna get any better. This is who I am. Love me, love my snakes."

"Sorry, I don't have to love your snakes," I say and return to my position face down on the carpet.

"See, I don't get no respect," she complains.

"Yeah, just like Rodney Dangerfield."

"Ooze." Lon tugs on my bathrobe sleeve. "There's nobody left, Ooze."

I look up to see her expression darken into fear. "What about Jackie Marz?" I offer with a false bright note.

"That Martian girl? She goes to Sunrise School. That's three schools ago, Oozy. Can't you keep up with us aliens?"

She's right. Lon has blitzed her way through so many special schools for the mentally ill and mentally retarded that I can't keep up. Just when she's befriended by some open-minded boy or girl who doesn't mind her monster magazines and chatter about mutants, she encounters an extra-cruel teacher or a bully who picks on her for being more different than all the other different kids. Mother and Daddy have almost run out of schools to enroll her in, and any pals have drifted away to new schools or to better health.

Something cold lands on my thigh; the bloody rubber hand has tunneled its way under my bathrobe! I wrestle it away from Lon and, without thinking, tear off its pinkie finger. Both of us watch the tiny digit fly across our vast living room.

"You're a cruel Homo sapiens, Oozy. You're going to die alone, ya know." Lon stomps off to her room, muttering about my premature death.

In Lonnie's wake, a new LP plunks down on the turntable; a spunky Carole King song filters through the gloom. How inappropriate, what blasphemy! There is no spunk in Tarzana, hasn't she heard? Damn her, Carole's beat is infectious, inconsiderately bouncy. It's her massive hit, "It's Too Late," the song Claire and I love to perform with our oh-so-clever hand jive. I nearly manage a smile, recalling how we always pantomime glancing at our watches when we sing the words "It's too late" and how, when Perry joins our chorus line, he points to his groin when we sing "make it."

Against my will, what is left of it, my fluffy slippers tap the carpet. My chin moves up and down like one of the undead. Slowly, numbly, I draw myself up from the floor. Loosely wrapped in my chenille bathrobe—what I throw on each af-

ternoon because I can no longer pretend that life is normal—
I begin to mouth the lyrics: "Something inside has died and I
can't hide / And I just can't fake it."

But this is a song of vengeance. "It's too late" is the ultima-
tum I would never deliver to Nate, yet it gives one strength to
repeat these words with conviction. "It's too late, it's too late."
It almost feels good to define myself like this—to say what I
will and won't tolerate. I suppose that convicting your lover
with pop lyrics is safer than doing so with your heart. My
heart still feels beaten to a pulp by Nate's mysterious ways.
But now there's another beat in the background, Carole
King's beat. When you can't jump-start your heart on your
own, it's always music that comes to the rescue. Maybe—if I
don't kill myself—the doctors can hook me up to the stereo
until I'm able to produce a beat on my own.

I   ▌   I

Carole King, the flesh-and-blood Carole, is rehearsing her
Tapestry album medley in the great outdoor amphitheater. Hit
after generous hit wafts into the office where I am trying hard
to concentrate. Doon has helped me snag a job at the Greek
Theater in Hollywood, a position that offers ample diversion
from The Nate Problem if only because everyone moves at
high speed, talks at high speed, and acts like they're auditioning for a part in *A Star Is Born*.

This summer, I've left Lonnie to her own devices, left her
alone in the pool. I've been hired as a rookie switchboard operator. My job: to wrestle with the cords of an old-fashioned
switchboard and hand out show information like a friendly
robot. "Ms. King goes on precisely at 8 P.M. No, you may *not*
be connected to her, she is not accepting phone calls. Sir, I do
not believe that you are her cousin. That's not a nice thing to
say, sir!"

Although I don't have the physical skill to handle the zillions of calls we receive, I am extraordinarily kind to callers. The most perceptive callers comment on my dulcet tones, which makes me happy and encourages me no end. I guess I'm practicing kindness when I don't feel the least bit kind. Maybe it's an effort to mask my depression. There, I said it: *Je suis* depressed. I am utterly, stubbornly depressed, adrift in a world that's cloaked and veiled, wading through a river of glue. But when I pass through the gates of the Greek Theater, I'm quick to adopt the kind of showbiz snappiness that is required here. For sluggishness is not tolerated, nor is depth. Most of the other operators, save for Doon and two spirited lads from Minnesota, spend their time at the Greek perfecting shallowness. The more cruel and insensitive you are, the more you're accepted. Since I'm lousy at acting callous, I stick out like a sore thumb. Silly me, I really care about how people are treated and who's fucking who over.

Thank God my boss, Darla, understands this about me and has tried to encourage my sensitive side. She admires the lyrical women I doodle on the company message pads. To ensure that I don't feel lonely, Darla has gifted me with a book of Botticelli paintings of even better-drawn lyrical women. She says that a person as "emotionally delicate" as I am shouldn't ever have to work. On the contrary, she insists, I should be painting portraits of wraithlike heroines and writing confessional poems, sequestered high in a tower off of Laurel Canyon. She thinks people like me should be protected from the dirty, street-level world of business. I'm seriously flattered. But I know I have to make it in the real world, as much as I long to be secreted away in a tower with a thick sheaf of poems. I'm learning that my sensitivity must be shrouded in a layer of toughness. I don't own a castle and can't afford to be secreted away. Besides, one look at Darla and I'm terrified I'll end up like her. She's a total flipped-out wreck—a pill-popping redhead with dark roots who fashions her hair in braids like Heidi, laughs too loud, wears prim little-girl dresses from Sears, and believes she was *the* Darla from *The Little Rascals.*

Well, it's possible; she could have been a child star who lost her sheen long ago. While the other operators make fun of Darla behind her back (unbalanced on multiple fronts, she shows up for work high as a kite and then crashes recklessly on our shift), I detect in Darla a wise old soul. For whoever sees greatness in me must have some cockeyed intuition. How could I deny them their special vision when I need this vision so badly myself?

"Lorna! You're on! Please take position number one." Darla waves her hands at me like she's having an epileptic seizure. For reasons I've been unable to pin down, she's eternally optimistic. She even harbors hope that I will excel at switchboard work in the way I excel at kindness. But she will have to fulfill this dream with another operator, for I am the worst of the lot, the runt of the litter.

In a trance, I shuffle from my backup position at the phone bank to the swivel chair that faces the master board—a Medusalike contraption that boasts twenty-four tentacles dangling over it in a tangled mess. I only see chaos here. All the incoming lines are ringing at once, and it's my job to shut them up by shoving the tentacles into their proper holes. No matter how many calls I answer, though, the confounded ringing won't stop. It's like a game version of my home life—I wish I could stuff a cord in Lonnie's mouth, but she'd find another way to make noise too.

"Lorna, you're spacing out!" Darla freaks. "Patch number fourteen in to me. Give number five to Doon."

I imagine the cords coming to life as snakes in some zany Warner Bros. cartoon. I picture them strangling all of the operators, one by one, ending with me. Then the noise would stop and we could all go home, despite the fact we are dead.

Gaining a little confidence, I fantasize about handling a few calls myself instead of passing them off to the other operators . . .

"Greek Theater. May I help you?"

"When is Liza Minnelli coming to the Greek? She blew my mind last year."

"She's blowing minds this year on August fifth and sixth."

"Greek Theater."

"Honey, connect me to the VIP ticket office—and pronto! I am a Very Important Person."

"The Very Important Person line is jammed. Would you like to speak to the Almost Important Person office?"

"Hello, the Greek."

"Is Neil Diamond returning this year? What about Lola Falana? Three Dog Night?"

"Um, the answers are: yes he is, she's sold out, and you've got to be kidding!"

"Lorna, darling," Darla interrupts. "Have you been shot with a tranquilizer gun? You've got to pick up the pace, sweetheart."

All twenty-four lines are still lit up: Answer me! Me! Me! I always hope to make the callers feel cared for, to let them know someone out there is really listening. But each time I confront the switchboard, I'm lucky if I can accommodate three or four callers, max, before my own brain circuitry goes haywire.

Bravely, I pull one of the cords all the way out and rest it on my shoulder, like I've seen Darla do. Then, after taking a deep breath, I decisively shove it into line five and bray "Greek Theater, may I help you?" When no one answers, I sink lower in the swivel chair. Finally, after maybe twenty blinks, I answer line seven, croaking "Greek Theater . . . help you?" Shit, it's Miss Bufano, our pompous general manager who's the spitting image of Mrs. Hathaway from The Beverly Hillbillies.

"Who is this?" she challenges. "Name, please. Give me a name!"

"This is Lorna, operator four." I swear I can hear her seething. "Miss Bufano? Are you there?"

"Operator four, you did not answer in the requisite number of rings. So what do you have to say for yourself? What could you possibly say?"

"Um . . . I tried. I wanted to. I wanted to be there for everybody but there's so many bodies!" The buzz in the room drowns out her reply.

"Lorna!" Darla cries. "Who the hell are you chatting with? Answer the goddam phones!"

I cup my hand over the microphone on my headset. "It's Miss Bufano, she's really unhappy."

"Tell her to take a hard look in the mirror. Meanwhile, the whole board is lit up like Christmas in July. Jesus, Lorna, answer anything!"

"Miss Bufano?" She's gone, leaving no visible trace, like all the other callers. I'm lost in a world of white noise and disembodied voices. When I gather the courage to answer another incoming call, I can't even remember the name of this place. "Um, Theater?" I venture. I throw up my hands, mimicking Darla. "I just can't do this, Darla. My head is swimming, I'm totally confused. Line two wants to speak to somebody I've never heard of and line eight needs to get in touch with God or Goop or Big Gulp. Please take me off of this thing."

"Okay, pumpkin. Doon, you're up. Please relieve Lorna. Lorna, take Doon's seat."

The ever-competent and sultry Doon rises to the occasion. I hang my head low and surrender the swivel chair. Settling into Doon's seat at the phone bank, I feel the other operators' contempt at my back; I have gummed up the works, and Doon has inherited my mess. Ginger, a worn-out rag doll of a groupie who swears she's slept with all the Stones except maybe Charlie Watts (she can't remember), jabs me with her vampire nails: "Maybe you could get a job with the phone company, darling-sweetheart-honeybuns. That Darla thinks you're really something, but we're still waiting to discover what that is, ha ha."

I bite my upper lip to stave off a barrage of tears, and nod my head in consent. "Um, none of my skills are put to good use here," I whine into my T-shirt. "Guess all my genius is cerebral." I try to make Ginger smile with this feeble half joke, but she arches her heavily penciled eyebrows and shakes her pathetic shag haircut in my face like a narcissistic collie.

"What do you mean your genius"—*cough! cough!*—"is made of cereal? Are you shit-faced or something? Are you high? Ya know, I can hardly make it through the day without a little help from my friends"—*wink wink*—"I mean, Lorna, if you want to keep up with the pace, ya gotta help yourself to the tricks of the trade. How do you think I stay out all night with my boyfriend in the Iron Butterfly without a little extra something?" She applies a silver-blue shade of lipstick to her dry, skinny lips and picks up a call at the same time. "Do ya wanna try this Yardley lipstick? It's peppermint flavor."

No thanks, I shrug. The smell of her patchouli oil is enough of a high. I would hate Ginger's insensitive guts if she wasn't such a complete airhead. Here she thinks she's a member of rock's royalty, and I think she's just hanging in there on the bottom rung of human consciousness. Miss Missing Link. But when she's not late for her shift, flying high on speed or dulled by quaaludes, she's a trip to be with. Broken people like Ginger interest me because they have a tough time hiding their past; all their grief floats to the surface, and no amount of makeup can conceal it.

Doon tugs at my Fiorucci T-shirt with the two kitschy cherubs and announces that our shift is over. We are free to do the things that aging teenagers do. She's dressed in fluid harem pants, a green velvet bolero, and lace-up granny boots; on her back is the ubiquitous rucksack. Admiring Doon's dramatic style, I almost forget what a dunce I was today. "C'mon!" she urges, "the twins are ready to *groove* with us!"

I laugh because she's stressed the word "groove" to lighten my spirits; we would never use hippie slang so sincerely. "I'm sorry, Doon. I never ever mean to screw up, but I really don't get the rhythms of this job. It's a wonder they don't fire me."

"Well," Doon concedes, "Darla always covers for you—you're her pet, you know. Still, it would be easier on all of us if you were assigned to another office." She looks me frankly in the eye. "I'm sorry, Lorna, but you really are all thumbs."

I flush with shame and tremble noticeably as we walk up the steep ramp to the amphitheater. Even Doon thinks I'm a problem! Nate's left me and now this. "Okay, okay. I'll quit." I walk away abruptly, forcing Doon to run after me. Eyes lowered and mind clouded, I don't see Biff One and Biff Two in my path. The Biffs are the most upbeat boys we know, the plucky twins from Minnesota. They came to Hollywood to pursue careers in film musicals, but the genre isn't too popular at the moment.

"Hey girlie-girl, going my way?" Biff One stops my momentum with one flip of his wrist, like he's one of the Temptations. He looks genuinely happy to see me. Biff Two busses me on each cheek, European-style. "Hey, mama, you look like you're going places." It's obvious I'm all shook up, but they've clearly decided to ignore this fact. "Hi, sugar," they greet Doon and peck her on each cheek too. "We're going to sit in orchestra and have a picnic before the show—can we count you foxy ladies in?"

"If Lorna feels up to it, then I'm up to it," Doon says decisively. I toss a smile her way; she really *is* my best friend, despite all my goofs.

"Yeah, yeah, I'm all the way in."

"Right arm! Far out! Outta sight! Outta mind! Outta town!" Biff One raves, rhythmically tapping his way up the terraced steps. Biff Two mimics these Fred Astaire moves, adding a Temptations-like spin for a final flourish. Taking our turn, Doon and I pretend to tap our way into the hearts and minds of an invisible audience, making our way up the steps to join the two Biffs. After the four of us have noisily assembled on a bench in row F, we indulge in shameless Carole King gossip and our daily dose of Darla stories. But as the sky darkens, we fall into a reverent silence, gazing up at the Greek's stage, which is completely bare save for a baby grand piano.

A shiver of electricity travels up my arm; an inarticulate tingle rises in my chest. The power of this wide-open space reminds me of something—something ancient and yet modern, a thing constantly lost and perpetually found. It's on the tip of my tongue, but I can't pronounce it. I let the majesty of the vast proscenium, the vacant stage, and the purple-pink Hollywood sky wash over me. I find myself nodding in rhythm to "I Feel the Earth Move," the song I heard Carole rehearsing hours earlier. It's as if I am being converted to some unknown religion.

And then the near-religious vision comes, the one I have practically every night at the Greek: I am poised on a tall stool in the center of a tight white spotlight. The long-stemmed microphone in front of me brushes my lips, and I dramatically throw back my shimmering mane. I'm encased in a skintight, black-sequined dress—probably that number the original Barbie wore—with satin gloves up to my elbows, belting out a song that penetrates the skin and works miracles at the cellular level.

I'm not a raging egomaniac. I have this recurring vision whenever the need to offer myself to others becomes overwhelming. Acting, singing, dancing are the most efficient ways I know to wake people up—much faster than taking people by the collar and shaking them until they confess to long-buried feelings of love, hurt, and alienation. But I am not alone in this dream. For Doon, the Biffs, and me, the Greek returns us to our real purpose: the burning need to make art. Art that moves and thrills people. Art that gets us through the night and, for an incantatory moment, returns us to our original condition—a place where we're safe, we're whole, and no longer separate.

If only I believed that! What a bunch of baloney. My separation from Nathaniel feels real enough. The depression, real enough. My grief has enough body you could shape it into a fucking statue. But of what? A woman whose facial features have been sawed off, that's what!

As we snap out of our collective stupor, the Biffs produce pieces of fragrant fried chicken and Tupperware bowls of coleslaw from their canvas army satchels. Doon reaches into her bottomless pit of a backpack and produces a box of Screaming Yellow Zonkers. All I have to offer is my gratitude and a few more "sorries."

"If you say you're sorry one more time, Lorna—" Doon warns.

"Love means never having to say you're sorry," Biff One interjects, coming to my rescue.

"Okay, okay. I'm sorry that I'm sorry so often. I know it's a crutch." I stand and begin to pantomime walking with a crutch, limping broadly enough to stumble over his long legs.

"Look!" Biff Two points toward the stage. We turn our heads to discover Miss Bufano sitting stage right, at the baby grand, zealously playing the overture to *Porgy and Bess*. This hateful woman seems to be pouring her heart out to the empty arena; her eyes are closed as if she's in another world, and her bad perm bounces up and down with each attack on the keys. Unfortunately, we can't control our titters. I turn away, because Bufano deserves her privacy and I'm not sure I want to see her as a sympathetic character.

"Let's make like a tree and fly!" Biff One decrees.

"Trees can't fly," I protest.

"Exactly my point," he counters as the four of us flap our arms, squawk, and exit down the aisle.

Engrossed in her music, Miss Bufano never raises her eyes to witness our exodus. As I round the bend to slip into the ladies' room, I hear her croon, "Oh, my Porgy!" and the sound stops me in my tracks. So this woman who appears to hate every living thing loves to sing her guts out. If only she could sing onstage rather than pontificate on the phone. Art solves so many problems.

■ ■ ■

The full moon has cast a spell on the over-amped audience. After applauding like seals for an ecstatic five minutes, we dutifully place our hands in our laps and wait for Carole King to walk out on the stage for her third and final encore. I have no voice left, I've been cheering so loudly, and I've no feeling left in my palms. Doon gives my numb right hand an affectionate squeeze, and I return the gesture, whispering "Thanks" in her ear. Holding onto small things, like the occasional hand, helps more than Doon could know. Still, the memory of Nate holding me tight around my love handles looms heavy; I will never forget his touch. In fact, I cannot think of anything more real and less flimsy.

Carole runs out, breathless, glistening, euphoric. She sits down at the baby grand, and the spotlight tightens around her until we see only her head bobbing up and down, her signature curls projecting a halo of happiness. Within seconds, the audience recognizes the introductory chords to "You've Got a Friend," the most soothing song in the universe, and sighs collectively (a couple of jerks hoot as if it was a raunchy Stones song). I snuggle deeper into my fuzzy blue mohair sweater and instinctively take hold of Biff Two's hand in addition to holding Doon's. Doon and I and the two Biffs begin to mouth the words to "You've Got a Friend," words we've known by heart for ages. By the second verse, the requisite tear makes its way down my cheek, but I do nothing to erase it. Instead, I behold the sky, now pitch black but salted with stars, and try to reconcile this feeling of fullness with the intense emptiness I've acquired this summer. I lift my head to the canvas of stars and, shaking with sadness and wonder, ask for things I'm not sure I'm deserving of. I want Lonnie to get well—as well as she can. I want Mother and Daddy to stop fighting. I'd even like to lose fifty pounds. But I also pray that Nathaniel finds peace, that he finds refuge from what's ailing him. I ask for the key to the puzzle of our abandoning each other. I trust that this key will come in handy later in life, probably too many times.

"To brighten up even the darkest night," Carole wails, and the audience answers by sweetly singing the chorus and swaying to and fro. So this is what love is about: swaying in the dark with your friends in the middle of a horrible loss.

I lift my face to the moon and say the word "Nathaniel" out loud. I whisper, "My love is unshaken. I love you for all time." With that, I blow a little kiss skyward, asking the heavens one last time for an answer. But they reveal nothing; the heavens are speechless.

I squeeze Doon's hand so tight she cries "Ouch."

Part Three

Out of Los Angeles

1971

verybody's doing it. Leaving. My parents have decided to divorce, what a concept. Here I am doing my best to believe that, on a higher level, no person is truly separate from any other person, and my own family is literally falling apart. But the break is long overdue; for years I have waited for my mother to screw up the courage to walk out. A long time ago, when I was in grade school, a shady but otherwise attractive man approached Mother in the Cold Remedies aisle at Sav-on Drugs; he made small talk while his eyes took inventory of her every limb and curve. I remember that his cartoonish lust had sickened me but also how disappointed I was that Mother had so expertly deflected his oily flattery. Looking away to give them some privacy, I had fingered a bottle of milk of magnesia, reading the contents over and over again, praying that

Mother would go home with this man. At the time, I didn't worry about me; I just wanted her to be loved in a big way—something my father couldn't figure out the formula for. But Mother wouldn't go off with a stranger any more than I would. We were both too decent and too concerned with our personal safety. Instead, Mother smiled her fetching Rita Hayworth smile, blushed from top to bottom, and turned on her heel to fetch me. I recall that we left the drugstore without buying anything. On the way home, I stewed in my juices. I mean, what kind of daughter prays that her mother will have an affair? Even then I placed love at the top of my list. I only wish that Mother had too.

The Persons have a master plan. Lorna is going off to the mystical University of California at Santa Cruz; Mother and Daddy are going off in opposite directions but remaining in the Valley nonetheless; and Lonnie is simply going off like a rocket. She's supposed to find shelter in some fabulous halfway house in an anonymous suburb, but with this change has come the traditional explosion.

Twenty years old now and dressing like an overgrown child—albeit an eccentric one—Lon has become heavy and slow. Her overeating has overshadowed my own, and her fears of growing old and being discarded have shaken her mightily. Terrified of having to leave our parents' house and feeling newly abandoned, she's begun a terrorist campaign to live in an apartment by herself, surrounded by her reptiles and fish and oddities. But Daddy and Mother won't hear of it. They clearly don't want her to join them in their new lives—they're renting separate apartments in Encino and Tarzana—but they don't feel Lon can handle living alone either. In some strong-arm, state-sanctioned home, they reason, Lonnie will be watched over, medicated when necessary, and allowed out in public only when accompanied by an attendant.

With no real friends in the world and nothing to keep her

occupied all day, Lon has entered a phase she calls "The Big Snooze"—long, solitary hours that can't be filled with enough drawing and writing and late-night monster movies to absorb her energy. After "graduating" from a succession of schools for the emotionally disturbed (the curriculum was always beneath her intellect, yet she remained too untamed for public school), and after renouncing the Heinz-Heinz Clinic last spring (the day she set fire to Mrs. Mancini's chaise lounge; her apology—"Go to hell, Mrs. M!"—wasn't considered contrite enough), Lon has become too dependent on the three of us to make her happy. And her unhappiness scares me to death.

From the looks of it, I'm the only one with a genuine chance to escape my family's fate. For this I already feel guilty (surprise!) and secretly, physically raring to go. After a summer of treading water at the Greek Theater, trying to submerge all thoughts of Nathaniel but watching them float to the surface like dead bodies do, I am doing myself a huge favor and swimming out to points unknown. Last winter, I read all about UC-Santa Cruz in *Life* magazine. The photo-essay almost frightened me off with its report on Santa Cruz coeds ("perhaps the most intellectually and artistically realized bunch of youngsters who inhabit the earth"). After such a rave, it appeared that only the offspring of Buckminster Fuller and Timothy Leary would fit into campus life. I wondered, would there be room on campus for a neurotic teen who's hitched her wagon to the stars of Hollywood, Broadway, and *The Paris Review?*

I was especially intrigued by the photograph of theater students prancing merrily atop a hill overlooking the Pacific Ocean, an image that suggested kindergarten and love-ins and unparalleled freedom. Okay, I admit it: I am terrified to join these students. I'm not sure I can prance well enough, merrily enough.

I I I

My two arms reach for the sky, flailing about in classic hippie style. I'm auditioning for a Beginning Theater class, and find myself skipping along a grassy mound, attempting to express joy, embody joy. At least that's the assignment. In truth, most of us haven't a clue about joy. I see anxiety in all the faces circling me and, in a few intriguing cases, strong hints of despair. The guy next to me could have experienced a psychotic break, he looks so blank.

Our instructor, Pierce Winter, is a man of few words but countless grunts. A practitioner of the little-known Murray Moskowitz school of acting, he insists that we let out our "natural" voices without censoring the most primitive of human sounds. While our arms sway above our heads and we run in a loose circle, Pierce scans us for genius, looking for those students who are willing to "go native" and show their true selves. I'm doing my best to act "free"; though I could care less about appearing pretty, I'm still not ready to go all the way to gross. Clearly, the young woman on my left is too invested in her beauty to howl, snort, and bark, and I fear she won't make the cut. When Pierce spots saliva foaming at the corners of my mouth, he shouts, "Cool drool!" and flashes a "V for victory" sign.

Our ragtag circle quickly loses its shape, and we are instructed to spin out at any time and find a private spot on the hill. I allow my body to roll away from the others and come to rest under a scrawny pine tree. My breath roars heavy in my chest, and I try not to think too hard about what I'm doing or what I look like. I am reminded of playing with Lonnie, the fact that she never censored me, and how I found secret pleasure in losing myself in her marginal world. Lonnie could tolerate any aberration: in her eyes, no behavior was considered alien. But I'm not sure I'm ready to trust anyone new with my secrets.

Pierce uses this pause in our activity to lecture us on "creating a character in the belly." "Imagine a character forming in your tum-tum." He slaps his stomach like a self-satisfied Santa. "This is especially tough for the guys. Then, when you have a clear image of this person, slowly give birth to his or her physicality. Begin by closing your eyes and thinking of someone you know. Feel this person growing in your stomach—cell by cell, feature by feature—as if you're pregnant."

My eyes let in a little light; I want to see whether the others are taking this exercise seriously. I hear titters on all sides of me; a few male students groan comically as if giving birth to hundred-pound babies. I remain quiet, trying to conjure up a fascinating character I would like to conceive. But I can't think of a soul. My head hangs over my chest as if I'm nodding off. I'm blank, blank, blank. Then I detect something tiny making itself known at the edge of my mind. It's a soft-focused image of a three-year-old girl: she's painfully shy, awkward . . . yet imaginative, spirited, kind of heartbreaking. The image becomes instantly embedded in my stomach, and before I know it, I am pregnant!

After five minutes of this exercise, Pierce instructs us to slowly open our eyes and rise from our places on the grass: "Keep in mind that the person inside you is growing at an impressive rate." I tuck my legs under me and delicately stand as if I carry something precious and new. Pierce asks us to walk around with our cargoes until they begin to take up all the space inside us and demand to come out.

Soberly, I tote my little girl, making a figure-eight pattern on the hillside. I experience her shyness from the inside and also her wacky sense of humor. This makes me smile despite my fear that she may be too vulnerable for life in the outside world. Pierce asks us to begin a dialogue with our characters, to speak with them freely, and again, not to censor anything that bubbles up from the unconscious.

This is easy. I say, "Hi there, Bitsy. Welcome to the new world." I tell my little girl that I am crisscrossing the top of a hill at UC-Santa Cruz in an effort to gain acceptance to a Beginning Theater class, that she is a part of this process.

After a long minute, she answers, "But isn't this hill the same one you saw in *Life* magazine—the hill with all those students you *assumed* were braver and brighter and tons more sophisticated than you? The hill where all the geniuses pranced?"

"Oh God, it is!" I respond, surprised that I hadn't thought of this myself.

"So, do you understand what this means?" she challenges me.

"Not really. What are you getting at?"

"This means that you are every bit as brave—that you have the right stuff!"

"Really?" I exclaim. "I'm here on that same hill, doing those same things and—can I say this?—it's not that hard. In fact, it's kind of where I belong."

"That's the ticket!" Bitsy agrees.

"You know," I confide to her, "I've no fear of expression. Only the opposite."

"You mean *re*-pression?" Bitsy asks.

"Now where did you learn such a big word?" I tease her.

Just then, Pierce Winter swings by and shouts, "Good work. What's your name?"

"Lorna Person."

"Lor-na Per-son. Yeah, I can dig it. Lorna Person, how's the birth process going?"

"I'm afraid I gave birth to myself—is that cheating?"

"Honey, this whole business is about cheating! If you can't steal from yourself, who can you trust?" With that, he slaps me on the tush as if we're football players, and silently creeps up to the young man on my left, who appears to have given birth to a lunatic. The student is wrestling with his own leg, screaming, "Off of me, asshole! I swear, you're not going to take over my life!"

Pierce places an affectionate hand on the student's back and encourages him to calm down. "Now, the point of this exercise is to create any character you want, so why in God's name have you created someone you can't live with?"

The young man wipes a bead of sweat off his forehead and explains, "I discovered something evil brewing inside of me—my older brother Stan. He's really dementoid!"

To that, Pierce offers a manly hug and says, "Be gentle with yourself, man."

The student kicks up a plug of grass and declares, "Stan's the man. He's in control now."

Pierce shakes his head ruefully, then races over to observe a tall, angular student wearing a purple felt beret; the fellow is staggering around in circles, mumbling to himself and bumping into other students' chests and elbows. When he forces me and my three-year-old against a tree trunk, at the same time pointing to a vein in his right arm and imploring, "Hit me!" I look up to greet the prettiest face I've ever seen on a young man. His lips, like his beret, are the color of grape jelly, his dark-blond locks cut into a medieval pageboy. "Can you help me?" he mutters, "I could really use a fix."

"You gave birth to an addict?" I ask, stunned.

"Everyone's in some kind of pain, man. Can you just give me a hit so I can get a little rest here?"

I'm confused; I've just given birth, after all, and I'm a bit exhausted. But my character hasn't emerged from my body yet. "Um, I've got a three-year-old on my hands and don't carry drugs, sir. I'm clean. I mean, *we're* clean."

"I don't think I'm gonna make it," he says with a convincing shiver that rattles his shoulders and travels all the way down his mile-long, blue-jeaned legs. "Do you have a blanket?"

I look into the prayerful blue eyes of this mysterious, gaunt man and chivalrously donate my Guatemalan sweater. "This is the best I can do for now." He returns my gaze, and I blink nervously. As he slumps against the tree trunk, I wrap the heavy sweater around his chest, then slouch down beside him, genuinely concerned. I take stock of his face, an artistic blend of Mick Jagger and Amelia Earhart, hoping to ask, "What in the world made you choose a character who's a total emergency?" But I'm way too polite. The "addict" begins to draw deeper breaths, and a faint smile warms his violet lips. If this is a new way to meet women, he's taken me in completely! His right elbow intrudes disturbingly on my private space, but perhaps he can't help it—he's extremely lanky.

"What's your name?" I inquire.

"Hitch. Hitch Jackson. Got the name from hitching around the country, playing the blues in the worst dives." He shifts restlessly in place, as if my sweater isn't enough of a drug to calm him. "Yours?"

I'm stumped. My little girl, Bitsy, never got the chance to come into the world before "Hitch Jackson" bumped into me. "Um, I'm Lorna. Just lost my child. A miscarriage of sorts. I really should go to the clinic now, I don't feel so good." I hold my stomach defensively, as if Hitch might take it away from me.

"Maybe we could go together," he suggests, rubbing his "needle-punctured" arm.

"Sure," I answer, realizing that I've just arrived in Santa Cruz and already I'm adopting the caretaker role, casting aside my own "emergency" in favor of another imaginary one. "Maybe the Wizard will give you a new arm and I can get a new baby," I say without a trace of sarcasm. I look down at the grass so he can't see that a black mood is coming on fast, one that could scare away the devil. I attempt a broad grin, but a murky tide is towing me under, threatening to drag me to the bottom of the sea. "Please," I beseech the beret-headed boy, "I'm having a . . . moment."

"What?" His elbow treads deeper into my personal space, lightly poking against my shoulder.

"I'm sorry. I'm not so well. You know, depression. Didja know that Virginia Woolf thought of depression as 'moments of being'? She defined these moments as profound stirrings under the surface—like cracks in the pavement made by tiny green roots. Little beginnings that eventually fed her writing. But I don't trust them like she did. All I feel is very, very dark. I'm warning you," I point my forefinger theatrically at his nose. Then I flash a more convincing grin. "A little craziness is productive, no?"

"You bet," he nods sympathetically. "If only a little craziness remained a little. I think I inherited my whole family's worth. My real name's Heinrich. Henry, if you'd like."

"My real name's Lorna," I blush. "The same as before."

Pierce Winter blows his whistle to signal that our birth exercise is over. We are instructed to return tomorrow for the final audition. Henry and I pull ourselves up from our tree trunk and move with the rest of the herd down the hill. I take in a whiff of crisp Northern California air, squinting at the silvery sea below us. I think of my darling Norwood, the devoted cat I left behind, and wish he could navigate this wilderness with me. *I'm not in Los Angeles anymore, Norwood, and I have no idea who I am.*

I I I

The next morning I am still terrified and have the fat to prove it. Last night in my damp and lifeless dorm room, I sat up in bed and finished off three poems—fertile city! Unfortunately, they were fueled by three bowls of shredded wheat followed by the same number of Kit Kat bars. The Kit Kats have the lowest calorie count of any candy bar because they're really cookies, not candy.

My melancholic mood was in perfect harmony with the Wuthering Heights rain that fell all night on the windowpane behind my shoulders. I was both grateful and bewildered. In the San Fernando Valley there is no barometric accompaniment for low spirits; the weather is notoriously, eternally sunny. Come to think of it, there are few physical obstacles to happiness there—if you have the depth of a hot tub. But in Santa Cruz you get certifiably dank days, and nights so heavy with moisture that you feel justified to make poems that are drenched and despairing.

So while my stomach processed too many Kit Kats for a woman my height, I activated my creative juices. Nothing went to waste.

The first poem—a paean to Nathaniel disguised as a curse on all men—came out effortlessly if not completely encoded. The second, a portrait of Doon, was set in language so playful that I couldn't penetrate it myself this morning. Like Doon, the poem gives off a troubled air: beautiful, capable, but damaged in some way I can only guess at. For me, Doon, a woman who acts invincible but insists she has the fragile heart of a waif, shall always remain a mystery. It's hard for me to accept that powerful women have problems too.

But the third poem, the poem that sucked all the air out of the room, was completely uninvited. I was hoping to capture the fairy-tale atmosphere of this campus, a place where you meet noble princes on the wooded paths to your class and nod formally to these lads in tall boots and fanciful caps, as if you've been transplanted to the sixteenth century. As if you never knew the hard facts of Los Angeles, the endless, labyrinthian freeways. My goal was to show the violent contrast between my two worlds—the poem would make sense of it all. Instead, I created a portrait of the fellow with the beret, the one who had the nerve to stick his limbs in my face and agitate my heart. Really, how dare he! He's way too good-looking (I always go for the so-ugly-they're-beautiful types) and too off-kilter. I'm a nut for oddballs, but he takes the cake and ice cream too. Really not my type. Probably as needy as me.

The poem that dared show its face was not about this man per se but a tone poem about his beret and color-of-blood lips: how these two things can affect one's balance. A meditation on the unfairness and sheer nerve of sensuality. It always shows up when least expected.

Ever since I landed here, I have viewed the campus as a sensual wonderland, and I'm not even counting the student bodies. The come-hither meadows splashed with sunlight coupled with the fragrant patches of mossy forest give off the scent of a dream. There is no way to confirm that this place is for real. Each day, as I make my way through the woods, I pinch myself on the tender skin at my wrist, just to make sure I'm not dreaming. Then I tell myself, I *deserve* the dream.

But this poem has unraveled me. I tear it out of my notebook, and before I can poke holes in it with my fountain pen, I decide to read it one last time. Just to make certain it's hopeless.

> your grape skin
> glistens on the horizon
> are you a man or a mousse
> moving onto my plate?
> my own juice embarrasses me
> I used to be dead but now I drip
> along already wet paths
> hungry for fruit that won't bruise my idea
> of life liberty

> and happy other people
> I shall dry up doomed
> in my belief
> that some food never ripens never softens
> I am as hard as a pomegranate
> in my dreary seedhouse
> my full starvation home
> while you and the lips you bring to the table
> have other ideas about eating
> well and good

Why am I spending my poetic imagination on the beret boy? I don't need a new obsession. I tuck the poem back in my notebook. Who knows? Tomorrow it could look like a keeper.

My plump, burping frame rests against the cool concrete in the hallway of the Theater Arts building. I'm still ruminating about "that poem," waiting for something to defeat the notion that your senses can do you in. Colors, shapes, textures are dangerous—they can arouse you like a kiss, pull your mind off your studies.

"Guess this is my last chance. After this audition, I can honestly say I tried to get back into the Thee-ay-tah. After I'm brutally rejected, I will go live the life of a hermit crab."

I look up to see not a crabby woman, but a wholly vibrant one. A deep, resonant voice has issued out of her uncommonly narrow body—a body not unlike Jules Feiffer's pen-and-ink dancer: elongated waist and twiglike limbs interrupted by a surprisingly ample bust. And shoulder-length, pin-straight blond hair that swings along with her rhythmic gestures.

She removes a comb from her jeans pocket and methodically works it through her pale strands, section by section, until she has removed every snag in the universe. What kind of woman is this? I typically rip through my sandy-brown locks with a cheap brush, pulling out half my crop each morning.

After every last hair has been calmed down, the woman kneels beside me on the linoleum and stares me in the face like an X-ray machine. She smiles to let me know she comes in peace.

"Last chance? I feel the same way," I tell her. "Theater departments are exclusive clubs. They exist to make outsiders feel like they can never come *inside*. I hate feeling like an untouchable," I grumble. "But this place feels different. It's small. We just might have a chance." I raise my eyebrows to show her I mean it and quietly offer my name.

"Person! You're a person?" she howls, hitting the floor with her palms.

"Do you know other Persons?" I ask excitedly.

"No. I don't know one person. But you have a great name, honey. I'm Charlotte Digby from the Atomic City. You know, Los Alamos, home of the Big One?"

I nod. The blond woman uses her small, white hands to mime an atomic explosion and, to complete the picture, creates blast noises in the back of her throat. Since I've only heard teenage boys make crass sound effects like these, I'm not sure if I should priggishly condemn this behavior or sit back and enjoy it.

"It's a terrible legacy," she continues. "For publicity, the city sells silk-screened T-shirts emblazoned with mushroom clouds. Can you believe it? They're really kitsch but totally shameful. So it's really not so odd for me to consider the theater as a profession—I come from a place that created the biggest theatrical event of all time. Ba-boom!" After this second outburst, she folds her pale hands in her lap, and I notice that they're glistening. This woman is utterly composed and yet her hands are dripping. This woman who speaks in complete sentences, so formal yet slightly wacko. I suspend all judgment and forge ahead.

"If I don't get into this class," I say, "I will be forced to sell poems on the corners of busy intersections. My poems will get run over, as well they should!"

"If I don't get into this class, I will have to sell finger puppets of Sir Laurence Olivier and make dirty hand gestures with them!"

I giggle and tuck the drape of hair that successfully hides my face back behind my ears. "If I don't get into this class, *I* will become a dirty hand puppet!" I say, upping the ante.

Charlotte retaliates, "If I don't get into this class, I will insist that dirty hand puppets have their own university!" She rises from her spot on the cold linoleum and pretends to speak into a microphone, a rabble-rouser at an antiwar rally: "Are you with me, puppets, or agin me?"

I double over laughing. "Charlotte, you're a nut!"

"Why thank you." She takes a bow.

"Wherever did you come from?"

"I told you—from the sacred Indian land that we blasted to smithereens. But hey, I think you're wonderful too. A gust of fresh air."

"As fresh as they come from Los Angeles. You were born under the bomb and I was born under the smog. We have a lot in common." I blush a wee bit; I'm so thankful I've found someone with whom to share the lunacy of college life. And Charlotte's so physically wild, like Carol Burnett or . . . Lonnie.

I look up to discover that the few students who'd been milling about have disappeared. Pierce Winter cranes his neck out the door to his studio and hollers, "Last call! Enter at my own risk!"

With equal portions of dread and daring, Charlotte and I make our way into a cavernous, dark room surrounded on two sides by heavy black curtains. I spot Henry in the group of students already splayed out on the carpeted floor. His eyes follow me as I search for a space big enough for Charlotte and me. The scent of musk and lavender and my own strawberry oil clouds the air. The whole scene makes me a little dizzy. I feel completely at sea, and yet I long to make this place my home.

In my ridiculous way, I scan the room for the faces of beautiful women; this helps support my opinion that I'll be one of the ugly ones here. In the theater, as in life, it's the sylphlike, symmetrical types who'll get the ingenue parts, while I suffer the infamy of character roles.

"Guys and dolls, *attenzione!* The final audition for Beginning Theater will begin momentarily. You will soon learn that I have little patience for stupidity, inattention, and laziness, but I have bottomless patience for bottomless creativity. I expect that anyone who attends my class is going to work his butt off, and I promise you, I will work my own off." Pierce whirls around and displays the immensity of his hindquarters for comic effect. Charlotte and I eye him with renewed respect.

"Oh God, I have nothing to work with," Charlotte whispers, pointing to her near-invisible behind.

"Don't worry," I whisper back, "I've got enough meat for two."

We are bonding so effortlessly I can't remember why it's usually impossible to make a friend for life. I always seem to know within the first five minutes whether it's going to happen or not. Maybe the missing ingredient is the very thing I ran away from: honest-to-God craziness. But such craziness should be tempered with an *attempt* to live in the world, no? Right now, *I'm* attempting to live in the world, each breath, each step requiring a brand-new decision to stick around.

I sense that Charlotte feels the same way; she has the manic quality of someone who makes the decision to live several times a day. Yet she appears more rooted than I do, has a way of planting her body on the earth that demonstrates the physical world is not an illusion. As a person who hardly touches down myself, it feels good to sit next to someone who's so solid. I can learn something from Charlotte. I would like to hug her forcefully but remember, in the nick of time, to keep my hands to myself.

Pierce explains that each student will get one chance to run into the studio's far wall. He doesn't look gleeful about this; in fact he appears doleful. And he doesn't tip us off about what quality he's looking for, what kind of release into the wall he expects. My mind races. I decide that he's looking for someone who takes risks. Although all my risks to this point have been emotional, I decide to throw myself at the wall with as much vigor as I can muster. I will approach its hard surface without hesitation and crash not so much recklessly as with full-bore intention. I will not protect myself by bracing my palms against the wall at the last second. At the last second, I shall appear happy about getting seriously injured.

One of the beautiful faces is selected to go first. She removes at least seven shiny bangles from her tanned right wrist and unhurriedly unclasps her turquoise bead earrings. Then she hitches up her long Indian-print skirt and tucks a few inches of material into its elastic waistband. This creates a miniskirt of sorts, a frock she can run in. Next, she ties her blue denim work shirt in a knot at the waist—she wouldn't want to trip on that! After a few furtive looks around the room, the young woman prances like a filly toward the wall, her glossy braid trailing behind her. When she reaches the wall, she comes to a full stop, then daintily throws herself at it, shoulder-first. After contact, she falls to the floor as if she's given everything to this wall, then leaps to her stockinged feet, suggesting she's got enough surplus energy to throw herself at the wall all day long. I sneak a look at Charlotte and roll my eyes. Charlotte cups her mouth to my ear, "Tomorrow she'll be covered in color-coordinated Band-Aids."

Henry is next up at bat. Before Pierce can say "Go," Henry has cruelly slammed his wiry form into the wall; he collapses in a stick-figure heap on the floor. We hear him moaning and laughing and coughing, and shake our heads in unison, big grins plastered on our faces.

A Paul Bunyan–like guy is chosen as Pierce's "next victim." His head is ringed with golden curls, and despite possessing the girth of a bully, his manner is as gentle and sweet as a kitten's. But before he runs toward the wall, the big guy frowns and thinks in place, the brooding intellectual. Then his feet paw the ground like a bull's, and he's off and running with such gusto that he appears to disappear into the wall's interior. The class witnesses a violent, awe-inspiring crash. Paul Bunyan has gone through the wall and no longer can be seen! What *can* be seen is the ragged outline of the massive hole he's gouged; it's a cutout of his body, like in a Road Runner cartoon. We laugh ourselves silly as Pierce runs through the hole to see if he has a major injury on his hands. After a few tense seconds, Pierce and the big guy emerge triumphantly from the hole, hands raised in victory. The class breaks into thunderous applause.

"So *that's* what it takes to get into this class!" Charlotte quips. Only now can we see that the "wall" is actually a fiberboard partition that divides our studio from a sister studio. It's as if Paul Bunyan has created a wormhole into another dimension. For a poorly spent minute, I worry about the existence of a Lorna Person on the other side of the wall—a Lorna who's a better actress than me.

Charlotte is the next candidate for greatness and blithely sprints to the wall, carefully missing the gaping hole but expertly flinging herself at the wall's mercy. Like a rag doll, she crumples on the floor after impact and, just when we think she won't rebound, springs to her feet like a Slinky and rumbas into the hole.

"Lorna Person." Pierce calls out my name, and I hear the chorus of titters I've grown accustomed to. Then Charlotte hollers, "Break a leg, Person!" and I lug my body full of Kit Kat bars off the floor and steady myself. But I don't have the finesse of Charlotte, and my flat feet propel me toward the wall in a zigzag course. Nevertheless, I invest all my feelings about risk into my fling at the wall. I tell myself, *For a change, use your body instead of your mind.* The wall gratefully accepts my blow, and although my knees and elbows sting with pain, I must admit, I'm having a ball!

When I return to my spot on the carpet, Henry sidles over and congratulates me in a gravelly voice, "Very cool, Lorna Person!" I smile shyly at the floor and wonder why such a handsome fellow is so vocally authoritative yet so emotionally shaky. It's his hyperanimated limbs that give him away; some of us bite our nails, some of us drink or do drugs, and others simply have exploding bodies. I do feel the beginnings of tenderness for Henry but inch away out of fear of the Other. What a stupid defense! If anything, I'm a card-carrying member of the Other.

After the remaining students take their turns at wall crashing, Pierce announces a half-hour intermission before he reveals the results of "who gets into my esteemed theater class and who goes home without esteem, wagging their tails behind them." He's a curious mix of empathy and brutality.

Charlotte and I venture outside the building to get some air, Henry shadowing us from a few feet behind. Everyone crowds around Paul Bunyan, slapping him on the back goodnaturedly. After a half hour passes, we shuffle back to read the list Pierce has posted on the studio door. I sneak a peek at it sideways. My name always startles me, yet I always expect to find it there, theater being the only realm where I have quietly acknowledged my gift. There's my name (thank God) and Charlotte's and Henry's. But Paul Bunyan, the student who surely gave more of himself to get into this class than anyone has done in the history of the theater department, has not made the final cut. That is impossible. I can't imagine spending a whole quarter in this studio with his black hole staring me in the face. I should mount a protest. I should speak up for the gentle giant. But I am new here, a nobody, and can hardly speak up for myself. I resign myself to living with this inconsistency. The theater is an illogical place, and who am I to question why the big guy won't be joining us.

Stop the World, I Want to Die Off

1971

harlotte and I are madly in love with nine homosexuals. None of them is out of the closet and, to be fair, it's unclear who is and who isn't gay. But our whole world has turned fabulously gay, and we don't care to find out the truth. We are happy in our ignorance.

Working slavishly on the crew of *The Boys in the Band*, a politically backward but oh-so-witty play about a group of urban gay men, we are captivated by both the taboo subject of this play and its alluring, all-male cast. Each night after rehearsal, Char and I retire to Denny's for a deft psychological review of the cast and what we consider a penetrating analysis of gay culture. Our conversation is buoyed by cup after cup of potent Denny's coffee, but we're young and don't feel the need for more than four hours of sleep.

First, we run through our favorite lines in the play, giggling like guilty co-conspirators. The bitchy wit of *The Boys in the Band* is new to us, and it feels daring to say these caustic lines out loud. Gay culture offers us something we hunger for: it weds style to intellect, tragedy to ecstasy. The outsider becomes a hero, and justice is served!

In our outwardly hetero skins and in the safety net of the wee hours, Charlotte and I confess to harboring ambivalent feelings about our sexual desires. "People are people," I tell her one night after a sweaty run-through. "You can fall in love with either sex—it's the *person* who makes the difference. His or her spectacular insides. Unfortunately, I happen to be a sucker for the 'difference' in men. Men are the second greatest mystery of life, after life itself. I mean, why the hell are they here? The moon I can understand, the ocean I can grasp. But men? Yuck!"

After a protracted swig of coffee laced with Sweet'n Low and Cremora, Charlotte comments, "Personally, I love dogs. They don't betray you. Dogs make the best lovers."

"Really?" I ask, bug-eyed. She has a way of taking me in.

"Yeah, sure. But only gay dogs. *Gay* dogs."

After our nightly forum on the bright side of homosexuality, we typically digress and get all giddy over the actors in the cast, allowing that their acting chops have blinded us to the fact that most of them are probably straight. Not surprisingly, it's the three actors who are the most androgynous whom we find the most attractive. After musing about the faces, voices, and blatant charms of Davey Dellaluna, Jakob Schwartz, and Joe Vermeer, Charlotte and I conclude that androgyny is the sexiest state of all, that a delicate blend of male and female attributes is a powerful aphrodisiac. But experiencing a schoolgirl crush on nine men makes us nine times more vulnerable than before. Surely we are setting a new school record.

Since the first day of class, Charlotte and I have gotten very chummy ourselves. Some people even have taken to whispering about us, saying we're "connected at the goddam hip," a signature line in the play. But we have no romantic designs on each other; we simply match each other's rhythms for feeling hopelessly bleak *and* deliriously happy—all in a good day's work.

By the second week in rehearsal (Charlotte's assigned to props and I'm pounding nails), we are utterly mesmerized by the Broadway savvy of our student director, Kenyatta Kitchens. He's completely, professionally brilliant and totally, personally deluded! Yet despite his affection for us, we remain social pariahs, underappreciated by the cast and crew. Most of the actors don't know we're alive, and I'm not scoring any points with a hammer. Clearly I'm miserable with any sort of tool—I have no business backstage—and Charlotte's artistry with her paintbrush has gone sadly unnoticed. For unknown reasons, though, the director has taken us under his wing. An over-the-top, male version of Josephine Baker and the rare black student in a sea of white faces, Kenyatta keeps our hearts pumping and eyes dazzled with a blinding love for the theater. Today, he's asked us to spare a few minutes for a covert meeting in the Barn Theatre auditorium. We oblige, our hopes and curiosity running high.

"Girls, listen up!" he hisses conspiratorially (he calls everyone "girls"). "I have a special kiss-up-to-your-director request." He places his smooth, manicured hands on his hips and poses coquettishly like a quiz-show model. "If you sweep the theater each night before the performance, I will personally french kiss you, take you out for sundaes as chocolate-y as my flawless skin"—he pats both cheeks—"and promise you juicy roles in my next extravaganza. What do you say, my sweet petunias?"

Charlotte grabs the broom that Kenyatta has gallantly extended and begins to perform a sweeping ballet. She leaps and pliés and practically pole-vaults. "I'll sweep with the director anytime, anywhere!" she says, sweeping literal circles around him.

Kenyatta laughs extravagantly, "Oh darlin', you're good."

Then Charlotte slips the broom handle suggestively between Kenyatta's legs. "Is it bigger than a bread box?" she taunts him in her low, mocking voice.

"I don't know, honeybuns. Shall we take a *poll?*"

I smile bravely at their punning, then notice that my left hand is shaking. Little earthquakes under the skin began to make themselves known almost the week I arrived on campus. I had tried to ignore them, but they kept getting louder, commanding more of my attention. Although I don't understand their deeper source, I am certain the shakes have something to do with not being accepted into the inner circles of the theater department. Yes, I have a good friend in Charlotte, but I find myself repeating the phrase "I'm being locked out of paradise" and know this to be an important clue. There's also the inconclusive fact of Nate. With all the novelty of Santa Cruz, its thirty-one flavors of eccentric students, its primeval forests and bucolic meadows, I'd hoped that the age-old—well, months-old—sadness of Nathaniel's disappearance would dissipate into the soil. But my widowhood is alive and ticking. And with it comes a spooky pressure in my head.

Of course, I've always had an uneasy time with my body— one could say I'm perpetually "shook up"—but this is different. Before, only my thoughts were jumbled; now the feeling is manifest in my arms and legs. Sometimes when the shakes get really bad, I think it's not me at all but the earth under my feet, just like Carole King said.

Quickly I grab a coffee mug from the bleacher behind me and grip it firmly—it's a useful little anchor. Observing my awkward way with objects, Kenyatta projects his charisma in my direction. "And you, my little doe?" (You have to give him credit: there is nothing petite about me and yet he sees me as a small forest creature.) "Will you accept the role of the lovely chimney sweep who comes to the theater at the stroke of six and makes it so clean you can eat off my lap?"

"Yes, sir," I respond to his wreck of a metaphor, staring down at my scuffed black clogs. "I can handle that, Mis-tah Kitchens," I say in my best Cockney maid accent. "But you don't have to promise me anything. Please don't promise me a thing."

Kenyatta looks downcast. He lives in a land of gotta-sing, gotta-dance make-believe, and I of all people have brought him down to earth. He's probably reliving his troubled teen years in Harlem and hating me for it. Then I see the light return to his eyes as if an electrical cord has been plugged back in. "Baby, I really mean it. I see you as my Ophelia. I can already taste it, it's so good!" I perk up noticeably. "I'm going to do a musical version of *Hamlet* set in the sixties—you'll absolutely triumph in the role!"

I blink away the possibility of tears. "But I can't sing, Kenyatta. It's my failing. I think I understand Ophelia's character, though. I've got real insight into her tragic-romantic personality. But does she really have to sing? Can't she just talk-sing like Rex Harrison or Yul Brynner?"

He moves in close to hug me, and soon I'm suffocating in a mist of Brut cologne and hairspray. "Darling creature, Kenyatta can move mountains! I will make sure that Ophelia is too out-of-it to sing like a bird. She will talk-sing like all great manic-depressives, and these songs will be heartbreakers! But first, the sweeping." He winks and throws me a broom.

I catch it in one hand and kiss the top of the handle like a tentative lover. Kenyatta laughs on cue, then takes the steps to the stage like the Broadway gypsy he is, his task complete. Right before he exits, he pivots around on his heel and throws both arms in the air like Auntie Mame. "Doncha just *love* the smell of the theater?" We nod like Stepford Wives. "You girls are my favorites! But you've *got* to have more faith. I can feel the doubt rolling off of you. You've got to believe in fairies! Clap a little louder or I'll die!" He giggles lustfully, then does a Bob Fosse hip thrust into the curtains.

Charlotte and I clap hard and long to show our Tinker Bell of a director that we believe in him, in the theater, in ourselves. I exhaust myself from clapping. Even so, my hands still vibrate with tension. I hurl the broom at the front-row seats and run out. My belief has bottomed out.

∎ ∎ ∎

Henry has been cast in *The Boys in the Band* as the beefcakey stud, the big-hearted, inarticulate party favor bandied about by a clan of wisecracking men. From the stage, he watches me while I do my lowly sweeping. I wish I could return the favor of his festering affection. But I've got an arrow in the heart too. The star of the play, Joe Vermeer, is a magnetic personality who is critically unaware that he's pulling me on a conveyor belt to his mysterious core. An olive-skinned, half-Dutch, half–Puerto Rican actor, he exudes androgyny, and in the midst of all the hippie, waspy, white-bread students who populate our campus, he's the rare ethnic student, like Kenyatta.

Joe has materialized out of nowhere—some say he's from the gangland turf of Brooklyn—but I don't care what depths or heights he came from. Of all the actors in this play, except Mickey Macchiato, who plays the one stubbornly hetero character, Joe is the most obvious candidate for real-life homosexuality. But who knows? Offstage, he shamelessly flirts with men and women alike, a naughty scamp, dishing out and feeding on bon mots.

My attraction to Joe runs deep. I can't explain it. Here I've been waiting for another Nathaniel, the king of intellect and psychology, to come my way. I've been waiting for a man with the word "BRILLIANT" written on his forehead in brilliant red ink; for a longhaired, lithe Jewish prince to come along in high-top sneakers. Someone familiar. And here comes Joe with his almost chunky, feminized curves, round moonface, and shock of ebony curls. My savory exotic. My vulnerable man-child. I ask myself: Joe, why you and why now?

Maybe it's the part he plays. When you play a charismatic gay man (albeit drowning in self-hatred), the charm is bound to rub off on all who come in contact with you. But the off-stage Joe shimmers like the onstage Joe, with a radiance akin to the aurora borealis. I can almost touch his halo, hear his body crackle with electricity. And so the journal I began only weeks ago begins to spill over with odes to Joe—descriptions of the pain I feel when he doesn't recognize me and the pain I feel when he does. Henry, who is fighting his own demons, lets me know that my lack of romantic interest in him doesn't "help the cause." He would probably pass out if he read my journal. But I have no intention of hurting him. If I could exchange my predilection for the possibly gay actor who is all pain on the outside for the hetero actor who is all pain on the inside, I would in a flash.

Today, Henry insists on taking me to lunch at my favorite dive on the Santa Cruz Pier. I smell a heavy agenda. In a weatherbeaten seafood cafe, I toy with the oyster crackers bobbing in my untouched, gluey clam chowder. I stare into the broth for an answer that will soothe Henry's ache and make his life a joyful thing. I could care less about me right now.

Henry pushes away his wineglass with such force that wine spills into his soup and all over the tablecloth. "Listen, Lorna. It's simple. I love you. I could give you a really good life. I'm dying here. If I need to, I will repeat every last cliché about a guy hopelessly in love, because they're all real."

Struck, I say nothing.

"I'll repeat what I just said—"

"No, you needn't," I caution like a heroine trapped in a dime novel.

"Yeah, I needn't. I mean, I *need* to." Henry's difficulty with expressing himself always touches me. But it doesn't make me fall in love with him.

"I love you, do you hear me? I could give you a better world. But I can't watch you watching everybody else in the theater department! Please do something about this. It's an emergency." He mops up the wine on the oilcloth with his slice of sourdough and, with his doleful eyes, applies for a passport to my soul.

"I know something about emergencies," I counter, looking fiercely into those blue eyes. "I know something about loving someone who doesn't love—" Something in my chest cracks. An ancient anger breaks loose, dislodges. After nine months in the deep freeze, am I finally thawing? Is the iceberg Nathaniel left in his wake—that immense hurt I've been lugging around—finally melting and flowing into the Gulf Stream?

My shocked expression melts into one of kindness, charity, devotion. "I don't take your love lightly, Henry. It touches me. *Really.* I have been loved in my life only a little bit, so your feelings mean something huge to me. Something beautiful. I will never feel smug about your love, and I'll never toy with it. Trust me. I'm sure we'll work something out. Something will come to us, don't you think? Let's be creative." I reach my hands across the table, but he withdraws his just in time.

Henry's chest caves in, and he shakes his head as if I've just crashed my car into his mother's Mercedes. "Just don't leave

me alone with these feelings," he gags. Then he begins to torture his slice of soggy sourdough with his knife.

"I won't leave you, Henry. But I can't promise that I will
love you the same way you love me. I'm in terrible shape. Too
sad to have the kind of feelings you desire. I guess I'm still in
mourning for Nathaniel." Images of myself veiled in black,
compulsively chain-smoking, come to mind. I hope my coun-
tenance conveys a thick grief and not the blush of pleasure
that comes with knowing that someone loves you.

"If you're in mourning, then how come . . . how come you
seem to come alive around Joe? Huh? I see you come alive
when you talk to him."

I feel found out. Humiliated. "I don't know, Henry. Joe's an
amazing actor. He lives a life of total fantasy, and I can relate
to that."

"He's gay, you know."

"Nobody knows for sure," I say defensively. "Maybe I'm anima possessed. Though only guys are supposed to be that
way. See, Joe's a total anima figure."

"What's the big deal about being animated?"

"I mean he's got so much female in him. I'm mesmerized by
that."

"Well, I hate to say it but people tell me I've got a really
feminine face too."

I have to laugh. "Yes, yes," I pat Henry's hand as if reassuring a child. "That's true, you have a beautiful face for a boy *or*
a girl."

"But that's not good enough?" he demands.

"If attraction were only based on faces, I would be
screwed!"

"Don't say that. You have the face of an angel."

"Yeah, right," I say with a measure of self-disgust. Then I
twist around in the booth and raise the back of my vintage
lace blouse; this reveals my candle-white shoulder blades and

my crummy, yellowed bra. "Getta look at these wings!" I point at my back. "All broken, broken."

Henry stares at my bare waist. "All I see is beauty," he says flatly. "Nothing broken on you, babe."

I nod in silence, actually believing him for a couple of seconds. How could I refuse this compliment? He sees something I've been trying to see my whole life.

▮ ▮ ▮

"Sweet Twat, please pay attention!"

Kenyatta has taken to calling me "Twat." All my life I've waited for an endearing nickname and now this, a name I can't take home to Mother.

"Are you here with us, darlin', or lost in the Bermuda Triangle?"

I seem to have dropped out of our nightly play review and bull session. The pressure in my head is finally unbearable, and my occasional body shakes have evolved into daily 6.5 earthquakes.

"I'm here, Mister K!" I smile as proof, but he pounds his forehead in a gesture of despair.

Kenyatta blows his whistle and yells, "Take seven!"

"SEVEN?" everyone echoes, never fully at home with his eccentricity.

"Yes, seven, doll-babies. I need to conference with Twat."

Kenyatta and I cloister ourselves behind the dusty maroon curtain that rings the stage, and huddle like a tiny football team. He takes both of my cold hands in his warm ones and squeezes them hard. "I adore you, girl, but you've *got* to get with the program! I fear I'm losing you. Say, what do you think of my new tap shoes?"

"They're lovely," I say mechanically.

"Hmm, perhaps it's time that my darling sees a shrink?" He bats his Revlon-coated lashes.

My chest heaves up and down as if I'm about to detonate or implode or just bawl my head off.

Kenyatta persists. "Honey, help is just around the corner. God knows *I* could use it!"

For no reason, I laugh hysterically at that. Then comes an unrehearsed barrage of complaints mixed with tears: "Kenyatta, why am I on set design? You know I can't build anything! Why am I not using my talents *onstage?* Why the hell am I sweeping? Why won't anyone in the cast except Henry talk to me? Am I invisible? Do they think I'm a leper? I know I have missing parts!"

As my nose fills with water, Kenyatta extends a linen handkerchief that had been crisply folded in the pocket of his nautical blazer. I grab it hungrily and honk my way through another monologue. "I'm thrilled to be working with you, really. And with Charlotte. Charlotte and I get on like . . . like . . . you know, that 'house on fire' thing. I'm completely gaga about this play. I think Joe Vermeer is the most sensational . . . actor! Everyone in the cast and crew is probably great, but they don't want to get to know me, really *know me.* But guess what? I'm writing more poems here than ever before. I mean, I am a fertile woman!"

"Oh, absolutely fertile," Kenyatta agrees.

"But these black moods, they come in like the red tide—"

"Oops, color clash!" Kenyatta slaps his cheeks.

"—and completely wash over me. It's like my world is being swallowed up by tidal waves, and I can't run fast enough. I'm so cold here"—my teeth chatter for effect—"and I can't stop this awful shaking. Look." I show him my hands, but they are uncommonly still. "Well, on the *inside* I feel like the soil is collapsing. My tectonic plates are shifting."

"My God!" raves Kenyatta. "We got tidal waves, mudslides, earthquakes! You really *are* from L.A., aren't you, dear Twat?"

"Yes, I really am." I almost crack a smile.

Henry peeks his head around the curtain and winks at me. "Hey, babe, do you need some help?"

I nod my head up and down like a three-year-old. He helps me up from the rough wooden planks of the floor and wraps his weathered bomber jacket around my shoulders. "Didn't we meet like this?" he teases. Again, I shake my head, sopping up water from my nose with Kenyatta's swatch of linen. Henry steers me out of the theater and in the direction of his mother's car, a vintage midnight-blue Mercedes. He guns the motor, and we vanish into the chilly October night.

When we stop in a cornfield, somewhere in the flatlands of Santa Cruz, Henry keeps the engine running and the heat on full blast. "So baby, help me out here. Tell me what you need." He looks away to give me some privacy.

I fiddle with the zipper of his leather jacket, at the same time taking inventory of the stars in the sky. They're no help. "It's time for me to see someone," I state without inflection.

"Who is it? Who do you want to go out with?" he accuses.

"No," I tell Henry. "Not a date. I need to see someone professional—like my sister does. I'm tired of handling this myself. Of handling myself, myself. Maybe I need to take pills."

"Maybe you just need to calm down."

"Calm down? Calm down!" I shriek in his ear. "What's that? Can you tell me what *that* is? Bubble baths and long walks in the country? No more caffeine?"

"Hey, I'm not the enemy." Henry folds his arms tightly to shield his chest. For a few minutes we give each other the silent treatment. Then he clicks on the radio and makes a big deal out of dialing in a San Francisco jazz station. For several more minutes, we listen passively to the sounds of cool jazz, staring out the windshield at ghostly, shaggy cornstalks.

Finally, I feel compelled to offer up an explanation. "I'm sorry, Henry. I just can't remember *how* to calm down. I don't think I have ever known what that is. When I take a bath, in-

stead of relaxing, I'm paranoid. I think the warm water wants
to disarm me, wants to lull me to a quiet death. But I won't let
it. Got to stay alert!"

"For what?"

"I don't know. For something awful—just take my word for
it. When I go to bed at night, I bite my nails to nubs and
scrunch my body into a tight ball, lying in wait."

"For what?" Again the same question.

"You know. To be ambushed by . . . some interruption, some
scream, some phone call that signals disaster."

Henry shudders and pulls a pitifully small joint from his
jeans pocket. "Do you mind, baby? I'm a little rattled myself."

I shake my head no and stare at a particularly sinister row
of corn. From my unreliable unconscious spring memories of
a horror film about children with cold, headlight eyes, standing defiantly in a field of corn. The lit-up eyes tell the whole
story: evil is more powerful than good, evil gets its way. Then
I remember the trailer was so scary that I never actually saw
the movie. Maybe I'm not crazy, maybe I'm just possessed like
those children. My eyes glow in the dark and no one has the
nerve to tell me.

"Let me take you to someone I trust," Henry offers in his
reassuring baritone. He takes an extra-long drag on the joint.
"A family friend. Someone who's counseled me and my broth-
ers and a whole lot of folks. Doctor Flowers is a maverick, a
total madman, but he's got a lifetime experience with . . . your
sort of thing."

"If only I knew what my sort of thing was. Do you?"

"Well, you're just a little depressed."

"A lit-little?" I stutter, incredulous. "God, I'm about to crum-
ble into a hundred pieces, Henry. I swear it. I'm afraid for my
life."

"If only you'd let me love you. I could save you if you'd let me love you." He tenderly brushes a strand of wet hair from my cheek.

"There's nothing to love at the moment. But I'll let you take me to your genius friend. Let's start with that." I look up at his flawless face veiled in marijuana smoke and see that he's telling me the truth: he sees something to love. What a notion.

I, Tragedienne

1971

enry is driving heroically along Highway 17, the precarious death route that connects Santa Cruz with the rest of the world. We're off to see the wizard, Henry's therapist friend, Dr. Flowers. He's promised to give me a new brain.

In the last few days, Henry's verbal insecurity has been replaced with a cool and confident caretaking. It turns out that he excels at being in charge of me, my movements, and my moods. And he's begun singing Motown songs nonstop, taking the lowest parts of four-part harmonies, and stressing the very words that chronicle his blazing but unrequited love for me.

I can only guess that what has brightened Henry's spirits is his newfound knowledge of the exact spot on the earth where my feet touch down every day. To make him happy while I can't possibly be, I have allowed him to sleep with me, well, up against me and sometimes holding me. At least one of us can get some sleep this way. And I have decided to spend whole days with him—not really a decision since my will is waning, but the best thing to do, considering my fascination with self-destruction. Though I have often confused the real Henry with his role in the play as the hunk who can't get a grip, I now see that I have done him a disservice. For all of Henry's outer beauty (which remains difficult for me), I detect a flowering intellectuality and, even better, a sense of virtue that matches my own. But my heart is sunk so deep in the ground that I can't hear it. It doesn't make a peep when I receive the quality of attention I have craved for so long. I must have a mean streak, to steel myself against Henry's affections the way I do. As if I would only let in love from certain approved individuals. "What a fool I am," I say out loud. "What a fool!"

"Say what, honey?" Henry twists his head to regard my utterance as if gold had spilled out of my mouth.

"The trees upset me," I say dully, changing the subject. "They are too beautiful, and that hurts me. I can't feel anything for them. It's like, I can remember beauty, I can recall van Gogh's *Starry Night* and remember that it's *supposed* to be beautiful. But that's just a memory. I don't feel the beauty in my *gut*." I pound my stomach a little too roughly.

"That's just temporary. The feeling will come back."

"NO IT WON'T!" I scream, surprising myself. "It's permanently gone. Kaput!" I smack my palms on the dashboard for emphasis, and they sting with heat. But I like feeling something, stinging is something.

Henry is stung too. For minutes, he drives the worst hairpin turns with intentional carelessness, singing like a broken record: "I don't like you, but I love you / Seems that I'm always thinking of you / Oh, oh, oh, you treat me badly, I love you madly / You've really got a hold on me."

I listen to this morbid singing telegram and watch the tall trees mock me. I stick out my tongue at them when Henry is preoccupied with passing a slow trailer. All this nature was supposed to do me some good. But it only serves as a reminder of my anesthetized life. I am a corpse, a stiff, a cadaver. The green color that Henry says is healing just annoys the hell out of me. As he makes a risky move to pass two campers, my fury turns inward; some demon girl insists that I bash my head against the window. This sounds logical, like a good idea. My head, which over the last two months has refused to cooperate, deserves to be worked on.

To test this idea, I press my head hard against the glass. I like the pain; it feels logical. I hold my head there, pushing my right foot into the floor mat, wishing it was in control of the gas pedal.

The demon girl tells me a story: *If you die, you will get some relief. All of the people who ignored you, who thought you were nothing, will be forced to reconsider.* My premature death brings tears to my eyes; I see Charlotte and Henry and Nathaniel and Doon staggering over my grave, leaning against each other as if my death has felled them too. The four of them can hardly walk, they are so overcome with grief. Charlotte begins reading one of my poems, but her voice cracks and she faints, the poem fluttering out of her hand and into the wind. The poem is lost!

My poem is lost, that can't be. I can't leave these shreds of paper unattended. Maybe I'd better stick around for my sad poetic efforts to see the light of day. I lift my head from the window and sit tall in my seat. For a moment, I have an absolute, Windex-like clarity: I see a future made out of really good poems. Plays I have written slay people metaphorically. Then I slump with the realization that if I don't stick around, I won't *have* an imagination. I won't be here to write dazzling poems and plays.

"Look, honey," Henry points, "there's a sight you never see."

Obediently, I look to my left and lock eyes with a doe that has decided to cross two lanes of heavy traffic, her nervous fawn trailing behind her. I wish this sight alone could make me happy; I wish I could chat with Henry like we were on a holiday outing, laughing all the way to some cheery resort. But I can't. Instead I think, "Deer don't need to be caught in headlights to *look* like deer caught in headlights." I smile weakly in his direction.

"Lorna, isn't that far out? Isn't that incredible?"

I want to tell him yes. I want to say that a mother and daughter on their way somewhere special have a poignancy that's unparalleled. I want to say I'm touched, that a mama and her baby are an eternally sweet sight. But I can't. I can only think of my own mother, how I have just crossed the street without her and will never come home. That perhaps mothers and daughters are not natural friends and shouldn't mingle—even if they look good together, poignant together. I want to tell Henry that I've forgotten about my family, and the sight of one doesn't help.

I notice that he's still waiting for an answer and say, "Yes. Incredible. Not to be believed."

"Oh, we have a cynic in the car," he snorts.

I punch him in the side lightly, not with the force I reserve for myself. "*Incroyable!*" I exclaim in French because it sounds more jubilant. The cars in front of us creep by the deer, each passenger gawking in turn. I can hardly gawk; I don't have enough depth of feeling. Nevertheless, to be a good sport, I try my hand at jaw dropping. But a weird, strangled cough surprises me. A river of tension gushes into my throat, and the damn floodgates open. I don't say a word but let the water streaming down my face tell the story.

"Should I stop?" Henry asks politely, surely at a loss.

No, I twitch my head violently. But I want to stop. I want to stop all the nonsense and leap out the door, heading into the wild to become a wild thing myself. That would be the honest thing to do.

I must be turning into Lonnie. I hate the woods. Wouldn't last a day out there. But isn't my *point* to end things? I read the license plate directly in front of us—CLOUDZ—and think about how the jagged *Z* ruins the whole image of puffy white clouds. I watch the breath of a dog as it clouds up the back window of a station wagon. His slobber disturbs me. I remember that my cat is waiting for me when I return to Los Angeles. That he will take me as I am. I imagine Norwood's fur as a silver-gray cloud that I can breathe in deeply. Finally, my racing mind comes to a halt. Not at peace, just worn out by bad ideas.

Under his breath, Henry's still humming "You've really got a hold on me." I take hold of his shoulder to let him know I hear him.

■ ■ ■

Godfrey Flowers is no god. Henry promised me a god, but Dr. Flowers is just a man, albeit a heavyweight. A rotund, Berkeley-based therapist with a frizzy Hasidic beard, he looks more like a sixties version of Santa Claus than Freud. He is squeezed into what appears to be a very expensive suit, accessorized with love beads, a tooled-leather belt, and dark tan leather sandals.

"Hello," I say evenly, feigning equilibrium. He says nothing, which gives him the edge. The unruly gray hairs sprouting from his nose and ears are terrifying to behold. I'm quivering again.

Finally, after much forethought, Godfrey waves us into his office; it's lined with bookcases stuffed with gold-embossed, leatherbound books, the kind meant to intimidate. Opened cans of Dr. Pepper litter the surface of his cherrywood desk, and his ashtray overflows with the carcasses of dozens of cigarettes. I stifle a gag. The whole place reeks of body odor and Gauloises.

"Heinrich, it's good to see you, man." Godfrey gives Henry a belated bear hug, then pats the cushioned seats of two cherrywood swivel chairs. He insists that I take the chair farthest from him, halfway across the room. I sit down and hide behind my curtain of long, sandy hair. My legs swing back and forth like a three-year-old's.

Godfrey takes a full minute to settle into his own, more important chair. Then he tugs on his awesome beard and, with a tone of regret, laments, "Lorna Person. Lorna Person. What a name to hang on an impressionable girl." He takes a robust swig of Dr. Pepper, then nods methodically, as if he's already arrived at a diagnosis.

"*Woman*," I say with a tortured grin. "What a name to hang on a woman."

"Oh! And belligerent too? That's good, that's very good."

"Not really. I'm actually painfully shy. I was just teasing you."

"Oh, we have a passive-aggressive in our midst! I like that, I like that!"

I toss a sharp look at Henry that says, "What have you got me into?" Henry shrugs back.

Godfrey whips out a handkerchief from his suit pocket and wipes his deeply lined forehead. Every inch of his face and neck glistens, looks about to pop. With considerable ceremony, he lifts his great belly out of the massive chair and strolls over to regard his new patient. After making a complete circle around me, he bends down and peers into my face as if gazing into an aquarium. "Story?" he snaps his fingers.

"What?" I say, shifting back in the swivel chair, away from his menacing bulk.

"Your story. What's your particular story?"

I can't speak. This is too weird.

Godfrey draws a difficult breath. "Why the hell are you here, Lorna?" he blurts out. "I mean that in the most compassionate way."

I look him in the eye. "Because . . . Henry said you were the best."

"And right he is. And Henry told *me* that you are from a Jewish family, that you have a crazy sister, and that you feel earthquakes under your skin. Is all this true?"

"Uh-huh," I nod.

"Well, try this on for size: Do you feel that you have nothing that's really and completely your own?"

"I have a cat," I declare. "My cat is all mine."

"Mmm. But nothing else?"

"I have my cat," I repeat.

"If that's so, then why are you crying, dear?"

Godfrey's face is one inch away from mine and, as much as I want to shove him facefirst into his great books, I think he's struck a chord. I don't know why his idea makes so much sense, but it does. I have my poems, I tell myself. I have a cat. What else could he mean? And what does being Jewish and having a crazy sister determine about me?

"Now, dear, I'm not being blunt to hurt you. I'm Jewish myself. Crazy myself. But a person like Lorna Person has *got* to have something to call her own. Or she won't see the point of sticking around. That's why I have my law practice." Flowers' thick hand waves at a diploma hanging on the wall behind him. He waddles over to straighten it.

"What?" My eyes dart over to Henry, who, up till now, has looked impatient but supportive. "I thought you were a therapist. You're a lawyer?"

"Right on! I dropped out of my graduate psychology program when I had my own breakdown. But don't worry, kiddo. You'll make it," he winks. Then Flowers promenades over to my chair, gives it a whirl, and begins to aggressively massage my shoulders.

Breaking his silence, Henry rises from the swivel chair and slaps Godfrey on his fleshy back. "Sorry, man. Our time is up. Thanks a mil." Before Flowers can open his big mouth, Henry adds, "We gotta fly." With authority, he leads me by the hand out of the office.

When we are safely out of Dr. Flowers' reach, Henry pauses to buy me a Tab from the vending machine in the hall. I am shell-shocked, bruised, but bloody curious. "I don't get it, where does your friend get off grilling me like that? With those bedside manners, he probably makes suicides out of happy people!"

"Drink up," Henry instructs, pouring Tab down my throat like I'm a helpless little bird. I shake off his ministrations.

"Jesus, Lorna! I'm just trying to help you!"

Henry skulks off to the parking lot. I run behind him, wailing "Sorry, sorry" at least twenty times.

On the trip back to Santa Cruz, as we wend our way along hateful Highway 17, I still resent the trees that are supposed to be beautiful and healing. But a little room in my heart has opened up. I watch Henry drive and listen to him sing with a different kind of attention. I feel softer toward him, more inviting. Maybe when he curls up with me tonight, I can be more present. Maybe I can even sleep with him, in the romantic sense. No one has ever come with me this far.

I   ■   I

Back in my dorm room, the rain coming down in glassy sheets, I find myself alone for the first time in three days. Henry's gone to a rehearsal where I'm not needed. My roommate is a phantom—I've seen her a total of five times since I arrived on campus. She's unofficially moved into her boyfriend's dorm room for more private sex and more frequent drugs, so her absence is not personal. Even Charlotte's out in the world without me tonight, eating tortilla chips and drinking coffee with a girlfriend who's probably easier on the nerves than I am. But that's a good thing: people will see that we are not connected at the hip, that we have lives of our own.

The life I have claimed for my own is on the brink of something big tonight. It seems that every time I think I can't possibly sink lower, I do. Each time I am absolutely certain I have hit rock bottom, somebody moves the rocks.

It's only dusk, and I am lying in bed, scratchy wool blankets drawn up to my chin. I am surrounded by the things I love: a bowl of crisp, dead roses; a Pre-Raphaelite poster of Ophelia floating like a log down the river; my all-time favorite poetry volumes, *Ariel* and *Transformations;* a ghostly image of my profile I created by pressing my cheek against a copy machine. But my once-precious notebook has been tossed across the room by a woman I don't know anymore. A woman who can't stand the sight of her poems. A woman who can't think of a reason to wash her hair but still has the chutzpah to apply dark-violet lipstick to her lips.

From my nightstand drawer, I sneak out the pack of cigarettes I have sporadically sampled over the past month. Everyone says I look ridiculous smoking—far too innocent— so I have taken to smoking in private, where I am allowed to be ridiculous. I *am* ridiculous, I don't mind telling myself. The feeling of sorrow and bile that I've been trying to force down all day has now risen from my stomach to my throat. I want to throw up sorrow, but it sticks there like a bloated rag, taking up too much space. I feel tentative, like a connect-the-dots drawing that's been left untouched. Nathaniel was wrong to leave me like this! I did nothing to him but love him to the root. But I don't wish to exact revenge; I just want to know why I was left alone on my iceberg, like an old Eskimo who is no longer useful.

Clad in a sexless flannel nightgown, I scramble out from under the blankets and retrieve my scorned notebook. The women's faces I've doodled over every last inch of the cover look freshly insane. I climb back into bed, snub out the silly cigarette I've taken two puffs of, and cast the notebook open to its last page. Slowly, compassionately, I draw a portrait of a beautiful woman whose face has been distorted by too much grief. When I notice how funereal she looks, I viciously cancel her out with a thick *X* drawn across her cheekbones. Below her neck I write: "School of Intensity: Inquire Within." Then I tear out the page and tape it to the side of my door that faces me. The picture looks great, but I'm not ready to go public with it. Back under the blankets, I find a page in my notebook that feels safe enough, private enough, and begin a poem that I could never send to Nate:

> Beyond envy
> your wildest dreams your superhuman powers
> your ruined specialness your genius fingers
> your broken ideal of beauty
> beyond your paradisiac memory you chose to go
> beyond me
> I am not beyond knowing
> we mean nothing to you

This feeble exercise is interrupted by a surprise dribble of water from my lashes that bounces on the page and smears the word "beauty." I rub the edge of my right fist on the word until my flesh turns blue from the ink. Then I wipe my fist on my cheeks, hoping to color them too. My notebook now looks junky to me, full of nothing useful. Too many stupid, painful diary entries, fledgling poems, and eccentric words I had hoped one day to use in novels! My hands tingle with angry adrenaline. I attempt to rip the notebook to shreds, but it fights back, refuses to tear. The power in my hands swells, is bent on destruction. When the notebook's cover finally flies off, a fever enters my body—a hatred, really—like a fire on the inside. I take the notebook in my hands and slam it hard against the crown of my head, slap, slap, slap. Then I slam the book on each side of my head, hoping to pound the bad feelings that live there to death. For once, I can't cry. The pounding feels deserved, the right kind of penance. I realize that I don't need a book to do this and begin pounding my head with my fists. "Crazy, crazy girl!" I chant.

Finally something tells me to soften the blows so I won't get brain damage. A broken heart is enough, I tell myself.

When my head hurts too much to continue, I try to snuff out all thoughts with my pillow and slink like an eel under the blankets. I lie in wait for nothing, hoping nothing arrives soon. Losing track of time, I finally slip into the coma I've been craving. At least I'm not aware I've been sleeping until it's over. I crane my neck to check the time on my clock radio: it's only 9:30, the night is horribly young. But an unfamiliar peacefulness has pervaded my mind. As hard as I try, I can't get upset. My body feels lighter. I sit up straight against my headboard and jiggle my head: it feels clear of ideas, deliciously empty. "It's time," I say out loud. "It's time to make the call."

I throw on my chenille bathrobe with the faint blood stains from old periods and fish my phone book from the knitting bag I use as a purse. Then I check out my swollen face in the mirror and work my bird's nest of hair into a ponytail. Cracking open the door a few inches, I survey the hallway. The coast is clear. Hobbling down the hall on bare feet, looking more like an inpatient than a coed, I can't believe I have the

guts to make the call. It's been almost a year since I've seen
Nate, heard his voice. But there's no turning back. My fingers
tremble as I punch in the numbers to an anonymous UC-
Berkeley dorm.

"I'm calling for Nathaniel Berman," I say hoarsely into the
receiver.

"I don't know if he's around," a woman with a cold French
accent replies.

A dark vision of Nathaniel cohabiting with a young Cath-
erine Deneuve threatens my mission, but I blink it away. I
wait for untold minutes before I hear a man chirp, "Thanks
beaucoup, Solange," and then, "Hello? Nate's Delicatessen!"
Nathaniel is happy; I can already tell.

"Nathaniel, it's me. Lorna. I hope I'm not interrupting—"

"Lorna? Lorna-loo! Lor-*na*-cious! How wonderful, I can't
believe it's you."

"You can believe it, Nate. It's me all right. *Who*ever that is."

"Oh, come on. That's someone supergroovy!" I laugh like I
always did at his fake hippie jargon. "Lorna, how *are* you? I
mean that sincerely. How—are—you?"

"Um, fine. Busy. Busy."

"Uh-huh."

"Well, *of course* I'm not fine! I'm really having a lot of difficulty. But I wish I could say I was fine, because I want you to
remember me as fine. Not as a mess."

"Lorna, what's wrong? Let me guess. This has something to
do with me."

"Yes. Yes it does."

"Okay, that's a start. Something to do with what happened
to me."

"No. This is about what happened to *me!* After you made
your decision. The decision that left me *out* of the decision.
I'm sure you had your excellent reasons, Nate, but truthfully,
the whole thing continues to eat away at me. I deserve an ex-

planation, don't I? Just because you're noble doesn't mean I don't deserve an explanation. I mean, I was your best friend and—" I shake my head ruefully. Already, I have lapsed into an incoherent rant.

"Lorna. You deserve a lifetime of explanations. I just couldn't . . . I just needed to be by myself."

"I thought so—"

"But let me finish. It's just that you saw me as this god, this guy who was practically holy. But I was a kid. Scared. Overwhelmed by the fierceness of your feelings for me. Scared. Did I say that already?"

"Yeah."

"And, as articulate as you think I am, I had no words. No words to express that I needed to be alone. I was a total baby."

"Well, that baby hurt me deeply."

"I'm sure I did. I couldn't face the fact that I was acting like an idiot. That's why I couldn't call or write. You're the only one who knows I'm a baby."

"Well, I'm honored. But were you planning to tell me someday? Because I think this lack of closure is getting in the way of a lot of things for me. I'm not sure I can have a new relationship until I know if ours meant anything to you. I don't want to put you on the spot—see, I'm terrified of you now. But I would like to know that my love meant something. It meant a whole world to me!"

For seconds, I hear nothing on the phone but light breathing, and I wonder if Nathaniel is crying or if I just wish he was. Finally, he speaks up in a tender, raspy voice: "Lorna, Claire tells me you're in the theater department at Santa Cruz. I bet you're a wonderful actress." I don't answer. "Well, this is what I believe. Our lives are made up of many kinds of plays: dramas, comedies, tragedies, mysteries, and, of course, tender love stories. And when you fall in love with someone for the first time, that someone is the first person who walks out onstage in your personal play, your own love story. You never forget her. This person in the spotlight who commands all your attention. Who opens your eyes. Who stirs your heart. You are that person, Lorna. You were the first person in my life to walk out on the stage. I honestly was in love with you, please don't think that I wasn't. You played a part in my life that no one else can ever play. I just had to—"

"You don't have to say it," I tell him. "Please don't say it."

"Okay. But are you okay?"

"Sure. Yeah. I'm okay. I've really no choice, right?"

"I've done a terrible thing."

"I've got to go to bed, Nathaniel. I wish you well. G'night."

"Lorna, I'll always remember . . . you on that stage."

"Me too," I say after hanging up the phone. I drift back to my dorm room, a complete zombie. I can't remember climbing into bed but notice that I'm back under the covers, shaken but tautly smiling. Nathaniel's words were soothing but completely incomplete. Not the words of a god. I suppose I'll have to let him go; I don't have a choice. But I don't want our love to become so faint that no one remembers its glory. Is that the fate of all love—to become ancient and forgettable?

I feel older than I should tonight. Almost wise. I'm not sure that wisdom will make me happier, though. I've witnessed how it carves away at the wholeness of love. Sure, everyone says I'm still young enough to have lots of loves in my life, that I have my whole love life ahead of me. I wish that sounded like good news. But from now on, romance is going to be mixed, tainted, weighed down by the past. Of course, for an artist, a wound of unknown proportions could be looked on as rich, complex material. But damn the artists! Not everything is fodder for poems and paintings! At least five percent of a powerful experience can never be turned into something else. It is what it is.

I peer at my newly wise face in the mirror. It still appears unlined, unlived in. It betrays nothing of what I'm going through. And then it comes to me, the secret of all time: *I don't have to stop loving anyone.*

"I don't have to stop loving you, Nathaniel," I say out loud. "No one said I had to kill off my feelings. I just have to make them bearable. That's the trick, isn't it? To bring your darkest feelings into the light?"

I pick up my tattered notebook from my nightstand and reread the poem I began hours earlier. It's bizarre, but I'll make something of it. Below the poem, with my Sheaffer fountain pen and in nice round letters, I write Nathaniel a letter:

Dearest N,

I promise to pack you in a secure place in my suitcase so I can carry you with me for a lifetime. Perhaps you will evolve into a sweet memory, one that doesn't hurt me anymore—one that helps me love again and forgive things I don't understand. But right now, for a little while, I'm going to leave my luggage behind. You're a genius, so I trust you'll understand. I need to travel light.

Kisses,
L

Glinda: The Dark Side

t's showtime, like Daddy used to say. I wish I was at the Bubble Bakery in downtown Santa Cruz, guzzling coffee and spilling my guts to Charlotte. Instead, I'm backstage at the Barn Theatre, about to spill my guts to total strangers. If I have the guts.

I walk onstage and wait for my cue, fidgeting behind a ten-foot-tall "bubble" that has been fancied out of silver Mylar. Tethered to near-invisible fishing wire, the bubble drifts downstage, and I tiptoe behind it, as if we're inseparable.

An irritating, high-pitched rendition of "Over the Rainbow," sung by a phony Buffy Sainte-Marie (why, it's my hammy friend Charlotte!) assails the audience. Charlotte's sitting on a bar stool, stage left, sampling a cappuccino between strumming power chords on her cheap acoustic guitar. The audience howls. I'm not sure why, although when we first developed this bit, Charlotte and I howled for days. And then I remember: amnesia is a vital part of the creative process; it helps make things new again.

More high-strung singing from my girlfriend and laughter from the audience. Charlotte's probably mugging, she's got to be mugging. I sip in some air and wring my bloodless hands. I'm shaking like a leaf, ever the virgin each time I set foot onstage. It never gets easier—entering the public arena, slipping on a new persona and leaving my less interesting self behind.

I peek around the bubble and spot Pierce Winter, my drama professor, in the front row. He's flapping a notepad against his thigh, a pencil gripped firmly in his canine teeth. Sheesh, he looks worried. Only he knows how hard I've been working these last months on my first major piece of performance art—a monologue to settle the score with my "Glinda the Good Witch" past. Pierce has been nothing but supportive. But he cautioned that my performance could be perceived as "over the top," even verging on offensive. Just like me, I'm afraid.

Peering around the bubble, I'm heartened to discover a sea of unknown faces. My audience could be anybody—friends, foes, potential lovers. But no parents; they couldn't fly up just now. And no Lonnie. This is not her scene. Besides, she's holed up in a halfway house in Sunland, just far enough away from Mother and Daddy to make visits inconvenient. Lonnie says, "Anyplace would be inconvenient for you, Oozy," but I'd never let her know she's right.

Hidden behind my bubble, I clear my throat a neurotic number of times. I press the tip of my pinkie finger until it throbs. A shiver runs up my spine because, with this performance, I'm about to eat my young. Soon everyone who used to like me will be forced to reconsider.

When Charlotte belts out the lyric about the tiny little bluebirds flying—viciously demanding "why can't I?"—she breaks down and sobs (viscous tears squirted out of a poorly concealed toy gun) until a stagehand is forced to remove her along with her obscenely large guitar. On her way out, Charlotte thrashes about in a pique of jealousy: "If those fucking bluebirds can fly, why the fuck can't I?"

The audience approves this juvenile stunt, stomping wildly. I shake my head yes! and bite my lip, silently debating the limits of courage. I mean, I could decide right now to leave everything the way it is; I could keep my dignity intact. But it's showtime. Somebody out there needs me. *I* need me if no one else is willing.

Deep inside a concealed pocket in my gown, I fondle the clear marble that Ollie Jonson gave me so many moons ago. It's just a little ball, but it seems to grow in my imagination, the model of a calm, clear world.

I climb through a narrow slit in the Mylar bubble and emerge clumsily, my billowing taffeta hoopskirt getting caught, as planned, and my oversized crown slipping down over my eyes so that I can officially see nothing. When I pull myself together, patting down the skirt and repositioning my headgear, I realize that mouths are gaping. For the moment, I am victorious: I look as foolish as I had hoped!

Gathering the material of my hoopskirt with both hands and flashing a brazen smile, I sashay to the edge of the stage and stare into the hearts of my paying customers. I screw off the star end of my sequined wand and toss it out into the ether. Somebody yells "Ow!" Then I finger a cigarette in my concealed pocket, slip it into the empty end of my wand, and proceed to light the tip with the long matchstick that has been holding up my bun. As I draw the matchstick from the heart of the bun, my voluptuous auburn tresses drop past my shoulders, almost dragging on the floor (I love the drama of a good wig!). I strike the match against the floor, and it sparks;

the cigarette catches fire; the audience wakes up. I inhale the Marlboro magnificently, then blow smoke into the eyes of the students in the front row. I want to direct the full weight of being human at my audience. Not as a weapon but as a wake-up call. I trust they're here to help me too. I *know* they're here to decide whether my show is competent enough for me to pass my finals, but also to consider who I am. This is a blessing of no small magnitude. I want to weep but remember that I have a show to do. I want to say, "I love you all, so please go home and be kind to yourselves, but think of me fondly at the same time." But my music cue sounds. Instead, I am compelled to share something universal and as old as the hills; at the same time, I am here to offer something unprecedented. Such is the burden of the Theater.

Clutching my chest with my free hand, I let go of a sigh heavier than a black hole. Then I amble center stage and address a young male student with cute whiskers and a pale, fawning girlfriend at his side. "Am I a good witch or a bad witch?" I do a turn on Glinda's line in the film, tilting my head to the side inquisitively.

The young student coughs and squirms in his seat, squeezing the hand of his fair lady even tighter. I reach out with both hands to let him know that I am totally at his mercy. But his head pulls back as if my presence is too rich.

"I repeat: Am I a good witch or a bad witch? That is the question. That is one hell of a question." I hear two more throats clear, then one nervous giggle flies free.

I throw up my hands to the heavens. "Oh my darlings, my poor unmagical darlings! I am so worn out, if I have to do one more good deed it will certainly break me."

I sense hostility from the young, smitten couple; the seen-it-all eyes of my professor narrow. But there are four students in the second row who are available to me, who have come here tonight to be converted. I swear it. I have a very good nose for transformation.

I begin to pace the apron, my hoopskirt trailing obediently. "Listen, my dears, to my nightmarish tale of goodness and judge for yourselves. At birth I was a good-as-gold witch. A baby mensch! This mensch grew up into the best little girl witch rat tails could buy. And today? As *tout le monde* knows, I am a full-blown, good-to-the-bone witch. Ptooey!"

From the audience, utter silence, the kind that burns like Arctic air.

"I mean, if I have no purpose other than serving up Goodness, life becomes empty real fast. So I ask you, is there life after Goodness? And where on earth do those bluebirds go after they've had their fill of ice cream and rainbows? I've certainly had mine." I cross stage left and mount Charlotte's stool. By now, I am smoking like a chimney. I have hitched my take-no-prisoners skirt up to my knees to reveal two pantalooned legs swinging madly in time with my soliloquy.

"Once upon a time Goodness meant everything to me. I helped the sick and the tired, the downtrodden and the untrodden. In fact, *all* the trodden were beholden to me. I poked my nose into other witches' business like *nobody's* business. I stopped the rain, reversed curses, made giddy proclamations that really worked. I enabled fish to fly and birds to swim, and escorted AWOL girls home to their aunties and uncles. This was very rewarding work, mind you. I was grateful to be handed a mission. But even the good, the excellent, the superlative, need a rest. We need to reveal another side. We need to 'get real.'

"It's not that I'm *not* a goody-goody. Jesus Christ! No one would recognize me without my peerless charitability. But I am other things too—things that most of you would rather not think about.

"Let me put it this way"—I lean toward the audience con-spiratorially—"I've a few feelings that have gone unnoticed, that need an outlet, that aren't . . . pretty. And if I don't allow them out, it could get ugly real fast. The Wicked Witch of the West wasn't the only bitch in town, you know. She had com-pany. I need you to know this if we are going to work to-gether."

To make my point, I snuff out my cigarette by dipping the tip of the wand in Charlotte's cold cappuccino. I stretch both arms over my head, stifle a yawn, then leap off the stool as if I am about to assault the audience. Instead, I run a frantic lap around the stage. Then a second lap. My hoopskirt bobs vio-lently up and down. When I am sufficiently breathless, I stop center stage and play with my hair like a nervous twit, strug-gling to compose myself.

"I can't tell you how sorry I am, how much I wanted to ful-fill your image of me. I wish I could keep my feelings to my-self like all the other witches. Glinda! Arghh! Even my name smacks of sweet, gooey things.

"I suppose you want details, facts. Okay, all right. Well, I have conflicted feelings about nearly all of my actions. Take that little girl, Dottie—Dorothy Gale of Kansas? Yes, *of course* she earned my intervention; she suffered profoundly before I tossed her the silver shoes and, later in the game, told her how to make the best use of her feet. But believe me—I swear on Oz's bald spot—Dottie was a whiner. And that dog of hers? He was a no-brainer, and *foul*. He stunk as badly as those mis-erable flying monkeys. But I am getting offtrack here. The point is, I helped the girl because her dreams created some-thing more powerful than my magic: they generated a great deal of barometric pressure in these parts. I mean, our cli-mate was *seriously* off-kilter. But while Dottie had launched the Cyclone of the Century, she was a total innocent. She just didn't have the *skills* to handle a Code Ten situation. So when she crushed the Wicked Witch of the East—Number Two, we called her—and then proceeded to get the willies, I had to take my best shot. I had to appear before Dottie as an object of Grace and Beauty, to dazzle her back to her senses. And this I did. I was the embodiment of equanimity, the all-loving, all-forgiving mother. And, it hurts to say this because, as a person of profound resources, I am truly this good—the goodness is not an act. But the goodness is mixed, more mixed than I care to let on.

"For example, on the day the Kansas girl partook of my generous magic, she did not know just *how* tired I was. For I was bone tired. I had been dealing with all manner of consequences from the cyclone. Emerald City was a mess, my hair was even worse, and the talking trees were tangled up in one hell of a knot. Add to that the death of an extremely uncharismatic witch and watch one's stress go through the roof!

"Although my bubble usually conceals a lot of emotional turmoil, I am certain the Munchkins caught sight of my nervous rash that day. And they *always* expect perfection. They would never allow me to be sharp or impatient, headachy or the slightest bit blue. Being a good witch is a kind of prison, you see. You have to wear dark sunglasses to mask the telltale flickers of depression."

I sit down on the edge of the stage and dangle my velvet-slippered feet. "This need to show all my moods has taken its toll. If only I could cast a spell on my own nature and make myself less ornery, more perfectly good! Even Dottie complained, 'You are certainly as good as you are beautiful. But you have not yet told me how to get back to Kansas.' See, everyone's a critic! Believe me, I was so spent that day it's a miracle I remembered the power of the silver shoes. By the way, they *are* silver. Hollywood had to go mess with their essence, turn them into *ruby slippers*. Didn't they read the original text?"

I remove my own slippers and toss them into the dimly lit air above the audience. "These are worthless! They have no special powers beyond looking really cool." I lock eyes with an older student who has "Women's Studies" written all over her. "I mean, they impressed *you*, didn't they?" She laughs heartily and flushes red. "Check out my posture," I instruct her. "A bit caved in for a good witch, no?" I slump as if all the magic has drained out through my toes. The woman nods in agreement. "Just once I would love to cackle like the Wicked Witch of the West, to paint the sky black, to tell my people that I am off duty." I leap up. "Yes, that's it! A little dab of evil goes a long way. I shall be moody and off duty. And needy? Yes, indeedy!"

I spin in circles on the stage, aglow with my decision to get real. My hoopskirt bounces up and down with renewed vigor. Too dizzy to focus, I stagger around the stage, intoxicated with the power of my new decree. Then I let go with an un-censored cackle: "Yaa-haa-haa-hee-hee-hee!"

"Oops!" I smirk like Wile E. Coyote, then cover my mouth with my hand. The trite background music, which has been hardly audible to this point, now swells to atonal extremes.

Totally green at acting evil, I try out all manner of curses:

"You mangy lion, you couldn't find courage if it was biting you on the butt."

"Hey, Scarecrow, you got crops for brains?"

"Yo, Tin Man! For a man without a heart you've got a really big—"

I am interrupted by a "little girl" with braids, wearing a blue gingham dress and ruffled apron—the indomitable Char-lotte—who is fleeing down the right aisle toward the stage, carrying a stuffed animal in an unusually large basket. She mounts the steps, stage left, bleating, "Oh dear, oh dear! The house must have fallen on her, Toto. Whatever shall we do?"

I cast a sarcastic glance at my audience: "Now doesn't that ring a bell?"

Charlotte/Dorothy skips in place, all perky and winded. I recite my lines dully as if reading cue cards: "You are welcome, most noble Sorceress, to the land of the Munchkins. We are so grateful to you for having killed the Wicked Witch of the East, and for setting our people free from bondage."

"Excuse me but . . . who the hell are you?" Charlotte demands in a falsely polite voice.

"Why, I am the Witch of the South. Who the—fudge—are you?" My struggle to exude warmth is painfully obvious.

But Charlotte isn't listening; she's making goo-goo talk to her stuffed pooch. "Toto, you are so furry-wurry. I wuv you so much, I could just crush you!" She smashes Toto into her nose, then abruptly throws him over her shoulder into the orchestra pit, with girlish insouciance. "Bad dog, you made a ugly-wuggly fart!"

The students cheer. I strut my stuff, hoopskirt empowering every move, over to Charlotte, and strike the classic Glinda pose: glittery wand in the air, silver crown glistening. I am oozing, leaking grace, all the power tools of my trade at my command.

"Are you a good witch or a bad witch?" I ask, fully in character.

"I'm not a witch at all!" Charlotte insists. "I'm Dorothy Gale from Kansas. Witches are old and ugly."

"But *I* am a good witch, and the people love me. I am not as powerful as the Wicked Witch was who ruled here, or I should have set the people free myself."

"You mean you have no power?" Charlotte whines.

"How unkind. How unjust!"

"I'm sorry, but I'm a little traumatized here. I don't have *time* to be just."

I let the audience see that my patience has run out. "Well,

you could go back where you came from, little girl. I hear Kansas is uncommonly *flat*. I mean that in the nicest way." I cross my arms and begin to walk away.

"Please don't leave me here, ma'am!" In a flash, Charlotte is down on her knees, begging at my heels, tugging on my legs so hard they're about to cave in. "Kansas is real pretty, but I don't have a mother there. And there's not anyone nearly as pretty as you."

I stop in my tracks but resist facing her. "Oh! Well, it must be a very unpleasant place then. And the name's not 'ma'am.' The name's Glinda the Good Witch, *Ms*. Good Witch to you."

"Okay, okay. Mrs. Goodwrench, can ya just steer me in the right direction? I'm very lost." Charlotte lets out a river of crocodile tears, supplying her own sympathetic "ohs" instead of waiting for sympathy from the audience.

I whip around to confront her. "Sure thing, dearie. Second to the right and then straight on till morning." I turn on my heel and proceed on my way with cartoonishly strident steps.

Charlotte stares blankly at the audience, scratching her head. Then she leaps once more for my ankles, causing me to trample on my hoopskirt. "Please don't give me that Peter Pan spiel! I know this ain't Never-Never Land."

"So we're disrespectful too? Unkind, unjust, disrespectful. And with painfully poor grammar. Little girl, obviously you have never been to charm school. So what is it?" I gesture grandly with the wand. "What exactly do you want from me?"

"I wanna go home to my Auntie Mame!" More crocodile tears. Charlotte's hidden squirt gun is working overtime.

"So we're talking direction? Mmm. Direction, direction, direction. It's what everybody wants and nobody has."

"Wow, that's really beautiful. Remind me to embroider that on a sampler when I get home."

"Now that's very hurtful, Dot. Remember, sarcasm will get you nowhere in Oz." I brighten. "Come closer so I may see who you really are." I practically poke her in the eye with the wand, insisting that she come within strangling range. Dorothy pitches herself so close to me, she's almost gagged by the flouncy ruffle on my bodice. Everyone can see that she's trembling, intimidated. Placing a maternal hand on each of her shoulders, I gaze into her eyes. "Oh, my dear, dear lass! Shall I tell you what I see?"

"Yeah, sure," she shakes her head up and down, "if it doesn't take too much of my time. I mean, *our* time."

"Oh, we have an agenda! Good, sit." With a firm push, I force her to the ground. Newly obedient, Dorothy looks up at me. "Listen girlie-girl, I hate to pull rank because I am older and wiser, but you might actually learn something here."

"Yeah, sure, sure." Dorothy puts on her best student face.

"So, where shall I begin? At the beginning?"

"Oh, shit!" Dorothy hisses under her breath.

"Okay, I will begin at the end. How about the end?"

"Sounds fine to me."

"Yes, I will begin at the end and end up at the beginning."

"I think that's called mind fucking," Dorothy whispers to the audience.

"Oh, how colorful! I shall remember that, dear girl. So let us begin. In the end, you realize that you have always been home, that there's no place else to go, that you carry your home with you wherever you go, that home is not really a place but a belief that you are cared for, that you are loved fully, that your imagination takes you to new places but also brings you back to yourself. That home is a portable concept. Got it?"

Dorothy nods mechanically.

"And in the beginning, you realize that you are walking on an endless road paved with golden opportunity, that you are in for a great adventure. In the middle, you assess correctly that this adventure requires an inordinate amount of suffering, that the obstacles in your path appear insurmountable but tend to disappear when you remember who you are. And, all the while, you have the sneaking suspicion that this adventure is a dream from which you long to awaken. Now, how does that fit?"

Dorothy nods again, seemingly with new reverence.

"Good. Now we are getting somewhere."

"But where?"

"Ah, that stuff was the easy part. Now on this adventure, especially when things get hairy and you are without direction, it's important to remember to treat all humans and beasts well—even though you perceive this is a dream. In other words, you might think twice before flinging your dog or criticizing someone who cares about you. Someone like . . . me, *par exemple.*"

Dorothy looks up, flabbergasted. "But why should you care about *me?* A girl without a mother?"

"What else could I do? You are deserving."

"But you were so harsh with me." She stares dejectedly at the ground.

"Oh, that. Well, I was mirroring your own harshness. For every curse you place on me, for every instance of disrespect, I know that you are doubly hard on yourself."

"You mean, you *like* me?"

"Well, I can *remember* to like you," I say, tenderly patting her head. "At least that is my intention. I can remember if I focus on who you really are."

"So who am I?"

"Oh dear!" I gasp. "I'm not sure." We regard each other in silence.

"You're not sure?" Dorothy shrieks. "That is, like, really scary. What kind of a witch are you?"

"We're all students here," I shrug, inviting her forgiveness.

"What? What kind of an answer is that? I wanna talk to a smarter witch!"

"You do, do you?" I administer a tiny pinch to her nose.

"Yes, I insist on it!"

"Very well. I will leave you now." I warmly embrace Dorothy, but she manages to wriggle free.

"Please send in the next witch," she commands.

I laugh extravagantly.

"What are you laughing at?"

"My dear, I'm laughing because *you* are a smarter witch. After all, you created a cyclone of grand proportions. Therefore, I will leave you with yourself. Good-bye and Godspeed." I blow her a kiss and exit in a flourish, catching my crown on the heavy curtains, stage right.

Dorothy/Charlotte sits crosslegged on the stage, shifting restlessly and pouting. Bored, she takes her squirt gun out in full view of the audience and spritzes her eyes, eventually soaking her entire head in stage tears while forcing out blubbering sounds. "Oh woe! Oh woe! I'm really screwed now!"

Nothing happens. Apparently nobody cares. Scared, she tosses away the water gun, then leaps up to fish Toto out of the orchestra pit. She sits down again and begins to rock in place, cradling Toto in her arms and stroking his coat of acrylic fur. Visibly calmer, Dorothy breaks out in a toothy grin. Then, with a great deal of exaggeration, she scratches the crown of her head. "Toto, I'm having a major thought. This could be very, very big!" She makes the dog say "Ruff! Dorothy is smart!" in response.

"Guess what, Toto? Glinda said this place could very well be our home. That *I* could be a home. That this is the direction. Can you believe that? I'm somebody with a direction!"

It soon becomes clear that real tears are rolling down Dorothy's cheeks. She forces Toto to lick the sides of her face and bark, "Ruff! Yum! Real salt!"

Pricking up their ears, the audience hears the theme most fondly associated with the Emerald City: "You're out of the woods, you're out of the dark, you're out of the night / Step into the sun, step into the light."

Dorothy springs to a standing position, hands on hips, looking confident for such a gawky creature. The lights dim around her, creating a small pool of light. Then, in the silliest spoof of Bergman's *Persona* ever conceived, footage of Dorothy's face is projected onto a large scrim center stage alongside footage of Glinda's face. In seconds, the two faces merge into one—Dorothy into Glinda, Glinda into Dorothy. And then a third face joins them: the face of Margaret Hamilton, the most celebrated Wicked Witch of the West. In seconds, her scary mug has merged into the combined personae of Glinda/Dorothy. And this new face, still recognizable for its equal parts Glinda, Dorothy, and the Wicked Witch, radiates peace and love like a feminized Buddha.

An explosion of light and smoke ignites the spot where Dorothy just stood. When the smoke clears, the audience sees Glinda (me!) standing in Dorothy's place, Dorothy's white apron tied to the waist of my bouffant skirt, her picnic basket slipped over my arm. Toto has been stuffed back in the basket, and a strange happiness has invaded my whole being.

I raise one eyebrow and address the audience. "I've found my way back, boys and girls. I've found my real goodness: it's an exotic blend not unlike black tea. A little bitter, a little sweet, a little nutty." I kiss Toto a bit lewdly, eventually coming up for air. "When you're whole, there's no place you can't go! Embroider that, my dears."

Newly young at heart, I skip down to the apron, returning to the young couple I had originally embarrassed. "Hi," I wave politely. I sit down and dangle my legs over the edge of the stage. "Thanks for listening," I say in my own voice, as Lorna. "You were great. No kidding." I reach out to make contact, and this time, the entwined man and woman grab hold of my hands. "Now it's time for your story," I tell them. "I promise to listen to *you*."

The lights go black; I creep offstage. On tape, we hear Charlotte finishing her acoustic-guitar version of "Over the Rainbow." But this time, no expletives, just a sweet, soulful rendition that soars high on the last note and hovers there.

Once behind the curtain, I exhale a breath as full as my hoopskirt and shed my hefty auburn wig. I hear a robust, affectionate round of applause, and can hardly believe it—everybody knows my secret and I'm still here! I hold myself tight just to make sure.

Sister Savior

1972

phone booth in the middle of a meadow. Surrealism at its finest. But this is my realism, my twice-a-year phone call to Lonnie. A mission impossible provoked by 182 days of accumulated guilt. At least in a meadow I can savor the distance between us, can rock the glassy sides of the booth when I can no longer bear to hear her litany of woes. I can lay my head down on the plush Yellow Pages and sigh, pretending my life is here in a meadow that knows nothing of wild sisters. At least I'm not *there*, with her in the trenches. The trenches of madness. I should make a point to write that down. But I have never been able to write about Lonnie. It would take some distance, no? Like about six thousand years.

It's moderately warm, but I'm bundled up in typical Santa Cruz garb: long-sleeved thermal underwear shirt, a fifties

Mexican peasant skirt, chubby Guatemalan sweater, yellow construction-worker boots. A Navajo necklace of silver birds rings my neck. The look is ethnically indecisive, but I am flaunting it. I believe that clothes should confuse, that identity should be fluid. But these clothes won't protect me from feeling terrible when I hear Lonnie's voice. My clothes will surely fail me.

Debi, the dorm supervisor, made me do it, made me call her. A week ago, Debi received an urgent call from my mother, who disclosed to this complete stranger that Lonnie had attempted suicide with one of Daddy's razor blades. And just for show, she had arrayed her backup plans on her bedspread: a bread knife, a vial of pills, and a red-and-green-striped jump rope. On the phone, Mother had intimated to Debi "how helpful it would be if Lorna checked on her little sister."

Little sister! Because I am in the trenches myself right now—coincidentally I have been cast as a suicidal nurse in an avant-garde country-western musical—it's taken a week to find the time to make the call. Really, I have been sensationally busy, totally committed to this play, and couldn't come up for air let alone *think* of dealing with this thing that's a part of me and yet far, far away. It has been exciting to forget who she is, my sister. The kind of amnesia that's permissible. I mean, who can live in a state of complete remembrance? Wouldn't that be masochistic?

Anyway, I am in a rare good mood, on a delicate high, and really can't entertain a puncture wound right now. I am in a selfishly good mood and refuse to give it up. The role of Sally the Fallen Nurse allows me to wail, croon, and occasionally crack wise. I even get what we in the theater call "a moment," a scene where I swallow a whole bottle of pills, stagger to my bed, and then, when the audience is certain I am "buying the farm," sit up and belt out a ballad. About the cardiologists I have known and loved. How each one has broken my heart but has the technical know-how to put it back together. Yes, the director's given me the rare chance to sing, with express instructions to sound "as bad as you do in real life." With this role, I've discovered a new secret weapon: I enjoy making people laugh almost as much as moving them deeply. When I can do both at once, I am beside myself!

Until now, I never realized how caring it is to be funny. Humor had always been a distraction from important things, not the business of healing. God, if you could melt someone's insides *and* make them titter at the same time, it would be like practicing medicine. And here I thought the only way you could teach people The Truth was by shooting arrows at their hearts. Before now, pain and suffering had been my medium, the key to waking up the masses. Adrift in a world of sunny Los Angelenos, I had looked upon anything less than pain and suffering as shallow or stupid. Well, stupid, shallow me!

The air is hotter than I expected, the meadow alive with insects and musty leaf smells. I am perched on a tiny phone-booth bench that only supports half my butt. My left hand robotically takes the receiver as my unsteady right hand punches in a series of digits that I swear I will never memorize. Lonnie has moved so often now that it does no good to envision her in any particular place. I prefer picturing her in a cabin in the woods, or on a ranch, to the endless stream of halfway houses and state-run homes to which she's been exiled. In the months since she left the Sunland home (after punching a schizophrenic teenager who insisted on calling her a "her"), Lon has kept moving at a breakneck pace, the result of starting and being drawn into heated, bruising arguments. She's even set fire to two of her nastier residences, leaving small black scars that, she explained, marked her bitter frustration with "the system" and condemned the heartless treatment and poor food she routinely receives. She's a fighter, my sister. The kind that goes up in flames.

I clear my throat of as much tension as possible; it's been six or seven months since we've spoken, and I know I'm going to get it.

"Hello, I'd like to speak with Lonnie, I mean Johnny Person," I say to a man who recites the alphabet as he answers the phone. Should I have expected less?

"You want to speak to a person? I don't know any persons! A-B-C-D!" he shouts, then hangs up the phone.

I try again, punching in the number more confidently this time.

A new voice answers on the eighth ring, a woman who sounds drugged to the point of oblivion. "Uh-huh?"

"Yes, is this Lemon Tree Lodge . . . in Bakersfield? This is Johnny Person's sister. May I speak with . . . him, please?"

I hate this change in pronouns more than anything. As much as I want to honor Lonnie's request to refer to her as a man, I desperately want to call her "my sister." The wrong pronoun can give me serious indigestion. Although the state of California has refused Lon's demands for a sex-change operation—she flunked the psychological tests—Lon is adamant that everyone at her residences treat her as a male. Anyone who doesn't go along with this pretense ends up with a knuckle sandwich.

Despite my liberal outlook, I wonder if I will ever be able to go along with this male business. I wonder, too, how Lon looks. Mother tells me the state *has* approved of Lon taking bus trips to the Gay and Lesbian Health Center in Hollywood to receive male hormone pills. This scares the hell out of me, but if it makes her/him happy . . .

"I said, may I speak to Johnny, please?"

"Ya wanna speak with Johnny so'll get Johnny. Is this okay

with you, it's okay with me." The medicated woman is very good at reception.

"Yes, it's perfectly okay with me," I answer in a squeaky voice. But she's gone; the phone must be hanging by the cord, because I hear a lot of background noise: baseball game on the radio, running footsteps, and what sounds like an argument or a cop show. Through the glass of the phone booth, I see a lone cow in the meadow and blow her a kiss. Or is it a *him?* I pretend to hum, which is absurd since I'm really not a hummer.

Lonnie finally picks up the phone. "Hey, Ooze, it's me. The Big Hulk. What's cooking?" She breathes heavily into the receiver, her voice lower than any man I know.

"Hi, sweetie. It's your good-for-nuttin' sister." She cracks up. "I'm checking in because I heard you were having a rough time. Are you in one piece? Because I know you hate to wake up and find yourself in more pieces than you can count on your fingers."

More supportive laughter. Then she changes gears. "Uh, Ooze? Can ya get me out of this joint? I gotta come live with you. This place is tearing me up just like you said."

Gulp. "Honey, you know that won't work, I don't have any money. I'm just a student. I don't even have a place for you."

"Yeah, but you have room for your boyfriend, the dumb-waiter, I mean dumb *painter!*"

"What a potshot! The painter is out of the picture, so to speak. A very dumb move on his part." Wow, Lonnie is right: he *is* a dumb painter. Mother must have told her about Will Boone, an art student I went out with for three weeks. He subscribed to the Ashcan school of painting—a little late to catch that wave—but he didn't subscribe to me. "I don't even know where he is or what he's doing."

"Probably molesting little kids."

"Lon!" I shriek appropriately. "No fair. He was a good guy."

"But he left ya in the gutter, riddled with bullet holes."

I have to admit she's right again. "Yes, Lon, he did manage to shoot me through and through. Metaphorically."

"Nah. He used real bullets," she maintains. "My little sister is full of lead."

"And *you* are full of it!"

She laughs at my joke in her punctuated way—heh-heh-heh—like a dirty old man. "Yeah, I really *am* no good. I'm rotten to the core. *I* should be shot, not you. I can't even go to college—they wouldn't let me through those pearly gates."

"That's not true," I counter, but I have no defense. No one in their right mind *would* let Lonnie, with her wrong mind, through. "Lon, let's get off this subject and on to one that's more appetizing."

"Yeah, Ooze, let's talk about chewing up my baby sister and spitting her out!"

"That's not what I had in mind," I say, ever the prude. "How's your drawing coming along?"

"Aw, let's not talk about that. I'm not doing the drawing thing because these bastards just don't understand my pictures. They're scared shitless of my anatomically correct mutants. And well they should be!" Lonnie's volume is now cranked to the max.

"Well, what about your writing? Are you writing any devilishly good poems?"

"Poems, yeah! But nobody here can read. I mean, I'm locked up with idiots!"

"Then why don't you send some poems to your idiot sister?" She usually loves this line of thinking.

"Yeah, I'll send you some shit. But really, Oozy, ya gotta get me out of here. I'm dying!"

My heart, already sunk to my stomach, threatens to hit the ground. "I know," I sympathize, "it must be awful not having an audience for your work." It's ironic that we share the same concerns for our art. But as weird as my poems get, they can't touch her necrophilia-themed light verse, her drawings of creatures with multiple penises that wave like menacing tendrils in worlds beyond my ken. In the two years since Lonnie's been living away from home, the naive gangster stories of her past have given way to morbid pornographic tales and sketches. If I stumbled onto these pictures without knowing the artist, I'd pray he was locked away for good!

"Lon, let's play a game. I'll ask you to make up names for things. For example: If you had your own rock band, what would you call it?"

"Yeah, heavy metal, AC/DC, what a blast! I would call my band the Anus Angels, heh-heh."

"Mmm. Let's try something else—"

"I don't wanna play no more stinkin' games. I want you to get me outta here—pronto!"

"Lon, I have no power. You know I have no power."

"You have *all* the power, you people on the outside are reekin' with it! Listen, I am isolated with stupidity. The caretakers here are a bunch of ignorant assholes. They treat me like a criminal."

"Okay, Lonnie, calm down. Sounds like something really bad has happened to you."

"You bet your bippy! They think I took Lester's radio and are accusing me of being a no-good thief!"

"So, did you or didn't you take it? I mean, why did they pick on you?"

"Because if you're isolated with a bunch of nuts, no one believes you. I am totally bad because no one believes me. That's the worst thing that can happen to a guy. They claim they want to hear both sides of the story, but they don't want to hear."

"How awful for you," I sigh.

"Yeah, awful ain't the word, it's downright heinous. I've just suffered too many bad days here. I'm totally disgusted with this place. The workshop where we make these outrageous pet toys is closed, so there's no more dough to buy live rats for my snakes. There's nothing to do here but smoke and watch the box. Everybody here just smokes and watches soap operas and game shows. I don't want to be suppressed like all these pod people. I don't want to end up like Charles Manson. I'm not a criminal, but if they say I am, I must be as bad as Charlie. I deserve to be here."

"Oh, honey, don't say that. Believe in yourself, not what they think of you. But listen to me, did you or didn't you take the radio?"

"Uh, Ooze, I'm not a thief. I just borrowed the thing to listen to the baseball game. I returned it, and then Lester lost it. I'm not a lousy crook. They—Mrs. Schnook-face and her cronies who run this joint—better not lay a hand on me, because I *choose* who lays a hand on me. If anyone puts his hand on me, it's because I let them!"

Oh God, we've ended up here; I hate this particular turf. "So, sweetie," I sigh for the umpteenth time, "where would you go if you could get away?" I'm closing my eyes so that even the pretty meadow and the cow will disappear.

"I'd take my show to Hollywood Boulevard, where things are a-happening, if ya catch my drift. Where people like me are tolerated. Where all kinds of weirdos peacefully coexist. By the way, you people are destroying the environment!"

"Yeah, yeah, yeah." She's been saying this since I was a tot. You people. We really are villains in her book. "So, let's recap: you want to move to the city, where you think life is easier?"

"Yeah. Where I can get a sex-change operation and buy exotic pets and decorate my groovy pad."

"But every time you've lived in the city people have been less . . . sympathetic . . . less kind to you. The city is a merciless place, remember?"

"Ooze, if you don't rescue me I don't know what I'll do. Meeshy won't let me live with her and her new boyfriend. She loves him more than me!"

"Now Lon, that's just not true."

For a second, I wonder if it *is* true. Kenny Mink, Mother's first gentleman friend since she divorced Daddy last year, has given her a new lease on life. He makes her laugh by tenderly crooning "People" and substituting our last name: "Persons . . . persons who need persons . . . are the luckiest persons in the world."

Mother and Kenny seem determined to have a better life—they go dancing at sports bars in the Valley and take bucolic road trips to Santa Fe and Montecito. They love to go out for Sunday brunch at the local Jewish deli, snuggling up with each other and the *Los Angeles Times*. One of the new sensitive males, Kenny's even in therapy. He's showered Mother with flasks of Babe perfume and is openly affectionate. The few times I've met him, he seemed genuinely decent, a real find. Because of this, Lon and I can't be too sure if Mother and Kenny's "better life" campaign includes us.

"Lon, you know Mother deserves to have a good life."

"Yeah, a life without *me*, Conan the Barbarian."

I just can't stand this. I'm at my limit, *was* at my limit minutes ago. Body gone limp, I tell Lonnie it's time for me to go, that I must leave my little booth and go into the forest to screw my head back on. I'm hoping she'll catch *my* drift, understand the need for head screwing.

"Leave your little booth? Booth-schmooth! Ooze, I'm demanding that you come here and rescue me or it will be on your head. My murder will be on your head."

Just like all the other deaths she's ascribed to me. In Lonnie's eyes, I am a serial killer. But like most murderers, I feel altogether powerless. "Okay, Lonnie. I'll come see you for a short visit. You can read your poetry and show me your drawings."

"You'll really come, Ooze? You'll visit my Chamber of Horrors?"

"Meeshy tells me it's a regular museum. A treasure trove of terrifying knickknacks."

"They're part of my body, Oozy. You'll see. You'll go native out here in the boonies. Ya can take the country out of the crazies but ya can't take the crazies out of the country!"

"Uh-huh, gotta go now. Energy almost gone."

"Yeah, I really drained your blood just like always, I'm a good-for-nothing—"

"Stop it right now! I won't allow you to say bad things about yourself."

"Then why did you abandon me in this hell-house if you care so much? Huh?"

"Gotta go, no more oxygen in the booth. They're sucking it out. Aghhhh. Bye."

"Bye, Oozy."

I throw the glass door open and slump in a heap outside the booth. I slip off my heavy sweater and spread it over my face. The afternoon light creeps through the thick weave, and I try to blink it away. For a long time, I lie motionless on a floor of prickly brown grass and listen to the crickets and frogs and birds. If I had an ounce of energy left, it would take a particle physicist to find it.

The Dance

1972

t's noon and I'm not even halfway to Lonnie's halfway house. The bus ride to Bakersfield—"Baked-to-Hell" in Lonnie's book—takes five hours. That means five anxious hours to prepare myself for the visit or five precious hours to spend adrift in fantasy.

I made the choice at birth. Eyes closed, I am already committed to a scenario wherein Dick Cavett is interviewing me about my life as a poet-slash-actress. I field his questions with a poise and honesty unusual for my age, and with more than a soupçon of wit. This fantasy is not idle play; the interview gives me a way to discover if I have anything to say for my twenty years, anything to add to human discourse. All my life I've wondered whether I even *had* a philosophy. I mean, you can't just go out and buy one. I wonder why a person can't be recognized for her inner life instead.

"Why can't a person be recognized for her inner life?" I ask Dick Cavett.

"I'm sorry, I don't quite grasp what you mean."

"I mean, I wish that a person's merit wasn't based on a fully developed philosophy. That takes time, you know. What's worse is that our culture judges people on their personality— cute quips, bright remarks, batted eyelashes—stuff I don't have," I explain, uncertain whether I have batted my lashes in the process.

"What do you propose in its place?" Dick puts me on the spot. The audience grows awfully quiet.

"I propose that a person be judged for his or her degree of self-reflection, on the depth of his empathy and on . . . his or her choice of shoes!" The audience gasps. "I mean, really ugly shoes can destroy a person's whole appeal."

Dick smiles like a leprechaun. "Okay, Ms. Fashion Police, what do you think of *my* shoes?"

"Oh, Dick," I fawn, "you're a *king* of self-reflection, plus your wing tips are to die for! They're so polished you can see your reflection in the leather. Yep, high aesthetic marks all around."

"Thanks, kid. Now tell me a little about your family."

"Well, I grew up in the San Fernando Valley. But I was not a beach babe, I never learned how to tan. My mother is a divorced housewife who is just beginning to raise her feminist consciousness, and my father works in television. He wrote a couple of *Rawhide* episodes and has written a great pilot about Peace Corps spies—"

Impatient with this chitchat, Dick cuts to the chase. "I hear you have an unusual sister."

"Unusual? Well, I really don't know what to say." I go blank.

Help, Dick. The idea of Lonnie doesn't seem to produce any words.

Picking up on my fear, Dick switches the subject. "Uh, haven't you been cast as Glinda the Good Witch a phenomenal number of times?"

"Oh, yeah, about fifty times! But I love her. She's great."

"Then would you mind doing a little Glinda for us today? I hear you do a mean Billie Burke impression."

"Oh, I don't know . . . I really couldn't." I shift in the leather chair, my face heating up under the merciless lights.

Smelling blood, the audience begins to applaud, then yelp, encouraging me to do the Glinda-shtick. I shake my head and my hands, protesting all the way.

"Come on, Lorna," coaxes Dick. "Just a smidgen of Glinda, or is it a glidgen of Sminda?"

I let go with a laugh and prepare to cave in. Giving the audience what they want is a famous person's duty.

When my fantasy fizzles, I am left with the echo of two conversations from the night before. As much as I try to fill my head with thoughts of an imaginary boyfriend or a new sitcom starring *moi,* I can't hear anything but my parents' voices. Before embarking on this trek, I had telephoned Daddy, then Mother, explaining that I needed some tips, needed to know what to expect. Would I be able to look at Lon without flinching? Would her behavior prove too disturbing, even for me? Lonnie is famous for her shock appeal and I wanted to be as informed as possible.

I had caught Daddy in a chipper mood, almost verging on frisky. "I've just bought the most amazing Siamese fighting fish, Lorna. The colors are knockouts. You've never seen such beauts!"

"Uh-huh, Daddy, that's great. Hope you're doing well."

"Yeah. Well, as well as can be expected since your mother

left me." He exhaled audibly, then spoke something unintelligible to the fish.

"Daddy? Are you still there?"

"Lorna, one of my guys just leaped into the other guy's bowl. I better call you back. I got a wrestling match on my hands."

"Daddy, I can't call back, I'm leaving for Bakersfield tomorrow morning to see Lonnie and need some advice."

"Lorna, you wouldn't believe the fight that's going on!" I heard some faint splashing sounds and imagined Daddy trying to separate two badass fish.

"Daddy?"

"Almost lost one, Lorna. These specialty fish are very expensive. Do you wanna guess how much I paid?"

"No, Daddy. I want to ask about Lonnie."

"Lonnie? Same old story. Last time she visited, she stole twenty dollars from me and raided the medicine cabinet. Your sister's very cunning, you know. She's gotten even more crafty since she left us."

"She didn't exactly *leave* us."

"Oh yeah? Well, you weren't around, Miss Bleeding Heart, when we managed to move her into the first home. It was a nightmare to get her things packed and get her settled in, only to move her out three weeks later after she slugged the supervisor."

"Lon slugged the supervisor because the bastard called her an idiot!"

"Well, she was acting like one, wasn't she? Listen, Lorna, your sister is not going to get any better, so don't try to put a gloss on everything she does. You are going to have to face the facts. Someday, when you're in charge of her, you'll finally understand why I say the things I do. She just exhausted your mother and me. You'll know this firsthand in about twenty years."

Getting worked up, I began breathing little clouds on the glass of the booth, writing my name in the condensation.

"So," Daddy continued, "let me tell you about this redhead I'm dating. Selma. Selma Sands. She's a widow with three grown daughters—her family's kind of like a female version of *Bonanza*. There's a heavy, jolly daughter; a pretty, shy one; and a dark, mysterious girl."

"That's great, Daddy." I was too tired to upbraid him about calling a woman a "girl."

"Great, yeah. But Selma's not as young or pretty as your mother. And she doesn't like sex."

"Oh, well, maybe you can change her mind," I offered, uptight about talking about parents and sex in the same breath.

"Nope, don't think so. The women of my generation were taught to hate sex. They hate it! So, uh, how's school?"

"Um, fine. I was in that country-western avant-garde musical, you know? The one I sent you an invitation to?"

"Oh, right. Did I tell you about that Western I want to write? Not a pilot, a *feature-length* Western."

"No," I gulped and wrote the word "no" on the glass with a big exclamation point after it.

"Well, it's probably going nowhere. Sooo . . . let me tell you more about Selma and me. We're thinking of tying the notorious knot."

"Marriage! Daddy, so soon?"

"It's not soon enough for me. I hate living alone."

"Do you, um, love her?"

"Hey, I like her. She's good company. Things are comfortable, what's wrong with that? Her daughters are all very smart."

"Okay, but what about *her*? You're not marrying her daughters."

"Don't get smart with me."

"But Daddy, you *know* I'm smart, I'm just as smart as her daughters."

"Yeah, you're a brain, but theater isn't going to get you a cent in this world. And poetry? Forget it."

"All right, Daddy," I conceded, "maybe I'll follow in your footsteps into television." He said nothing. "Well, congratulations if you really are going to marry Selma. I want you to be happy, of course."

"Yeah, happiness," Daddy repeated, his voice drifting off.

"I'll write you a poem for the wedding and then I'll sell it for big money to Hallmark," I teased him. "Listen, I don't have much time here. There's another student waiting to use the pay phone." I held up two fingers to the glass to signal "two more minutes" to a young man in army fatigues waiting outside the booth. "So Daddy, quickly, do you have any last-minute advice for me when I see Lonnie?"

"Advice? Jeez, I don't know, Lorna. Just don't let her near your purse. She's a devious one, your sister. Always looking to steal something from you. But, uh, tell her you care. Hell, you know what to tell her. Tell her we *all* care about her. Tell her that."

"Okay, I will. Bye now."

"You really got to come down and see the fish. You can't imagine how gorgeous they are. And Selma would like to meet you. Her daughters are all professionals—one's an orthodontist, one's an OB/GYN, one's a lawyer for Lockheed."

"Great, the military-industrial complex. That's really impressive."

"Hey, *you* might consider a job at Lockheed. You can always write poetry on the side."

"Okay, Daddy. Love you. Bye."

"Sure. Uh, take care. Good-bye then."

I hung up the phone, exchanged places with the young man in fatigues, and let out a gallon of air. Then I walked in ungainly circles around the booth until it was free again.

My call to Mother was shorter and less painful, except she repeated everything I said to Kenny Mink, her new lover.

"Mother? It's me, Lorna."

"Lorna! How wonderful! Kenny, honey, guess who's on the telephone? It's Lorna. Kenny says hello, Lorna."

"Hello, Kenny," I said dutifully.

"Kenny, Lorna says hello to you."

"Mother, I don't have a lot of time. I'm seeing Lonnie tomorrow, you know, and I was hoping you had some advice for me. It's been so long, I'm a bit scared."

"Well, there's no reason to be. Lon's so excited to see you, she's called me three times this week. She wants you to be prepared, though. She's heavier than you've ever seen her, huge, actually. She's also on medication that slows her down a bit—this really embarrasses her—and she's binding her breasts now, with wide surgical tape. What? Oh, Kenny wants you to know that Lon needs all of our support."

"Of course," I groaned.

"Kenny, Lorna says she knows that."

"Mother! I really need to feel that I'm talking only to you, okay? No offense to Kenny. Now what's this about Lon's breasts? Will binding them hurt her? I mean, can it cause cancer or something?"

"Lorna, I'm not happy about it either, but binding her breasts makes Lon feel more confident. If her housemates see her looking more like a man, they'll treat her like a man."

"God!"

"I know. And for your information, the reason I tell Kenny everything you tell me is because he *is* part of this conversation. He's a big part of my life now. You'll have to get used to it."

"Fine. I just need to know that your attention is here, Mother, with me."

"Sweetheart, I *know* you needed more attention from me when you were little, and I can't do anything about the past—"

"Let's not get into this," I begged her, rolling my eyes and twisting a couple of split ends until they broke off.

"Okay, we can follow your rules. What do you want me to say next? Just give me instructions."

I shrugged, but of course she couldn't see me. Mother sounded newly aggressive, more in command than I was accustomed to. Although I was proud that she had, in feminist terms, located her source of power, her new tone of voice made me uneasy. Would she now be impervious to my criticism, to my attempts to blame her for everything that had ever gone wrong?

"Mother. I simply want *you* to have a conversation with *me.* Then, when you get off the phone, tell Kenny whatever you'd like. You can share anything with him that you feel is important. That part's up to you."

After a formal pause, I heard, "Okay. I can do that. Kenny!" her voice rang out. "I'm not going to relay everything Lorna says, okay?"

"Great, Mother," I sighed, disappearing into tangles of wavy, unkempt hair. "It sounds like you guys are really close now. I'm happy to hear that."

"Yes, Kenny makes me feel, oh I don't know, extra special. Like I have some value in the world."

"Your mom is worth a billion dollars!" Kenny hollered in the background.

"Tell Kenny I agree with him, that I'm pleased you found a billionaire who can afford you!"

"I will, honey."

"Um, Mother, one more thing. Daddy just told me that Lonnie will never get better. He said *never*. Do you believe that? I mean, that's not how I see it. We shouldn't limit Lonnie like that. Don't you think she could get better someday, if she, like, had a great teacher the way Helen Keller did?"

"Yes," Mother replied, her voice shaking with conviction. "Yes, I do. I believe Lonnie just might surprise us someday."

"Thanks for saying that," I said, sniffing up tears. "Bye now, better go."

"Lorna, remember: I love you."

I sipped in some air through my clogged nose. "Yeah, love you too, Mother. Love you too."

Then I placed the receiver in its cradle, sat down on the little bench in the booth, and covered my face with both hands.

I I I

Glancing at the world through the bus window, I've been working on the nail of my left thumb for more than an hour. I'm always challenging myself to leave it alone, but nevertheless I'm drawn to its ragged edge, its almost glowing physical reality. Chewing on this nail, what is left of it, does not comfort me, but I enjoy the fact that it is always there for me to grab hold of—something you can't say about people.

I keep hiding the nail from myself, sitting on my hand for a few seconds at a time, until a magnetism, like a tractor beam on *Star Trek*, tugs this hand directly in front of my mouth, lures my thumb to my lips, and plunges the thumbnail hard against my teeth for one more round. Telling myself not to indulge, not to give in, reminding myself of the shame and the ugliness that follow in the wake of chewed-up fingers, I notice that the black woman sitting across the aisle—she's wearing a "Save the Whales" T-shirt, Levi's, a colorful batik turban, and purple high-top sneakers—is watching me. Okay, I won't bite 'em into oblivion while someone is watching, but there'll be a next time, I swear it.

The woman smiles at me, revealing huge, square teeth and gums that go on for miles. I like her already. She says, "You have pretty eyes," and I wonder if she's trying to distract me from my nails.

"Thanks," I wince, then regard my lap intently as if I were studying the weave of my sweater.

"You have shyness too?" she asks with a lilt.

"Yes, I have that in spades," I answer, head bowed. Of all the dumb American phrases!

"My name is Sabine." She reaches into the aisle, and I shake her hand; it's lovely, with beautiful, unvarnished nails. A worker's hand.

"I'm from West Africa. I'm on my way to see my brother's son. How do you say, my uncle?"

"Your nephew," I answer. "I'm on the way to see family too—my sister."

My face is trying to look pleasant, but a sullenness must be leaking through, because she asks, "But you're troubled?"

"Yeah, I suppose I am," I tell her. "My sister lives in a place that's full of trouble."

"But you are bringing it with you?" she asks in all innocence, or maybe she's telling me. It's hard to know.

"I suppose I am," I repeat. "My sister is living in a government-run house, a place for those who don't fit in. A place with other people who aren't well—well, *she's* not well. It's a sad, sad place . . ." I realize that I am trying to break down the complexity of my sister's life for this foreigner, like I'm speaking to a child. I want to protect her from what I know.

"I don't understand," Sabine tells me. She's playing with a heavy necklace of shells and smiling inappropriately.

"My sister is considered 'crazy' in this culture," I try to explain, gesturing like an academic. "She can't take care of herself, she can't be counted on to wash herself. Sometimes she removes her cowboy boots and I see feet that haven't been washed in months. She screams a lot. She fights a lot. She's interested in stuff that's dark. Very dark." I look up at Sabine, her radiant smile still catching the morning light, and blush. *She's* very dark, after all, and I don't know if I have offended her.

"Ah, ghosts and shadows."

I nod and purse my lips. "Maybe. She doesn't make sense a whole lot of the time."

"No!" the woman yells, almost violently, and slaps her knees with both hands. The other bus passengers regard us crossly. "She *must* be listened to. There is screaming for a reason. She has an important message, yes?"

"A message?" I ask, already tearful. I am that wide open.

"You must listen to the screaming ones," Sabine continues. "Certain people scream because of what's inside them. Like, you know, having bees in the mouth. But after the message is delivered, these special ones can rest. You will see."

I study my lap again. "We—my parents and I—*tried* to listen to Lonnie when she was little. But when she spoke, her feelings came out exaggerated, so much bigger than most people's, that they blew us away."

"I do not understand," Sabine said, matter-of-factly. "She blew on you?"

"No, I mean her feelings pushed us away. For example, my sister howls and cups her ears if someone at a restaurant even drops a spoon on a plate. The first time she tasted chocolate, she thought it was the most horrible thing in the world. Then, after a few weeks, she decided that Nestlé Crunch bars were heaven and couldn't get enough of them. When she was just five, she complained about the smog, the noise in the city, how cruel people are. I guess she told a truth that was too painful to hear, so maybe we shut it out. Frankly, she wore us out. I mean, she constantly reminded us that the world is too painful to live in. Who could listen to *that*?"

Listening to my own story, my age-old rationalizations, I remind myself that I am equally kind and cruel. I have sinned against Lonnie, have avoided her like the plague and have also given her everything I have: my entire childhood. What was left after that?

Sabine silently removes her necklace and I wonder if she's going to bestow it on me. "*Listen again.* Your sister has a message that's not about pain. The pain came later, when no one would listen." Sabine smiles at me with the commanding teeth and gums, then closes her eyes. Just when I think she's nodding off, her eyes pop open and she removes her contact lenses. "These are killing me," she confides and slips on some dorky Buddy Holly glasses.

"Thanks for your advice," I whisper, and shift in her direction. I reach across the aisle to make physical contact, to tap her gently on the shoulder. "I'm Lorna, from Los Angeles."

She sees my hand floating in the aisle and impulsively grabs me by the palm. "You have beautiful hands," she says.

"Oh, thank you!" I redden and quickly retrieve my hand. Feeling exposed, I tuck both hands under my hips.

From a crinkled brown grocery sack near her ankles, she removes a jumbo-size box of Milk Duds and a single can of Coors. "Want to share?" she asks eagerly. She lets go with a playful fake burp, then laughs like a rowdy schoolboy.

Not wanting to ruin the moment, I accept a couple of Milk Duds, but I wrinkle my nose at the thought of beer. Again, Sabine bursts into giggles and, holding the candy box in the air, pitches a large number of Milk Duds into her mouth. After a few minutes of robust chewing, she smiles at me, her teeth all gluey with caramel. "Sisters can be a mystery, you know? How do you say, a bitch?" Hearing the bell, she looks up. "So this is my stop. Good luck to you and the special one."

I wave good-bye as if hypnotized. I'm so surprised at this strange intervention that my hands are trembling. And then I notice that they are worker's hands like Sabine's, and though my nails are shot and my fingers red from gnawing at the flesh, I see my hands have a strength that someone could admire.

The wind blows through the tiny crack above my window. I watch Sabine bend her long frame down to kiss a small boy; he's wearing a Dodgers baseball cap and a Black Panther T-shirt. A bit chilled, I slip my chin under the neckline of my Ragg wool sweater and try to get some sleep.

I I I

From the ratty Greyhound bus station in downtown Bakersfield—not exactly overflowing with optimism—I take a city bus to the outskirts again. It deposits me in front of the gates of Lemon Tree Lodge, where I pause to take in a remarkable scene. A lush oasis in the midst of badly ignored and overrun lots, Lemon Tree could be a private girls' school. At first glance, it boasts a vast lawn of perfect blades of grass, bisected by a single concrete walkway, a modest grove of fruit trees (I see only oranges but have faith the lemons are just around the back), and a white clapboard house, circa 1920, that looks both cozy and institutional. Two dusty cars sit in a gravel driveway; I bet they haven't touched asphalt in ages. The only sounds I hear are bird whistles and an occasional bark from far off.

My legs feel rubbery and unreliable. I remind myself that I am more reliable than most people who dare to come here: I arrive with a shred of respect for the residents! Though they seem weirder than weird on the outside, I suspect the Lemon Tree residents have a sixth sense. Their antennae are more sensitive than most people's, more sensitive than mine. This puts them on the cutting edge of our culture, gives them a value that cannot be denied. Wiping my sweaty palms on my long floral skirt, I remind myself that I am on a mission for

Lonnie. Not everything revolves around my comfort, my well-being.

I take one giant step in the direction of the house. An orange-and-black cat materializes out of thin air and rubs ardently against my leg. Of course this is a sign. "Hello, creature," I whisper, and pet it timidly. "Is this your home?" I ask. "Are you a bit nuts too?" The tabby answers with more vigorous rubbing, adding drooling to the mix. "Ah," I say, "that's a yes. You *are* a crazy cat. Well, guess what? That's my secret too! I'm a crazy woman masquerading as a sane one. Isn't that a hoot?" The tabby answers with a demonstrative gurgle—half meow, half purr. "Thank you," I tell it. "May I enter now?" Abruptly, the cat takes off, chasing a whiff of something spicy on the wind. I turn toward the house and, without further ado, walk straight up the concrete path, mounting the steps with a confidence that's arrived in the nick of time.

I press the buzzer a bit longer than necessary. An older woman blanketed with liver spots opens the door in slow motion, as if she has more time than most of us. Her hair is greasy, and she smells of cigarettes.

"Hi. I'm here to see Johnny Person. Could you show me to the office?"

"I'm the office," she answers.

"Oh!" I exclaim girlishly, never letting on that I assumed she was a resident. "I'm Johnny's sister, Lorna. She . . . he's expecting me." Damn! Lonnie hates it when I blow her cover.

"Well, come on in. Johnny's real excited that you've come all the way from Santa Cruz. He's been yakking about your visit all week. We told him he'd better wash up or you might not wanna give him a hug, ha ha."

How thoughtful, I think. Especially coming from the queen of hygiene. "May I see him now, please?"

"Suit yourself, honey. Room 13. Johnny's favorite number."

"Of course." She leaves me alone to contemplate a door

with *13* scribbled on it in pencil; the number is encircled by a ring of spooky skulls and crossbones. "Knock-knock," I say, in suspiciously high spirits.

"Who goes there?" Lon barks from the other side.

" 'Tis I, Saint Oozy of Santa Cruz."

"Oh, Ooze!" she squeals, and throws open the door. She crunches me with her famous bear hug. "How's it hangin', Oozc?"

Lonnie's wearing outmoded bell-bottom jeans that are so long the cuffs drag on the floor; her small feet are encased in giant alligator-hide cowboy boots. She has squeezed her broad chest into a too-small denim work shirt with torn sleeves; her belly hangs over her snakeskin belt like a beer gut. Mother had told me about Lon binding her breasts to hide all vestiges of her sex, but if I didn't know she was my darling sister, I would swear Lon was the toughest dyke I ever laid eyes on. Or some baby-faced Hell's Angel.

I enter Lonnie's room and flop on her bed, already inexplicably exhausted. "Wow!" I exhale, "your space is more potent than ever!" My eyes scan the small room, which is jammed to the gills with morbid objets d'art and nauseating pictures ripped out of questionable magazines. To make her happy, I single out a few outstanding items. "Gosh, Lon, a bloody rubber foot and a jar of icky eyeballs and a cardboard cutout of a man with a shovel in his head and a picture of insects devouring someone's nose. Ughhh!"

She giggles approvingly. "Hey, Ooze, get a load of this." Lon forces one of her pencil drawings into my hands; it appears to be a man copulating with a corpse that has four penises.

"Uh-huh," I nod. "Very deep stuff. What can I say? Skillfully drawn, but not my kind of thing."

"Yeah, Ooze, *your* kind of thing is a painting of daisies drenched in powdered sugar in the hands of a little girl wearing a pink, fluffy party dress."

"Now that's not fair," I whine. "My taste has expanded a little bit too. I like stronger images now."

"Oh yeah? How about a bouquet of writhing snakes that have gone bonkers and wound themselves around the little girl's neck? And her party dress is shredded after the snakes have had their way with her! Now *that's* what I call a strong image!" She hangs her head low like the Neanderthal men she admires, and laughs at the ground, heh-heh-heh. Vintage Lonnie.

I change the subject. "Why don't you show me some of your new writing?"

Lonnie rustles in her desk drawer and hands me a sheaf of yellowed, curling papers on which she has typed her poems on a manual typewriter. The sheets stink of cigarette smoke. I recognize these sheets from my last visit with her, over a year ago, and wonder why she won't show her newer work. Maybe there isn't any. Prudently, I select one of the more benign poems from the bunch and read it out loud:

Savage Genesis

by Johnny Person

The Child ambles over the fallen and
Rotting debris, his pervaded mind
Wondering, pondering, pondering
Over the brutally mangled body
Of his newborn sister, lying supine
On the dining room rug,
A large sticky puddle of crimson
In which she lays, bordering her delicate
Baby skin.
The Child brandishes a large Bowie knife
In his tiny hand, and he utters one
Vaguely recognizable sound:

"KIL."

Our Child is growing up . . . !

"I really like this one!"

"Gee, thanks, Oozy." Again she crunches my bones in gratitude. On her arms I see the usual self-inflicted scratches with
dried traces of blood. I have to look away.

"Ya wanna see my new tattoo?" she asks, fired up by my
presence.

"Sure."

She rolls up the right sleeve of her work shirt to reveal the
head of an angry sea witch with MEESHY inscribed beneath it.
My eyes practically fall out of my head, no doubt something
Lonnie would really like to see.

"Wow, 'Meeshy'! Does she know about this?"

"You bet your life! And look at this."

Lon strategically pulls up the work shirt a few inches. On
her lower back, I make out a circle of distasteful tattoos: the
devil himself next to a nonwhimsical, bloodthirsty dragon;
the infamous Creature flanked by an almost demure Dracula.

"What a rogue's gallery of ghouls!" I exclaim. Lonnie flushes
with pride. "Did it hurt? Aren't those big tattoos painful?"

"Painful, yeah. Torturous pain! And expen*sivo*. Man, they
cost me an arm and a leg! I had to fight to get my arm and leg
back from the guy."

"Oh, right," I say with heavy sarcasm. I've been playing her
straight man my whole life. "So, Lon, are things improving?
You seem in a much better mood."

"Well, they got me on this mood-altering shit. New drugs
for an old monster like me."

"Stop it." I hate to hear this stuff. "So do you have any
friends here? Any pals?"

"Yeah, Lester. He really digs my stories and poems, but the

rest of them can't read. I told you that! This is a dead-end place for nobodies. We're locked away so we can't interfere with anything. We're anarchists, we're against the status quo, we'll eat the status quo and spit out its carcass!" She stares at the ground, at something I can't see. "Hey, Ooze, ya gotta take me outta this place. I swear I'll be good."

"You're already good. Listen, I brought you something." From my Danish book bag, I retrieve a rolled-up comic book. It's the most stomach-turning thing I could find in a hurry.

"Wow, Oozy, you remembered what I like! *Sex 'n' Drugs 'n' Stuff: Comix for the Compleat Sociopath*. Thanks for nothing!"

I nod, watching her excitement. Sitting down on the bed, she becomes lost in the pages of this rag. I use the time to recover, trying to remember how to breathe.

"Listen, Lon, there's something I have to ask you."

"How many people I've murdered?"

"Not exactly. I want to tell you about this woman I met on the bus. She's from West Africa and she told me that I'd better listen to you more carefully."

"Yeah, man, do what I say. I'm a megalomaniac!" Lon pauses to stretch her denim shirt over her ample gut. "Does this woman own a monkey?"

"What? I don't know," I answer impatiently. "Can I just ask my question?"

"Sure, but I can't promise anything. You *know* my IQ is very low. How low can you go? Heh-heh."

"Lon, pay attention! I want to ask you what your unique message is. The African woman told me that you have a unique message, and I'm ready to hear it."

Lonnie lurches off the bed and begins to pace back and forth in her tiny museum. She eyes me suspiciously like she's dealing with a therapist. Finally, she joggles her head sharply from side to side, indicating no. She positions her face within inches of my own, and I see coarse blond hairs growing on her upper lip. The hormones Mother told me about.

"Oozy, you're not going to analyze me, ya hear? I don't need a blinkin' autopsy. You're not gonna get to the root of *my little problem!*" She shakes an accusatory finger at my eye.

"Sorry," I whisper and stare at the floor, ashamed of my pitifully transparent agenda. "I just thought you had something to teach me, something I've missed all these years because I was too arrogant."

"Arrogant, yeah," she agrees, then sits down beside me. We swing our legs back and forth over the edge of the bed like two little kids. I wish I had a comic book to get lost in or a watertight excuse for leaving. When I turn to Lonnie, expecting more curses to fall on my head, I watch a confusing light pass through her eyes; a smile wiser than both of us takes possession of her mouth. Lonnie is vigorously shaking her head up and down. I have never seen anything like this.

"You thought of something?" I ask, hoping my question doesn't hurt her in some new way.

"Yeah, man, I got a damn message. I'm here to tell you Earthlings somethin'." Although she points specifically at my nose, I know she's accusing everybody she's ever met.

"Yes?" I encourage, hanging on every word.

"I'm here to tell ya that this world stinks!" Uh-huh, I nod again. Big surprise. "You people hurt each other, ya go to war and kill, kill, kill. Ya persecute anything strange and different and call yourselves humanitarians—*hu-mans.* Ooze, my message is: this is not my world. This is not *the* world. I'm in the wrong place, man. Ya got it all wrong!"

"I see," I nod soberly. "But that's because you grew up in the wrong culture. But let's say you were born in Africa—in the jungle or on the plains. Let's say you were treated well there and fit in. I know this seems impossible to imagine, a place that treats you with respect. But remember, no matter where you grew up, in Burbank or in Nairobi, you came here to tell us something special, I just know it. Can you imagine what your special message might be?"

Lonnie considers my words seriously, toying with a bottom lip that threatens to unravel, it is so chewed up. "Hmm. My message?" Without warning, she leaps from the mattress and strikes a boxer's pose, fists protecting her face. "My message is ya gotta be free and wild! Remember the animal in ya, Oozy. Get down with animals! They don't go crazy like you humans. They are naturally crazy, man!" She laughs at her joke. "You've never seen a mentally ill lion, have you?"

"That's true," I concede. My eyes begin to fill with water, the curse of "my people." I press on. "But what is it about wildness that turns you on?"

"Oh, Oozy! Stop with the questions! Can't I just squeeze ya to death like always?" She cuddles up to me, and I smell a mouth that hasn't seen a toothbrush in days.

"Lon, please. Just one last question: What would you do with freedom if you had it?"

"I told you, I'd choke you."

"Lon!" I can't bear to hear a trace of her hatred of me, even couched in a tease. "Be serious, now."

"Oh, I dunno, Ooze. Guess I'd just stalk the hills, play with monkeys. Eat humans for lunch. Dance the dance."

"The dance?" I repeat.

"Yeah!" And then she demonstrates what appears to be a very old dance, weight low to the ground, feet pounding the earth, arms akimbo. Lips closed, she's smiling nonetheless, eyes rolled back in her head.

Slowly I join in, swaying alongside her. I always try to be supportive. But this is different; I hear the same inner beat she does and feel an acute need to answer it. For two minutes, in total silence, we flail at the air with our arms and stomp the hardwood floor with our feet, awakening spirits, shaking up the netherworld. Though her room is small and crammed with curios, the space seems to expand with our ritual.

"Say-hey, Jim!" Lonnie cheers. Jim, Lonnie's retarded friend whose room is next to hers, enters the room and seamlessly, silently, becomes part of our dance. He practically topples over with enthusiasm trying to mimic our body movements, rocking fiercely, cartoonishly.

On her way down the hall, another of Lon's friends spots our group and giggles softly, hand clenched shyly over her mouth. She's got spit on her lip and a rash on her cheeks. An Asian woman about thirty-five, she's dressed in a worn purple bathrobe, ripped black tights, and a blue baseball cap. "Okay-okay-okay-okay," she repeats rhythmically at least twenty times, then begins jumping up and down in the hall, trampoline-style.

Impressed with her choreography, Jim and Lonnie echo her up-and-down gyrations, and I swear the room banks sideways. "Sara, Sara!" they call out to her in unison like she's their queen for a day.

For no discernible reason, Sara stops hopping, perhaps struck by the oceanic good feeling. She begins to hum an up-tempo version of "America the Beautiful," which, on the second verse, miraculously segues into "I Wanna Hold Your Hand." A huge Beatles fan, Lonnie waves her into the room and takes her for a dance partner. A fourth resident, Lester, appears from out of nowhere and begins to walk frantic circles around our party, methodically chanting "Bang a gong, get it on!"

"Rock and roll!" Lonnie cries and begins singing along with Lester.

Dazed and gasping for air, I spin out of the action and beach myself on Lonnie's bed, head landing on a pile of orange-and-blue boa constrictors. Stuffed animals. How could I have missed them?

For untold minutes, I watch the four remaining dancers collide with each other like it's the funniest thing. They slam into each other's hips, mercilessly tickle each other's sides, slap each other's rotating butts. Then, without warning, Lonnie and Jim break into a ferocious game of patty-cake, while Lester and Sara hook arms square dance–style and swing around the tiny room until they succumb to the Earth's gravity, finally collapsing in a heap on the floor. It's then I notice that even Lonnie's floor is crazy, every inch covered with garish fanzine images of Kiss, Alice Cooper, and other repellent rock stars.

All four friends are breathing hard, their foreheads shiny. I'm no longer dizzy but feel an inner chill. Outside, a choir of birds trills. I vaguely remember that I'm on the outskirts of a city, in a secret wild place. I don't recall how I got here and haven't the faintest idea how to get home.

Our collective panting gives way to a profound silence. There are no breezes to cool our hot bodies. In the sudden stillness, the meaning of the dance becomes clear: Lon and her friends may be fighting for their lives but they are having a decent moment, a moment soon to be buried in a punishing landscape of boring days and interminable years. Somehow Lonnie's gang has made the unbearable bearable. They have found a way to be free.

On the heels of their celebration, the four friends become curiously withdrawn, lost in four separate and impenetrable worlds. Make that five: a little river of fear rises within me, and I clutch an orange boa to my chest like a life raft.

"Ooze?" Lonnie breaks the silence to address me. "Can you please leave us alone now? We're kinda busy."

For the hundredth time today, I nod. I wrap the floppy boa

around my neck like a muffler and walk down a dark hall to the smoky rec room. I join a small group of smokers on a tired couch, but no one looks up to greet me. *Star Trek* is on TV, and the Klingons are bombing the hell out of the starship *Enterprise.* The Lemon Tree Lodge residents find this hilarious, and while I don't see what's funny, I fade into the background nicely, chuckling too, and clutching the silly snake. I am having my own decent moment and almost missed it.

The Circle Game

1972

ying for a job at the University of California at
Santa Cruz, I sit twitching in a circle of anxious
candidates, each more qualified and bohemian
than the next. The school plans to interview
twenty of us at a time in the name of democracy and I think
somebody mentioned Marx. It's here in this golden circle I am
asked a question that only Miss Universe pageant contestants
get the heady opportunity to answer. Namely, "What was the
best moment in your life and what was the worst?" Because I
have a high fever, I have no peak moments to offer.

Looking around the room, I eyeball the talent and tacitly
give the job to each applicant down the line. They *all* seem
right. I seem wrong. Save for one shimmering sensation: I
know I will be chosen. So I clear my throat and humbly tell the

truth: that my best and worst moments are the *same* moment. Only, they both lasted a lifetime, at least my whole life up until this point. I report that the worst moment in my life *is* my life with my mentally ill/emotionally disturbed sister. That, yes, it has been a long moment and one that could be classified a living hell. Conversely, I note that the best moment in my life has been this same god-awful experience—that what I know and who I am has been immutably shaped and pummeled and informed by Lonnie the Wild One. That because of Lonnie, I am an ultrasensitive creature, an empath by necessity, and that I wouldn't have it any other way. No one in the room applauds, but I feel as if a winner's bouquet of roses will soon press its way into my arms and I will be obliged to cradle it, weep, and smile simultaneously.

In my feverish state, I run long at the mouth and hear myself add a bit about growing up with my sister's pythons and boa constrictors, insisting they actually make sweet pets: "They crave affection just like dogs and cats!"

When I catch myself in the middle of this woozy non sequitur, I acknowledge my fever and am allowed to go home, trusting my instincts that I have been chosen over eighty other exotics for the very banal position of housing manager—a two-hour-a-day job that pays exactly three dollars an hour. Truth has triumphed, but I have no interest in this job, only a faint desire to scratch a boa under its neck, crawl beneath the covers of my lumpy student bed, and sleep without listening to the screams of the past. You understand, Lonnie is a noise, a white noise, and like chaos, is involved in everything I do. I can't escape the noise; I even hum its tune on occasion. Even now, in my twenties, when I go to bed I cringe. As if the devil was playing the piano, I cringe, and pretend something wonderful in my life is so loud that I can't hear anything else.

I   I   I

In the morning, I get the call. Surprise! I'm the new housing manager. But there's more. Because of my "experience" with reptiles, I've been appointed to the University Animal Board.

"No thank you," I tell the kind administrator. "My fever's lifted, and now it's so obvious: I should pursue a job in the arts. Even if I just sell tickets." I laugh self-consciously but hear only silence in return.

"My," the woman finally responds. "Whatever brought about this change of heart?"

"Gee, I'm not sure. I just saw a picture of me doing something that saves lives—metaphorically, I mean."

"Very well. I don't suppose I can change your mind?"

"No, I'm really sorry I wasted your time."

"Then there's nothing more to say. Best of luck to you, dear."

"Mmm," I mumble and hang up the hall phone. "Way to go, Lorna!" I mutter under my breath, looking one last time into Ollie Jonson's clearie to make sure I've made the right decision.

Victorious but set free in a sea with no name, I pad down the hall to my dorm room in my stocking feet and slam the door. To enhance my rapidly darkening mood, I put Joni Mitchell's "Blue" on the record player and plug in the hot plate to make a mug of instant hot chocolate. Everything's just great. I have no job for the summer, nowhere to live come June, and no boyfriend to make up for all the bad stuff in life (although, I have to admit, Henry's still hanging in there, and this means the world to me). But, lest I forget, I have been true to myself.

I'm so accustomed to feeling crazy-depressed, that I barely notice I'm a little less depressed than usual. For a moment, I can almost sense the future intruding on the present, a preview of feelings a tad less intense than all-out despair. To better understand this novel sensation, I liberate my notebook from under my pillow and prop myself up against my headboard. As always, I plan to capture the ineffable in poetry! But my pen begins to draw instead. On a bare page in the notebook I draw four circles. Like I used to when I was innocent and hopeful and disappointed in life far too early. Now I remember: the circles stand for faces, the wide-open faces of each member of a family.

The making of families is a long-lost ritual that used to come in handy. When I was desperate for a different family. When I could surprise myself with the outcome. How I loved to mix and match the features of the mother and father, creating offspring of infinite variety. This practice could occupy my thoughts for hours, filling me with a palpable faith in the future.

My pen hovers over one circle and then another, waiting to lovingly fill in the details but finding nothing loving to say. Filling in these circles once proved therapeutic and quietly entertaining. I excelled at birthing whole communities, families that would surely take me in. But I was also taken in by the destinies these faces suggested, how drafting a subtle change in the angle of a nose could affect a whole life. In a second, a pug-nosed, ponytailed girl could become an outcast with a hawk nose and messy hair. And vice versa. I was especially interested in the vice versa.

Today, I find myself staring into the centers of my circles. I am bankrupt, cannot imagine a single fortuitous feature to fill them with. Not one novel nose, not one curvaceous mouth. No saucer eyes or fringy bangs. Not even a sprinkling of freckles. I am visually clueless.

Suddenly, in the absence of clues, my own family comes to mind. And then I can see no other faces but my family's, no other possible arrangement of features save for those permanently inscribed on the four Persons. Is this what the Buddhists call acceptance? Or am I incredibly stubborn, refusing to see another way? Perhaps these empty circles are symptoms of clinical depression, the final proof of an incurable sadness.

Close the book, I tell myself. *Leave the four circles alone.* But the faces of Lonnie and Lorna and Julia and Burton intrude, flooding the circles and staining them with a history I have avoided and also technically studied to death. Now, as long and hard as I stare at the page, I can't change the identity of these faces—they even repel Groucho Marx noses and furry eyebrows.

Lorna, close the book; your story is written in indelible ink. It's ancient history. Close the book and begin another.

I slam the notebook shut as if it had tried to bite me. Maybe circles are too cartoonish a medium. Maybe I need to sketch lavish, intricate portraits that reflect lavishly complicated lives? I've never even attempted to draw my own family, afraid of the karma such a portrait might unleash. Perhaps, like most offspring, I'm not even capable of seeing my family in an attractive light. Could it be that my family is handsome in some way I can't detect? Because I'm a part of the picture, I can't really step back and know this. I squint, imagining a beautiful portrait of the Persons—one taken on vacation in Lake Tahoe or at the San Diego Zoo. Could such a photo lie? I mean, can you take a beautiful picture of a disaster? Just consider the ethics.

As I sneak a peek at my four impoverished circles, my mind drifts toward those heart-stopping pictures that, over the years, have jumped out at me from *Life* magazine. Coolly detached images of devastating fires and volcanoes and tsunamis. I recall that disasters have a seductive, even gorgeous side to them. No question that families are natural disasters too, but their gorgeous side has been lost on me.

In a hurry to uncover the truth, I unearth a cardboard box from under my bed. From it, I extract a badly bruised photo album, literally in pieces but overflowing with somebody's truth. I hold my breath and feel my hands go numb. I begin at the beginning. Flip, flip, flip. I find little evidence of a family, though. Most of the photos are of friends or of me with friends. It's as if my family has been edited out of my life. I guess Mother and Daddy have held on to the baby pictures, the group shots.

As I turn the last page, a loose photo flies out of the album and lands on my knee. It's a discolored snapshot of Lonnie posing next to me: two gawky sisters adrift in the fifties, one slim-hipped and pale blond, scowling comically while shaking her Cecil puppet at Daddy's Nikon lens; the other, an unremarkable, full-calved strawberry blonde, head twisted sideways to the sun, squinting painfully at the camera. I can hear Daddy shouting, "Open your left eye, Lorna! Smile for chrissake!"

Both girls are wearing white seersucker sundresses that tie around the neck movie star–style, and white tennis shoes gaily decorated with Magic Marker ink. Although they are posed in front of the famously fun Teacup Ride at Disneyland, both girls refuse to smile for the camera. Because there's nothing to smile *at*, nothing amusing or distracting enough, nothing to make their lives go away. Lonnie is probably furious at Daddy for insisting that she wear the dumb white dress of a delicate little girl when she'd rather don his dungarees and heavy oxford shoes. And I am probably furious that my teeth didn't turn out well—well enough to smile confidently for snapshots—and that I have trouble looking in the direction of the sun. Because of this, I will never appear starry-eyed in any photograph throughout history. Certainly, I am furious about being dragged to Disneyland with three people who inhibit my style and put a stranglehold on my life.

I should have been born into the singing King Family and forged my talents on a weekly TV show. Instead of this, this black hole of anonymity and weirdness.

Looking past the two girls in the photograph and into the purplish blur of the dizzy teacups, I recall how much I hated the Teacup Ride; whirling like a dervish was a cruel and unusual punishment, not to mention a total throw-up fest. Just when you and your sister were given charge of a teacup, the management would allow an older kid into your cup, some muscle-bound freak who wrested control of the wheel and arrogantly spun you into his own brand of oblivion.

I wonder why Daddy had posed Lonnie and me in front of this ride from hell and then had the nerve to coax a smile from us? I guess he must have seen that the spinning teacups would create a spectacular background for showing off his daughters. He had an eye, after all. But it usually went right past his daughters to alight in some other world. A strategy I can finally understand.

If I didn't know these girls, if I had chanced upon this photo album in a friend's attic, no doubt I would have stopped to ponder this poignant snapshot of radiant youth. I would have even been jealous of the sisters, assuming that behind their scowling and squinting, some amazing camaraderie was at play. I concede that I would have found the puppet-shaking, towheaded child especially comical. I would have been impressed with the way she challenged the status quo of family photographs, breaking with the tradition of smiling widely, bravely, falsely. By replacing the compulsory smile with a goofy, in-your-face affront to the camera, this strange young thing would have given me faith in the absurd. Gosh, she would have made me proud! Her humor, her fierceness, her raw unsociability.

And the strawberry blonde? Uncertain, exposed, and a bit shaky (I can see this in the way the sun affects her whole being, how she pulls back from the light and into herself), she would have interested me artistically. Just the fact of her imperfection, the Virginia Woolf bone structure, the Botticelli nose, the extra-fleshy body. I have a soft spot for girls who look damaged, who look beautiful *because* they are damaged.

This girl who twists her face up to the sun against her will, who looks dreamy and half haunted, I would have liked to help her out. I would have celebrated her ungainly feelings, given her room to express herself. I would have sat down with her and listened intently—for hours at a time—for her story must be one of endless compromise and unwonted courage. And by telling her story, she could transform it. Put herself at the forefront. That would have made her wildly happy. Then, I would have kissed her on the cheek and told her that everything was all right. That love has been with her all along. That I am sure of this.

About the Author

Laurie Fox was raised in Burbank,
California, and has been involved in the
Los Angeles and San Diego literary
communities as a poet and bookseller.
For the last eight years, she has worked as
a literary agent in San Diego and the
Bay Area. She lives with her husband,
author D. Patrick Miller, and her cat,
Chloé, in Berkeley, California.
This is her first novel.

This page constitutes an extension of the copyright page.